OLD SCORES

OLD SCORES

Frederic Raphael

ORION

First published in Great Britain in 1995 by
Orion
An imprint of Orion Books Ltd
Orion House, 5 Upper St Martin's Lane, London WC2 9EA

A CIP catalogue record for this book is available
from the British Library

ISBN 1 85797 641 X

Filmset by Selwood Systems, Midsomer Norton
Printed in Great Britain by
Butler & Tanner Ltd, Frome and London

FOR BEETLE

I

My sister was the pretty one. As far as our parents' self-esteem was concerned, Pansy and I represented the good and the bad news. When Mickey and Toni parted, Pansy's charm and beauty promised them both, separately, that they had some compensation for their marital disaster. My quite good 'A' levels and subsequent university career led only to apprehension; although she did not say so, I suspected that Toni feared that a graduate daughter might also prove a harsh judge. Everyone called my mother Toni, though she was baptised Antoniá, a name Granny Rougier had borrowed from the library.

Taking myself to be a sort of worthy disappointment made me more dutiful than my sister; I elected to pose as the sane one. There was a spice of concealed accusation in my regular memory for birthdays and in my apt selection of Christmas presents. Pansy was lovely; I, it seemed, was loving. Thanks to me, we continued to have family occasions, even if we had no family. After Mickey had kissed Pansy for what had actually been my choice of golf-balls, or Toni had clapped grateful hands at the three-pack of herbal soap which Pansy had just given her, although she had, in truth, been too busy to go and buy it for herself at Floris, my sister's big blue eyes pleaded with me for discretion. Golly, she was grateful; where would she be without me?

Being clever, or clever*er*, offered me the satisfactions of blameless duplicity; I was a deceiver without being dishonest. Heart and head were, in my case, very communicative partners. Having decided to be Pansy's trustworthy, reliable and thoroughly decent sister, there was something more than a little wilful in my virtue. It was tasty to know that it remained within my unexercised power to lower my sister's stock. By way of a dividend, I became a secret sharer in Pansy's glamorous life: her passionate ups and downs offset the flatness of my own emotions. She lived; I observed.

When Pansy started modelling, she asked me to share this heavenly flat she had been told about in Pont Street. What could dress a pretty girl's life better than a reliably less attractive, but really, really nice older sister? My degree had qualified me for a rather dull, very demanding job with a bright, if simian, solicitor called Norman Pereira, but when we moved into 73e, Pansy was already earning much more money from modelling than I could by devilling for Norman. If proximity to Pansy made my life infinitely more amusing, I was, at the same time, made unmistakably aware of what was always likely to be beyond my scope. Gratitude and envy led to the same consequences: I was the most conscientious flat-mate in the world. I never forgot a message and I knew where everything was, not least because I had been left to put it there. Pansy often said that she really, really did not know what she would do without me; Norman Pereira said the same. Their sincerity sometimes left me smug; and sometimes suicidal.

Since friendship with me now offered access to Pan, a surprising number of males were soon asking me to premières and private views. My reputation for coolness was a relief to men like Simon or Giles or Brice, or either of the Georges, or even Bartolemeo. It exempted them from having to express desires which my second-bestness did little to stimulate. Since their purpose in escorting me was to curry favour with Pansy, it suited them to think that I liked nothing better than their restraint. Nearly all of them told me, on different occasions, how much they admired my mature attitude, by which they meant that when they broached the question of sex, I almost invariably invited them not to bother, which they greatly preferred. Asked what I really liked doing, I told them that I read a lot of books.

When the evening's recruits arrived from their dealing rooms or from their chambers in order to sip our Chardonnay, they would chat politely to me while their less polite eyes followed Pansy as – 'Help, help! Late as usual, I'm afraid!' – she hurried around the place, entrancingly half-dressed, new telephone under her chin, irresistible with unfinished phrases. If, later the same night, my delegated escort was chivalrous enough to make husky noises and sought to unbutton my blouse or persuade my hand to abate his virility, I gave no indication of having guessed that he might be stiffening his resolve by imagining me to be Pansy.

It was not until Pan told me that Brice Cavendish wanted to marry her, and I had the prospect of being left by myself in 73e, that a desire for marriage leapt into my head and thence, I suppose, to my heart. Only then was I shaken by the shameful possibility of being discovered to be a virgin on my wedding day. Dear God, I was twenty-four and I *had* read a lot of books!

I first saw Roger Raikes in Norman Pereira's office, scanning an interleaved blotter of correspondence which I had left for signature on Norman's desk. My boss had been delayed in court and one of the more ignorant clerks must have let Roger into the front office. When I came in, on my sensible and silent soles, he had no time to pretend that he was not doing what he was doing. He gave me an ingratiating wince of shame; I was reminded of Pansy, when she had done something unforgivable and expected to be forgiven for it.

'Oh I know,' he said. 'It killed the cat. But to be perfectly honest with you, curiosity's never done me any harm.'

To my surprise, I colluded with the grim hint of a smile. By intimating that I should say nothing (it was always my speciality), I became Roger's protector as I had so often been Pansy's. What could he have seen to his advantage in cribbing Norman's dull letters? The tightness in my chest promised that I was excited by the evidence that he was an opportunist, even though – on this occasion – no profitable opportunity had been presented to him. After I left the office, I looked back through the frosted panels in Norman's door; Roger's pleasing, dishonest face was blurred by the glass. I fancied him in the shower, without the glasses and with the water needling those pink cheeks.

The evening after I first saw him, my sister and I were taken to the ENO's *Don Giovanni* in a party of six, including Brice Cavendish, who had just been elected to Parliament in the wake of Mrs Thatcher's second electoral victory; it meant he had to have a quick word with masses of people in the stalls. My escort was Roland Savory, whose wife Prue worked (and was working that night) for a junior minister. Savory was a florid, fair-haired man, with a shining prong of a nose; he said there was ant-eater in his family. It was a joke, but he looked decidedly flushed about it. After people had laughed, he seemed quite angry.

Roley had got a Blue for cricket. He had begun his journalistic career as a sports-writer, but he was now a chalk-striped city journalist in his truculent thirties. His whispered hints and disclosures, during the interval, about the Eton and Oxford life of Pansy's fiancé, whose best man he was slated to be, seemed intended as a down payment on an understanding between us: they guaranteed that he was wicked and that he was tolerant and that he was preparing to grace me with the same qualities. So how about it?

In the taxi after the opera, he said he would give me his day and night telephone numbers on the assumption that I should never call him in the country or dream of displacing his wife. I promised him that I was interested in him only as a sexual object. Roley honked his incredulity. Men often do when they hear the truth.

He took me back to a Horseferry Road *pied-à-terre* which he was sorry to say that he was only in the earliest stages of rendering habitable. He apologised for the uncarpeted and bedless bedroom but said that what he really liked about me was that I wasn't bothered about frills: I was obviously too experienced to expect subtlety or soft furnishings.

Once it was clear that I intended to allow him to do whatever he wanted, he felt obliged to tell me how much he really liked me. If I didn't mind him saying so, my kind of intelligence was a pretty rare commodity; had I ever thought about journalism? When I looked at my watch, he cut out the small talk and went to search for something we could put on the uncarpeted floor. His shouted commentary told me that all he could find were some tea towels in a drawer in the kitchen. If he hoped that I should be naked on his return, I disappointed him, but less than I feared my nakedness might.

As he spread the towels on top of one of the paint-speckled canvas sheets which the painters had been using while they did the woodwork, his with-you-in-a-minute anxiety induced a smirk from me which threatened to dispel the erotic atmosphere. He responded with a sudden all-right-then attack. Giving me no time to take off any of my clothes, he dumped me on the floor and threw up my skirt and set about fumbling himself urgently into me. Since the angle seemed not to be very convenient, he used my legs as handles, rather like a man coming to terms with a wheelbarrow. Energetic noises suggested that it was a decidedly uphill struggle, during the course of which he kept bumping into me. The end was quick and sticky and then he was saying, 'God, I think I love you, darling. I think I truly do.'

He lowered my hips to the floor, and leant down over me. I kissed some stubble and said how sweet he was. As far as effort went, it had been a captain's innings. I was not sure if I was bleeding, but I thought not; after a number of Welsh ponies and adolescent explorers, my virginity was probably technical. Roley hobbled to the window-sill, with his trousers round his ankles, and sat down. He looked relieved to be back in the pavilion.

'How are you fixed?' he said. 'It's not that late. Great thing about opera: no encores.'

'I really ought to go,' I said.

'Christ,' he said. 'Jesus Christ. Jesus CHRIST!'

'It was fine,' I said. 'It was perfect. Don't worry. Once was ample. I'm in no hurry for a thousand and three.'

'Don't worry? I'm stuck. I'm . . . bloody painters, bloody damned painters. Probably Irish. They've bloody well skinned me. I hope I'm going to see you again. God, this is embarrassing. It's all over *everything*. It'll never come off, will it, for ages? Talk about whited sepulchres! Hairy hell! Sod it, honestly.'

'There must be some turps somewhere.'

'It'll sting like buggery.' Indignation was beginning to excite him, although at a very odd angle: his erection went out sideways and then straightened up. 'Look at that!'

'I was doing.'

'Pity to waste it. What's so *bad* about a white sepulchre?'

I said, 'You were jolly here-comes-Charlie, you know.'

'You liked it. Admit it, you bitch.'

'It was fine,' I said. 'For a first time.'

'I don't imagine you're the sort of woman who just wants the same old thing. If there are things you like, you only have to say. Or . . . indicate. If you want me to pitch it in the rough, I'll gladly pitch it in the rough. Or not.'

'Turps!' I said. I had been looking among the painters' pots and bottles. 'And a rag.'

'I'll . . . do the necessary. More practically, when am I going to see you? We've got unfinished biz. And I really do like you.'

'I'm probably going to get married,' I said.

'*Are* you? You never said. You're not! Who to? Anyone I know?'

'I'm not entirely sure.'

'Meanwhile, where do you propose I put this? You're always alleged to be the clever one.'

2

When Pansy suggested that Rachel buy her out of her share of 73e, Rachel had a better idea: she decided to change her life. She sold the lease, profitably, and then she gave notice to Norman Pereira and became a copy editor with a women's magazine, where she stayed until she considered herself qualified for a job in Wapping. There was a want of secretaries willing to run the gauntlet of picketing printers. Once established, Rachel elected to look for a flat in the Barbican, where she made an appointment to meet an estate agent called Andy Basso.

She was side-saddle on the cindery stonework of an angular fountain, which had not yet been plumbed in, and reading *Staying On*, when a voice said, 'Mrs Gibbons?'

She looked up and saw the blazer and the pink cheeks.

'Good heavens!' he said. 'You don't remember me, I hope!'

'Of course,' she said. 'Curious coincidence!'

'Oh dear,' he said. 'And now you're Mrs Gibbons, are you?'

'Not in the least.'

'*Aren't* you? I was supposed to meet a Mrs Gibbons. All right: hold it! Because you know what's happened, unfortunately, don't you?'

'Yes,' she said. 'I've failed to meet Mr Gibbons. Roger, isn't that your name?'

'Yes, it is. Raikes. Fancy you remembering. And you're ... ?'

'Rachel Stannard.'

'Of course you are. What's happened is, I've picked up the wrong bloody folder. I've got you, and Andy's got that very boring Mrs Gibbons, which has to be somebody's good luck. You are looking for a flat, aren't you?'

'I am, yes. Have you got some?'

'I like it,' he said. 'What a seriously nice surprise!'

'If you're an estate agent,' she said, 'you can't be *that* surprised.'

'Seeing you again. I've often thought about you.'

'That's funny,' she said. 'So have I.'

'Meanwhile, I've only got the wrong keys and the wrong particulars, but otherwise there's no sort of a cock-up, is there? Luckily, plan B is always available: we make a sharpish little sortie to the site office and with any luck their invaluable Mr Lockhart will reveal all, or most of it. You may not be Watson, but I do have my methods.'

'And are you still reading people's correspondence, when left alone in their offices?'

'I'll tell you truth,' he said, 'which is a bit of a limited offer. I do when I have time. Unfortunately, I've been unbelievably busy. And quite successful. Pretty soon people will be wanting to read *my* letters! What are you doing tonight?'

'I'm supposed to be going to something at the Wigmore Hall, I think. With some people.'

'Wigmore Hall? What's that? Boxing?'

ii

'Bring him along,' Pansy said. 'There's always a spare seat if you know who to smile at.'

'I don't think he'd mix all that well.'

'Turn up the juice high enough and they all mix. You are enterprising suddenly, Raitch. I do terribly want to see him.'

'No, you don't.'

'I always show you mine. Where does he come from?'

'All right, he's an estate agent.'

'So's Giles Harmer. He *is*! Only Giles is a glorified one.'

'Roger isn't in the least glorified.'

'Roger! Sounds on the ball. You honestly like him, do you?'

'I don't know about that,' Rachel said, 'but I'm probably going to marry him.'

'I sometimes wonder if I really *like* Brice. Bring him to the wedding, why don't you? It's going to be jammed with people wanting houses, probably. Is he hunky at all?'

'He's got very even features.'

'What colour eyes?'

'Oh God!' Rachel said. 'Browny green, I think. Greeny brown.'

'Nose?'

'Definitely, but not unduly. He wears specs.'

'Buy him contacts.'

'I like him in specs. It makes him look like a little boy.'

'Sweet! What kind of hair?'

'You'll see when you see him. Brown. Straight.'

'You're obviously in love. Hey, you haven't done it yet, have you?'

'I only met him this morning. He showed me a flat.'

'Bare boards can be terrifically sexy, I find. Especially if they're chestnut, and not varnished yet. I remember a place in Chester Square. With those nice shutters that fold back into sort of boxes. Unfortunately, I got something in my knee. What's Roley going to say? They do seem to like me on my knees; do they you?'

'Roley's married.'

'I know *that*. But what's he going to say? He told me you were wonderful. Did he get you to yap? He does like his girls to yap.'

'He *can't have*. Told you.'

'Roley tells me everything. There's no known cure. He likes to yap and he likes you to. He said you were wonderful and unbelievably . . .'

'What? Did he get you to, ever?'

'Even-keeled. This is you he was talking about. Me? Only once or twice. He was so hellish low, I felt a moral obligation. Charity work, basically. He must have looked a sight with a white bum *and* appendages.'

'He even told you about that?'

'Poor Roley! He's concluded that Prue almost certainly prefers ladies. So who does he work for? This Roger?'

'Reece, Streatfield and Pollock.'

'Never mind. You will bring him, won't you, tonight?'

'Of course not,' Rachel said.

'Raitch, can I ask you something important? I'm beginning to wonder. Should I really do it?'

'With whom?'

'Don't be silly, darling, marry; Brice.'

'You told me you were mad about him.'

'He's everything I've ever wanted. He's handsome – fairly – and a bit of a pig and a swine and he knows absolutely everybody.'

'He's also going to be extremely rich.'

'Which is not necessarily all that much of a drawback. Only tell me something: does he remind you of Mickey at all?'

'I don't think he reminds me of Daddy in the slightest.'

'What about that sort of honking noise he makes when he thinks he's said something funny?'

'I've never noticed it.'

'I always thought that that was what I loved about him and then I realised, it was on Wednesday actually, at that beastly Berkeley buffet, where he *will* go, that it sounded *exactly* like Pops, and since then I've had this alarm-bell ringing in my ears. You never noticed it? What *have* you noticed?'

'Well, the dandruff. And the choice of socks, obviously.'

'I'm dealing with those. Those I can deal with.'

'If he's like Mickey, then he's like Mickey. So what?'

'Also he and Toni get on alarmingly well. He tells her all his stories about Number 10 and she absolutely *creams* herself.'

'Pansy, really! You're talking about our mother.'

'Oh Raitch, I do love you; you're the only person in London who still has the decency to be shocked when I say things. I think it's the HRT that's done it for Toni. She told me she fancies very young men suddenly. A lot. It's a bit unnerving, I find, having a mama who's younger than you are. The thing is – if I can go on for a *second* longer without having you look at your watch – I can't make out exactly *why* I still want to marry Brice. I'm terribly afraid it may be because I love him, and we all know how deeply fatal that can be! I should so, *so* much like to be the calculating minx he wants me to be and suddenly I'm not *totally* convinced. That bloody alarm just rings and rings.'

'Too late to worry now,' Rachel said. 'Goode's are cleaned out by people buying you all the Minton in the place. I even know someone who forked out for the salad set.'

'That's another horrendous probbo: did I or did I not choose the right pattern? I've seen tons of it lately, absolutely everywhere.'

'Any minute now, estate agents will be deciding to have it.'

'I *know.*'

When Roger drove up in his at-least-second-hand, powder-blue Triumph Stag, Rachel was relieved to feel a spasm of disappointment: it stimulated an effort on her part to appear impressed. It was difficult – and happily proved unnecessary – to distinguish between the pleasure to be taken in deceiving Roger and the pleasure to be found in his company. Knowing that he was unscrupulous lent his candour an amusingly dubious sincerity. What made him tell her so promptly about his mother and crippled father and of his regular visits to their Pinner semi, where the good son had paid for a little lift to get the old man up to bed? If she had believed that Roger was disclosing his suburban origins in order to win sympathy, Rachel might have had no appetite for him, but her faith in their common future was restored by the implication that he was an apple who was determined to fall as far as possible from the family tree.

He drove, snarlingly, to a roadhouse on the river at Marlow. After a Tio Pepe, he went for prawn cocktails and the beef Stroganoff (why not?) with a bottle of Beaujolais (Rachel's eyes met those of the wine waiter and warned him against saying a word), followed by *crèmes brûlées*. Roger's chosen venue was a hundred yards from the renowned restaurant to which Brice had brought Pansy and Rachel, and a dozen people who were seriously concerned about Europe, in order to celebrate his first PPS-ship. Agriculture was not glamorous, but one had to accept some dirt under the fingernails before choicer pickings could be reached.

As the fairy lights twinkled, Roger asked Rachel whether she had ever eaten in Marlow before. She promised him that she had not. He put his hand over hers and said, 'I'm going to keep you in all this, Rachel. Remember that.' He seemed so moved by his prospective generosity that it was all she could do to prevent him ordering up another round of *crèmes de menthe frappées*.

The possessive way in which he raised those almost colourless eyebrows when the waiter asked about more coffee gave her the frightfully reassuring feeling that they were as good as married. The rumple of his forehead – the hairline was already rather sweetly receding – implied 'Darling?' without his saying a word. If he was a bit of a devil, it told her, he was also the kind who could be relied on to help her jacket around her shoulders before stepping aside and allowing her to lead him into temptation.

She waited without impatience for his next move. Whatever the outcome, it would not markedly displease her. She was really pleased to have found him (imagine everyone pretending really to like him!) and she was not going to break her heart if he never asked to see her again. Indifference graced her with more charm than eagerness could ever have supplied. It gave Roger the chance to impress himself by his ability to seduce a classy girl who showed no urgent appetite for his company: she was not getting him, he was getting her. As he looked at himself in his blazer and his buttoned-down, graph-paper shirt, he reckoned he must have unexpected charms. Why else would someone of her sort be going along with him? Having discovered that she neither resisted his kisses nor demanded them, he decided to postpone temporary pleasures in the pursuit of more long-term objectives. He had read a couple of books on career management; both emphasised the importance of timing. As for Rachel, she recognised that it might have been humane to assure him that the objects of his ambition, herself included, were less inaccessible than he might think, but she also knew that such kindness would be cruel: Roger's appetite fed on challenges. At school, he told her, he had been quite a useful hurdler. He might have been a South London Harrier, but his ankle went.

Rachel was becomingly implacable in her postponement of that weekend together in the country. Roger boasted of access to a furnished luxury cottage, worth three hundred a week, or a thou per month, near Thame, but he totally understood that she had to be sure of what she felt, for his sake as well as hers. Rachel was touched by the sharp operator's respect for what he took to be scruples. It suggested that she could always rely on the distance between them to bring them closer together.

When, finally, they made the date, Folly Cottage was grander, if less frivolous, than its name. Roger opened the door with a flourish of cleverly secured keys. His gesture of illicit achievement invited Rachel to enjoy the luxury which he had no right to offer. The cottage was furnished with what she guessed to be the least attractive pieces of a legacy. The immaculate dreariness of the place – there had to be hunting prints, didn't there? – reminded her of Granny Rougier, whose distant French origins impelled her to such ostentatious Englishness that she had never even possessed a passport and gave them spotted dog, with diluted treacle, for Sunday dinner.

'Just the job,' Roger said, 'wouldn't you say?'

'Is there any heating, do you think?'

'Flick-of-a-switch-time,' Roger said.

'You've been here before.'

'I'm not entirely as young as I look, duchess.' He opened a cupboard under the stairs and considered the range of boxed switches which it concealed. 'Whether or not that's an entirely good thing.'

'It's an excellent thing,' Rachel said. 'How many times?'

'That would be telling, wouldn't it? I tend to keep tabs on things that might be useful and this place, well, it's had its uses and I wouldn't want you to think it hadn't.'

'Why?'

'Why? Because I don't intend to deceive you, is probably the best answer.'

'Short of the truth, you mean?'

'I do like you, Rachel. You're not like anybody I've ever known.'

'How much of an honour is that, would you say?'

'You might not think it one, but I damned well mean it to be. I think that should raise the old temp in a relatively short time. What we could do is eat meanwhile.'

'Meanwhile?'

'Until the old boiler gets itself geed up. I do quite a decent line in omelettes if you feel like trusting me. Or is there something you'd sooner have?'

'Who are these people?' Rachel said. 'Omelettes are fine.'

'I imagine you can give people merry hell if you feel like it. I wouldn't care to catch the rough edge of your tongue when I wasn't ready for it.'

'Be ready for it,' Rachel said.

'God, I do like you,' he said. 'Quite surprisingly much. Chives or not? They spend most of the year in San Pedro. South of Spain. Be ready for it! Ten golf courses. Quite a thought.'

Roger was competent with the provisions which they had brought, to which he added the owners' condiments in unobtrusive quantities. His appropriation of the blonde-wood, Boffi kitchen had the allure of something both clean and improper. As a user of other people's amenities, Roger the chef had the style of a tactful embezzler: he never made an ostentatious hole in anything.

'So are you going to tell me her name?' Rachel's flirtatious tone was so foreign to her usual character that she could imagine that someone from the old Pont Street set might wonder who this girl could possibly be who so closely resembled, yet surely was not, Pansy Stannard's sister. 'Or should it be their names? Presumably it should.'

'I don't make a habit of this kind of thing, if that's what you're suggesting, duchess.'

'Unless it's what I'm hoping,' she said. 'Has that occurred to you?'

'I'm seriously glad we did this finally.'

'What were you beginning to wonder?'

'I like them a bit runny, don't you?'

'A bit runny suits me fine.'

'I'll have to think about what you mean by that. Hoping. You're a bit of an unknown quantity so far as I'm concerned. Not to say virgin territory!'

'By no means say that.'

'So, we're pretty well quits in that department, are we?'

'Put it this way: I don't think we need call in an accountant.'

'That's what I like. That look on your face. I love that look. It really gives me a strong desire to do things.'

'I must wear it at all times,' she said. 'Pending discovery of what these things are.'

'Have a feel,' he said, 'if you don't believe me. All your fault. I hope you like tinned peaches. Yellow cling! For some reason that always gets me, always did. What do you want to do this after-noon? Do you want to go into Oxford?'

'Not really,' she said. 'I've already been to one university.'

'So you have. Did you like it?'

'Did I like it?' she said. 'There's nothing quite like three years in Hull.'

'It at least gives you the chance to say that, doesn't it, going? That's something you'll always have over me. I've never had an opportunity to waste my time in any way whatsoever.'

'What about now?'

'I wouldn't describe this as a waste of time, by a longish chalk. By no means.'

'How would you describe it?'

'There you go: the famous look! I don't want to go into Oxford, least of all when I see you looking at me like that.'

'So what do you want to do?'

'Christen the upstairs room, basically. Unless you've got other ideas.'

'They've got a lot of books, whoever they are.'

'And records,' he said. 'You could probably find all kinds of good things I don't know anything about.'

'What sort of people normally rent this place?'

'Visiting professors, bankers, people who are using other people's money mostly. Are you a bit warmer now?'

'The toast is about to pop up,' she said.

'You intrigue me, honestly.'

'In what regard?'

'There you go! You say all kinds of things as if you meant something secret by them. OK: as if you were talking to someone who wasn't exactly me. "In what regard"!'

'But then again, who are you exactly? I certainly don't know; that's probably what I like about you. Never make the mistake of telling me, will you?'

'What about what I want? Do I get to tell you that?'

'Is there something exact that you want?'

'There might be. Am I never to tell you when there is?'

'It can sort of come up then, can it?'

'Damned right,' he said.

'All right then,' Rachel said. 'Out with it.'

'To be serious,' he said. 'I'm thinking long-term. I'd hate to think that I was *never* allowed to tell you precisely what's on my mind. You probably don't realise it, duchess, but you throw quite an intimidating shadow.'

'I shall evidently have to exercise.'

'Because of what you don't choose to disclose basically, about yourself.'

'Whatever is basic is usually no more than that. This duchess talk of yours, is there any chance of your dropping it?'

'With a clang, if so requested. It's the tiara, darling, that's all. Don't you like bended knees at all?'

'It makes me self-conscious.'

'Nuff said. Deleted in all future correspondence! Yellow Cling Peaches. Del Monte they always were, weren't they? I don't suppose you had them. Childhood fave of mine; I loved that slippiness, silent slippiness; I loved that for some reason. Would you hate it terribly if I watched something this afternoon? Say, if you would.'

'For instance?'

'France–England. At Twickers. Would you hate it? I don't have to.'

'I'd like to watch it myself.'

'You weren't secretly hoping, were you, by any chance?'

'I wouldn't go that far, quite.'

'How far would you go, Rachel, if seriously pushed?'

'No idea,' Rachel said. 'I've never had a serious push.'

'Assuming it meant getting something you really wanted?'

'Such as?'

'You've never been short of it, have you, money? Or . . .'

'What's the alternative?'

'We don't have to watch the rugger. You certainly don't. If you've got better ideas.'

'You'd sooner watch it on your own, is that it?'

'Far from it. Absolutely not. I just didn't reckon with it being on with you.'

'You'd be amazed at what's on with me. I'm a very conventional sort of a girl.'

'Isn't there a bit of a contradiction in there somewhere?'

'Oh, I hope so,' she said.

'God,' he said. 'You're the sort of girl I always imagined myself scratching my head over.'

'That doesn't sound particularly appetising.'

'In the sense that . . . oh, I see what you mean. Not like that. Fancy you liking rugger. What other games do you like?'

'None really.'

'I'm quite a big squash man myself. And tennis.'

'I'd forgotten tennis. This means we're not going to the christening, presumably?'

'Christening.'

'Upstairs. This afternoon. As advertised in earlier editions.'

'We certainly can if you want us to. Or we can save it.'

'What about half-time?'

'It is rugger. They have very short half-times, remember. Just time to suck a lemon, bit of a pep talk and get the breath back.'

'Right.'

'You were probably thinking of soccer.'

'I must have been.'

'You are a hell of a difficult read sometimes, ladyship.'

'I've gone down in the world,' Rachel said. 'Are we having coffee?'

They took their mugs into the living room, where they had a leaded view of the Oxfordshire countryside. The television was built in under the bookshelves. It had a pair of louvred doors in front of it which Roger rattled open with been-here-before lack of hesitation. When he threw cushions on the floor below the sofa, Rachel assumed that he had done other things before as well.

As the match began, but after the national anthems, of course, he put a hand on her haunch and left it there. It meant that he had to duck repeatedly at his coffee, since he could raise it only as high as the elbow on which he was resting his weight. He watched the screen with thorough attention, while the hand (which had now brushed her skirt lightly up her thigh) made progress, like some quietly misbehaving puppy, between her legs. About twenty minutes into the first half, she sighed and moved a cushion under her hip-bone. Roger's eyes switched from a penalty-taker, whose feet were about to make a stuttering approach to the ball, and made a rapid survey of Rachel. His expression was such a comic balance of anxiety and complacency that she had to close her eyes. She sensed him leaning towards her and his breath was warm on her face before his lips were. He kissed her keenly, but with an air of capping rather than beginning something.

'Love you,' he said. 'And tell you what: let's slip those off, why don't we, the knicks? Look at that, would you believe it? Right between the posts and he's gone and missed it!'

iv

Mickey said, 'How's your mother?'

'Why do you ask? Do you want to be sure she's unhappy?'

'You're very unkind sometimes, Rachel.'

'Look, I've got some news,' she said. 'In case you're interested.'

'You're going to get married.'

'Not quite.'

17

'You're not going to have a baby, are you?'

'By no means.'

'I give up,' Mickey Stannard said.

'I *am* married. I got married on Saturday.'

'Why? Why?'

'Because I wanted to, and so did he.'

'Was Pansy there?'

'Pansy was there. Every show needs its star.'

'Am I going to be told who he is?'

'His name is Roger Raikes.'

'And what does he do?'

'He's a partner in an estate agent's. A junior partner, but...'

'Will I like him?'

'I don't know.'

'And you don't care, is that it?'

'You might well. He's quite a big squash man. He's number twelve on the ladder. He may be eleven after tonight.'

'I've been told to stop. It's unwise when you're over fifty. Especially with this hernia. Where are you going to live? Or where are you living, should I say?'

'We're still looking. Aren't you going to have an op? Meanwhile, he's still got his place and I've still got mine.'

'That sounds impressively modern,' Mickey said.

'You're in and out the same day, if you get the right man.'

'And then you hobble for a month. I've been told to lose some weight, but meanwhile I'm fine. Is there anything else I richly deserve to be told?'

'Mickey, you're not upset, I hope?'

'I am your father, you know. I'd hate to let you down. Of course I'm upset.'

'We did it the way we did because Roger was terribly afraid of being ... outgunned. Socially.'

'And I'm sure you did little or nothing to allay his anxieties.'

'Heck, no,' Rachel said.

'Do I understand you? I suppose I do. You don't like to be seen to be angry, do you? Or is it simply that, like me, you rarely dare?'

'Who do I have a right to be angry with? Who do you?'

'You blame me, don't you? And always have. Why? When you understand very well why I did what I did. Are you going to go on working?'

'Why else do you think I didn't have the baby?'

'Baby? What baby?'

'The one I didn't have. Of course I'm going to go on working; I've got this new slot to edit on the Weekend section. Opera and ballet mostly. I'm even getting to write a few pieces. Please don't be visibly upset. Emotional. No need.'

'Are fathers forbidden to care, or is there someone in here you know or something? Under your own name are you doing this?'

'Initials. I just don't want you to be under an obligation.'

'I'm all right,' Mickey Stannard said. 'Whose baby was this?'

'Mine,' she said, 'mostly.'

'Rachel, why you've waited all this time to be like this is what mystifies me. You seem to be doing all the things you want to do, and yet...'

'Perhaps being like this is one of the things I want. How about considering that distasteful possibility?'

'Am I supposed to be amused or offended or what?'

'Try both. I thought you might want to know that I'm married.'

'I hope you haven't ... done this ... No, I'm sure you haven't.'

'Go ahead and say, because I bet I have.'

'All right: to spite us.'

'Us?'

'Your mother and me.'

'That constitutes "us" these days, does it? Well, well! And what's the rest of the news this hour on the hour?'

'Rachel, Rachel. I wish you all the happiness in the world. Anything you'd particularly like as a wedding present?'

'Sure. What did you give Pan?'

'Pansy did ask me to the wedding.'

'As you were paying for it, she possibly would. Ten grand, it cost you, didn't it, at least? How about giving us twenty-five?'

'I've never known you like this.'

'Me neither. That's what I principally like about it. Oh Daddy, you would have *hated* it. It was a desperately suburban occasion. His father's an invalid, of the most unglamorous imaginable kind, complete with wheely-bin; I couldn't humiliate him by inviting a lot of haw-haw-hawing friends and relations.'

'Haw-haw-hawing? Which ones are those?'

'Have you ever heard Pansy's Brice when he starts honking? He sounds like some kind of a rare sea-bird. Not quite rare enough.'

'He's doing exceptionally well. The Lady likes him.'

'He's a coming man. Honk, honk, honk. Here he comes.'

'I'd like to at least meet him, your ... chap.'

'Husband. He's my husband. You have to get used to these things. Like we did Mummy not being your wife.'

'You couldn't resist that one, could you? He's doing well, is he?'

'I think he probably is, yes.'

'And he loves you?'

'He certainly seems to want me.'

'That's half the battle.'

'No, no; he *seriously* wants me. He thinks I'm ... an asset.'

'You could do with some money, could you, to prove it?'

'Thanks. There's this house apparently.'

'I do wish one thing, and that is you'd given me the chance to ... prove how generous I was.'

'You can always make it fifty, if you want to do that.'

'To think you were always so ... so ...'

'Dull?' Rachel said. 'Did the word escape you? It can't have got far. No need to watch the Channel ports exactly.'

'He seems to have done you the world of good,' Mickey Stannard said. 'No, not dull; nice. You *are* getting tart: with a vengeance!'

'That's the journalism. Nice equals a drop in salary and prospects. He thinks I'm a *catch*, Daddy. Can you imagine?'

'If you don't want to talk about it, we won't, but tell me something: did you get rid of this baby deliberately, or ... ?'

'Obviously.'

'And then you married the father?'

'Indeed.'

'I thought you wanted children.'

'Just at a time when I'm beginning to get pieces in the paper? *Per-lease!*'

'Have you always told a lot of lies?'

'Quite a few,' she said. 'But recently I've got better at it.'

'I suppose you really are married.'

'Oh, I'm afraid so.'

'Are you having regrets?'

'For your sake. Did you hope I was conning you? Or is it just that you never thought it would happen to little Miss Muffet?'

'You think I behaved like a shit, don't you? Going off with Patricia. You think I should've stayed with your mother.'

'I don't think you should've done anything,' Rachel said. 'Unless perhaps get rid of us. Before we were born, I mean.'

'Pansy doesn't take that view, I don't think.'

'No, that's right. But then . . .'

'For God's sake finish your sentence, Rachel.'

'She's got Toni's eyes, hasn't she? *And* she hasn't got your nose.'

'Where is this house?'

'Essex. Near Chelmsford. The right side of London for both of us. What is a tuffet exactly? Has life taught you?'

'Is Essex necessarily a good idea?'

'Perhaps that's why I did what I did. When I had the abortion. Tried to get rid of myself. What do you think, Micks?'

'I'd sooner pass on that one. And stick to paying the bill. I don't want to start having opinions that cost me even more than the lunch. You will get a survey, won't you?'

3

Was it that I wanted to see what would happen when I could afford to say something tactless to my father? It had always been my policy to make things easy for him, for Toni, for everyone. Allowing the family to get away with things had been my furtive way of amusing myself at their expense, or was it at my own? I had had no consciously aggressive intent when I arranged lunch with Mickey, but his flushed appearance and the razored grey in his newly layered hair provoked me. The evidence of his mortality reminded me of how long I had spent protecting him, and myself, from brutal truths. As I turned the knife in his wounds, I felt more affection for my father than I had for many years. The one generosity which I craved was his admission that I could hurt him. However, the cheque which enabled us to buy the Old Mill, Badham, and the willow farm which went with it, was also very welcome.

I did not sever myself from Pansy's world when I married Roger, but I was careful not to introduce him to it. Fearing that I might be amused by his humiliation, I avoided exposing him to Brice and to Roley Savory, who became my Wapping colleague soon after Prue had set up house with Vivien Cazelet. Roley was flattering enough to be quite unpleasant when he told me the news; knowing perfectly well that Prue's decision had nothing to do with me, he saddled me with credit for a feminine plot.

'I've got a nose for these things,' he said.

'Is *that* what it's for?' I said.

His concocted grievance gave Roley an excuse to press me to resume what he insisted on calling 'our little *numero*'. He had put on ostentatious weight after the conclusive split with Prue; the extra pounds supplied a less embarrassing reason for his wife's departure than her Sapphic predilections. When I gave as my excuse that I was now a married woman, he said, 'Oh, for *Christ's* sake,' and began a campaign of public sarcasm around the office. As a result, I became a favourite of Michael Lea, the associate editor, who felt his own place menaced by Roley and had set about establishing a network, to which I was now a natural recruit. Michael even suggested that I sit in on the Tuesday conference. When Roley vetoed the idea (on principle), I was compensated by having my full name replace my initials on the mini-profiles (450 words) which were now my scathing speciality. My lunch with Mickey, together with Roley's insinuations about a bitches' coven, liberated a cutting attitude – with an abrasive feminist edge – towards people whom I should previously have found intimidating.

If my journalistic promotion had preceded my marriage, I might never have set up house with Roger. However, rather than regret my improbable choice of him as a husband, I elected to regard him as the talisman who had brought me luck. My pleasure in him was neither sexual nor domestic; it was – to use utterly unpublishable terms – both moral and spiritual. Our life was one of uxorious regularity, but what I treasured – what comforted and uplifted me – was the fact of his existence, particularly when I was not with him.

On Saturday afternoons, we played tennis with Greg and Cyn Barraclough at the local club; Roger even invested in the tie. We went to Garden City on Sunday mornings and in the afternoon we usually had a return with Greg and Cyn. I waited for Roger to say 'Even-Steven' as we came off the court at one set all; he seldom failed me. During the week, he and I found frequent opportunities to ask each other how it was all going, but we rarely stayed for answers. No small part of what I appreciated about Roger was the way he kept things from me. Although we spared each other the details, the apparently new white BMW in which he was waiting for me at Hatfield Peverel station one Friday evening was his coded way of announcing that he had achieved a full partnership. I couldn't tell it was second-hand, could I?

When, after just over a year of electric windows, the BMW yielded to a manifestly second-hand, wind-down, red Ford Escort, I accepted Roger's explanation that in-house market research had proved that clients could be well alarmed by showy motors. A few weeks after that, he stopped me in the kitchen doorway, after we had had Saturday lunch (ham and salad and an M & S sticky treacle pudding) and said that he loved me, very much.

I said, 'All right, Roger, what's the matter?'

'How much does this newspaper job of yours really matter to you, Raitch?'

'Is it money?'

'It's money. It's just about everything.'

'I can let you have some. How much do you need?'

'How do you feel about a complete change?'

'A complete change in what sense? And of what?'

'Like going abroad for a while. That sense.'

'Hadn't you better tell me what this is all about?'

'It's all about pulling up stakes, to be frank.'

'I think you'd better be a lot franker than that, don't you?'

'All right,' he said, 'so I've been stuffed. Good and proper. By people I trusted. Royally. Back passage time. To the hilt. Satisfied?'

'Meaning, presumably, that you thought you were taking advantage of them and all the time they were taking advantage of you?'

'All right, duchess, I thought I was doing something clever. I took advice and the advice was that I was.'

'And then unfortunately what?'

'The advice . . .'

'. . . turned out to come from someone who was cleverer than you. Who also happened to be in on whatever it was. How did I guess?'

'You haven't been reading things I left around, have you?'

'No, but I did wonder why you left them.'

'Do you love me at all, Rachel? I truly hope you do.'

'Dear Christ,' I said. 'Do you need as much as *that*?'

'All right, I've done the house. I've done the lot.'

'You've done the *house*?'

'In the sense that, if we don't give them the house, it's my name on the bloody bulletin board. Calling all cars time.'

'You certainly *have* done the house. How much money are we actually talking about?'

'I can always do a runner. You don't have to know where I've gone. You'd have *not* to know, in fact. Why did you marry me, as a matter of interest?'

24

'Probably my short legs,' I said. 'I also liked your eyes. I thought you were someone who was going places. And I was evidently right. Roger the Dodger, as Pansy so rightly said!'

'It at least gives you a chance to come it, doesn't it, ladyship? *When* did she? Tart! This gives you the chance you were waiting for, then, does it? Roger the Dodger, highly original that is!'

'How about the details, as you estate agents say, don't you?'

'All right,' he said, 'I've been stuffed, which – OK – means I'm not as clever as I thought. It also means I'm now cleverer than I was, because I can see where I went wrong. And accordingly won't again. I don't think of them as short. The legs. If we move quickly, I can save quite a percentage of what we can get for the house, which I happen to have had quite a decent offer for already ...'

'You've *sold* the house already? Without even asking me?'

'I only said "offer". I happened to be showing somebody the place. While telling them it wasn't for sale. Just for the sake of example. And the response was surprisingly positive.'

'Was it just? That *is* heartening. When was this exactly?'

'A week ago, ten days? Do you trust me, Raitch?'

'Don't worry,' I said. 'It hasn't come to that yet.'

'Look, before you ... it's nothing *criminal*, what we've done.'

'You and who else is this we're talking about?'

'Do you remember Quigley? I went in on something with Quiggers and this supposed mate of his. It was an option situation. No-time-to-think time. Ivor Tubbs.'

'Using the firm's money?'

'Technically, yes.'

'How does that differ from "yes"? Except that it's criminal.'

'It wasn't actually me who did it. Which is the good news. This is purely temporary, Rachel. Nothing more than a blip.'

'Selling up and leaving the country under plain cover is a fairly hefty blip, as blips go.'

'If that's how you feel about it, you don't have to come.'

'It's how I feel about it all right,' I said, 'but I'll still come.'

'I couldn't blame you if you wanted a divorce. The only problem is, I have signed a few things which, strictly speaking, need your endorsement too. Rather sharpish actually.'

'I don't want a divorce particularly, though I can't imagine why not. Produce your dotted lines, you'd better, hadn't you?'

'I'll never forget this, Raitch.'

25

'It's unlikely either of us will.'

'I'll open a special account, as soon as I can, and make sure you eventually get your full share back, with compound interest.'

'What's mine is yours, Roger. And *vice versa*, isn't it?'

'I'm not sure I can live with that. Can I think about it?'

'Where are we going to go exactly? Have you got that one worked out as well? Have you got the tickets? Or must we walk?'

'France, I thought.'

'What the *hell* do you think you're doing? One thing at a time, if you don't mind.'

'We never do naughties downstairs any more. And I do like it downstairs, don't you?'

'You've got one hell of a nerve,' I said.

'And it's getting longer even as we speak. You parleyvoo a bit, don't you? Over the back of the chair, darling, with you, I thought. I've always imagined it like that.'

'Always, have you? Look, one thing at a time, Roger, don't you think we should?'

'Not a bit of it,' he said. 'I'll get those down for you. Life's very short. Just kneel up and make yourself comfortable.'

'Not the Riviera,' I said. 'There are too many ... people there already. Turning into a crook and selling things up before I'm even allowed to know about it certainly seems to do quite a lot for your confidence.'

'That doesn't hurt, does it? That's nice, isn't it, like that? Girls often like it more they think they will.'

'With a clear view of Mrs Staples' washing, why wouldn't they? It's certainly unusual. I wonder what she uses.'

'Amazing, the things you can do, if you want to.'

'Have you done the furniture as well?'

'That was the offer. I thought I'd better take it. We can always get other chairs when we get down there. To tell you the truth, I wish we'd done this a lot sooner.'

'Down where?' I said.

'The Dordogne. Magic, apparently. Anything else I can do for you, while we're at it? This is the time to say.'

I looked round at him. He was still wearing his designer glasses and his tennis-club tie. 'This is fine,' I said. It was too.

Roley said, 'Rachel, let's talk this over like sensible, grown-up people. There's a line for you! But let's, because this man sounds frankly dangerous.'

'But can I be sure of that?'

'You never could resist being clever, could you?'

'You'd be surprised how interesting life can get, Roley, when you've given up any idea of being happy.'

'He's a suburban flash boy, from what you say, and now he's got himself into a mess. How big a mess, we have yet to see, because when someone like ... Roger ...'

'Yes.'

'When someone like Roger admits he's in a *bit* of a mess, depend on it, it's a lot messier than that. You've got to dump him. A.s.a.p. What possible reason have you got to stay with him?'

'I married him.'

'I see no reason why you shouldn't hope to be happy. You quite often seem happy to me.'

'*Seeming* happy is an art form, Roley. I'm hot on art forms. That's why you didn't want me at conference.'

'Look, sausage-face, he's dumped you right in it. *Sauve qui peut* is my advice, and you can. Conference is a total waste of time for you. You'd only get bullied by Handy Andy. First thing you ought to do is home in on that ugly little sod Pereira and check out the legal pos-ish. You can't go permanently on the run with a man who wears trainers at the same time as a tie-slide.'

'I should never have told you about that. I thought it was sweet.'

'He's going to bugger your whole life. How sweet is that going to be?'

'You get used to it. I want to see it through, Roley. I know it's mad. *And* perverse. So what choice have I really got?'

'You haven't seen the flat.'

'I'm sorry?'

'The flat. You haven't seen it since the paint dried. Why don't you come on up? We can have coffee there.'

'I'd like to see what you've done to it.'

'You do lie handsomely. I finally let Prue have The Old Rectory. I hate unpleasantness and it was hers originally. She and Viv are breeding dogs. Those Chinese things. I expect they eat them in

Sechuan or wherever it is. In Wiltshire they just run about and look as if they need ironing. The girls practically lick the same plates. Just as well I got the flat before the prices went doolally.'

'That's what I don't understand,' I said, 'how he's managed to over-extend himself when property prices are supposedly rocketing? Wouldn't it have been much easier to make a fortune? Schnauzers, is that what they're called?'

'If he's been a naughty boy and signed contracts what aren't really his size, it doesn't matter which way the market goes. They could be Schnauzers, I suppose. They're not Sulikis. *Or* Suzukis. I sometimes think I shouldn't mind being a Lez myself; do they take male converts at all, do you know?'

'What do you think made him do it, Roley?'

'He wanted you to think he was a clever chap, didn't he? That's what makes us all do things.'

The flat was on a higher floor than I remembered. We looked out at St James's Park from between nicely lined curtains and Roley started breathing audibly. The sitting room had an oak refectory table for his word processor and intelligent shelves of books. Matching Chesterfields faced each other across a Chinese table with flagged review copies on it. 'Move in here, Rachel. Disappear as far as he's concerned. I'd love to have you here for as long as you feel like it. We've got an unfinished agenda, you and I, haven't we? Take a look at the bathroom. It might just tip the balance. Talavera tiles. All the way from El Ebury Street.'

Whether or not it was deliberate, he had become a parody of an estate agent. He might as well have been wearing a tie-slide. The bathroom had all the usual toys, including a high-speed shower. There was even a bidet. 'In case you sit on any more wet paint, I presume.'

'I don't want to get pregnant, do I, particularly? Look here, come to bed, Rachel. Now that I've got one. Come to bed and forget all about this eminently forgettable character you've been stupid enough to marry.'

'I'd love to,' I said.

'You know the real problem, don't you? Michael.'

'*Michael?*'

'At the office. The real problem is Michael bloody Lea. He hasn't got a proper job. They brought him in to unsettle Frank, which worked perfectly in the first over and now, of course, they need someone to unsettle Michael. You know the logical person, don't you? You. Short and bouncy.'

'I like Michael. He's been very nice to me. And I'd only have to come to conference.'

'He's been very nice to everyone,' Roley said. 'You'd have a rightful place there once you were performing arts supremo, which you could easily be if you'd let me run your campaign. All you've got to be is reluctant, in a totally ruthless sort of way. Do you like them at all, Schnauzers, if that's what they are?'

'Roley, on second thoughts, I think I ought to go.'

'I've already taken the cover off. You said you wanted to go to bed and I've taken the bloody cover off. Hang second thoughts.'

'I'll help you put it back on again.'

'You're going to ruin your life, Stannard. I can see you are. Why? What for? The man's a pronk.'

'I married him,' I said.

'I married Prue. You didn't know what you were getting into any more than I did.'

'Anything that I've known I was getting into I've always ended up hating.'

'She shaved HQ, was the first indication I had that it was all spinning out of control. He's going to cost you absolutely every-thing you've got. All right, watch me cut my bloody throat, because it's not between him and me necessarily: there are stacks of people who go for girls with by-lines.'

'Too late now, Roley.'

'Why the fuck did you agree to have lunch?'

'True.'

'You wanted someone to tell you what you wanted to hear. Well, I'm telling you: dump the little sod. Dump the little sod and come and live here until something or someone better turns up. And meanwhile get your clothes off. I've got to get back to the office and finish a piece.'

'You're right, that's exactly what I wanted to hear you say.'

'You are a tantalising bloody bitch, Rachel, if you don't mind my saying so.'

'Not at all,' I said. 'It's really nice of you.'

'People pretend they're disgusted. I've pretended it myself, but I'm not. On the one hand, I can't really believe that she likes it so much better with Vivien than she did with me, and then again . . .

do you happen to know how they know when they've finished? I've been down there a few times at weekends, but I can't quite bring myself to ask them. Aren't you going to at least do *something* to help me bring down inflation? It doesn't bother you, does it? If it bothers you, don't do it.'

'Got it!' I said. 'They're called Shiatsus, aren't they? It doesn't bother me in the smallest.'

iii

Having been a careful clipper of our travel pages, Roger decided that the Dordogne was remote enough from England, but sufficiently popular with the English, to provide the ideal place for the new life he had in mind. Who could fail to admire the speed with which he converted a disaster into what might as well have been something which he had always intended to do? Thanks to his dexterity in transferring what remained of our cash from London to Geneva, we had enough money for a modest property which had, nevertheless, to make the right impression on the clients whose business he was reassuringly confident of acquiring. Our flight had all the allure of an often postponed holiday. Roger smiled at me as we drove off the ferry at Calais as if he had finally redeemed his reputation by keeping his promise.

When we found a property at a price we could afford, its name – '*Les Noyers Tordus*' – enchanted me more than the house itself. Any twisted walnut trees had long since been cut down. The principal charm of the limestone farmhouse, with its flagged front-terrace above the arched cellars where animals were once stalled, was that it stood on a spur overlooking three valleys. We reached it up a narrow track which continued only as far as the Lacombes' farm. A single untwisted walnut tree grew on the far side of the track, opposite a studded oak doorway in the wall of what the particulars called '*le patio*': a gravel space, spiked with weeds, between the barn which faced the house and the stone steps up to the terrace.

The owner of *Les Noyers Tordus* had died in Martinique over a year before we were shown the place by Maître Lespinasse, the notary from Ste-Foye-le-Fort. The shutters had not been opened since; saltpetre blistered the bedroom wall. Bats hung in folded rows, like shrivelled umbrellas, from the rafters of a barn whose tiles sagged picturesquely and would need a lot of money to rectify. As Roger said, with an estate agent's practised optimism, the place had considerable potential.

Maître Lespinasse was a weighty man in a brown suit. The purple rosette of some order distinguished his lapel. His favourite phrase was '*Je ne suis pas le bon Dieu*'. One had the feeling that he meant it to be taken with a pinch of salt: he certainly seemed to have elastic discretion over the price of the property. Roger made adroit use of his ignorance of France, and French, in bargaining with the notary. He had instructed me to reveal no knowledge of the language; I was to play the little woman who was innocently gratified when Maître Lespinasse was lulled – as well as discreetly bribed – into reasonableness. It occurred to me that, if I were ever to find my way back into journalism, there might be quite a larky piece on Roger's recipe for stuffing a *notaire*.

I had informed Michael Lea that I had to leave the paper because I was pregnant. I quite agreed with him about the folly of giving up my job, but what could a girl do when her bio-clock went off? Had I been telling the truth, I should have felt a fool, but the bogusness of my ante-natal spiel gave me the feeling that I had got away with something (I was plausibly contemporary in my maternally green concern about clean air for the little one).

Although I had been deprived of a job which suited me, I had no vindictive reaction so far as Roger was concerned. However, respect for his vanity demanded that I pretend that he had been a scoundrel and that I could never entirely forgive him. Good-humoured sympathy might have unmanned him; hence my attitude of rueful complicity as he explained how we could save more of our skin than had at first seemed possible. I had very nearly loved him for his casual 'Our turn next week then,' as he (and I) waved adieu to the Barracloughs after they had paid for the court on that last Sunday afternoon before we loaded everything left to us into the Avis Transit, at four in the morning, and drove down to Dover to catch the ferry. Roger may have been a shit, but he was *my* shit. I could no more put him down than I could an unfinished thriller; if he had been in paperback, I should have had to find out what happened to him in the end. I am one of those people who never walk out of a show, even when I have been given free tickets.

In the short term, Roger managed to appear unbruised by his

fall. Once we were safely at home in *Les Noyers Tordus*, his first businesslike move was to have cards printed. He made contacts and discovered the lie of the land with all his old confidence. The gold-buttoned blazer and the well-pressed trousers and the barber's-pole stripes of the Hatfield Peverel Tennis and Croquet Club gave him an Old School panache which proved ingratiating in expatriate circles. The trustworthy handshake (confirmed by a little turn of the chin and sometimes by a second hand clapped on top of the other) crossed the Channel with an unimpaired capacity to reach out for new friends.

I had prepared for a change of names, but Roger promised that it sufficed to put distance between ourselves and any unpleasantness. 'It's not as if I'd broken any laws, you know,' he said. When he swore that, before leaving, he had fully paid back our share of whatever money had to be made up, I was touched by what I was pretty sure was his thoughtful dishonesty. Pressed to say whether I believed him, my lips promised that I did. My performance made him almost vindictively randy, which was interesting.

As soon as we had aired and painted *Les Noyers Tordus*, and replaced rotten shutters and warped doors, Roger began to invite new friends to visit us and see what I had done to it. He had a knack for making himself useful to people, and for finding uses for them: he had soon knotted together a network of acquaintances, most of them retired and eager to rent their houses during advantageous months. Roger proved himself to be just the man they needed. English, Dutch, Scandinavian, or French, none of them would normally have struck me as worth knowing, but Roger's opportunism turned social drudgery into a form of sincere and appetising trickery. We did not cheat our clients, but it was exhilarating to be in the business of gulling them, however modest the commission.

Roger's linguistic limitations amused his French contacts. Assuming that he would never be able to follow their quicker tempi, they fed him phrases as one might a grateful puppy. What would they have thought if they had observed him frowning as he went through the small ads in *Sud-Ouest* with his dictionary or willed himself to follow the *actualités* on the television?

Thanks to whatever it was that I now felt for Roger, in view of the life which his peculations had obliged us to lead, everything that I did was seasoned with realistic falseness. Even my labours in our economical vegetable patch, hacked from the rough ground below the oak tree under whose shade we stationed the car, was more the kind of gardening to which an Englishwoman who loved country life was expected to devote herself than anything that I should normally have chosen to do. My pretence of being an earthy expatriate endowed keeping up appearances with all the charm of a secret vice. In much the same spirit, when I solicited the Lacombes' advice on how to prune our vine (*'Surtout pas trop de pousses'*) or put down the martens which infested our roof (their prescription against *fouines* was fresh eggs spiked with strychnine), I put myself in our neighbours' debt with disarming gratitude. It might have been fully discharged when Roger was twice asked to drive Simone to Caillac, one harvest-time, after she hurt her eye baling hay, but I took care to maintain the impression that we still owed more to the Lacombes than they did to us.

I became an involuntary *antiquaire* after selling some pine furniture, which we had brought with us from Essex, to a Swedish woman. Astrid spoke excellent English, but the way she would say 'Yah!' instead of 'yes' provoked me to ask an improbably high price. When she wrote me a cheque right away, I discovered my new vocation. I was not certain that Roger's charge of desire for me that same night amounted to congratulations for the unexpected bonus I had earned, but it inspired me to go into Caillac the next morning and buy an encyclopaedia of antiques.

After we had been at *Les Noyers Tordus* for two years, Roger formed his own company, 'Périgord De Luxe', and had new cards printed with our telephone number on them. He was one of the first to see that old *châteaux* and *gentilhommières*, often abandoned to dry rot or termites, and presumed to be unsaleable, could yield bigger profits than routine properties, especially if they were seductively refurbished. We devised a cut-price way of doing this by taking Polaroids of the empty interiors which I then 'furnished' with photographs of antiques culled from magazines or catalogues. As time went profitably by, I sometimes searched out (and then surcharged) the furniture, or provided similar chairs and tables and *armoires* from my own sources; Madame Harlin in Ste-Foy-le-Fort was often my genial accomplice. I did not cheat anyone, of course, but I was not above suggesting the remote possibility of finding something which was already in my cellar (it had been cleared out and rendered damp-proof).

33

It was Thierry de Croqueville, a local architect whom Roger met as a guest at a Rotary Club dinner at the *Soleil d'Or* in Caillac, who alerted him to the possibilities of *La Fontaine du Noyer*, a *maison de maître* further down the valley which led to the Dordogne. Its aristocratic owner had shot himself – the inquest said by mistake – while out hunting rabbits. The widow, an Englishwoman, wanted to dispose of the property and return to London. There were complications with M. de Roumegouse's two sons by an earlier marriage; however, an offer no one could refuse would, as Thierry put it, 'deblock' the situation.

Sometimes I accompanied Roger when he took clients to see a property. It amused us to make it appear that I had been conscripted to the unusual role of playing the hostess. Given my apparent distaste for commerce, I would make a show of slowly coming round to a grudging recognition of the merits of an unsaleable house and, under Roger's jollying, concede that there was rare scope for budgeted improvement. Sometimes, to vary the routine, I would remain obstinately sceptical, despite his apparently desperate requests for endorsement; on those occasions, I would either whisper to the clients to beware of termites (that would be the cue for the story of the Australian surgeon who had had to retire from retirement in order to pay for his roof) or ask too loudly who Roger imagined would mow those thirty temptingly cheap hectares. In irritation at my staunch disloyalty, Roger would then slam us back into the Cherokee (Roger's idea of a rustic gentleman's ideal transport) and we drove on to another house, which we had had in mind all along. In the light of my now established integrity, my enthusiasm would have an honourable ring.

Under normal circumstances, I would probably have gone with him to collect the Greshams from the *Relais St Jacques* before they went to inspect *La Fontaine du Noyer*, but Fernand Lacombe had promised to deliver a load of manure; I wanted to be there to thank him and to spread some of it before it was time to plant my peas and beans. Fernand cleaned out his sheep-pens in the early spring and was glad to make a favour of dumping some of the muck on my patch. He was a short, thick-set man, whose mother still lived with him and his wife, Simone.

Simone suffered from regular misfortunes, of which her mother-in-law was the most constant and her failure to produce a male

34

heir the most unforgivable. The hobbling old *mémé* also had her litany of lamentations; she often showed me her varicose veins. When she came to our terrace door, she played scales on the glass with her finger-nails and adopted a posture of deferential insolence. Once she had been left alone with the *bêtes* and mislaid a heifer, which had to be found before Fernand returned and blew her up. I put the old woman in the Cherokee and, by a lucky fluke, we discovered the creature in somebody's corn, halfway to Caillac. The second sight with which I was alleged to have located the errant beast earned me an ambiguous reputation. Some months later, I was asked peremptorily about some missing ducks whose whereabouts I was presumed rather malevolently to have withheld.

Fernand's heavy body was improbably faced with his mother's small features; the old lady's demanding nervousness could be seen, like traces of female make-up, on her son's wind-thickened complexion as he manoeuvred his winking tractor between our two apple trees. A hot heap of manure steamed on its scoop. As soon as Roger had driven off to collect the Greshams, I had changed into jeans and an anorak and a pair of green wellies, but Fernand still saw me, no doubt, as a dilettante.

'*On travaille un peu?*'

'*Un peu,*' I said.

Fernand worked his levers and jerked the load of mucky straw onto the verge near where I had been digging. '*Il y en a davantage,*' he said, '*si vous en avez besoin.*'

'*Ça suffit largement. C'est déjà beaucoup.*'

He blew through his lips, as if my accusation of generosity were less than complimentary. He then backed and pivoted the tractor with abrupt skill. As I started forking the manure onto my patch, he was already riding past the gate of *Les Noyers Tordus* on his way to the farm. Was I wrong to connect his backward glance and its accompanying wave, a rustic compound of derision and benevolence, with what I found, a few minutes later, in the middle of the heap of manure?

35

4

Before Roger turned left and drove the Cherokee up between the chestnut trees towards *La Fontaine du Noyer*, he checked in the mirror that the red Porsche 944 Turbo was following. Baptiste – the Roumegouses' caretaker – was already wheeling back the iron gates to the courtyard at the side of the house where the stables had been. He did not wait to see Denis Gresham push open the chunky door of the Porsche and display his olive-green corduroy suit and Tricker chukkah boots.

Roger indicated the way up the steps to the long terrace dominating the vineyard below the house. Denis had a spring in his step and a way of lifting his chin as if he were trying, cheerfully, to see over some obstacle. Perhaps he was only trying to be as tall as Carol, who was blonde and long-legged and was dressed with becoming unsuitability in Italian heels and a tight, wraparound camel-hair skirt. The knotty Missoni jacket was ajar over a mauve silk shirt which blinked at the nippled bob of her breasts as she skipped up the steps to where Baptiste was waiting to unlock the French doors.

The caretaker was a muscular man in his fifties, whose legendary father had been even stronger than he; there was something both burly and delicate about him. He shook hands with Roger and snatched off the black beret, with scowling politeness, when Monsieur and Madame Gresham were introduced. Suspecting other people of being up to no good was a routine courtesy with him. With ostentatious gracelessness, he opened the shutters, one set after another, and then he went away along the terrace. Soon they heard him shouting, perhaps at his mother, perhaps at an animal.

The long house was still furnished. Family portraits hung on the walls; sheeted *canapés* stood on oriental carpets which had been brought home when France had colonies. 'It's got atmosphere,' Denis Gresham said. 'It's certainly got that.'

'Don't worry: it goes away after the windows have been opened for a while.'

'No, I mean it.'

'I know,' Roger said. 'And I agree. That's why I was trying to put you off realising how exceptional the place is, because I'm beginning to think it's under-priced.'

Carol walked a few steps and then, without turning round, she said, 'How much is it again?'

'Emma Chizzit? I said eight mill. But I won't ever say it again. It'll be ten to the next people. Seriously.'

'What next people? How much land did you say?'

'Thirty-two hectares. Something over sixty acres.'

'And what would they take?'

'They'd probably be unwise enough to accept seven-five, strictly against my advice, if most of it could be cash.'

'Might that not leave us with smelly fingers?'

'I know where you can get plenty of soap. Everyone bungs people around here. It's a way of life.'

Carol said, 'Can we go upstairs?'

'In your case, Carol,' Roger said, 'I can't imagine anyone ever saying nay to that suggestion.'

As she gave him the required look, Denis was admiring a Louis XV display case which contained some antique Limoges. Rachel had appraised its contents, encyclopaedia in hand, when they first came to check out the house.

'This staircase is a bit special, as I'm sure you've observed,' Roger said. 'Walnut wood, hand-carved, by hand.'

In the master bedroom, Carol walked over to the mullioned window and looked out over the valley. Leafless walnut trees stood in ranks; their pale shadows lay in front of them like grounded arms. 'I suppose it's got a history, hasn't it, a place like this?'

'Oh listen, these old French families, they never have a cupboard without being sure to leave plenty of skeletons in it.'

'It'll be needing some money spent.'

'Less than you think. I got this frog friend of mine, an architect, to give it the twice over. His verdict was, it needs so little spending he was quite depressed.'

37

'And what other lies did he tell you?'

'Not the same ones he'd tell you, Carol, I can promise you that for *absolument rien*. You'd like Thierry; proper Frenchman. Plays hard, works harder. He reckons it could do with about thirty grand spending on it.'

'And then there has to be the furniture. I'm not sleeping in that.'

Roger looked at the heavy, narrow bed, as if he had not seen it before. 'My wife is ace on furniture, if we can only persuade her to stop worrying about her garden for twenty minutes and get her hands to the pump. She really ought to be in the business. Sadly, she prefers the garden.'

Carol said, 'What's happened to Denis?'

'This place has actually come down in price since I last showed it to anyone. He's probably lost in admiration somewhere. It wasn't my idea to knock anything off, but they would do it. The people who inherited it all want out, preferably by different doors. Family values!'

'It must look wonderful in the summer.'

'Does it not? If we haven't got rid of it by May, it's going to be A-number one irresistible at that point. No offers time! Hence you'd actually do me a service if you could talk Denis out of buying it now. Shall I go and see what's happened to him?'

'Den'll be all right,' she said. 'He can find his way about.'

'Are you Australian at all?'

'My first husband was.'

'Wherever did you find time for a first one?'

'You're a pretty smooth article, aren't you?'

'Takes one to recognise one, Carol.'

'You know what worries me?'

'No, but if there's anything in the whole wide world I can do about it, don't hesitate. Day or night.'

'Getting people.'

'From where I stand, I can't imagine that ever representing much of a problem for you. Which side do they queue?'

'To do things. *Denis!* Gardeners, plumbers, electricians, those sort of people. Sweetie, we're up here.'

'If that's a worry, worry not! Rachel's got those kinds of people all sussed and sorted. My wife.'

'I gather.'

'Some hunt, some gather. She's a very shrewd judge of a plumber is Raitch. And our friend Thierry de Croqueville, who's this architect and seriously loves the place, and knows a *hell* of a lot about the family, is more than clued up; he's downright cynical and *very* sharp.'

Carol said, 'You're a very experienced man, aren't you?'

'I've cut back since I got married,' Roger said.

Denis backed into the bedroom, looking up at the oak beam which formed the lintel. 'I have to say so as shouldn't, it's a knockout.'

'Not if you duck your head in good time.'

'Isn't it, sweetheart? All the things I swore I wouldn't say, I can't help saying them.'

'*And* his wife knows all about plumbers,' Carol said.

'You're talking about the very woman I've always wanted to meet.'

Roger said, 'She'll hate me for having told you.'

'That's the price you'll have to pay, if you want us to pay the price *we*'ll have to pay. It's definitely got to be a little bit less than eight mill.'

'Guess what: Roger asked if I was Australian.'

'He can still hear Craig; so can I sometimes. Miserable bastard, not that I'd ever, ever say so.'

Carol said, 'It could be a bit lonely, society-wise, around here, couldn't it?'

'Imagine someone knocking her about, Roger.'

'As far as company goes, more and more prince-type people are buying out here. If you can't find anyone you like, you can always ask us round. We'll probably be busy, but...'

'You know who have a place outside Biarritz? The Rices.'

'I don't want to snow you,' Roger said, 'not over your ears anyway: you're looking at three hours if you want to get to Biarritz.'

'In that case,' Denis said, 'Biarritz can bloody well get to us. Why would anyone ever want to knock that about? When can we see your wife?'

'You can pop up now,' Roger said. 'If you want. Alternatively, pop up whenever you feel like it.'

'How about you both dine with us tonight? At the hotel. Unless you've got better things to do.'

'We'll cancel them,' Roger said. 'Anyway, we haven't.'

As he drove up, Roger could hear the telephone ringing and ringing in *Les Noyers Tordus*. He jumped out of the Cherokee and ran through the archway and up the steps to the terrace. Assuming that Rachel had strolled up to the farm for some wine, he thrust the key into the lock, only to discover, as the telephone continued to ring, and ring, that he was trying to unlock an open door. He stamped in as the telephone fell silent. Then he saw that Rachel was sitting, with her back to him, in a tub-chair near the telephone.

'Raitch? What's wrong?'

'*Is* something wrong?'

'Who was that? On the telephone. I thought perhaps ... perhaps someone had been pestering you. A nutter maybe.'

'Do we know any nutters?'

'A voice from the past conceivably. Was it someone being a nuisance?'

'I wouldn't know. I didn't answer.'

'All right: why not? It might have been important.'

'What constitutes importance at the moment?'

'Work it out. It might have been ... it might have been a client. It might have been someone who was ill, in England. It could even have been me. Then again, it might have been ET phoning home! So what's the story?'

'I didn't feel like answering.'

'Right. Fine. Only ... next time, put the machine on for me, all right, and *then* throw a moody. Jesus! Now where are you going?'

'Upstairs. If that's all right.'

Roger picked up the receiver and made sure that the line was still working. Then he sighed and climbed some of the stairs after her. On the landing, he took a self-controlling deep breath before continuing to the door of the bedroom, where Rachel had gone.

'I hope this won't upset you,' he called out, 'but the Greshams're wriggling on the hook. They want us to have dinner with them. Tonight. At the *Relais St Jacques*, which can't be altogether bad, can it?'

He nagged his top lip with his teeth and then he went into the bedroom. Rachel was standing under the unplaned oak beams which still carried wires for the tobacco which used to be dried in the *grenier* during the winter.

40

'All right,' he said, 'let's have it: something's happened. What?'

She took a dress from its hanger and held it against her; it was the white one with the red spots. 'Do you think?'

'Why not?' Roger said. 'Ideal evening for an attack of the measles. All right, you looked at me like that before and now you've looked at me like it again; so now I've definitely clocked it. Suppose you now tell me what's it all about.'

'It?'

'I'm selling them *La Fontaine*; we're down to the short strokes. It. Whatever it is, I want it out of the way before...'

The telephone rang again. She looked at him with what might have been affection. 'Do you want me to get it?'

'It's a bit on the late side, isn't it?' He clattered down the stairs and jumped the last four. Rachel stretched her neck and looked out towards the Lacombes'. The cooling sky was like clarified butter behind the empty trees around their farmhouse. His voice came to her up the stairs: 'Raitch?'

'Something wrong?'

'It's bloody Baptiste, from *La Fontaine*, and either he's pissed or I'm too stupid to understand him. Could you possibly come and parleyvoo...?'

Rachel went downstairs and took the receiver from Roger.

'*Monsieur Roque, bonsoir!*' While the loud voice blared in her ear, Roger frowned for a translation she did not hurry to give. She nodded; she frowned; she asked a question and nodded again. '*Je comprends, Monsieur Roque, et je vais parler à mon mari. Je vous rappelle dès que j'aurai quelques nouvelles.*' Rachel put down the telephone and looked at Roger with a steady face. 'You didn't take something from *La Fontaine* just now, did you, by any chance?'

'Take something? What do you think I am? What sort of thing?'

'As a joke perhaps. From the china cabinet.'

'That's not my idea of a joke. I prefer the one about the bishop. What's the accusation exactly?'

'There's a piece of Limoges missing.'

'A piece of Limoges?'

'You report me correctly. Someone who wasn't you, it seems, took a piece of Limoges out of the cabinet in the *séjour*. Who does that leave from a cast of less than thousands?'

'Why the hell would he do that? It was Den, if it was anyone.'

'*Den?*'

41

'Denis. She calls him Den.'

'And it seems to be catching. Baptiste went back to tidy up and he saw that it was missing. He wants it back before anyone blames him. What a bastard!'

'We don't know the first thing about him, do we?'

'Den?'

'Baptiste. You sound really strange.'

'Would that be my voice or your ears?'

'The way you're talking. For all we know, Baptiste is hoping for some hush money.'

'Give it to him. It'd be a public service if he lost a decibel or two. He says he doesn't want to make any trouble.'

'That's what trouble-makers always say. What do you think?'

'People have been known to take things. It'll be a nice exercise to get whatever it is back from your friend Den and re-insert it whence it come.'

'Without blowing the deal, it'll be a bloody miracle. It might be more advisable just to slip Baptiste whatever it takes and say nowt. Is it valuable?'

'An eighteenth century *saladier*?'

'It just might be a damn good sign. Den obviously sort of feels the place is his already. Denis.'

'Except that it isn't,' Rachel said.

'Unless Baptiste broke it dusting last week. It looks as though we're a bit stuffed at both ends. However ... Look, I'm sorry if I was snappy; didn't mean to be. I actually thought I was bringing the good news from Aix to Ghent and then ...'

'Do you not want me to wear that dress?'

'I like that dress. I like it a lot. I'm obviously changing my shirt and tie, but I still think the blazer, don't you? The full monty for the *Relais*!' Roger went into the bathroom. 'Wait till you see his chukkah boots.'

'Yes, and then what do I do?'

'Jesus *Christ*, Rachel. What the *hell* is going on? I mean, *Jesus*! This is dis*gusting*!'

'Oh, yes,' she said. 'I forgot: sorry about that.'

'*Sorry* about it. What's it doing in the kazi? Where did you *get* it?'

'Fernand gave it to me.'

'Fernand gave you a dead lamb covered in shit? What for?'

42

'I don't suppose he knew.'

'How do you give someone a dead lamb covered in shit and not know?'

'How do you steal a Limoges *saladier*?'

'No. No, Rachel, I'm sorry, but no. Have we got a plastic bag or something? I mean, what is this *about*?'

'Mary didn't have a little lamb, probably. Certainly.'

'Oh, I see. I see. Well, it was your decision. You decided to do what you did. I left it absolutely to you.'

'So you did.'

'I'll get a bin-liner,' he said. 'He came down and gave you the thing, or did you actually ask him for it?'

'It was in the manure,' Rachel said. 'He didn't know it was there. Unless it was his idea of a joke.'

'Well, it bloody well isn't mine. You were a grown woman, and you decided what you decided. That's something we're both going to have to come to terms with. I have; you'd better. End of story.'

When he came back with the blue bin-liner, she said, 'I'm sorry, Rodge; it wasn't all that good a joke really.'

'Stuffing it down the bog? It was a stinker. You don't often call me Rodge.'

Rachel said, 'Steady now. Don't crumple the dress.'

'Be a honey,' Roger said, 'and don't ever do that with the telephone again, will you? That's yellow-card stuff, OK? I seriously think this could be the big one tonight.'

'I'm sorry?'

'The Greshams. I think it could really be the big one. We just need to pull the stops out, subtly, and they're in the bag. What did you think I meant?'

iii

'*Tiens!*' Sibylle Argote came running as they pushed open the glass door of the winter terrace. '*Les amoureux!* 'ow are you?'

'*Bonsoir, Sibylle! Nous sommes très, très bien,*' Roger said. '*Et vous êtes très, très belle ce soir!*'

Sibylle kissed them urgently on both cheeks, but there was nervousness in her welcome: her beauty made her uneasy. '*On vous attend.*' She held onto Rachel's forearm and kissed her once

43

more. '*Ils ont l'appartement face à la vallée. Montez-y! Et merci de les avoir logés chez nous.*'

'*Il n'y a pas de quoi,*' Roger said.

'*Il fait des progrès,*' Sibylle said.

'*Toujours,*' Rachel said.

'*En français.*'

They went up the stairs to the suite which overlooked the valley of the Dordogne. In the moonlight, Rachel could see down through the *oeil de boeuf* window to where the river twisted a silver trail through unseen limestone bluffs. She stopped to check her appearance in the mirroring glass of a lit display case. There were sabre-tooth tiger teeth and ibis horns, bracelets and earrings and splintered bones from megalithic times. A fading card announced '*La collection Félix Argote*'.

Rachel said, 'I hope he isn't planning to take a souvenir from here as well.'

'Keep the volume down, honey, shall we? You know what these old places are like. Sound's a funny thing.'

Denis appeared to have put on weight since the afternoon. He was wearing a dark grey pin-stripe suit, with a floral waistcoat, what looked like a half-Blue shirt and a Sulka tie with a modest diamond stick-pin. The shoes were black casuals, with a droop of gold chain over the instep. 'We decided it was time to make a disgusting exhibition of ourselves,' Denis said, 'and I hope you'll be the first to approve. Is this stuff all right?'

'Dom Ruinart never did anyone any harm.'

'It's all lies, is it? Denis Gresham.'

'I'm Rachel.'

'From all we've heard, that's excellent news.'

The suite's wide bed was on a high platform reached by wooden steps from the sitting room. Carol was still rustling up there while Denis winced over the champagne cork.

'Your husband is a salesman *sans pareil*, are you aware of that?'

Carol came to the top of the steps. She had schooled her hair into a burnished bun. Two or three truant curls gilded the whiteness of her neck and set off the Bogaert earrings. She wore a ruched black dress, with a red underskirt; the square neckline flattered breasts which needed no flattery. When she stopped on the second step and reached back for her stole, it gave them a chance to see that the stockings – and the suspenders – were black and the legs

44

slim. 'So sorry,' she said. 'I can never be ready on time.'

'You should meet my sister,' Rachel said.

'Rachel Stannard!' Denis said. 'Rachel bloody Stannard!'

'No, that's me.'

'I know it's you; of course, it's you! You just don't happen to know it's me. This is amazing.'

'Is it?'

'Women's Press. You used to work for.'

'Very briefly.'

'Pansy Cavendish's sister or I'm a Dutchman.'

'Oh don't be a Dutchman,' Rachel said. 'We're already over-subscribed around here.'

'The model,' Carol said. 'You're *sisters*?'

'You don't remember me,' Denis said, 'and why should you? Lady Olivia Platt.'

'We're talking about before he had the operation,' Carol said.

'This is all well over my head,' Roger said. 'Might that be why I'm enjoying it so much? Bound to be!'

'You wrote articles,' Rachel said. 'About country gardens. Good heavens!'

'Ultimately, the girl has a memory. In them days, your editor didn't want men writing about that there kind of thing – you tell me why – so I turned into Lady Olivia. Contrary to malicious rumour, no radical surgery was required. At least that's what I told Carol.'

'Who believed him.'

'The darling! We seriously love your *manoir*. Here's to it.'

'It is a bit of a beauty, isn't it?' Rachel said.

'And then, of course, you became a journalist yourself. I read quite a few of your things.'

'For a while.'

'You had the style. What made you give it up?'

'True love,' Roger said. 'And also I had this gun.'

'You should do what I did, you know, with your talent. Because guess what they're paying me for six thrillers in the next three years. I'd tell you myself, but it's absolutely disgusting and I do want you to enjoy your meal.'

'Can you really get people to do things around here?' Carol said. 'Only we know some people in Ischia and their septic tank boiled over and they had an awful time. For months.'

'I know people it happened to in Thame,' Roger said. 'It happened to these friends of ours in Thame. The thelf-thame thing.'

'You've done that one before,' Carol said, 'I'll bet you. Denis, I think I'm overdressed. I think Rachel's absolutely right: I should change and wear something simple.'

'You look fine to me,' Roger said. 'Don't change a thing.'

'She loves to take her clothes off,' Denis said. 'It gives us a lot in common.'

'Thrillers, eh?' Rachel said.

'Are the thing to be doing at the moment. I'm doing this big one about Euro-fraud. Murder and worse among the Brussels nabobs. With a TV mini-series built-in. When in doubt, bump off a technocrat or hump a lobbyist. Lady Olivia Platt never had that kind of fun. Show 'em a specimen chapter or two, a full synopsis and de golden rain begin to fall. Two million-three. Oh God, I've let it out now.'

'They must have had a bit more than a specimen chapter to go on.'

'Oh, I did also show them the very viewable Carol. On one of the rare occasions when she was fully dressed. I had a bit of form: some as-told-to stuff about famous people understandably too busy to spell their own names. Nothing much you haven't got, apart from the nerve ... You should give it a go, Rachel.'

'I'd never be able to think of plots.'

'Think of other people's. I'm modernising Monte Cristo for one of mine, plus a few embellishments. Find a disused quarry, preferably with a dead owner like the late, great Monsieur Dumas. Biff, bang, wallop and away you go. Rachel Stannard!'

iv

On second thoughts, Carol had selected a green silk dress with an autumnal leaf pattern; it further revealed her very viewable shoulders. Denis wagged the empty bottle of Dom Ruinart and said that there now seemed to be nothing much for it but to go and eat. Roger squeezed Rachel's upper arm as they went back past the *Collection Félix Argote* and gave her the good old wink.

As Rachel led the way into the dining room, a solitary woman in a black leather jacket and trousers was being shown to a table overlooking the terrace. Across the valley, far below the *Relais*, the lights of La Roque-Gageac were doubled in the black river. In the distance, beyond the hills, the unseen brightness of Caillac was reflected on the clouds above the town.

Denis insisted that they all have a series of specialities.

'After all,' he said, 'unless we can have the Fountain – what's the name of the place?'

'*La Fontaine du Noyer.*'

'Yes, unless we can have it for far, far less than Roger swears it's worth, we may well never come back here.'

As if to indulge him, they had the *Ravioles de Homard* and the *Escalopes de Foie Gras Frais*, after which they voted unanimously to wait a few minutes for the *Omelette Norvégienne*. Denis had put on Yves St Laurent half-glasses to choose a Chambolle-Musigny 1981. He resumed them to check out the Sauternes. 'Madame has a bit of a sweet tooth,' he said, 'among other choice parts. Look, might they not meet us, these roomy-goose people, if you put it to them in a suitably disinterested way?'

'Denis, give me a good reason – apart from desperately wanting to be in Carol's good books – why I should be disinterested.'

'I did have one vulgar thought,' Denis said. 'The first and only one in my life: suppose, just for fun, that I pay you commission on the full eight mill come what may. If the price were a little more ... buyer-friendly, you wouldn't be doing yourself down, whatever else might be going on.'

'You're asking me to play both sides against the middle.'

'I'm asking you to play the middle against both sides.'

'Denis, you're corrupting the young,' Carol said.

'I just want Roger and Rachel to be rich and happy. Call me a sentimental fool, and pray hurry up about it.'

'Rotcher, good evenink. Have you heard?'

'Gunther!'

'My apolotchies, everyone, but ...'

'Gunther Strasser. This is Denis and Carol Gresham. Our new best friends. And Rachel, of course, you know.'

'Rachel!' Gunther Strasser kissed her hand. 'I am behaving batly of course, as expected, but the Van Schlictenhorsts – you've hurt?'

'Magda and Theo, what about them?'

'Cleaned out. Cleaned completely out.'

'Cleaned out?'

'Zey came back from Caracas and ze house was toadily empty. Toadily. Not a shtick of furniture left in it. Zey even took ze bidet and ze high-speed shower.'

'The Van Schlictenhorsts have got a high-speed shower?'

'Zey *hat* a high-speed shower. Zey no longer do. Zey no longer have any sink at all.'

Catching a look between the Greshams, Roger said, 'Thanks very much for telling us, Gunther.'

'So you see ze sort of sink zat's heppenink arount here.'

'These are people,' Roger said, 'who live in a very isolated house, with no servants and no one in the vicinity. Nothing like *La Fontaine*.'

'Zey took sinks it neeted four men to deliver. An *armoire* vayink about two tons plus. So zis is vot is heppenink at ze moment unless ve're *ferry* careful. I sought you would like to know.'

'Very considerate of you, Gunther.'

'Forgive me interruptink. Enchoy your dinner. Ferry nice to have met you, Mr and Mrs Gresham. I am brinkink ze Heidelberg Ballet zis summer season to Caillac. Also the Kreuznach Quartet, so I have not peen idle. Good appeteet. I see you arount.'

'Absolutely,' Roger said. 'Good to see you again, Gunther.'

Denis said, 'All I can say is, Roger, you're unlikely to have put him up to it!'

'Gunther will do anything for anybody,' Roger said, 'and, unfortunately, he more than frequently does. These Dutch people – the Schlickies – go away and leave their place unsupervised...'

'It happens everywhere,' Carol said. 'It happens on the Riviera all the time. You have to take precautions.'

'Unless you want triplets you rather do, I'm afraid,' Roger said. 'These days.'

'They must've been professionals.'

'Well, you don't sneak in and pop a two-ton *armoire* in your side pocket as a souvenir exactly, do you?'

'It's not like snaffling an ashtray when no one's looking, is it?' Rachel said. 'Or a piece of Limoges.'

'They must need such nerve,' Carol said. 'People like that.'

When every table had been served with its *plat de résistance*, the kitchen door was bumped open and Olivier Argote came out in his unspotted whites; his name was embroidered in red longhand on the breast. He was over medium height, fair-haired, slim and dapper, with an upswept moustache; cooking might have been something he had learned in the cavalry.

'*Tout s'est bien passé?*'

'*Très bien*, Olivier,' Roger said.

'The lobster raviolis,' Carol said, 'were extremely wicked.'

'I take the idea from a restaurant in Parme. Parma. Italy.'

'Chefs can steal things too, can they, Olivier?'

'We prefer to call it *hommage.*'

'*Hommage, homard*, call it whatever you like as long as it always tastes this good.'

Rachel said, 'I like the new plates. Aren't they nice, Denis? Limoges.'

'*Sibylle dit que maintenant il faut changer les cristaux.* There is always something. *Bonne continuation, messieu'dames.*'

Carol said, 'I think we've been to Parma.' Olivier wanted to move on, but Carol's hand was on the chef's sleeve. 'How long have your family been here?'

'My father come here during the war.'

'Your father was a chef too? Is he still around?'

'*Il nous a quittés,*' Olivier said, '*il y a longtemps.*'

'He means he's been dead for a long time,' Rachel said.

'I did gather,' Carol said.

Roger said, 'How goes the flying? *On joue toujours au pilote de ligne?*'

'*Toujours. Hélas, ça veut dire qu'une fois par semaine, maximum. Avec les rénovations, c'est le travail qui domine . . .*'

The *patron*'s eyes veered towards the woman who was dining alone. He took the opportunity to move on after they all jumped, and laughed, at a sudden beep-beep from the next table, where Patrick Delbos, a Caillac doctor, and his neat wife Monique were having their coffee and *petits fours*. Sibylle Argote skipped over and sat down with her *copine* as the doctor stood up, hands raised in apologetic surrender, and then felt for his car keys.

Monique said, '*Chaque fois qu'on vient manger tranquillement chez toi, il y a un vieux con qui se trouve le moyen de mourir.*'

Sibylle said, '*Mais elle est terrible, cette dame!*'

The woman in the black leather jacket and trousers was smoking a cigarette. She looked up at Olivier Argote with unblinking eyes. After he had murmured a few words, she interrupted curtly. Rachel

49

caught only the soft aggression of the woman's delivery. It was surprising when Olivier sat down at her table.

Roger said, 'Definitely one of the more memorable blow-outs! Denis, why don't ... why don't you let us do the wine at least?'

'Nothing would please me more, but unfortunately Carol thinks I can afford to keep her in this style without a moment's hesitation, so it can't be done. Don't damage my credit-rating, all right?' Denis seemed larger again as he stood up. 'It's been a pleasure.'

'Look,' Roger said, 'obviously I'm trying to rush you into *La Fontaine*, if I can, but if you want to see a few other places, that can easily be fixed.'

'Get them down to six-five and I'll rush into it with the best of them. After all, that urgently needed new alarm system is going to set us back a bit, isn't it? Will you give me a tinkle in the *mattino*? Not too early, because Madame likes a leisurely breakfast after I've watched her doing her exercises.'

'Perfect. That'll give Rachel time to get started on that new thriller she's getting down to first thing.'

'Gootnight, efferypoddy,' Strasser called out. 'It was ferry nice meeting you. I see you again, Rotcher, yes, before I shplit?'

'Absolutely. Give me a call, Gunther. Meanwhile ... enchoy.'

5

There was a fox sitting under the brambles by the side of the road as we came to the *calvaire* at the bottom of the drive which leads up to *Les Noyers Tordus*. Like actors, wild animals are often smaller than one expects. I said, 'Trust Gunther to come up with the goods.'

'If *he* calls,' Roger said, 'by all means don't pick it up. Den obviously didn't take that bloody salad bowl thing, you know, did he?'

'And how do we know that, Holmes?'

'The way he reacted. You sailed a bit close to it, talking about Limoges like that. You were a little wicked there, Watson.'

'Fancy the Schlickies having that happen! Now they know why they got such a bargain with that *moulin* of theirs. They didn't.'

'They'll be needing a few new *armoires*. I wonder if they'll possibly want to get shot of the place. I don't believe it, do you? Denis and the salad bowl. Why would he bother to nick a piece of china? Funny, the way he remembered you.'

'Yes. I wonder why he did.'

'He remembered you because he remembered you. Do you remember him?'

'I remember his articles. Couldn't write for toffee-nuts. Every single driveway was a riot of hydrangeas.'

'Memorable! And now he's making a bomb. Olivier can certainly dish out the sauces. Fun people, I liked them, didn't you?'

I said, 'Who do you think she was?'

'Carol? What do you mean?'

'The woman in black Olivier sat down with.'

'Was she buying or selling? I wasn't quite sure. You know, it seriously might be worth you thinking about some kind of a thriller. If you felt like knocking out a few ideas. You've still got the contacts.'

Our lane makes a hairpin bend through the woods before it straightens past my vegetable garden and goes on up to the house. As we came out of the bend, we could see a Peugeot parked, with its lights off, in our usual spot under the oak tree.

'Hullo!' Roger said. 'Unidentified conveyance. In our air space. Recognise it at all?'

'Ninety-two plates,' I said. 'Paris? That's a bit odd.'

'They won't be getting any *armoires* into that in a hurry, will they? All the same, I think we'd better box a bit clever, don't you? Plan A: I'm driving straight on by and up to the farm, all right? Can you see any sort of lights in the house?'

'Not if you go that fast . . .'

'Well, I do go that fast. And for a good reason. Because otherwise they'd maybe guess that our interest is more than passing.'

'Perhaps someone's just chosen to park there.'

'And then gone walk about at a quarter to midnight? Very like.'

'Roger, we can't knock up the Lacombes.'

'No one's getting knocked up. I just want to use the telephone and call the cops.'

'Fernand gets up at five.'

'You always know best, don't you, when it comes to *nos amis*?'

He stamped with both feet on the wide brake pedal, jerked the gear into reverse, turned on loud tyres and headed back towards *Les Noyers Tordus*. He parked the Cherokee so that my door was tight across the front of the Peugeot. 'Is that better?'

'Roger, what are you doing?'

'I'm doing what I'm doing is what I'm doing. I'm not waking the Lacombes and I'm doing what I'm doing. So now let's see what happens.'

His headlights shone full across the *chemin* and blazed against the plum-coloured stone of the archway leading into the patio. Then he both-fisted the horn. Dogs began to bark. 'As the Lacombes can't be disturbed and as I do not propose to be robbed, I'm going – always with your permission – to kill the bastards. If they come out, and if they've got just one item of our stuff in their bloody swag-bags, I am going to smash straight into them, zero to sixty in no time flat, and squash them against the wall. That won't have to wake anybody up, will it? Do we have a seconder?'

As he raged, a fuzzy figure in a silver fun-fur and a white beret had stepped forward, frowning and shading its eyes, from the archway. 'Rachel?'

'Fucking hell,' Roger said. 'What's this?'

Pansy came up to the driver's window and looked in as if she hoped it was her taxi. 'I didn't know where else to go, so I just got on a plane. I called you from Bordeaux; it rang and rang but there was no answer. The car was included if you paid a bit extra, so I thought what the hell, I'll just ... and I did. Was I wrong?'

'How could it be included,' Roger said, 'if it was extra?'

'At least we didn't wake the Lacombes for nothing.'

'I wanted to bloody well kill somebody,' Roger said. 'It's given me quite a stiffy.'

'I hope it's not inconvenient,' Pansy said. 'You will say if it is, won't you? I've got my case in the car.'

Roger raised one hand and, with a nastily amenable smile, lifted Pansy's keys from her gloved fingers.

'Don't you think I did brilliantly to find you first time in the dark? It's not all that warm, is it, for the South of France?'

'This is the South-West,' I said, 'and it's only April. We still have frosts.'

'He's not angry, is he?'

'Not with you, he's not.'

When I turned on the lights in the sitting room, I had only the smallest hope that Pansy might find something complimentary to say about the house. 'You were absolutely right,' she said, as she shed her coat and flopped into one of our high-collared wicker chairs. 'one hundred per cent.'

'Was I? What about?'

'This time I've absolutely and totally had it.'

'Are we talking about Brice?'

'We're talking about Brice, we're talking about Chester Square, we're talking about ... Do you remember Lindsey Lang I was briefly at school with?'

'Is she his latest?'

'*Is* she? I hadn't heard that. Who told you that?'

'I was asking,' I said. 'Not telling. Why did you mention her?'

'She's marrying Roley Savory. I thought you'd want to know.'

'Thanks,' I said. 'I am happy.'

'Oh, darling, do you mind?'

'If I don't mind, why have you told me?'

Roger came in, listing heavily with Pansy's large Vuitton suitcase.

'Oh, that's so nice of you, Richard! I just threw a few things into a bag.'

'Did you really? What made you choose concrete blocks? And the name's Roger. As in The Dodger. Remember?'

'I heard myself say Richard and I couldn't think why. Who is Richard?'

'There's Richard Maitland,' I said. 'Do you want something to eat?'

'I packed and flew and I couldn't face anything on the plane. It all looks like samples, don't you find that? Even in Club. I *hated* Richard Maitland. He stayed too late and he came too soon. Have you actually *bought* this?'

'Yes,' I said, 'this is our house. We bought it and we like it very much. Please be very, very nice about it.'

'I thought perhaps you were only renting, *pro tem* sort of a thing, until you found something you liked better. How old do you think the Harman-Paravicini woman is?'

'If you came Club,' Roger said, 'did you grab an English paper at all?'

'Oh Roger,' Pansy said, 'do you know, I never thought!'

'Do you mean today? Or in your whole life?'

'Can't you get English papers? Who used to defend lots of awful people in the Sixties. She got some killer off and then she married him and he did it again; unfortunately not to her. She must be nearly ninety, isn't she?'

'I interviewed her once, when she took silk. I liked her. Not that I let it show.'

'Brice has been going to these weekend seminars at her place in the country, supposedly to beef up his elocution. I must be the most stupid woman in the world, don't you think so? I always hated that word "seminar". It makes me feel totally inferior.'

'How about an omelette?' I said.

'I don't really care about him bonking people, although I do a bit; what really rubs me raw is when his perfectly sweet father rings up and asks me what the hell I think I'm playing at.'

'And what are you?'

'Nothing. Much. Nothing the old boy could possibly know

about. You know who's recently come back onto our screens and that's Babyface Lamotte ...'

'He hasn't got a hair on his head.'

'My scouts report that he's definitely got it elsewhere. He's been in Bogotá and now he's back. Hugely aged – he looks positively adolescent – and greatly improved. They're quite possibly going to give him Buenos Aires unless he's very, very careful. Did you know he spoke fluent Russian *and* Chinese? I never knew that. Do you think I probably ought to tell Brice where I've gone?'

'Do you want him pounding after you?'

'Well, obviously; but he can't. The House is sitting. They need all the votes they can get. Do you know what I wish? I wish his father would die and we could have the bloody title and the place and take it from there. You do have a spare room, don't you?'

'The house isn't much,' I said, 'but we do run to two bedrooms.'

'It must be heavenly in the summer,' Pansy said.

Roger had toted the floral suitcase to the door of the downstairs bedroom. Instead of joining us at the big kitchen table in front of the fireplace, he sat down, with his back to us, on the futon in front of the television and switched it on, with more volume than usual.

'Brice can be such a *pronk*; I mean, *such* a pronk. I don't know why he wasn't killed in the war.'

'He wasn't even born, was he?'

'His father, who I happen to be terribly fond of. In which case ... but I don't suppose it would have worked. I actually sometimes think I love Crispian more than Brice. Shall you mind terribly if I don't totally finish this? It's delicious, but you know what it's like when you've already chomped and chomped. Anyway, I bet you like to get up terribly early and do terrifically organic things in the garden before breakfast. You're such a saint, Rachel, but I still love you. Thank you so much for letting me come. Whoever else could Richard have been?'

'Raitch, come and see this. Quick.'

I left Pansy sitting at the pine laundry table at the kitchen end of the room and joined Roger on the unsaleable futon. Archive footage promised another glimpse of the war-time period when everything was black and white and the French like to believe that they were all heroic. A young woman was seen getting out of a liberated Citroën, of the kind previously used by the Gestapo; she

55

was embraced by young men in baggy trousers and garter-sleeved white shirts, with sten guns on their shoulders. The commentator told us that her name was Yvonne Langon.

What had excited Roger was that the film had clearly been taken in the Périgord. As we watched, Yvonne Langon, whose death, earlier that day, had triggered the item, was seen on the terrace of the *Relais St Jacques*, where we had just had dinner with the Greshams. '*C'est ici, en plein Périgord, que les règlements de comptes les plus sanguinaires ont eu lieu dans les heures chaudes qui ont suivi la libération du Sud-Ouest ...*' The commentator's melodious phrases covered lurching images of FFI fighters dragging three Members of the Milice towards the edge of the terraced cliff on which the *Relais* was built. There was the river and La Roque-Gageac hopping about in the distance. The three prisoners wore dark trousers with wide leather belts and heavy boots. As they realised what was about to happen to them, they tried to dig in their heels, like children who had come out to play and now wanted to go home to their mothers.

The film ran out and reprieved us from having to watch them being thrown over the edge. There followed a quick clip of the 1945 marriage of Yvonne Langon and Lionel Cator, '*l'agent Britannique*' who had helped to rescue her from Gestapo headquarters in Périgueux and with whom, so we were told, '*elle avait vécu ses plus beaux jours de la libération*'.

'Major coincidence time! I wonder if Olivier and Sibylle saw it. What those people went through, don't you agree?' The vision of war-time romance had quite altered Roger's mood. 'They were younger then than we are now,' he said, 'and think of all the things they did. But then they had a cause, didn't they? I thought about doing some free-fall parachuting at one point. I knew some people who were into it. Ivor Tubbs was. And another chap I was quite thick with.'

'How do people manage to do things like that to each other?'

'Needs must when needs must,' Roger said. 'Don't you think that's what Pansy'd like to do to Brice?'

'But it's not what she actually *does*.'

'Life can't always be as nasty as we'd like it to be, can it?'

'I've left the plate,' Pansy said. 'Because I didn't know what you wanted doing with it. I couldn't see where the washing-up machine was.'

'I'm right here,' I said.

'Oh darling,' she said. 'Do I look ghastly? I *must*.'

'If you were me,' I said, 'you'd be one of my better days.'

'It's the journey,' she said. 'Flying makes me blotchy.'

Roger stood up and stretched. 'I'm going up to bed, if nobody minds. I've got nothing to do in the morning except worry about really, really important things like Pansy's complexion, so naturally I want to make an early start.'

Pansy's look, as Roger left us, recruited me to a sisterhood of bruised females. 'I knew it,' she said. 'I shouldn't have come. I knew it, I knew it. But I momentarily lost it.'

I took her plate from the kitchen table and made a patient operation of tipping what was left of her omelette into the bin.

'Why don't you dump him?' I said.

'Who?'

'Brice. If this keeps happening.' I turned around and saw how prettily she had managed to blush. 'Is there someone else?'

'That depends,' she said, 'on how far back you choose to go.'

'Let's try the beginning of the week. The beginning of the week. Oh my God, it's not Kosta again, is it?'

'Kosta is a total Greek shit bastard. He's a narcissistic, pot-headed pig-person. He always was and he always will be. Of course it's Kosta. Do you think I should divorce Brice and marry him?'

'Why do you always have to marry people?'

'He's changed,' Pansy said, 'hasn't he? Roger. *You*'ve changed. So why can't I? He's a lot more...'

'What?'

'Positive. All right: *rude*.'

'He was a bit thrown to find you here.'

'I'll tell you what finally did it, if you really want to know. Brice wanted *me* to come down to the Harman-Paravicini woman's seminar and bloody well *join in*.'

'What was it on?'

'*On?*'

'The seminar.'

'All fours, if I know anything. All she ever does is talk about all the famous crooks and people she blew in the Sixties. She was number one in the world, apparently, for quite a while. She's still got this look about her.'

'There's something about having been a champion,' I said, 'isn't there? You never entirely lose it.'

'I thought he loved me. I always do. And then of course he had to make out that it was me who didn't love him.'

'And do you?'

'You still look at your watch! You know my problem? They will all start puffing and panting and making promises the minute I'm alone with them and I don't see that I can be blamed for thinking that they, well, mean what they say. A *bit*. If letting him do whatever he wants isn't loving someone, what is? But there is a limit; and seminars between the sheets with a dowager queen termite have to be getting pretty damned close to it. So I said I wouldn't go. And what do you think he did then?'

'Don't tell me he hit you?'

'Let's be fair: I'm always hitting him. He broke my American Express gold card. Well, he sort of bent it back and forth and then finally he ripped it in half. He really had to work. His nostrils flared, which I've never liked.'

'How did you get here?'

'Do you know what the latest idea is that's floating around? A bonking tax. It's been seriously talked about, Brice says. They've worked out that if everyone paid a flat rate per bonk, we could undertake quite a lot of capital projects that've got stalled recently. *And* they could raise family benefit.'

'What do you mean, you're always hitting him?'

'Only with rolled mags, usually. I got here strictly because I bumped into Kosta at Harry's Bar. He said he'd popped in for someone to eat on his way to Singapore. I do seriously love Kosta; he never asks any questions. There's something so reliable about people who only ever want to booze and stuff.'

'What's he going to Singapore for?'

'Something unimaginably shady, presumably. He doesn't like to waste his time.'

'So what happens now?'

'He'll come round in the end,' Pansy said.

'Who will exactly?'

'We shall just have to wait and see, shan't we? It's on the knees of the gods, as Brice always says. Five times out of six, anyway. Haw haw haw! Why *knees*, do you know?'

'Pansy,' I said, 'how can you and I possibly have the same parents?'

'I did once see Mummy kissing Major Geach. Do you remember him?'

'Didn't he only have one leg?'

'It was always said to be quite a good one. Does he ever hit you?'

'He must be dead by now. And why would he hit me?'

'Roger. Oh my God! Now I know who Richard is: Richard Notion. He wore a blazer just like ...' She pointed upstairs, with her thumb. 'Perhaps that's where you get your nose from. Peachy Geachy.'

'What *kind* of a kiss was this? And when?'

'Quite a good old gobble. He was staying at La Napoule that time when Daddy was allegedly head-hunted back to London in a hurry. The hols when those men used to peer at us through their binoculars when we went up on the roof and took our tops off.'

'They used to peer at *you*,' I said. 'You actually had a top for them to peer at. It's lovely to see you, Pan, and everything, but ... why have you actually come down here?'

'Give it some thought, darling. How else was I supposed to get him to give me back my Amex card?'

ii

Roger was breathing regularly by the time I went upstairs. I envied him his economic ability to make pretence and the real thing indistinguishable. I took a long time to fall asleep; I kept imagining that Pansy had managed to do something unwise to the electrics while she was water-picking her teeth. To have seen her and Carol Gresham on the same night was a double-feature which left me feeling that the world was full of women more beautiful, and artful, than I was. And then, when I did fall asleep, I saw myself being dragged towards the edge of the terrace at the *Relais St Jacques*. The men who were manipulating me did not seem to have any enthusiasm for what they were doing. Finally they dumped me, quite near the edge of the precipice, and went into the restaurant. One of them was completely bald, but carried a wig, like a trophy, tucked into his belt. Another resembled Monsieur

Despont, an electrician who left us three days without heat or light. I was reasonably sure that the third was meant to be Theo van Schlictenhorst, but he had been very unconvincingly made up.

Roger still appeared to be asleep when I woke. I was in the middle of a schoolgirl dream from which I parted with reluctance, as from a library book one had no time to finish. I liked school, except for the occasions when we were all expected to enjoy ourselves. Now that I think about it, does one ever see a dream from start to finish?

We are lucky on our hilltop; the mists which fill the three valleys seldom reach *Les Noyers Tordus*. On spring mornings, we ride above an undeveloped world which takes on substance and definition as the day warms. The spire of St-Germain-de-Grives is the first thing that punctures the clouds. Since I was still irritated by Pansy's arrival, I traipsed down to the sloping, dewy field to collect some cowslips to greet her when she woke. When I returned to the house, I could see Roger, in his dressing gown of many colours, sitting at the laundry table and frowning at his electronic diary-cum-calculator.

I sneezed and waited and sneezed again before I opened the front door. Would I have sneezed twice if he had not been there? He went on clicking and entering with the air of an examination candidate whose last hope is marks for trying.

'Do you think it's immoral?' he said.

'It?'

'Taking commission on eight if I only get six-five for *La Fontaine.*'

'How about illegal?' I said.

'Illegal I can live with. Sorry if I was asleep when you came up. You were rabbiting with Pansy and I dropped off. But at least *it* didn't. Another time, eh?'

'If they're willing to pay six-five,' I said, 'they won't run away from seven, and the commission on seven is quite enough to get us a washing-up machine that doesn't have two legs, so why not let's be legal *and* moral and only take what we're entitled to? Alternatively, hang out for the full price. I think you'll get it.'

'You don't understand people like Carol and Den. She wants the house, because then she'll have got him to spend the money, and he wants to prove that he can get it for less. That way, they'll both have got a result. Neither of them really *wants* the *house*, in the way that you – and I – wanted this place, for instance. They're not into homes and gardens; they're into power and ... and ...'

'Water-skiing?'

'Winning; they're definitely into winning. Sure, he can *afford* eight, he just won't ever pay it. I wouldn't be in the least surprised if they water-skied like bastards.'

'And hang-gliding,' I said. 'I bet they hang-glide like bastards as well.'

When the telephone rang, Roger held out a hand like a magician soliciting applause for his assistant. Then he trotted over and picked it up. As Pansy came out of the spare bedroom, with a kittenish frown, Roger sat down thumpingly in one of our rustic chairs and I heard him say, '*Non, pas du tout.*'

Pansy was wearing a pink-and-white brushed cotton outfit. It still had a manufacturer's tag on the hood. '*Bonjour,*' she said.

Roger waved her down. '*Je comprends, Olivier, ça je comprends. Et c'était quand, tout ce ...*'

'*Tout ceci,*' I said. 'What's happened?'

Roger waved me down. '*C'était quand tout ceci?*'

'Roger, what's happened? *Please.*'

He waved me down again. As Pansy tiptoed, quite amusingly and very meaningly, into the kitchen, I could understand why Brice might have been tempted to hit her more than once.

Olivier Argote had called because, when Hélène took them their breakfast order in the morning (including *oeufs à la coque*) our friends the Greshams were not in their room; they, and their car, had disappeared.

'Action this day,' Roger said. 'I'm going up to Sainte Foy.'

'Perhaps there's a simple explanation.'

'There is,' Roger said. 'They're a couple of fucking swindlers. They're a couple of professional fucking crooks.'

Pansy said, 'Is it all right if I make myself some coffee?'

'Help yourself, darling,' I said.

'You don't have to come, Rachel.'

'That sounds like marching orders to me,' Pansy said. 'Do I answer the phone?'

'You answer the phone; you take a message; you behave like any responsible six-year-old. Or is that straining your abilities?'

'Please don't be rude to Pansy.'

'They've stuffed us. They've stuffed us and they've enjoyed it.

61

I'll be rude to anybody I like, *and* anybody I don't like. And I don't need any bloody lessons in comportment at this stage.'

'Maybe they've gone off in the car to have a look at the country-side. Or see *La Fontaine du Noyer* as the sun comes up ...'

'Maybe they've gone hang-gliding, taking all their luggage – *and* a bed-side lamp – with them.'

'Bed-side lamp?'

'They took a bed-side lamp. One of those big Spanish ones. You said they were Spanish.'

'Why ever would they do that?'

'Presumably they wanted it for beside their bed. Don't know, don't care. Ballocks to it, frankly. Large ones. *Ferry.*'

Roger drove the Cherokee to Ste-Foy-le-Fort with the howling competence men always display when they want you to feel small. As he slowed down, very slightly, at the tight bridge which narrowed the road in the middle of a double bend, he said, 'That bastard Kraut, that's what did it. Bet you.'

'Did what?'

'Put das boot in. Gunther. He panicked them, didn't he, and scuppered the whole bloody thing?' Roger checked in both directions before crossing the main road at Pont de Cause. 'Enchoy.' A red patch in the side of his face changed shape and density, like the flux in an oleaginous suburban lamp. 'Never did trust people with a spiritual dimension. He's got too much white to his eyes. Bloody SS man in an earlier life.'

'He can't be much over fifty.'

'Some people are natural spoilers. They see something happening ... they have to spoil it. His fazer voss propaply ze Fuhrer's right hant. And those are the people we're supposed to be friends with. Crap, isn't it? Heidelberg quartet. Ballocks.'

'Kreuznach,' I said. I would.

Roger changed gear more often than usual before steering one-handed, with a blank expression, up the hairpinned road which led to Sainte-Foy-le-Fort. I had never been there before in the morning. Its turban of battlements and the Romanesque gateway gleamed as the sun struck their lichened gold. 'It is beautiful, isn't it?' I said.

'It's more than beautiful. It's a direct hit on the bloody goolies. It's straight in. From forty yards. Bang. If you think that's beautiful. Depends who you're up for.'

'Sainte-Foy, I meant.'

'Fuck Sainte-Foy. Fuck them. Where it hurts; the way they've fucked us. Slice it across or slice it longways, we've been very sweetly salamified. They were probably never going to buy it.'

'Then why did they bother to go through the motions? So *many* motions! That's what I don't get.'

'What do you get, Rachel? Apart from up early in the morning?'

Olivier was in hairy slippers and a pair of corduroy trousers and a check shirt. His moustache seemed to have lost a little of its elevation. '*C'était pas la peine de venir tout de suite!*' Olivier looked at me as if I should have known better. '*Ce sont des choses qui arrivent; ça fait part du métier, voyons!* Zese sings 'appen.'

'No, no, no,' Roger said. '*Non, non, non, Olivier.* I booked the room; we ate the dinner, and drank the champagne ... *Je suis personnellement responsable.*'

'*On prend quelque chose?*'

'*On a déjà pris quelque chose,*' I said. '*La lampe, par exemple. C'est honteux, vraiment, Olivier.*'

'*Un petit café, un croissant. Une lampe, c'est pas la fin du monde.*'

Sibylle said, '*Tiens, les amoureux!*'

Roger said, '*Bonjour, Sibylle; nous sommes vraiment désolés.*'

'*Il fait toujours des progrès,*' Sibylle said, '*son français! N'est-ce pas, Rachel?*'

'I seriously propose to pay this bill,' Roger said. 'Or we can never come here again.'

'I only think per'aps you have an address or a telephone number ...'

'Haven't you got their passports?'

'I give them back.'

'This isn't the end of this,' Roger said, 'by any means. *Rachel le connaît, ce mec. Ils ont travaillé ensemble.* We can find out his address.'

'He seems to make a habit of moving,' I said. 'I doubt ...'

'We can at least damned well try. It's not a joke. *Je veux payer leur ... leur addition. C'est un question d'honneur.*'

'*Une question,*' I said.

'No, I'm sorry, but that's how I feel about it. I hate shits and I particularly hate English shits. And I *particularly* particularly hate them when I was pretty damned sure that they were total prats and we were going to ... to make quite a bundle out of them.'

'*On n'a pas perdu grand'chose, je vous assure.*'

Sibylle put her arm through mine. '*C'est pas notre première expérience. Il nous reste très peu de premières expériences!*'

Her coppery hair shone and the enviable grey eyes gleamed as she took us towards the terrace where Hélène was prompt with coffee and *croissants* and home-made apricot jam. It was as if being robbed were an occasion for celebration; Sibylle took pleasure in showing greater insouciance than her husband. To judge from Roger's expression, her generosity had also deprived him of a grievance: he drank his coffee in a very monosyllabic way and looked down at where the Dordogne meandered, in gleaming silver stitches, across the wide valley below us. I so disliked the bitter line of his mouth that my heart went out to him.

iii

'I'd actually like to go to England and kill them,' Roger said. It was the first time he had spoken since we left Ste-Foy-Le-Fort, but it sounded like the conclusion of a long debate. 'I can seriously imagine killing them. In some detail.'

'They're not going to get away with it,' I said.

'Are they not? What's going to happen to them?'

'They're driving a Porsche,' I said. 'They can be traced.'

'With frog plates. Do you not understand anything?'

'You're talking a lot about killing people suddenly. I hope it's not something I've done.'

'They're villains, Rachel. They're crooks. People do these things because they're good at them and because they like it. They rent cars, they don't buy them; and then they dump them. They rely on other people's stupidity, and they're rarely disappointed. We're mugs, Raitch; we're mugs and we've been mugged and they're laughing. Somewhere or other they are sitting having their coffee and *croissants* and laughing, and that's why they do it. For laughs.'

'And what are they going to do with Olivier and Sibylle's bedside lamp? How many laughs are there in that?'

'They'll bung somebody with it probably, or chuck it over a cliff. The great thing for those people is getting away with it.'

'Why do you suppose he actually reminded me that we'd met before? Why did he do that?'

'Denis? Have a guess.'

'He was afraid...'

'Yes.'

'Afraid of ... what? Oh, I get it: afraid I'd recognise him!'

'Or had *already* recognised him. If you'd happened to have remembered what you *did* later remember, when he told you, you might have rumbled him; but by him recognising *you*, pronto, he made his story seem absolutely...'

'Charming. Which he did.'

'Which he did. And also *plausible*, very. And it worked – you have to hand it to him – because he wasn't *totally* consistent, totally smooth. That's something we ought to remember.' He caught my eye and did not quite wink. 'OK? In case we meet someone else like him. The trick being to concede right away what could otherwise be held against you. He made an open joke of the one weak element in his story. Eminently crafty!'

'You know what I can always do, don't you?' I said. 'Because that's call Mike Lea at the paper and give him the story. I mean, a man with a multi-million pound contract for thrillers who goes around stiffing country hotels.'

'Not a bad thought. It might even be worth a few bob.'

'Always assuming he really *is* some kind of an author, *and* he's well enough known to be worth exposing. Which we could then pass on to Olivier and Sibylle. No?'

'You know what's nice?' Roger parked the Cherokee under the oak tree and pulled on the hand-brake and gave me a look which indicated that the episode was closed. 'Olivier and Sib don't hold it against us, which I find seriously touching. They're a couple who've really ... well, they've really got something, haven't they? You can feel it. What do you reckon it could raise, the story?'

As we climbed the steps to the terrace, we could see through the glass panels of the front door that Pansy was on the telephone. 'I know that,' she was saying, 'of course I know that. And I feel totally the same way about you. Of course I want to come home. Only I don't know how. *Why?* Because I haven't got a bean. No, I can't. Because you ripped it in half. And I wish you'd seen your nostrils while you were doing it; Bricey, they were *white*.'

'She's been on the phone ever since we left,' Roger said. 'Since the minute we left. Bet you anything you like.'

Pansy waved to us in the same silencing way that Roger had at her. 'Can't you cable it? You can cable money still, can't you? Oh darling, of *course* I want to be your wife. More than ever. I *am* your wife. What else am I? That's not fair; Brice, that is not fair. I only did what I did because you did what you did. And you did it twice. I don't know; but I can ask them. Darlings, is there a branch of the Crédit Lyonnais in Caillac?'

'I'm sure there is,' I said.

'Yes, there is,' Roger said. 'Excuse me, but whose call is this?'

'How long do you think it will take?'

'Pansy ... WHOSE CALL IS THIS?'

'Roger, please ... I'm on the telephone to London.'

Roger snatched the receiver and turned round, several times, hot with self-control, before he spoke through very braced lips. 'Brice? This is Roger Raikes. Your wife needs money. Roger Raikes, your brother-in-law, in-law. Otherwise ... Yes, exactly. She needs money for her ticket; she also needs money for this telephone call. I beg your pardon? Well, would you really? And now I'll tell you what I'd quite like to do before you get around to teaching me some manners and that's I'd quite like to move into your bloody constituency and vote for the other fellow. And I'm more than prepared to bring quite a raft of friends to do the same thing.'

'It's Forty-two, Place de la Boétie,' I said.

'Crédit Lyonnais has a branch in the Place de la Boétie in Caillac. Number Forty-two. Don't ask me to waste money spelling things, just send her some dosh and send it now. I don't care if we're related or not.' He had to reach quite a long way to replace the receiver; he dropped it, with furious delicacy, an inch or two into its cradle. 'Next time, I'm voting Labour. And if they want to bring back the guillotine, they can.'

'That was unnecessary of you, Roger.'

'Don't use this telephone again. Ever.'

'Wasn't it, Rachel?'

'Rachel is not the referee. Don't appeal to her.'

'This is obviously the last time I ever come here.'

'Get that in writing, Raitch. Get it in letters of fucking fire. *Now!*'

He clearly wanted to go somewhere, but he could not decide

where; finally, he stamped upstairs, as though he had been sent there, but did not really want to go.

'Why does he hate me?'

'He hates being broke,' I said. 'He hates having our friends robbed by people we sent to stay with them. It's not altogether your average morning. How was Brice?'

'Is your coffee machine broken?'

'I don't think so.'

'I couldn't get it to make coffee. He was unexpectedly human. He'd just jogged six times round Blackball pond. Two of them backwards, which he finds particularly relaxing, and once hopping, which he only does when he really, really wants to punish himself for something. So . . .'

'You have to turn it on,' I said. 'It rarely makes coffee if you don't turn it on.'

'Oh,' Pansy said, 'that's like the one we've got at home. Why do you think Roger is climbing down the drain-pipe? Is it something he does often or has it got something to do with me? Are we supposed not to react, I mean?'

Roger dropped adroitly onto the terrace. He hardly needed to brush himself down. He bent his knees and paddled his fingers at us and then he opened the front door. 'I always wanted to do that.'

'And now you know you always can.' Pansy's applause implied that Roger's display of agility was in her exclusive honour. 'You might have to, if the house burns down.' As she spoke, the telephone rang and I turned to pick it up, since it was on the table behind me. 'Oh,' Pansy said, 'we're still allowed to *answer* it, are we?'

'Rachel Stannard?'

'Yes.'

'Mike.'

'Mike.'

'As in Lea. As in Wapping.'

'*Mike*.' I covered the mouthpiece and said, 'It's Mike Lea.'

Roger said, 'And?'

I said, 'This is amazing. Because I was thinking of calling you. No, no, because we've had a leedle bit of a drama with some English con artist who told us he was a famous thriller-writer and then buggered off without paying the bill at our favourite local hostelry. Denis Gresham.'

67

'Produces no instant erection, I'm afraid.'

Roger said, 'What's he know about him?'

I was happy to return the same wave he had earlier given me. 'Small matter,' I said. 'What else is happening?'

'Roley Savory's engaged.'

'To the long-lasting Lindsey Lang, I hear.'

'How the hell?'

'We've got a really, really good local radio station.'

'Then you'll also know that this Yvonne Langon lady has died.'

'Yes,' I said, 'they did a piece about her on the box last night.'

'Right, so here's the very long shot I thought you might be able to help us with. This Cator character.'

'She was married to.'

'Among other good things. Did they have him on at all?'

'He was mentioned *en passant*. They seemed more interested in the lady's distinguished later life as a lover of animals and some baron or other. Are you sure he's even still alive, Cator?'

'That's our possibly reliable information. And living right next door to you. In the Dordogne.'

'Which is bigger than Yorkshire. They were actually together in a place called Sainte-Foy-le-Fort, where we had dinner with this supposedly multi-million-pound thriller writer. We only missed them by fifty years.'

'Cator's English. A bit of a maverick, by all accounts. Which is Polish for shit. We thought it might be timely to do a piece about him, and her, and it. Very much in the Rachel Stannard cool-look-at-the-hero tradition. Your one about that footballer – "The feet were all right, but the rest of him was clay" – it's still on my personal green baize. Rusty drawing pins. How's the family?'

'The family,' I said, 'is all here. All fine.'

'No regrets?'

'Have you got any serious leads on where I might find him?'

'Can't you have a bit of a scout round? *Tire quelques ficelles.* He likes ladies, it seems. Roley thinks it might make a hell of a come-back piece for you. I agree. They gave her the G.C., but London didn't make too much of a fuss of him. Nudge, nudge.'

'Have you got any stuff from the morgue you could fax me?'

'Give me your fax number; it shall be done.'

'It's the same. You just wait for me to hang up.'

'We could use about fifteen hundred words, by Friday mid-day latest. Life and loves under the heel of the Hun. Whatever.'

'*Expenses*,' Roger said.

'Expenses?' I said.

'Within reason. But no helicopters, Stannard; not without a call back. Roley says to say "Hi!".'

'And I say "Hi" to him. Oh, and Mike. This Denis Gresham. Can someone check him out? He truly has behaved like a total bastard. And he is supposed to have this big TV deal.'

'Meanwhile get those stout shoes on and take to the woods, will you? Truffle-time in old Virginny. Oh, and lots of love.'

When I looked round for some interest or even a hint of admiration, I saw that Pansy had moved very close to Roger. 'I only want people to be nice to me,' she was saying. 'There isn't anything else I want in the whole world.'

'Then try not making long distance calls on their telephones, unless they're very, very rich or love you very, very much,' Roger said. 'Or both. He's not going to print anything, is he, about Denis without getting back to us?'

'He's not too interested in Denis.'

'Good. Because it occurs to me that all we need is to shop him and then find that he's some kind of an eccentric millionaire and he *has* got the *fric*, and we've corked the bloody genie.'

'You know very well that's never going to happen.'

Roger turned to Pansy. 'I know very well that's never going to happen, apparently.'

'Where do I start to look for a man called Lionel Cator who may or may not still be living somewhere around here?'

'You know who you should go and see: Olivier and Sibylle. They know everything that happens around here. And then some.'

'I'm not exactly the *first* person they're going to want to see, after we stiffed them with the Greshams.'

'Take the car. Pansy'll be more than glad to run me into Caillac, won't you, Pan? I've got these flyers to collect, and we may as well spread a few around at the same time. We can also check out the bank.'

Pansy said, 'All right, only how long does money usually take to come?'

'In my case,' Roger said, 'a lot longer than it takes to go, but I daresay that's not true for people in your jammy situation.'

Pansy said, 'If he sends me enough, do you know what I just

might do? I just might go and see Buzz and that terrible Trish of his in Monte Carlo on the way home. Those riveting Canadians of his gave Buzz this unbelievably golden handshake.'

'Pay your telephone bill here first,' Roger said, 'won't you? And then you can give us a long and very boring call when you get there.'

6

Daily Express, 15.5.47.

'Among those decorated by His Majesty the King at an investiture
at Buckingham Palace yesterday was the French Resistance heroine
Yvonne Langon. Raven-haired Mme Langon, 28, received the George
Cross for her part in the daring daylight rescue of a party of eighteen
English and Commonwealth airmen from a German motorised column
in May 1944.

'Mme Langon – wife of the British agent Lionel Cator, himself
dropped into occupied France in 1943 – was severely wounded during
the rescue but helped to hold off the Germans while the airmen made
their getaway. Captured and tortured by the Gestapo, she was later
snatched to freedom by a party of Resistance men which included her
husband. Lionel Cator, 26, was unable to make the journey from
France with his wife.'

*

Paris Diary, Evening Standard, 14.3.51.

'Rumours are circulating in Paris about the break-up of the marriage
between legendary Resistance heroine Yvonne Langon, 31, and her
English-born husband, Lionel Cator. Friends deny that the two are
planning divorce, although I understand that they are no longer living
together in Le Rouret, the South of France village where they have
made their home. Yvonne has been seen in Paris with the Franco-

Belgian socialite industrialist Baron Pierre-Henri de Castillonès, heir to the FranTiss textile group.

'Lionel Cator has excited controversy by alleging that a number of shady activities have been concealed by official connivance with people who have got something to hide. Yvonne Langon, by contrast, has declared that war-time hatreds must come to an end and that, while proud of what she was able to do in the Maquis, she has no spirit of revenge.

'Yvonne told me not long ago that she would prefer to serve some larger humanitarian role in the Europe of the future. The Baron Pierre-Henri de Castillonès spent much of the war in Guadeloupe where he has a large plantation house and a private zoo.'

*

The Times Literary Supplement (anonymous review), 22.10.56.

'*London Calling* by Colonel Gervase Bristow D.S.O., M.C.
'Few men are in a better position to reveal the nature and extent of British involvement in the French Resistance than Colonel Bristow, who, from 1942 onwards, was in command of Special Operations in the South-West of France. Units acting under his London-based command are generally agreed to have hampered the progress of the Hermann Goering Division, on its way to Normandy. The delays may have been decisive in the days immediately after the landings. It is less certain what political and military directions were given to the local *réseaux* during the darkest years of the Occupation. One looked forward keenly to Colonel Bristow's mature reflections, and perhaps revelations, on this aspect of Baker Street's planning and practice.

'A certain disappointment in this book springs from the author's failure to be more forthcoming – not to say trenchant – over certain matters which have long been mooted, more or less openly, in intelligence circles. The question of who suborned whom, how effectively and for what end, in the department of the Dordogne, where Captain Lionel Cator was in official command during the summer of 1944 remains a smouldering issue, which a book by a commanding officer might be expected to resolve in a definitive fashion.

'In secret activities conducted against an unscrupulous and better armed enemy, it is clearly necessary for cunning as well as courage to be used. No one should be surprised – still less scandalised – to discover that bribery, blackmail and bluff were among the arts of the war which were practised in order to intimidate, wrong-foot and confound the enemy. However, the circumstances which led to the arrest of the *quondam* resistance leader, Louis Leclerc, and the botched attempt to rescue him, remain entirely, and disappointingly, unilluminated.

'Col Bristow's reluctance to render a documented account of the operations he supervised – he prefers a frankly popular narrative, padded out with tracts of woodenly reconstituted dialogue – may be due to an honourable desire not to re-open old wounds. However, it is hard to accept his cavalier, perhaps ghosted, style as an appropriate one in which to record events so sombre and so fraught with drama (no mention is made of the events in July 1944 which culminated in the arrest and deportation of a number of refugees in the village of Ste Foye-le-Fort). It may be admirable not to take oneself too seriously, but some passages of this readable volume come close to being facetious, not to say factitious. We still await a properly authenticated and adult account of the tangled history of *Réseau* Victor.'

*

The Evening News, 8.6.67.

'Yvonne Langon-de Castillonès, G.C., the 48-year-old Resistance heroine, is today fighting for her life once again, but in hospital. She is reported critically injured after a road accident. She was, it seems, alone in her Alfa-Romeo when she hit a tree while driving back to Paris from the South of France. Mme Langon-de Castillonès was banned from driving for six months when, two years ago, she was convicted of being drunk in charge of her Maserati. She and her industrialist husband are said to be living separately.'

*

That's about it. Lotsa luck. Lotsa love. M.

I read the flimsy sheets and then I pressed them flat and read them again. The distant trumpet stirred the war-horse. I waited for the meaning of the articles to come together in my mind. Lionel Cator sounded a somewhat ambiguous character, but it was not unamusing to hear that there might be someone, somewhere in the landscape, from whom one could learn something more interesting than the rent he hoped to get for his house in the summer months. Although I had made a face at Roger's suggestion that I should go and ask a prompt favour from Olivier and Sibylle, I was soon driving to Ste-Foy-le-Fort to do so.

I looked both ways at Pont de Cause and I drove one-handed over the black hill where the previous summer's fires had made mournful columns of the pine trees. As I climbed the steep road towards Ste Foy and rounded the corner to see the battlemented gateway for the second time that day, I recognised that I was still the kind of woman who feels privileged to be called on to prove her reliability to people on whom she herself would be unwise to rely.

Sibylle seemed scarcely to recognise me as I walked alone onto the terrace of the *Relais St Jacques*. She said, '*Tiens,*' but Roger's absence forbade her usual dual use of '*les amoureux*'. I sensed that my singular presence called for a more personal response than she found easy; she preferred complicity to contact.

'*Excusez-moi, Sibylle, mais ... il y a quelque chose qui s'est passé, un peu à l'improviste ...*'

'*Ils sont rentrés chez vous, vos amis?*'

'*Je crains que non. Je cherche Olivier. Sur un autre sujet.*'

'You know where is the airstrip?'

'The airstrip?'

'Where he keep his little *choucou*? His aeroplane. You find him zere. He is a little boy, you know. He 'as 'is ...'

'Hobby?'

'You call it? Per'aps.'

The hangar of the Ste Foy flying club was on the plateau below the battlements. The runway was partly concrete, partly grass webbed with metal mesh. A footless wind-sock drooped on the morning air. Olivier was wearing zipper-pocketed red overalls, pigskin work-gloves and a leather flying cap; he reminded me of Jean Renoir in *La Règle du Jeu* (whenever it is on television, I try in vain to admire it). He waved to me as if I were expected. We did not shake hands, because we had already done so that day.

I said, 'Here I am again! I'm sorry but it's nothing to do with ... you know, our friends.'

'Oh, so much the better,' he said.

'In another life, I used to be a journalist at one time, and my old editor's just called me from London about someone called Lionel Cator ...'

Olivier snapped shut the clasps on the cowling of the little plane's engine and eased the fingers of his glove with his teeth. 'Lionel Cator.' On Olivier's lips, Cator sounded like an abbreviated *quatorze*. 'He is a long time ago now, that one!'

'He was married to Yvonne Langon at one time. Who died, yesterday, I think it was.' Was I explaining something Olivier knew already? If so, he showed no sign of being prompted. 'Because he was English – *is* English, I suppose – and was quite a hero, well, they'd like to hear what he thinks about her death, which I expect you heard about.'

'Why do you come to me?' Olivier remained polite, but his tone was one I had not previously met.

'Oh only because, well, you know everything there is to know. He was here, wasn't he, during the war?'

'And after it, now and then. But where he is exactly, now, who knows? They call 'im *le Renard*, do you know this?'

'I'm interrupting your morning. Again! I really shouldn't.'

'Do you know why? Because ... say it: say "*renard*".'

I said, '*Renard*.'

'You see? You are not French. The Milice make people say this word if they suspect you are not French.'

'During the war.'

'Only a French person say "*renard*" like a French person.'

'As far as I'm concerned,' I said, 'only a French person can say *anything* like a French person.'

'Enny-sing,' Olivier said. 'You are maybe right.' It was usual for him to be charming, but he was trying to be, which was not. 'Not everybody likes this man, this I can tell you. He is a bit of a fox. You don't know what 'e does always, or why. When I am a little boy, they do not talk very much about these days.'

'Did they not tell you about the things that happened at the *Relais*? I saw some film on the news ...'

'After my father disappears, my mother is not much occupying

75

herself with those businesses. For her, the family and the hotel, that is enough. For her, the war that matters it is the other one, *la guerre de quatorze*: she loses a brother and three uncles.'

'And your father?'

'My father disappears,' Olivier said, 'since many, many years. It is another time for me. Nineteen forty-something. I am sorry, but ... those days, they mean nothing to us now.'

I nodded and smiled. There is something sad, and sometimes touching, about the dishonesty of honest men. When I sneezed a couple of times, it was as if I had done it deliberately: how convenient to be able to parade so abrupt a symptom of help-lessness! I hesitated and then I sneezed again, one, two, three, four, five times. 'Oh my goodness!'

'You catch a cold? I know what to do, if you 'ave time. You have time? It takes maybe half an hour. Get in the plane. I can clear this. Get in. If you want. If you dare!'

I shrugged and took a big step into the cabin. Olivier's cookery seemed to certify him as a pilot. As I had once remarked, in print, in my profile of a doctor who had been in the Cabinet, if a man is officially qualified in one domain, it is hard to believe him entirely incompetent in another.

I fastened my seat-belt and said, 'They used to use the *Relais* as a ... rendezvous, didn't they, at one stage, the Maquis?'

'Many things happen there. Before it belongs to my father. He does not buy until after 1945.' Olivier turned the key in the controls. As the two-seater plane bumped across the grass, the radio came alive. Olivier announced his flight plan to some distant controller, in Bergerac or Périgueux. The routine phrases distanced him from me. Since I did not quite trust this con-venient retreat into jargon, it made him more attractive to me. As I sat strapped beside him in the broad little cabin, I wondered whether he had offered me the therapeutic flight *instead* of what I wanted.

The airstrip was a continuation of the limestone bluff on which the *Relais*, and the upper part of Ste-Foy-le-Fort, was constructed. As he opened the throttle, Olivier's glance at me matched reassur-ance with menace. The runway went up at the far end, like the deck of an aircraft carrier. Abruptly, there was nothing but the wide chasm of the valley into which those three *miliciens* – and who knew how many others? – had been pitched to their deaths on the day when some amateur *cinéaste* still had film in his pre-war camera.

The busy blur of the propeller chewed the air. The lurch of the plane as we throbbed northwards made it seem that we were riding a ribbed surface as solid as a road. The landscape diminished and widened below us. Olivier's casual command of my fate made me conscious of his physical person. I could imagine, with placid heat, agreeing with whatever he asked of me. Fancying neither his sex nor his company, I fell provisionally in love with his gloved confidence. Imagine a lover in gloves! I could see myself, like a third party, accepting and perhaps relishing whatever he proposed. I have always suspected it would be a pleasure to have nothing in common with a man in whose power one found oneself. I was not *happy* in the little plane, but it beat gardening.

'When do I begin to feel better?' My innocent voice made me feel clever. 'Or does that come later?'

He raised a single finger. His overalled knees were several inches apart; the feet, in a scuffed pair of brown pierced-leather shoes, were at an angle of forty-five degrees to each other against the frayed slope beneath the controls. I grew aware of the breadth of his hands; dark hairs clustered above his bald wrists where the unbuttoned cuffs of his overalls had been pushed back. In the vee of his half-unzipped overalls, the flesh of his throat and upper chest was mottled, perhaps from some childhood disease. I decided that I should prefer him to take me from behind.

We climbed into puffy clouds which paraded away towards the west. Olivier was relaxed in his soft black seat, his rakish moustache at odds with his mechanic's costume. After we had reached a certain height, the engine note changed and became almost silent; we seemed to have scaled some peak on which Olivier was content to draw breath. Could this be the climax of our excursion?

'Do you want to do this? You do not 'ave to.'

'I don't know what it is. I thought perhaps we'd already done it. Will it really do any good?'

'I do it for Cédric when he has the bad chest. It works always with 'im.'

How could I refuse to let him do for me what he did for his nine-year-old son? 'As long as I come out alive.'

'*Sait-on jamais*,' he said.

I leaned forward, as he did, as if to make sure that there was no one between us and the bottom. He had already lowered the nose. The sky started ripping past us. The ground came up like a lift. The river was a silver serpent wriggling on the floor of the valley. Olivier sat smiling humourlessly beside me, tilted yet balanced, as the altimeter quivered downwards. His calm fed on my fear. At not quite the last second, he pulled back the joy-stick – Mickey used to read me his father's old Biggles books – and, as gravity drained the congestion from my sinuses, the plane went sawing upwards again. Our dive had taken place only in order that we might climb out of it, just as we had gained height only so that we might dive.

'*Ça va? Pas de mal?*'

We banked and were soon coming in above the terrace of the *Relais St Jacques*. Hélène did not look up from sweeping the area where tables would soon be set out for Easter visitors. It took longer than I expected to circle and then crab towards the landing strip where I had parked the Cherokee. Olivier taxied in and cut the engine. The clean blade of the propeller stuttered into visibility. He leaned across me to unlatch the low, wide door.

'He has enemies,' he said. 'Your friend the fox, so do not be surprised if ... people are not so quick to tell you things.'

I said, 'Would you prefer me not to ... try and find him?'

'To me personally,' Olivier said, 'it does not matter.'

7

Pansy said, 'I'm sure you can drive, if you'd sooner. We could always call Avis and check.'

'I don't want to call anybody,' Roger said. 'I like it when women drive. It's the way they have to use their legs. If I had a chauffeur, I'd want her to look very much like you.'

'I'm not all that brilliant with cars. Especially when they've got gears.'

'That's what I like: two legs, one rubbing against the other.'

He had her drive him first to the printers on the outskirts of Caillac. The Communist ex-mayor had authorised the development of shops and self-service markets across the street from the *lycée* Marcel Picpus. Since his electoral defeat, he was under investigation for kickbacks and *fausses factures* to the benefit of the Party's election funds. However, no one could do anything to dismantle the breeze-block *Jardinerie* and the plywood fruit and vegetable wholesaler and the corrugated iron warehouse from which washing machines and refrigerators and '*accordéons traditionnels*' were sold. A *marchand de vin* advertised local wine '*en vrac et en containers*'. Léon Fongauffier, the printer, stocked stationery and office equipment. His mother wrote down Roger's name and went into the back of the premises. '*Il est peut-être là.*'

'What she means is, he's there if we've come to pay and not if we've come to collect.'

'I thought we *were* collecting,' Pansy said.

'You are quite exceptionally beautiful, Pansy, aren't you?' Roger said. 'And just as well.'

'There are some things people can't do anything about, aren't there?' she said.

79

'Collecting *debts*, I meant.'

After a few moments, Fongauffier came into the front of the shop with a stack of pink flyers. '*Tout est prêt.*' Fongauffier counted the bundles as if he feared that he might be giving short weight. '*Cinq cents.*'

'I'm going to ask you to do something, Pansy, which you absolutely don't have to do, and that's help me put these under people's windscreen-wipers. I won't tell anyone that your husband is a member of the British government.'

'Well, he isn't really.'

'I still won't tell them,' Roger said.

'When are we going to go to the bank?'

'I don't think they'll be in funds just yet. It's only a couple of hours since you spoke to Bricey.'

'You don't have to go on being unpleasant about him.'

'Now that you've stopped, you mean?'

A remarkable number of the owners of the cars on which Pansy placed the flyers advertising 'PERIGORD DE LUXE' returned to their vehicles while she was still to be seen in the Place Pasteur. They seemed eager to hear more from her about the services which the company offered. Her confession of ignorance only encouraged them to even more probing attention of the printed material. On the other hand, when she had gone to the bank and Roger continued alone along the Avenue Thiers, people simply scowled at his pink bumf.

He was pulling open the windscreen wiper of a Toyota, before inserting his literature, when a voice behind him said, 'No thank you, Rodge, very much.'

He turned and saw a muscular man in his late thirties with close-cropped, brillo-pad hair, a dragon tattooed on one forearm, one earring, and a half-moon scar on his cheek. He wore a sleeveless electric blue parka, orange stretch pants, green hiking boots and an XXX cotton T-shirt.

'Pretend you don't know. Pretend you don't.'

'I'm afraid I don't have to pretend. Know what?'

'Rodge the Dodge. Of course you do. Who I am.'

Roger took up another stance and sleeved the remaining flyers in their plastic container, he blinked at one or two places along the street and then he looked again at the man who had spoken to him. 'How are you, Quigs?'

'On the contrary, Roger. How are *you*?'

'As you see. Rich and powerful. What brings you down here?'

'Sniff and scratch,' Quigley said. 'And isn't it funny the people you come across? The missus still with you?'

Roger said, 'We haven't had an easy time, but we've hung in.'

'I'm very glad to hear that. I wouldn't like to think of you having an easy time.'

Roger said, 'You're obviously . . .'

'What am I, Rodge, obviously, would you say?'

'Flourishing. You look very fit.'

'What's the news of Lester these days? Old Les, what's his current story? I am fit. Very. You have to be.'

'I don't know anything about him. I only hope he's getting a tenth of what he deserves. In which case he can't be having all that good a time.'

'I had a soft spot for Lester,' Quigley said.

'He was a swindling bastard,' Roger said.

'He was a swindling bastard *poof* were your last words on the subject of our mutual friend Lester Gillis, as I recall them. Not that I *knew* they were your last, because weren't you going to give me a bell? Didn't you promise to?'

'He dumped you in it and then he dumped me in it. Classic.'

'How about a glass? Got time for one of those, have you, in your doubtless busy schedule?'

Roger said, 'Actually I'm with someone . . .'

'Big and strong?'

'Of course. My sister-in-law. We can go in here, if you feel like it.'

'I bet I was one person you didn't expect to see.'

'That is a little bit true. So what are you doing these days?'

'You know the mistake we made, Rodge, don't you, on serious reflection?'

'Trusting I. Tubbs esquire, for starters. And then Lester G.'

'You start small or you start big; you never want to start in the middle. Is what I've learnt over the years. We wasn't straight enough and then again we wasn't bent enough. Betwixt and between is nowhere at all.'

'I never thought of us as bent. I took Lester's word.'

'And I took yours. I did six months, Rodge. And what did you do?'

'I was lucky. I didn't think I was, but I was. What do you want to drink? I absolutely didn't recognise you, Quigs, not without the old collar and tie. I wasn't finance director.'

'I'll have a *formidable*, as it's you, Rodge.'

'*Un demi pour moi et un formidable*,' Roger said, '*pour mon ami*. You knock about quite a bit then, do you, on the conty-nong?'

'Nothing permanent like you. I'm basically your back-and-forth merchant.'

'We have been home. My dad died and we went back for that.'

A tall, thickly bearded man in a yellow anorak and striped overalls came diagonally across the Avenue Thiers carrying a plastic hold-all. Roger could see the end of a *pain* and a double deck of Heineken six-packs.

'Captain Haddock,' Roger said. 'Only get the red boots! Do you think he dances all night?'

'Twinkle-toes? I happen to know he does. Oy! *Jonty!* In here, my son. Because guess who this is. Jonty Goldstein, meet Roger the Rodge. As previously discussed. At some length.'

Goldstein had bluer eyes (not quite aligned) than the corsair's beard and Mediterranean lips seemed to warrant. 'Small world,' he said.

'We've never met to my knowledge,' Roger said, 'but have a drink anyway. How are you enjoying yourself down here?'

'Same as we enjoy ourselves everywhere.'

'You chose the right place, Rodge. You find it warm, do you?'

'Nobody's called me Rodge in years. And – do you know something? – I'm not all that sure I've missed it. It gets warmer.'

'That's a promise,' Quigley said.

'Have you visited the caves?'

'Very picture-skew, some of them, you found, didn't you, Jonathan? We also went to this funny church.'

'It's a shame you're too early for the music,' Roger said.

'Invite us,' Quigley said. 'We might well come back.'

'Or alternatively never go away,' Goldstein said.

'What about the food? How do you like the food?'

'The food, I have to say, we don't necessarily like.'

'You're joking. You seriously don't like the food?'

'We're veggies,' Goldstein said. 'And it's not all that if you're a veggie.'

'So,' Quigley said, 'at least that's one mystery solved. We now know where we can find you, you and ... Mrs Raikes. It's always nice, isn't it, catching up with old friends?'

'How did you actually get here, if you don't mind me asking?'

'We've got the van, haven't we?'

'The van. Of course. Big one?'

'There's nothing like a big one when you do what we do.'

'Which is?'

'All right: Antiques Road Show, us. We specialise in whatever we can get hold of. Your chests, your *armoires*, your hutches and then there's your general *bibelots*, of course. We buy and sell. Here and there. We eat and drink in moderation and that's pretty well it at the moment.'

'And you're also veggies.'

'Very much veggies,' Goldstein said, 'us.'

Roger saw Pansy go past the doorway of the café. She was chatting to three helpful men. 'I say,' Roger said, 'I'm terribly sorry, but that's my ...' He stood up and threw money onto the table. '... that's the person I'm ...'

'Oy! *Miss!* In here. Roger's in here.'

Jonty's yell brought Pansy's head back round the street door. 'Oh,' she said, 'this is where you've got to. Good news! Apparently it could be here as early as this afternoon. Certainly in the morning.'

'What's this then?' Goldstein said. 'The baby?'

'The money,' Pansy said. 'I'm waiting for some money.'

'Welcome to the club,' Quigley said. 'Allow me to introduce the committee, in fact.'

Roger said, 'Do you want something to drink, Pan?'

'I'll have whatever you're having.'

Goldstein held up his big tankard. 'Have a dip. It's yours. Look at this lovely woman, look at this lovely girl, if you don't mind being called that; *she*'s not feeling the heat in the least, are you, gorgeous? Not like Rodge. Rodge is looking exceptionally well done. Regulo number 9 is Rodge. Isn't that a funny thing?'

Rachel said, 'Olivier, I'm so sorry about those damned people.'

'Who is that?'

'Who drove away. Did a flit, as they say in England.'

'Did a flit. It is not important.' He had taken the white crash-helmet from where it hung on the handlebars of his *moto* and was steadying it onto his head. 'Beware of the *renard*.'

'I don't think he'll be wanting to do anything to me.'

'You are too modest maybe.'

She watched him go, tall in the saddle, across the grass to the roadway, and then she drove the Cherokee back into Ste-Foy-le-Fort. She parked on the white-slotted tarmac beside the covered market and went to see Madame Harlin, the *antiquaire* from whom she had recently bought a console table for a Danish couple. The deep, narrow shop had once been a *boulangerie*; an old cast-iron oven bulged into the middle of it. The jangle of the bell brought Madame Harlin creaking down the crooked stairs, first the head (with the vigilant black eye-patch!) and then the rest of her angular body.

'*Madame Harlin, je me demande si vous pouvez m'aider.*'

'I will do what I can, of course.'

'This is nice.' Rachel had the flat of her hand on a carved hutch, with a sliding panel in the seat. 'It's new, isn't it?'

'To say it is new is not very polite, I think, *chez une antiquaire*!'

'In the sense that I have not seen it before.'

'It is new,' Madame Harlin said. 'How are things at *Les Noyers Tordus*? *Monsieur va bien?*'

'*Monsieur va bien*. Madame Harlin ... I'm looking for some-body and ... Did you see on the television, or in the newspaper, that Yvonne Langon had died? She was ... she was in the Resist-ance, here in Sainte-Foy, at least for some of the time ... and she ...'

'I came to Sainte-Foy long after the war, Madame Raikes. I am a Lilloise, you know, a *nordiste*, as they say.'

The door opened and again jangled the brass bell on its stiff, dusty collar. A woman wearing a black suit with a ruffled shirt came in and nodded at Rachel and Madame Harlin, as if their presence confirmed her suspicions. She pointed a sidelong hand in a stiff gesture, like a hieroglyphic character, and rode it through to the back of the shop, where the glass and china were.

'Lionel Cator,' Rachel said. 'Does that name mean anything to you?'

'You discuss these things in the Périgord and very soon some people are not talking to you. It is a minefield, Madame Raikes, you understand? The mines are rusty, they've been buried for *decennies* but they are still there, and they are still dangerous. You never know when they could go off.'

'Decades,' Rachel said. 'Those are always the interesting things, I find, don't you?'

'Not particularly,' Madame Harlin said. 'Decades! Of course!'

'How much is this?'

'That has to be *douze mille*.'

'Do you have any idea where he lives, or lived? *Douze mille!*'

'Perhaps he has gone back to England. I came here in 1969, which was already a long time after ... those days. And the things that happened then.'

'They say he killed people. After it was supposedly all over ... don't they?'

Madame Harlin drew in a deeper breath than was usually necessary. 'They say also that he has a lot of money.' She leaned round the doorpost to look at the woman in the back of the shop, leaving only her feet to be polite to Rachel. 'He is the man to avoid.'

Rachel said, 'When you say he has money ...'

Madame Harlin turned back with a more friendly, and more forbidding, face. 'I don't say; *they* say.'

'Did you hear about the Schlickenhorsts?'

'It's foolish to leave things unattended. Some of the things they had in the house, they did not even know exactly what they were. So I hear. Not wise.'

Rachel said, 'Thank you, Madame Harlin. I do like the hutch. I don't like the price quite so much, but ...'

'Père Batzan.'

'I'm sorry?'

'Is someone you could talk to, if you wanted. In Villefranche-les-Evêques. It's on the edge of the *Double*. The far side of Périgueux. *C'est un Basque, de très, très vieille souche.* I could make it *dix mille cinq*. That's the last price.'

As Rachel left the old *boulangerie*, a red-haired woman with a chapped complexion, in a fawn and pink plaid poncho and white boots, was coming towards it. Rachel stretched the door open with the tips of her fingers, to stop it jangling again. The woman frowned and said 'Thanks a lot' in an Australian accent.

Rachel walked up to the box-hedged *Monument aux Morts* in the square in front of the *Relais St Jacques*. In the middle was the flag-draped statue of a *poilu*, with local names carved underneath on marble panels. The straggling column of those who had died between 1914 and 1918 suggested why the village had had few sons to give in 1939. A whiter, supplementary panel of '*Martyrs de la Résistance*' enshrined twenty-two men and four women.

While she was taking note of the more unusual names, whose families ought to be easier to trace, Rachel heard the slam of a car door. The woman in black leather had driven up in her black Turbo Saab. As she was walking towards the terrace under the cherry trees where Hélène had been sweeping earlier, Olivier emerged from the bar door. He was wearing a brown suit and suede shoes. With his hair brushed flat, he looked like another man, thinner and darker. He shook hands with the woman, but he did not smile.

'Excuse me. Excuse me.' The Australian woman was coming towards Rachel with one arm extended. A black snakeskin handbag dangled from it. 'I was looking for you, because you left this.'

'It's very nice of you,' Rachel said, 'but actually I didn't.'

'In the antique shop.'

Rachel took the bag, which hung heavily on the Australian's fingers, and shook her head. 'Much too smart for me!'

'Then why leave it in the shop?'

'*This* is mine.' Rachel swung her sack forward from her shoulder. 'I don't take a handbag when I'm carrying this.'

She was opening the fastener on the snakeskin bag, in case she could find out whose it was, when it was snatched from her from behind. '*Donnez-moi ça.*'

Rachel said, '*Et voilà! C'est à vous, madame, non, ce sac?*'

'*Bien sûr que c'est à moi. C'est pas à vous, ça c'est certain. Vous l'avez pris où exactement?*'

'*Cette dame vient de le trouver chez l'antiquaire.*'

'*Voilà!*' The trim woman checked the clasp of the bag, glared at Rachel and had no time for the Australian before she turned and pointed her nose towards the *Relais*.

'Now look who's a criminal,' Rachel said.

'I love gay men. I seriously love them. How did you get to know them? And where can we find some more?'

'Only one of them knew me. Quigley. The one with the short hair.'

'The way they all have these heavenly tattoos nowadays! I liked the beefy one. The nose alone! And the shoulders!'

'Jonty. He was married when I knew him: Quigley. And completely different. Well, very different. Mr Three Piece Suite. Straight as a Roman road as far as I ever knew.'

'We're all a bit bi though somewhere along the line, aren't we?'

'Are we?' Roger said. 'Look here, what do you want to do?'

'What do I want to do?'

'In the sense of shall we go home and come back, which means fifty minutes' driving, or do we hang about, have a spot of lunch, an omelette possibly, and then go back to the bank? Or a pizza. Up to you.'

'You're the man,' Pansy said. 'You decide. Only not an omelette.'

'The thing being, I don't know how long Rachel's going to be.'

'Or a pizza particularly. It's nice she's got something to keep her busy, isn't it?'

'Let's go as far as the river and have a drink and a bite. And then we'll come back and make you rich again.'

'Done,' she said. 'One does miss it, I find.'

'What's that then?'

'Money.'

'You've fancied other women, have you, in your day?'

'It's so beautiful,' Pansy said, 'around here. No wonder you're so happy.'

'Well, I'd be happier if I could go to the bank and get some of Brice's money now and again. You're not going to say.'

'Try me.'

'Whether you've fancied other women.'

'I prefer men.'

'That's a comfort. But it's not an answer, is it?'

'Men really, really like thinking of girls doing things with girls, don't they? Brice went on a delegation once, to one of those places like Bangkok, and that was what all of them wanted to go and see. Afterwards, one quite senior executive character stayed behind

87

and turned into a total Buddhist, if that's what they are out there. They can't do anything wrong apparently, which must be nice, especially when you've got acquired tastes, which he definitely had, although no one was quite sure where he'd acquired them. Except that I tend to quite like things, I find, when they're wrong. I don't know about you. What did you do to him exactly?'

'This is the place. Do to who? It's a bit penny plain, as my father used to say. I didn't do anything to anybody.'

'It looks *sweet*. I love these little French hotels. When you go in, they always look at you as if you were up to something and they didn't care a bit, don't they? The people. I love that. It makes me want to do something really, really wicked. Quigley, is that his name? Did you turn him down or something?'

'Down, no. What do you think I am? Alternatively, what do you want to drink?'

'I'll have a *kir royal*. You don't have to tell me if you don't want to.'

'*Deux kirs royals, s'il vous plaît, madame*. We did something together. In business. Which didn't work out. And that was it.'

'What about the other one? Jonty. What did you do to *him*?'

'I never saw him before in my life. And with any luck, I never shall again.'

'I thought he was heaven. How come they're so hunky these days? All my fag friends are *massive*. Do you think women will decide to get massive one day, and grow moustaches and have tattoos and shake people until their teeth rattle possibly? He blames you, doesn't he?'

'He did do six months. Which rightly or wrongly he chooses to blame me for.'

'Cheers,' Pansy said. 'Which? Rightly or wrongly?'

'All right,' Roger said, 'if you want to know, I was a total bastard.'

'Were you really? How?'

'A total and complete bastard. I sold him down the river. I couldn't do anything else. Turned him in, not down. And they believed me, because he was the only one who could sign cheques. I paid up. *We* paid up. Pretty well. But I did stiff him with the responsibility. All right and between ourselves, I told the cops it was all his idea, which it strictly wasn't really.'

'And now he's come down here to have a word with you, has he? I always fancied Brice was a bit of a bastard. But I'm beginning to lose hope rather.'

'People like Brice don't have to be bastards. Have you ever done any canoeing?'

'It's passed me by,' Pansy said. 'I'm sorry about using the phone, Roger. I'll give you the money, obviously.'

'And don't think I won't take it.'

'Do they kiss a lot when they do it, men? Or do they just get on with it sort of a thing?'

'What do you feel about eating?'

'You know what I think – and I don't pretend to really *know* – I think people do a lot of things because they imagine other people are watching. I mean, it doesn't matter *all* that much whether they're actually there or not; they still do things *for* other people.'

'And also against them,' Roger said. 'They'd like to know what we want to eat.'

'They'd probably have been much nicer with you if I hadn't come in.'

'I didn't think they were particularly unpleasant after you arrived.'

'They were though,' Pansy said. 'What's *friture* mean?'

'Is it something people do?'

'It's on the menu,' Pansy said.

'Oh. It's ... it's a sort of fry-up, isn't it?'

'You're the frog,' she said. 'I don't mind having that.'

'Women kiss each other a lot,' Roger said. 'Why shouldn't men? Women never stop.'

'Or an omelette. I didn't say they *shouldn't*, I just wondered if they *did*. Are you afraid they might come along and do something to you?'

'Personally, I've never kissed a man in my life. Or done anything else in that line. And I can't say I've missed it. Such as what?'

'Well, for instance, people sometimes kill people, don't they, if they can't think of anything else to do? And what's *gésiers*? Are they good?'

'Sort of ... a salad thing. Do people ever try to kill you?'

'Me? God, yes. I've been bumped off more times than I can

89

count. You see it in people's eyes when they're doing it. That's why they always shut them at the last minute. Bang! I love it.'

'Oh *then*,' Roger said. 'You can't help shutting them. Women shut them too.'

'*I* don't,' Pansy said, 'I like to look. I like to see them die on me. You know what's funny about men? Among other things, I mean. As soon as they're happy, they're unhappy again. As soon as they've done you, they wish they hadn't. They want it, they want it, and then they wish they hadn't had it. Am I right?'

'You're a bloody menace,' Roger said. 'But then you probably know that.'

'He looked as if he could break a bus in half, didn't he, the hairy one with the ...? Jonty. Do they put things in their crotches as a matter of habit, or are they really hung like that? I'll go for the *gésiers*. Twist my arm, I might even have another *kir*. I wouldn't want to get on the wrong side of that one. The boots alone! Do you know something? I'm feeling a lot more cheerful; I don't know about you.'

iv

Villefranche-les-Evêques lay in a long valley to the north-west of Périgueux. The bishops' palace was pinched in a bracket of ground between the *route nationale* and the pine-covered hillside behind the town. Workmen in white paper caps were wielding power-hoses to clean the flat Renaissance façade. Rachel parked the Cherokee on the pale gravel below the formal steps. When she asked for Père Batzan, she was directed by a postcard-seller to a small blackened church deep in the perpetual shadow of the town's back streets.

The priest seemed to be amused by Rachel's approach. She guessed that appearing benevolent was his way of giving himself time. The grizzled old man was wearing a *soutane*, patchily stained, and he was bare-headed. His face looked as if it had been badly ironed and the tonsured cap of greying black hair was no cleaner than his robe. His eyes were so black that, in the cat-soured gloom of the porch, Rachel could scarcely distinguish iris from pupil.

'First of all, Father, I'd better be honest with you.'

'If you think that is a good idea.'

'I'm a journalist.'

'An honest journalist!'

'I didn't say that.'

'I know.'

'Did you hear that Yvonne Langon had died? You knew her, I think.'

'Many years ago.'

'What about Lionel Cator?'

'What about Lionel Cator?'

'You speak very good English, Father.'

'I am a Basque. Basques either learn languages or . . . they speak only to Basques. I also knew Lionel.'

'And still do?'

'Why do you not buy me a glass of Alsace?'

'Why don't I?' Rachel said.

v

'That was *terrible*,' Pansy said. 'It was absolutely ghastly, wasn't it? What were those rubber bits?'

'Those were the *gésiers*,' Roger said.

'I don't think you should necessarily pay for a dish that tastes like that. I certainly think you should put up a fight.'

'You're a dangerous bitch basically, aren't you, Pansy?'

'What have I done now?'

'You're trouble. You like it and you like landing people in it.'

'Roger, you're being such a sod again suddenly! What trouble have I landed you in?'

'If you don't know what you're doing, I'm certainly not telling you. But you're still doing it.' Roger put money on the table and added twenty francs, in small change, for service. On reflection, he took two francs off the pile and put them back in his pocket. 'It also took forever. I'd sooner you didn't mention them to Raitch.'

'Them.'

'Quigley and friend.'

'Anything you say.'

'I don't think we have to go quite that far; which doesn't in the least mean I shouldn't like to go a hell of a sight further.'

'You know what's cute about you, Roger?'

91

'Cute? No.'

'You don't do anything for its own sake, do you? Not anything. Not even get annoyed. I love that. There's always something going on with you. Under the surface.'

'If you grow up in Pinner, Middlesex, there'd better be or you stay where you are. In the summer, the river gets quite low on this side of the bridge. It seems the water is quite high on that side and then down here, you can almost see the bottom. That's an island where you can see that tree sticking out.'

'Why did you marry her?'

'Rachel? She's a very bright, capable girl. Very.'

'We all know that,' Pansy said, 'but why did you marry her?'

'Why does anybody marry anybody?'

'Bad as that, eh?'

'Do you want it, Pansy? Because you're certainly asking for it.'

'Look, I'm just waiting for the bank to be honest.'

'All right, my turn: why did you marry Brice?'

'He amused me. Oh, not because he's amusing. Because he wanted me so much. He looked like someone trying to hide an outsize truncheon in his trousers. And what was giggles about *that* was that otherwise he was unbelievably pompous and smug and self-important. Wanting me made him all nervous and hand-in-pockety. Which was really very cute. For a time. Right up until we got married really. Why would anyone want to wear underpants with hippopotamuses on them?'

'He was also very rich.'

'Which didn't hurt a bit. Aren't they supposed to be sexy according to some people?'

'What you really mean is, why did *she* marry *me*? We all know it can't have been my money. It must have been my truncheon. You're going to have a title, aren't you?'

'I'm looking forward to it, quite. I think she married you because she didn't have to wonder what your motives were. She's clever, isn't she? So she probably knew.'

'I just thought I was getting lucky.'

'And you don't think you're cute! When anyone else would have said that they fell in love with her.'

'Oh I did,' Roger said. 'I did.'

'What about me?' Pansy said. 'Have you actively considered getting lucky with me?'

92

'You absolutely have to seduce people, that's the thing about you, isn't it?'

'It's the only thing I've ever been any good at. It always disappoints people if I don't remember to behave like a total Babylonian. I even get letters. What can I do?'

'Have a baby probably.'

'Oh *don't*,' Pansy said. 'I hate being reminded of why I've really got all the bits and pieces. Why did Rachel get rid of it? She'd be a terrific mother and it's not as if she's got much of a figure to lose.'

'We may as well wend our way back to Caillac and see if someone's pressed the necessary buttons. She didn't want it. I left it to her and, at the time, she strictly didn't want it.'

'Do you think we'll see them again?'

'Who? No, I don't. I certainly hope not.'

'Did you ever meet his wife? Quigley's. You said he was straight at one time.'

'Erica. Yes. She collected very small things. Her house was full of them. I'd forgotten Erica. I had to call by once and she'd made apple tarts. They were mini too.'

'What do you think she thinks about you?'

'Why ever should she think about me?'

'It's funny, isn't it, the way you can make people hate you and you don't even think about them from one year to the next? Because think of what you did to her.'

vi

'I came out of Spain in 1939. A few hours before Franco closed the frontier. Most of our people were interned. Various camps along the border. The French maybe hoped they would soon be able to send us home. They were ashamed, so they were ... cruel. *Vae victis*. I did not have to be interned, because I was a priest; I chose to be. The Church offered to look after us, I think because it disapproved of us. Kindness too can be a punishment; perhaps I was afraid of that. The Basque priests, we were more Basques then priests sometimes, in our superiors' eyes. They wanted to have us where they could ...' The old priest sipped his Alsace and his beard bristled at the taste. '... *mortify* us.' He might have been

93

tasting the word as well as the wine. 'You want to find Lionel Cator, you don't want to talk to me.'

'Which camp were you in?'

'1939? Near Hendaye. In the hills. Hot. We looked down towards St-Jean-de-Luz. You could see sailing boats, people holidaying on the beach. I was not like the others who were there. The scum of the earth. I *chose* to be there.'

'Do you think Jesus had a choice?' Rachel said. 'About coming down to earth? Did *He* decide or …? How could He have, when He didn't exist before He was conceived? Or did He?'

'You are not of our Faith.'

'I'm not of any faith, I don't think.'

'I can tell. You are very credulous. You ask an old priest – a *very* old priest – to tell you the truth about the nature of God, as if the answer was in the reach of any simple old soul in a *soutane*. Did He have a choice? Who am I to enter into the mind of God?'

Rachel said, 'I apologise.'

Père Batzan put an arched hand over Rachel's on the tin table which was tight against the wall of the side street. He hooded her fingers without touching them and patted the air. He seemed rather practised at it. 'Let me talk about myself,' he said. 'God can talk to you about *Him*self, if He wants to, in His own time. They hated us, the French; we had done what they should have done. We had fought the good fight. Unforgivable! They wished that we were dead. They hated looking us in the eye. Police. Priests. Politicians.'

'Did it make you angry?'

'Grateful; the French bishops, was it not a grace that they regarded us with suspicion? We had not entirely failed to do something. Isn't that part of the beauty of God's generosity in disapproving of human actions? He cannot *really* find it intolerable that men and women do certain things they do, but He is good enough to allow us to believe that He does. This lends them meaning.'

'You're a bit of a heretic, aren't you, Father Batzan?'

'I try,' he said. 'But I'm getting old now.'

'Eventually they released you, did they?'

'When the Germans came, we were moved to the camp at Rivesaltes. Bad rumours; terrible mosquitoes. People escaped. Perhaps we were let out. Who knows what a wink means exactly? I came, eventually, to be up here in the Resistance with … someone

I knew in Spain. A man, dear, a man. Lionel got us weapons and supplies from London. Yvonne, you know, was his wireless operator. Wonderful girl; a child almost. The skin! And the eyes . . . !'

Rachel said, 'Where can I find him, Father?'

The black-eyed old priest shook the greenish pitcher of Alsace. The last drops rattled like small change. He tipped them into her glass and brandished the pitcher at the interior of the murky café. 'They give you expenses, am I right?'

'You evidently know the newspaper world.'

Père Batzan's mouth drooped at the corners. The lower lip jutted upwards to age the beard and moustache with loneliness. The *patron* came with a fresh instalment of Alsace and Rachel filled the old priest's glass. 'You're married,' he said. 'You have children?'

'One day.'

'Why do people still get married? If God is of no importance to you, why take the trouble?'

'It's not all that much trouble. It's something people want to do.'

'You reveal your need for Him. Your anger possibly. Is that sentimental?'

'Where should I go,' Rachel said, 'if I want to find him? Yes, it's sentimental. Cator, I mean. Which doesn't mean it's not true.'

'This is a strange part of the world. You must not hurry things.'

'What was he like when you knew him well?'

'Young.'

'And Yvonne? He was happy with her, was he?'

'He loved her. He was happy with everyone. I never saw a man so reckless and so . . . Even when he was angry, or frightened, he was laughing. For me, he was a man who had never expected to be free, and then he found freedom. And then . . .'

'What? And when?'

'He found that freedom . . . was not always a liberation.'

'The mayor,' Rachel said, 'of Villefranche, what happened to him exactly? What was his name?'

'Life is a mystery,' the priest said. 'Who can say exactly what happens to anyone? Teyssier. Yves Teyssier.'

'He was murdered, wasn't he?'

'It was never certain.'

'He had done something, hadn't he, during the war?'

'Everyone did,' the priest said, 'or else they did not. That is something you will never understand, perhaps.'

'Did Lionel Cator have anything to do with him? During the war, I mean?'

'He will tell you himself,' Père Batzan said, 'or he will not. What you can do is you can drive somewhere and then you will see what happens, or what doesn't.'

Rachel said, 'You know something, Father? You're a man who can give inevitability the allure of a promise.'

The old priest's sudden bark of laughter sounded like a quotation.

8

In accordance with Père Batzan's instructions, which he passed off as hints and possibilities, I turned off the *route nationale* onto a narrow road through replanted woods. Saplings were springing their first buds; midday light strained through a blur of branches. At first, the area seemed a little different from the countryside I knew. Sawn wood made neat palisades along the sides of the road. Uncut spruce bristled behind new wiring. A beige *deux chevaux* van, with a rumpled roof, was parked off the road, at a steep angle, in the clearing between two copses. I had the exhilarating feeling, or fantasy, of being watched. Soon after I had passed the van, I heard a powerful motor rasping somewhere behind the trees.

On the far side of the pine-covered hill bracketing Villefranche-les-Evêques, I crossed a stream which surged under a plank bridge as if propelled by some invisible pump. The track curved with the contour of the hill and then dropped towards a mill which looked to be long deserted. The brown paint on the shutters had peeled to show grey boards. Two huge barrels, with rusty metal belts, were falling apart under the eaves of a deep tiled roof. The yard was overgrown with nettles and brambles and elder. Under another roof, a tyreless *traction-avant* Citroën – of the kind I had seen Yvonne Langon get out of in the newsreel – had been colonised by a fig tree.

I stopped the Cherokee and climbed mossy stone steps to the oak-beamed terrace outside the front door. Was I pretending to prospect, in case the house could be flogged as a bargain to some in-funds businessman who had got his timing right? Or was that really what I was doing, if only to avoid the humiliation of an entirely fruitless journey? Curiosity made me try one of the shutters over the main door. I winced (for whose benefit?) as it creaked and yielded. The house seemed to be inviting me to an indiscretion. My talk with Father Batzan led me to speculate whether there were those – including Eve? Including myself? – who could find God only through transgression. Without the chance to affront Him, one might never be conscious of His existence. My thoughts were sweeter for the knowledge that Michael Lea would think that I had lost my mind, should I ever make the mistake of sharing them with him.

A deserted house in the countryside becomes a lair. The traces of the humans who once occupied it cease to be those of particular people and become those of a tragic species which always prepares for a longer life that it can hope to enjoy. As I walked into *Le Moulin de l'Enclos*, I sniffed the tradition of miserliness. The faces in the buckling daguerrotypes on the wall, poxed with black where the damp had worked through from the back, were of unsmiling ancestors to whom generosity was cowardice; they had had the nerve to be heartless.

There were cupboards on each side of the narrow fireplace in the short wall. The doors had collapsed onto their bottom hinges. I could see tea-coloured medicine bottles and a glass bed-pan, the relics of a *grand malade*. I went up narrow wooden stairs, almost as steep as shelves, to the loft. It had warped and unplaned boards and the same kind of rusty wires along the beams which we had in our bedroom. Heaps of bottles, dim with dust, slumped against the tiles. Between the stones slotted unevenly along the low wall, I could see bright lozenges of the outside air. The long abandoned attic rustled with cagey movement from creatures who seemed to have recognised me for a blunderer; they presumed on my inability to do them harm.

In the middle of the *grenier* was a metal bassinette; its rusting frame bore traces of white paint. Nothing in the house had alarmed or moved me, but the whiteness of the empty cradle, almost luminous in the shady loft, danced in front of my eyes.

'*Vous cherchez?*'

How can a voice startle and yet not surprise? I did not hurry to turn. The tone was not so much aggressive as jeering. Its mildness implied that a female intruder could not be a threat. When I looked round, I was faced with a gaunt peasant in baggy blue cotton overalls, dark blue shirt and unsubtle sandals over grey socks. He wore a wide belt around the middle of his overalls and he had a tartan cap on his head, with a fat button on the top.

'*Vous m'avez fait peur,*' I said.

'*Qu'est-ce que vous faites ici? C'est une maisongue privée.*' The harshness of his local accent turned his French into another challenge which he dared me to meet. '*Vous n'avez pas le droit d'engtrée.*'

'*J'espérais rencontrer Monsieur Cator.*'

'*Connais pas.*'

'Lionel Cator. *L'Anglais.*'

He shook his head. '*Il n'y a pas d'Angalais dang le coing.*'

'*Si, si.*' It amused me to contradict him by pointing to myself. '*Moi, je suis anglaise.*'

He refused to be amused. '*J'aime pas tellemangue les Angalais.*' When I indicated that I did not care whether he liked the English or not, he looked at me with deliberately nasty eyes. '*Et puis ... une femme toute seule, même une Angalaise ...*' He paused for the sneer to make its salacious point before adding the obvious threat: '*Il y a toutes sortes de choses qui peuvent arriver à une jeuneux femme toute seule dans uneux forêt, nong? Tu te rends compte?*'

I adopted a practical, now-you-listen-to-me approach. '*Je m'appelle Rachel. Rachel Stannard. Je suis l'amie du Père Batzan de Villefranche.*'

'*Ah bong. Il a une amie, le pauvre! Tongue mieux pour lui. Pourquoi voulez-vous le voire, cet Angalais?*'

If I was encouraged by his returning to the subject of Cator, I was not about to be grateful. '*Si vous ne le connaissez pas, c'est pas la peine de m'expliquer là-dessus, n'est-ce pas?*'

'*Vous êtes fâchée.*' His tone became sulky, as if I had been unreasonably tart with him. '*Vous ne devez pas vous fâcher, voyons. Vous êtes ici sans autorisationg.*'

I now suspected that he was not the owner of the property, whatever else he was. We were both intruders. '*Et vous, monsieur? Le droit d'entrée, vous l'avez, vous, je suppose?*'

'*Angalaise.*' His eyes glittered again; he had the trick of it. '*Ici dans le coing, parfois on bouffe bien les petites Angalaises avec un petit bout de paing.*'

I had heard enough silly boasts from Frenchmen about the kind of sandwiches they liked to make with English females in the middle. 'Well good for you,' I said. 'Only you'll have to catch them first, won't you?'

He was between me and the head of the stairs. I was damned if I would show that I was afraid of a stroppy old peasant. His attempt at intimidation was absurd and disgusting. He seemed less like a man than an old turkey who could be clapped decisively out of the way. As I sidled past him to the stairhead, his evasive movement was a parody of politeness: he was giving me permission to leave, although he had no right to prevent me. I had gone a couple of steps, in no great hurry, when he said, '*Rachel?*'

'*Oui?*'

'*Vous êtes juive?*'

'*Pas du tout,*' I said. He was not the first person to think that being called Rachel meant that I was Jewish, but I still resented the insolence of his tone.

'*J'ai un mot à te dire.*' He called after me as I went on down the stairs. '*N'essaie pas de te mêler dans des choses dont tu de connais strictemangue rien.*'

I did not need his advice about whether I should stick my nose in other people's business; I wanted only to be shot of him. My heels clattered on the boards. I sensed that he was coming after me, but I heard nothing.

'*Je pars,*' I said. 'I'm on my fucking way, so don't worry about it.'

Whose voice was I using? It was a liberation to be someone whom I did not myself recognise. I was angry and I was a little frightened, though more of the freedom I had fallen into, like a trap, than of the mischievous old peasant who still seemed to hope for some profit from the occasion.

'*Attendez.*'

'No, I'm not waiting. I'm off. Fuck it.'

'*Peut-être je peux vous aider. Ne t'énerve pas, voyong.*'

'*Toi! Vous! Merde!* I don't want your bloody help.'

Now that I knew that I was doing what he did not want, I went as springily as a girl in a gym slip across the *séjour* towards the front door.

Before I heard any sound of his coming, the tips of his fingers were on my sleeve. I threw up my arm as I might at the clinging touch of a cobweb. I turned in the doorway, expecting to brush him away. With daylight full on him, he was not the same stick of a peasant who had been upstairs with me. He was lean and creased, as the other had been, but his breath was rancid with undeclared laughter; the clever eyes and the newly dapper definition of the wide, thin moustache blew the rustic disguise. This man was trouble.

'What is it?' I said. 'What do you want?'

'*Mais pourquoi vous énervez-vous? Le renard, vous voulez le rongcongtrer?* Doan chew wan' to meet eem?'

'*Pas tellemangue,*' I said. 'Not all that much.'

When he grinned, he took on the appearance of the fox Roger and I had seen sitting by the roadside as we drove home from the *Relais St Jacques* the night before.

'OK,' I said, 'so why are we talking French?'

'You're taking a bitva risk, in'cha?'

'You also imitate taxi drivers in old movies, do you? You've got an impressive repertoire.'

'You're taking quite a risk, in case you don't know.'

'Those are the times you do, aren't they? But then again, I'm not exactly in much danger at the moment.' I turned to go outside. '*Au revoir.*'

'I'm Lionel Cator,' he said. 'What's left of him.'

'No surprises there, I'm afraid. And so what?'

I walked towards the stone steps of the terrace, above where the Citroën crouched on its hubs. All of a sudden, yet quite as if I had expected it, I was being danced backwards off the terrace and dumped on my back in the lush grass. I felt nettles and thorns and then my head was eased to the ground and Lionel Cator had a shin across my chest and a knife at my throat and a fox was smiling at me with nasty teeth. 'Morning,' he said. 'Made in England, right?'

'Excuse me?'

'You. No wonder they hated us.'

'Who was that?'

'Turn your back on me, madam, and you're leaving the door open. We assumed it to be respect. That they felt. Was it? It wasn't. Am I hurting you?'

'I rather think you'd know if you were, wouldn't you, Mr Cator?'

'You think you're clever. You weren't clever enough to guess what I'd do. Or certain enough of what you wanted me to. Thought it was enough to guess who I might be. Put you in two minds.'

'True.'

'Never have a single thought. Knights' fork. F-X Batzan is an old troublemaker. He likes to put me up a little game from time to time. Saw you coming before you left Villefranche; had you in the woods; saw you break and enter. He likes to tease me; I like to tease him. Basques and Welshmen, tricky bastards.'

'The two of you have tons of fun together, it seems.'

'Did you get stung? Show me.'

'Nothing to show,' I said.

'Still worth a dekko. *Vous me croyiez un vieux paysang, nong?*'

'*Peut-être.*'

'The girls always used to say "perhaps". Now they say "fuck". Same race. Not a Jew, why are you called Rachel?'

'I expect my mother wished she was. Who knows?'

He said, 'Did you see me back there? No one wishes that.'

'Or she might have loved somebody once. I saw a *deux chevaux.*'

'Blind. Haven't got a car. Journalist. You're very ... modern, then, are you? Pride yourself, do you?'

'I don't know what I am,' I said. 'I'm waiting to see.'

'Haven't you left it rather? Do you want some tea? Said you were English.'

'And what about you?'

'I never said what I was.'

'How are we going to have tea?'

'Boil water; make some.' He led the way across to the shelter where the two barrels still flavoured the air with the lees of an ancient vintage. 'Man must have his tea.'

I said, 'Do you live here?'

'Do I live anywhere? What do you want from me? Clock's running. Always is. Bastard thing.'

'They never gave you a medal. Why was that?'

'She's dead, is that it?'

'You know she is.'

He pulled a primus stove from the darkness behind one of the barrels and lit it with a tilted touch of a cheap plastic lighter. 'I was offered one. Up the jacksie. Gong. Refused.'

'Are you sorry? She's dead?'

He marched away towards the well and pulled back its wooden

hood. He now had the drilled stride of a generation which had been taught not to slouch; I could see him in Oxford bags. 'Left sorrow in my other trousers. Not worn 'em for years.' The chain of the well rattled; he had used it before. 'There's a trick to getting water out of wells.'

'I know,' I said. 'I went to Guide Camp.'

'How about cutting throats? Trick to that too.'

'You learned that as well?'

'Twenty years old; wasn't anything I couldn't learn. Not that I knew it. Late cut. Square drive. Unfortunately only learnt what they taught me. Education's meant to do that: thus far and not a step beyond. You have a lot of feelings, I expect. Mine went in the wash. Like John's crown. Pipe your eye when you see a dead cat, do you? Avoid their corpses on the road as well?'

I said, 'Why are you still out here?'

'Money,' he said. 'Is that what it's about?'

'It being...?'

'Now you're being coy. Disappointment, that. This excursion. Is it to money that I owe the honour of your visit?'

'And curiosity.'

'I'll settle for money. Sent you out from England to hunt for an old fox, did they? Well, well.'

'You flatter yourself. I live near Sainte-Foy-le-Fort. They called me.'

'Live, do you? How can you tell? Alone?'

'With my husband.'

'And how many children?'

'We have no children.'

'Hubby does what?'

'He buys and sells. Houses. We do it together. He's called Roger.'

'Brave, young, beautiful; couldn't operate a wireless to save her life. Is that what you want to know? Yvonne. Got your notebook? Got your tape-machine? Chop-chop!'

'I've got my head,' I said. 'Which will do. How did they come to send you out here?'

'Do it together, do you? Lived in Hyères during my childhood, and school holidays. Bit of a frog, I suppose. Knocking around London, end of '42. Fumbling girls in the black-out; never even saw their faces; less of their other parts. Done by numbers. Introduced to Gerry Bisto. Howjadoo? Parleyvoo? Off you go. Set

Europe Ablaze. Got any matches, anyone? Volunteered. Mad. Bit in love with Bisto. He was good at that. The C.O. ... Ah, you do know something, do you? Assumed I could do the job, without saying exactly what the job was. They ran the world like that, our mums and dads. Never happen again. Been in the Balkans, Gerry, alone, in '39 and '40; last man out. Having done God knows what kinds of mayhem down there. Knew he'd done things, not polite to ask what. Had a great-aunt once called Rachel; never knew about it till some time after the event.'

'What event exactly?'

'Look at that,' he said, 'a man who can make tea. Sugar. Liberated. No milk; no cow. Shall you mind? My father was, as you've been told...'

I shook my head. 'I've not been told a thing about ... your background.'

'As you have *not* been told, was a – what is the word? – *Christian*. He was a Christian.'

I said, 'And you?'

'Of course,' he said. 'Like father, don't like son.'

'You've said that before.'

'Correction: he did. When I tried for his college. Oxford, 1938. And they turned me down. Luckily. Went up after the war; different college. Better one. Yvonne. What do you want to tell them about her?'

'He was something else apart from a Christian, presumably.'

'You have an orderly mind, Rachel. Won't make friends like that. You like tidy ends. World prefers 'em untidy. World always wins. Rev. Headmaster, my progenitor; regulation preparatory school. Cold baths. Bare bum swishings; leaving jaw; now to the Father, and later, if he was lucky, to the Son; the lot. Copper's nark, me, destined to be; learnt from quite an early age how to operate in enemy territory; shouldn't have survived eighth birthday otherwise. *All* territory was enemy. Green baize both sides of the door. You want to tell them that she was the great love of my life? Separation a tragedy from which foxy old fool never fully recovered? Tell 'em. True enough. Want me to say she never cracked under torture? Patriot and idealist? I've said it. Also true. And I still say it. Now you can trot along, can't you?'

'Is it not the whole truth then?'

'Whole truth; truth with a hole in it. I could've cut your throat, Rachel, do you know that? And buried you and no one would ever find neither 'ide nor 'air.'

'More or less anyone could do that to more or less anyone, when you come to think about it.'

'Doubt it, dear. You should try it sometime. Clear my throat, shall I, and ... ? I arrived in France, she was with a man called Leclerc. Sounded like a frog, wasn't. Catalan, he *said*; London reckoned otherwise. Louis. Luis. Louis le Loup. Loop the loo. Been a flyer in Spain. Steady hand. Hand in glove with old Batzan. Militant atheist. Spoke Spanish, Catalan, Arabic, mostly when he was angry. Word was he was some kind of a Berber. Not advised to say so to his face. Black beard, black eyes. Loved him. Man to die for. Fuck this, fuck that, that's your style these days, is it?'

'Not mine particularly,' I said.

'Sainte-Foy-le-Fort. I could tell you some stories. Master Félix Argote, name come up yet? Jews in the cellar. Put that on the menu yet, has he, up at the *Relais*, on Father's Day?'

'What Jews were these?'

'Ask them sometime, if you want to see what a look of innocence really looks like, *flagrante delicto*. When I dropped into the *double*, I was Captain Cator; twenty-three years' worth. Experienced soldier? I'll say. One cock-up landing on some god-awful Greek island; machine-gunned by our own planes. Poles. Waved at them; in they came; took us off at the knees. *Efcharisto pohlee!* You don't get it. Why should you? After which episode, much hanging about in gyppo-land. Spell in Cairo unpeeling a colonel's lady. Wendy Mackinnon. Sip before dins. I'd left the UK, twenty years old, in proper love with a Catholic girl in Basingstoke. Father disapproved; main thing in her favour. *My* father. Tricia. Lovely face, bit of a hump to her. Never *imagined* her without her clothes on; never saw her neither. Wrote to me: waiting for you, darling. Lie. I broke her heart, they said; never her cellophane. Couldn't get my finger in. So! 1943, Bisto said how's about it? Who, sir? Me, sir? Gosh, sir; yes, sir. Didn't even have the wit to shit myself. Trip to the continent? Beat hanging about West Wycombe, by three sets to nil. Bit of a sticky one on our hands, Cator; can you cope? Give it a try, sir. Slight case of anarchy, needs sorting out. Pop over, would you, and remind the sepoys: orders is orders? Renowned for his googly, Gerry B. Any questions? Um, upper hand, sir; how best to establish? Simple, Simon: tell 'em, do as you say or no more sovs and no more whiz-bangs. Heel, boy! Off you go then; just the boy to do a man's work. Oh, Cator, one thing: find some women in the ranks. My advice, treat 'em like anyone else. Clear? As mud, sir. Excellent. Unused to women under me. Despite Mrs Mackinnon. King's commission, licence to lie. Liberty and deception sleep in the same bed. With me?'

'How did Yvonne Langon come to be in the . . . group? Was she from around here?'

'Far from it. Very. Alsace. Near Strasbourg. Evacuated 1939, plus parentals. They hated it. No running water. Savages, they thought they were billeted with; sooner have been under the Fredas. The Germans. Otherwise Fridolins. You've heard of the Germans, have you? 1943, they were occupying the country.'

'All right,' I said, 'all right. Sorry about that.'

'Want an easy time, Rachel? That what you've come for?'

'I don't know what I've come for.'

'Money; established that. Same as I came for, in the first place: except that I came *with* money. Achieved instant popularity. Evie couldn't stick it with her parents, banged up with a family of Périgourdangs and all using one outdoor bog; buggered off into the bushes sharpish and found Luis. Nice girl. Till she learnt better. Time I was on the scene, she was smoking, she was drinking, she was a regular soldier. Expected tohu-bohu, found Luis was running the whole show pretty damn well; been in Spain, man with a mission. *Bloody* well, if the truth be known, which it seldom is, thanks to principalities and powers. Hated Fascists. London had him down for an enthusiast. Not a term of praise. Uncontrollable. Hence, all aboard, Cap'n Cator. Tell me something meaner than common sense. That was me, by moonlight.'

'They dropped you into France just like that?'

'Do them justice. Prior to Oper-wation Buggery, great care taken with costume. Pop down to Sussex-by-the-sea for insertion froggy dust in *pantalon* pockets, ditto turn-ups. Miracles of modern science? Second Nissen on the left. Forensic johnnies highly ingenious. Put you on a diet of snails for three days, in case the Gestapo analysed your droppings. Condemned man; French breakfast. Froggy flour in the lower intestine, if inspected. Assumed Fredas played by Queensberry rules. Imagine a row of Himmlers on their knees in the long grass, looking for evidence. Sooner stub their fags in your face. What did Baker Street know, or care, unless they knew all along? Probably Deauville dust they threw in our eyes so's we'd not guess what rough stuff was coming. Bluff and the real thing; two barrels, same gun. My orders: "relieve" Loulou. Not one of *nous*, dj'understand? First, make him 2-i-c; then ease him out. Upwards and downwards; same bloody *chemin*.'

'If he was doing such a good job, why not tell them he was?'

'They knew that. Red, wasn't he, Loulou? *Rojo* through and through. Wrong agenda, dear. And Yvonne? Under the spell, dear. Flat on her back. As required. Swore like a trooper; *was* a bloody trooper; couldn't get enough of the ramrod. Voice of innocence; tongue of fire; vocab of a squaddy. *Rien à foutre*. Still with me? Pick 'em up, pick 'em up! What were Bisto's orders so sealed I had to read them without opening them? Indicated already, haven't I?'

'I'm not all that hot at these things. What?'

'Pick 'em up, pick 'em up! What are you hot at? Must have a speciality; father's was Greek testament. Riot Act, mine. First rule of war: never trust your allies. Your enemies you can kill, or come to arrangements with, but your allies ... First job: Loulou out of the bloody driving seat. Take the wheel, Captain Cator, but don't run the show off the road. Call him Luis; call him Loulou; and meanwhile think dago, think red; think Abdul. Think Coco. Trying to use WD property to build *rojo* power base. Capital offence. Can you do it, Captain Cator? If you say so, sir. I say so, Cator. Then I can do it, sir. Up, two, three; down, two, three. Tried to write this stuff down at one time; couldn't. Why?'

'Not everyone can write.'

'Round objects, Rachel. Couldn't abide my young self. Ignorant, opinionated, arrogant; *that* part was all right, but the rest of it! Bloody Spartans at Thermopylae. "Obedient to their orders, here we lie"; like troopers. People at home make heroes out of the dead, stay alive themselves. Rule one of war: stay out of it yourself. Clever chaps never try to hold the bloody pass; send others to do it. And we're honoured; we're very, very honoured. Haven't seen a naked women in eleven years. Do you think she was murdered?'

'Do I think she was murdered?'

'Evie. What's the word around the building?'

'Why ever should she have been? So what happened when you got here?'

'True. Right, gather round. Smirk if you want to. Last word

on subject. Twenty-three years old, orders are (a) bump-a-dump Master Leclerc and (b), if time available, set Europe ablaze; within reason. Clear, Cator? Clear, sir. You're looking at your watch. Got an appointment? Go to it. Don't mind me.'

'I'm sorry,' I said, 'it's an old reflex. I worry about . . .'

'Him? They say confession is good for the soul. Concealment's better; it's got some life in it: confess and you're dead. Or not. Came out here, expecting to find aforesaid mess, *la pagaille*. Instead of which, what? Luis knew his way round literally with his eyes shut. Natural leader. Up to Ribérac, down to Montauban: king of the mountain; king of the plain. Friends everywhere; *compañeros por todas partes*. Know where Montauban is?'

'Isn't it where the Ingres museum is?'

'And can you also find your tit in the dark? Saw Luis thrash a woman once. Not Evie. Léah; spat when Germans passed, recce job; she was look-out. Showing off. They whistled; she spat on the ground; squeal of brakes, they piled out – understandably – and then, *"nicht var"* the Oberleutnant said, so they hopped back on board and drove on. Good old discipline. Just what we needed. All took about three seconds. Grinned at Luis when we came out of the shrubbery, Léah; assumed she was in for a pat on the back; if not more. Got it. Luis snapped a branch, pants down, thrashed her bloody. Elder; breaks easy. Lovely white bum. Never said a word, Léah; barely made a sound. Innocent me; never guessed till then what a bare bum must've done for my father; education unexpectedly continued. No time to be ashamed; stuck out a mile. Wiped herself after, gave him a look. Wish I'd had one like it, to be honest. Luis said to me later: "I'll have to plug her hole, blast it." In Arabic. In love with him, wasn't she? All were; and dared not speak our names: security. Léah spat to please Loulou, juicy little tart; thrashed her bloody, should've done the same thing to Evie. Can't see why, can you? *Pro bono pub.* Yapped, Léah; didn't blub. Loved it. You can't punish women, you see, that's one of the secrets of the universe. They don't take it the same way men do. Because what's punishment about? The regiment, dear. Jealousy, Evie's trouble. You'll never understand anything went on with us in those days; don't care how many bloody notebooks you've brought with you. Look at your watch if you want to. What are you late for?'

'I'm not late for anything.'

108

'I hope you're right. Rarely my experience. Love: one of Loulou's many enemies; female version, got in the way. Woman can be jealous of anything. Even a thrashing. Girl spits on the ground, the whole world moves over a quarter of an inch. Couldn't do the right thing, Loulou, then; forked. Made him angry with the whole sex. He'd've shot her, we'd've done nothing, carried on. Shot Léah, shot Evie. Ditto. Man's world.'

'What did you mean exactly when you said you were all in love with him?'

'Wanting to be with him, close enough to catch courage like a cold. You were with him, you laughed; it was all bloody marvellous, all of it. That's the bit you don't always own up to, Rachel; shooting people, frightening the shit literally out of people. Loved it. More particularly, in the now-it-can-be-told department, loved him; nothing queer about Carruthers, but ... And that was the man I'd been sent to budge. The Lord Cator! Imagine being one of the very few free men in a slave country; with a box full of other people's money, guns and ammo *ad libitum*; and your only accountant a black-eyed beauty who reported back what you told her – long, short, short, long – and didn't even know what she was sending. I was a lord of creation, Rachel whatever-your-name-is. *And* a traitor. Judas, the double disciple. I could not love thee, dear, so much, loved I not Baker Street more. Bliss it was, dear, God help me. And I was twenty-three years old.'

'Raikes is my last name. Were there other girls beside Yvonne and Léah?'

'Couple possibly. Hell of a long time ago; only wish it was longer.'

'Do you really?'

'Someone of my name, Rachel dear, has done some very strange things in his life. Things that'd ... if people knew about them.' He took a finger to his mouth and wobbled it against his lips. 'Can't believe 'em myself. Imagine if all the Spartans had died and there were none to go and tell. That's where we are today. That's where *you* are today, because L. Cator Esquire, he doesn't have a today. Surplus to requirement; over and out. All passion spent.'

'What about naked women? You still think about them, don't you?'

'I'll have one if you happen to have one with you.'

'How do you come to have money? They say you've got quite a bit of it.'

'Bloody father died is how. The Reverend Bum-bugger. Still got a father, have you?'

'I do. He's not all that old.'

'Only you are, right? Not given you what you wanted, has he, Mr Raikes, even if you do do it together? It's no good expecting me to be a gentleman, duckie. I'm a bloody gypsy; I'm a bloody Coco; everything they don't want around. Have been for years. Want to know why I married her and then you can bugger off, mission accomplished?'

I said, 'What happened to Luis?'

'Tortured to death, wasn't he? Before we could get to him. Want the details? Bit of a thrill; bit of a shock. Cream your bun for you. Why not?'

'He was captured, was he?'

'Wounded first. Out cold or they'd never have had him. No, señor. What about what you *didn't* ask? Viz: did I have anything to do with it? Answer that one for you, shall I? What happened? What do you think? What do you bloody think?'

'I can't say.'

'Hope I shopped him? Hope I didn't? You don't know what you hope. London still London, am I right? Fifty years. Tell 'em what they want to hear or they don't hear a thing.'

'What was it like, after the war, living with a heroine?'

'Working together with Georgie Cross between the sheets? Not telling. But she *was* a heroine. Bloody cow. She was that. Smirk if you want to, but don't ever forget it. *And* I loved her. I loved her all right. For a time. Loved him, loved her. Whatever it means. Didn't know much about love; not sure I do now. Optional extra; like the fiddle. This place; do you know about this place? *Moulin de l'Enclos*, do you?'

'Of course I don't.'

'You know about the Ingres Museum. Owned by a prize shit bastard. Mr Mayor. This place. Later decorated. Medal of the Resistance and contributions to right quarters. *Not* in that order, by a long chalk. Had a word with him about it. Another story; not for bedtime. He didn't talk, Luis; she didn't talk neither. Or spit. She didn't talk and she might as well have and we got her back despite everything. Not him. No, *sir*. Meaning? Speak up; smirk if you want to.'

'London told you not to get them out, is that it?'

'*Ordered* us not to, is it. Not to get *him* out. Might endanger the success of impending oper-wation Overlord. *Verb. sap.!* Followed by *quelques messages personnels*: such as, back orf or else. Facer, right? Luis in central prison in Périgueux. Luis. Six others. Leave them be, that was what the Spartans said; they had Ephors, we had Bakelisher Strasse. We also had the right dust in our pockets and we were told to do as we were told. Or don't come home for the party. Which I never fucking did. Disobeying orders is a serious offence, Captain Cator. Orders, sir? Never got the message, sir. Faulty W/T. Bloody girl pressed the wrong button. Horatio Nelson; battle of Copenhagen. Who's he? Telescope? Blind eye? What's that? You're wrong, Rachel: I'm not proud of it. *Pas du tout*. Least I could do; did it. Because?'

'Presumably, you . . .'

'Presumably! Word never used in honest speech. Blind. Fraud. Wotcha 'fraid of? I don't have feelings. I promised you. I can still keep a promise, even if I do pee more than I used to. So: why and how did we get Luis into aforesaid hole in first place? Dangerous oper-wation proposed; Luis has info troop-train scheduled, headed Normandy, ex-Montauban. Do we, don't we blow tunnel; block line? No problem, Loulou says. Many dead; home for tea. What would you do, chum? What's Cap'n Cator's problem now? Stop bugger winning another cup. Your war effort is not always my war effort, saith the Lord, but don't tell the troops. You smile: trust a woman, always smiles when nothing to smile about. David and Bathsheba; what do we know about it? Naboth, his vineyard; father used to preach on it, way over the boys' heads; that's what he liked, dirty old sod, dear old pater. Father, Son and Holy Ghost. It's all gone, Rachel; that world. Swish their bare little botties and give yourself a rub before you go upstairs to madam. Stiff hankies; thing of the past.'

'So what happened with Loulou exactly?'

Cator grabbed me suddenly by the throat. He really did. His thumb was under my jaw. His face was up to mine. 'Shut your conceited little face, would you please, dear? You can't call him Loulou; I can.' He let me go and I swallowed several times. 'Get some service in. Lou had the facts, he had the gen; decision was up to Lord London. "*Qu'est-ce que tu ponce, mi capitán?*" The grin; the teeth; the eyes. Look at the bastard. Dared me deny him; didn't, couldn't. God help me, wouldn't. Played on his weakness, didn't I? Played on his strength, same job: *vaya usted con Dios*. Either way, I had to win. He succeeded? *Our* success. Tap it out on the old W/T – long, short, short long – and for Christ's sake get it right this time. After which, wait for another *message personnel*; funny thing, they don't say Christ, do they, the frogs? Obscenity one thing; blasphemy another. Not so *chez les Anglais*. And if he failed? *Les cygnes chantent deux fois. My* success! Go tell the Spartans. They'll find out anyway. Dry your eyes and tap it out, you boo-hooing bitch; love and war, know the diff? I didn't *want* him caught; I didn't *know* he would be; I only knew he was off to the wars because I daren't deny him. He was pulling my bloody plonker, Rachel; yes, you do: people always know what things mean. He'd been pulling it since the moment I turned up with all the right substances in my bloody turn-ups. Wanted to take Langon with him. Called her that. Never Yvonne. Long Gone. I said I needed her with me, for the W/T. True? True. The decisive foot came down, two three.'

'I thought she was caught with him . . .'

'Wait for it. *Wait* for it! As you were, and wait for it, dear! Sent him without her; needed the W/T, didn't I? So I gave him a bunch of chaps, girl called . . . can't remember her name; smelt of onions. Make it quickly in, quickly out, Luis; risky this one, *hombre*, very, very. Oh I told him! But how long can you stop someone doing what he means to do, especially when it's what you mean him to? He went; *hasta luego, compañero. Luego* came, and went, band he wasn't back. None of them were. Finally, word from the jail-house. Myself evidently not only person plying the Suez canal; cuts both ways, you may remember. Périgueux *père de famille*, with the *maison d'arrêt* keys on his belt and only so many shopping days to Christmas, decided to open an account with us. Your money is safe with us, M'sewer, ditto secret. Strength of the English? No shortage reliable people of the second class. When I got the word, we were up at Château St Martial; know it?'

'I've heard of it,' I said.

'I've heard of Christian charity,' Cator said, 'and seen a few examples.'

'If Yvonne didn't go with him,' I said, 'how come she ended up in there with him?'

'I like you, Rachel; you don't like me. Always drawn to that. Mummy is telling the story in her own way. So wait for it or it's lights out right away. Luis captured, what's to do? Bisto's recipe: sleep on it. Four in the a.m., Château St Martial, Captain Cator obeying orders, Evie rolls up. Shake, shake. Not a word; a look. Looks at me and what does she do? As you were! Wait for it, wait for it! Look says: they've got him; your fault. Sleeping dog; bloody liar. Pure hate. Then she pulls down her bloody pants. She pulls down her pants, off with the shirt, angry tits jumping around, heat coming off her, steam off a horse and she's down on the ground with me and that was our first time. Might as well have been first ever. I don't know which of us hated the other one more. Bang, bang, bang. Shooting party. Two dogs, two bitches, and Luis the bone neither of us had; the one with the meat on it. Bang, bang, bang. *Période de chasse*. I wanted her dead; didn't know, didn't think what *she* wanted. Which suited her fine. Are you with me? I didn't want her bloody accusations, all of which were true, even the ones she hadn't thought of yet. And at the same time, public school boy. Golly gosh and what *does* she think she's doing? English mentality, can't ever quite shake the stuff out of your turn-ups: she loves me, she loves me, I was thinking, or why would she do those things? Take that and that, you bitch, you whore, dearest love. "*Mon amour, mon amour*"; she kept saying it, must mean it; must mean me, I thought. She certainly went at it, thought she was going to do Hampers irreparable damage. French girl'd never happened to me before. Loved me, didn't she? Yes and no, as previously instructed, *dès le premier jour*. Get it?'

'He'd already told her to . . .'

'Betray him first; then think clearly. Knew her; knew women, knew men: rarely think straight when hot; cool parts first, cool head follows. Knew her; knew me. More than I did. Chance of a lifetime, much appreciated. Gave her one and gave her two, without unloading. Lovely job. Followed by . . . C.O.'s calm appreciation. Rule one: under torture, people always talk, *y compris* the bravest. Assume Luis broken man. *Ergo* . . . act as if all revealed: names, addresses. Could not love thee, dear, so much. Could now. Time to grow up; Loulou's point. He'd told her: "I get caught, you don't cry, you don't mourn; you go and fuck the *rosbif*. Give him a dose of what's good for him and then, possibly, he can think straight. Doesn't mean a thing to me, *querida*." My reading. Yours?'

I said, 'I can't read people without my glasses.'

'You come after us; you can never catch us. That's the fun of it. So what did he want me to do? What was I supposed to do? Under whose law? What did she want? All right, I knew what she wanted and I knew what I ought to do. *Statim*. But I don't believe that's why he told her to do what she did. All the reasons in the world wouldn't quite cover it. You can see what God's about, can't you? What about you: what would you do, chum? Look at your watch? Got all you need, have you? Never take more, is my advice; lumps in the pockets give you away, lumps in the throat ditto. What's your next instalment then?'

'You went and got him. Or tried to.'

'You were there, dear, were you?'

'*C'est vrai, ce qu'ils disent: vous êtes décidément un vieux renard.*'

'What happened was, she told me we had to do something. *Mon amour, mon amour.* Cool head, my fanny! Call London, see what they could do. How about a RAF special: low-level, pin-point cock-up *à la Polonaise*? Tap, tap, tap. Long short long. Nix. Up to me, but no unnecessary heroics, please. *Muchas gracias por nada!* We cleared out of St Martial and when we got down to the *double*, I took the decision. I'd taken it already, but I didn't unwrap it until we'd had a chance to stretch the legs. Nastiest decision I'd ever taken. Cowardice gets a bad press, but it's not always an easy option. Write that down. Because I looked Evie in the eye and that's what I said. She looked at me. "*Tu es un vrai salaud.*" I said I'd go myself if I thought there was half a chance. "*Laisse-moi y aller,*" she said, "*et puis après ...*" "And if he's dead," I said, "*tu m'épouseras?*" Condition of sale. I said that; I actually said that. What did it mean? Not what it said; but *what*? No one will ever know, dear; don't bother looking. Ignominious? Could well be. Her eyes went up, two three, down, two three, and off she went; see if she could suck him out of there. Then *she* could spit. At him; at me. I should've stopped her, should I? Impossible to say; ever, ever, ever. God doesn't know the answer. Is no answer? Rachel Raikes. You married a man you didn't love, Gypsy say. Gypsy right?'

'She went into town and she got caught, is that it?'

'Did she want to be? Succeeded. Bloody heroines. So now what? *Père de famille* on the line again. *Un peu de chance, mon ami*: they're shipping them out, Germany; all the women; some of the men. This time, bugger London; had to do something; and did it. Ambush in *pleine campagne*. Yvonne and others debussed, two three. Cator's coup! Truth is, Luis's little oper-wation saved her more like; railway line blown, tunnel down; had to take them by road. Bang, bang. Miscellaneous bodies in ditch. None of 'em ours except the onion girl. *Tante* pee. Never liked her. How are you Evie, if that's you? She'd had a chat with the Gestapo, hadn't she? Otherwise safe and sound, so how's about a kiss? Hit me in the face, hard as she could. Luis was dead before she went into town.'

'And then ... ?'

'She was in my arms, of course. Promises must be kept. Why not? I loved her, as you will say in an exclusive interview, and so I did, in my way, and so did she me, in hers. More than your bloody little pen can ever say; because of everything and in spite of everything. Only way to keep him alive. Try telling them that and they won't understand a word of it. No, we never talked about him; that was how we kept him there. You're afraid I'm joking; I'm afraid I'm not. All I know for certain is what we did. At it like knives, we were; for weeks and weeks after Loulou was killed. Funny things, private wars. Also time-consuming.'

'And after that?'

'No such time,' Cator said. 'In some respects. Never heard the whistle, did I?'

'What happened that ... changed things?'

'Look at the time, Rachel. I'm ten bob in an old pair of trousers as far as you're concerned; well, there you are, you've found it; probably a lot more than you deserve.'

'She never loved you really, is that the story?'

'Tell it then.'

'You're good at smirk and you're also good at smoke, aren't you? As in screen.'

'I'm never telling anyone the truth, dear, not even a short-legged tart with a plum in her mouth.'

'You don't care what you say to people, do you?'

'Nice of me, I thought, giving you a chance to get on your high horse. Up you get! Click of coconut shells and away you go. But if you'd sooner limp, I can always arrange it. Likewise, I could've cut your throat and had you inside that bloody *tonneau* and no one would've known the difference.'

'Father Batzan might.'

'Franco-Xavier needs me more than he'd ever need anyone to know what happened to you.'

'Why would you want to cut my throat, Mr Cator?'

'Keep my hand in. Help me stay young. Suppose I didn't want people coming after me.'

'You came and found me; I didn't find you. So don't pretend you're not playing some kind of a double game...'

'I haven't seen a naked woman in eleven years. I could very well never see one again. Care to oblige? Sainte-Foy-le-Fort, you live near, do you? Funny that!'

'It doesn't come into what you told me. Is that what's funny?'

'Absolutely right,' he said. 'Absolutely bang right. Another story entirely. *Vieux renard!* Why shouldn't I bloody well be?'

'There are still a few things I don't get,' I said.

'The numbers have come down then, have they? Only a few? You're either stupid or you're lying.'

'Never forget both,' I said. 'You got tired of Luis, is that what happened, between you, eventually? He let you down, is that what happened? He died on you, I mean.'

'Get the hell out of here. Get in your bloody machine and roll on out before something happens to you. Go and roll out your bloody pastry, Rachel, and make mid-morning bikkies for the tourists. She was the love of his life but it was too hot not to cool down. You've written it already, haven't you? Particularly between the lines. Always the best bits. Words to the wise. *Méfiez-vous.* Don't like me, do you?'

'Not a lot,' I said. 'When can I see you again?'

9

'Is it all right if I wash my hair?'

'All right with me, you mean, or all right for your hair?'

'Oh Roger,' Pansy said, 'why are you such a flirt? What I mean is, if I don't use the telephone, is it all right if I go and wash my hair?'

'I'm a bit worried about Rachel actually. She might have called at least.'

'Perhaps she did while we were out. They took for ever, didn't they, in that bank? They hated giving it to us.'

'Except that I left the answer-machine on, didn't I?'

'That's a car now, isn't it?' Pansy said. 'It could be her now. Is it OK if I shower and wash my hair at the same time?'

'You can do anything you like. You can soap your muff three times and whistle the Marseillaise while you do it.'

'Just as long as I don't use the phone, right?'

'We're seriously short of money, Pansy; I realise that you don't know what that really means, but what it means practically is, if you use the telephone, I just might possibly do something unforgivable to you that we both might enjoy more than quite a lot. Meanwhile, call me when you drop the soap and I'll come and find it for you. Oh look where it's got to! And how one thing does lead to another!'

He turned away from Pansy's reproachful encouragement and walked out of the house and down the steps and through the arch, preparing himself for Rachel, and saw a van. It was a Transit like the one he had hired to bring the furniture from Essex. The wide door slid back and heavy-duty green boots were hanging out.

'Roger, hi! I hope this is OK. Because we suddenly realised something. You remember Jonty, don't you?'

'Of course I remember Jonty. Jesus!'

'Only we was reading your literature ... and – if this is in the least bit inconvenient, you've got to say so – it then struck me: you're the obvious man.'

'Am I just? To do what exactly?'

'Help Jonts and me find our dream house. "Our de luxe dream house in an idyllic landscape." Do I quote your well-chosen words?'

'Excuse me, but how long have you been around the region?'

'You're excused. How long have we, Jont?'

'A few days. Why?'

'I didn't think you liked it all that much.'

'You know our problem, of course.'

'Not entirely.'

'The food. Which is how come we thought suddenly if we had a place of our own, we might very well become considerable neighbours of yours.'

'You want somewhere to *buy*?'

'Rent or buy. Rent with a view to buy, if you like. Flexible, us. Only we do need expert assistance from long-term residents who are themselves wholeheartedly committed to the beauty of the area. As you and the missus are very widely rumoured to be.'

'How much can you afford to pay?'

'There you are, Jonts! I said he liked us. This is a very nice spread you have, Roger. This is an exceptional example of what an expatriate can aspire to, given the resources and their careful use thereof.'

'You should have seen it before we started.'

'You should have sent us an invitation.'

'If you're serious ...'

'Oh, we're serious,' Quigley said. 'We're very, very serious. Look how serious Jonty is. The beard says it all. Can we come and have a preliminary chat on a no-obligation basis? Only first, let's get something clear and out of the way; if we're being any sort of a nuisance, you're to sing out. Bad is the last thing I need to feel.'

'Come in,' Roger said, 'come in.'

'Oh my goodness, look through here! Look at this courtyard, Jonathan. You was wrong, wasn't you, about him? I know my

Rodge and I know how hospitable he can be. As advertised, after all! Your literature speaks in quite large letters of a catalogue available on request. Can I put my hand up possibly?'

'Why don't you sit down and I'll go and fetch one.'

'You can see why some people succeed, can't you, in life, and others don't?'

'What about a beer while I'm at it?' Roger called out from the front door as Quigley and Goldstein creaked together on the hammock in the courtyard.

'That would be very acceptable. Not that I knew you was at it. Wouldn't a beer be acceptable though, Jonty? Should've guessed perhaps.'

Roger was taking two tins of Heineken Export out of the refrigerator when Pansy's head and loosened hair appeared over the landing rail. 'Rodge ... I can't find the shampoo. Any ideas?'

'How about next time you bring your own?'

'Is that an invitation?'

'Cupboard under the basin. Do you want to borrow a robe? There's one on the hook behind the bathroom door.'

When Roger went out with the beers, glasses, and the catalogue under his chin, Quigley said, 'We're not interrupting nothing, I hope, are we? Are you not having one? A beer?'

'I'm all right,' Roger said. 'Book of words! And pictures!'

'Fallen on your plates here all right, Rodge. As widely predicted.'

Goldstein was pointing to a polaroid in the catalogue. 'How about this one? How much is that?'

'Look, don't be bloody silly, all right?'

'I was being bloody silly apparently. I wasn't conscious of that until it was pointed out.'

'That's an eight-million-franc job.'

'Roger, darling, sorry but ... I can't seem to find it.'

'*Jesus!*' Roger turned to see Pansy leaning out of the mansard window of the second spare bedroom. She had not borrowed a robe. 'On the hook behind the door.'

'It's seriously not there.'

'It's looks as if it's there to me,' Quigley said. 'What about you, Jonts?'

'Very much so,' Goldstein said. 'Janet Reger, and why not, if you've got it? Which she more than evidently has.'

'The shampoo.'

'Bottom shelf. At the back. In a pink canister with a plastic top.'

'Oh, is that shampoo?'

'Don't you love them?' Quigley said. 'I love them. They deserve a channel all to themselves, they truly do. Roger...'

'Yes?'

'You've torn yourself away. Very nice of you. Here's what's in my mind; I think I know what's in yours. And I admire your taste. It's going to take us a day or two, isn't it, to get ourselves satisfied? Accommodation-wise. So, would it be an intolerable imposition if we did something?'

'That might depend on what you did.'

'What did I tell you, Jonts? This is a very together character. You'd possibly be surprised, and conceivably flattered, if you knew how often you've come up as a topic of conversation when we're sitting at home in dear old Beckenham South, as we've come more and more to think of it, with the old fried chicken and our favourite video, which currently happens to be *Spinal Tap*. Some of us are still eagerly awaiting the sequel to that one.'

'I thought you were veggies,' Roger said.

'Got it!' Pansy called out. 'Got it, Rodge.'

'We normally are,' Quigley said, 'but chickens don't really have faces, do they? We don't touch nothing what's got what you'd probably call a face. Which doesn't include the odd chicken, we've decided. Would it be all right if we camped?'

'Camped? Of course.'

'See, Jonts? What did I not tell you on countless occasions? What we have here is essentially a very nice man.'

'I don't know how many sites are open at the moment,' Roger said, 'but I'm sure there are some. They do a guidebook.'

'Camped here,' Quigley said.

ii

Rachel said, 'Can I take you somewhere?'

'How do you think I got here? I've got transport; Harley-Davidson, up the back. Rolled down the *chemin*, that's how come you didn't hear me. Had it for years. Never rely on other people and you'll rarely be disappointed. Scouts' Law. Why do you want to see me again?' Cator folded down the little stove and replaced it behind the barrel. 'I'll tell you and then you can tell me I'm wrong. I broke off a branch of the past, didn't I, and thrashed you with it? Gently. And you're not sure if you want it harder or what you want. Want to know where I live, is that it? How do you know I live anywhere? You could probably walk straight through me, if you decided to.'

Rachel offered a sigh of resigned amusement and strolled towards the Cherokee.

'Something I didn't tell you, is there?'

'A great deal, I hope.'

'Hope, do you? One luxury I avoid. Think I lied to you, do you? Can you put a finger on it?'

'Oxford,' she said. 'You didn't go there, did you?'

'Never said I finished,' he said. 'Father died; that was one thing; hers. Women you don't know; they're the dangerous ones. Ask them one day in Sainte-Foy-le-Fort what happened there, July twenty-four, forty-four.' When Rachel turned and looked interested, he indicated the *Moulin de l'Enclos*. He cleared his throat like a man who had said the wrong thing and wanted to return to another subject. Was it another act? She could not be sure. 'Man who lived in this house, good reason to believe he sold some friends of mine to the Fredas. Doctor and his family; good people. Couldn't *prove* it; knew it: came to light after the event. Well after. Scot free is not part of the Welsh vocabulary, dear, not as spoken by yours truly. No one lives here because I won't have it. No one lives here and no one says why and everyone knows exactly. Sown with salt. Field of blood. There's Judas and then there's Judas. What do you do with vermin, Rachel? Strychnine, don't you? You don't cut its throat. Do you like motorbikes?'

'Never been on one.'

'One day I could scare the life out of you, if you've got nothing better to do.'

'I've got the garden,' Rachel said, 'and my husband –'

'I can also tell you a few things that'll keep you awake at night, if he doesn't. I could tell you what happened to the people who were staying at the *Relais St Jacques*, July twenty-four, forty-four. Left no forwarding address. You won't do it, of course; why shouldja? I could wise you up, but nobody wants that, do they? Last thing we need today, when we've all got our watches to look at. And our deadlines to observe, two-three.'

Rachel said, 'You wouldn't want to see it, would you?'

'See what?'

'The article. How would you like to come across?'

'I lived with her for years, Rachel, after the bloody war, and I never should have. I should never have stayed with her after July forty-four and that's the real truth. Day I stopped loving her. Something you won't put in the paper: I'm circumcised.'

'A lot of people are. My husband is.'

'Haven't seen a naked women in a dozen years, may well never see one again. Dozens of 'em about. The flesh, the flesh! Life is full of last times; and first. Rarely recognised for what they are. I didn't know it was, but it was.'

'What was what?'

'And who was who?'

'You didn't break up till a lot after that, did you? Nineteen forty-four.'

'Break up. No. I broke up; she didn't. Never noticed. I cover up better than what I do anything else. The green baize effect. Anyone can be what they are; no skill required. You know who she went off with, of course; got cuttings to that effect, I daresay. Excellent man, Castillonès; rich as greases; couldn't have chosen better. Rewards are the cruellest punishments; some say. First-class shit, the baron, you'd like him. Wore Evie like a button in his lapel; needed one too: certificate of clearance. You'd like him very much. "*Mes hommages, Madame!*" Kiss your hand and his nose up your skirt. Ideal. See me again? What for?'

'It might be interesting. Possibly.'

'Watering the gravy, dear, are we? Backing away, are we? Why did I tell you? I was circumcised. Why? Silly old man; had to expose himself; that what you think? Embarrass you?'

'Not a bit.'

'Much as that, eh? Had my reasons. Give you a clue, something for another time; father never knew. Mine. Destiny that shapes our ends; one of his favourite texts. And now to the Father, and to the Son ... I kicked her out in the end; couldn't stand her. Or *it*; probably latter. Not her fault; not mine. Lived a lie till I was ... a certain age. Till something happened. Met an old friend I didn't know. Turn right at the bottom, you hit the main road. Home to hubby.'

'How do I get hold of you?' Rachel said.

'Old Man of the Sea, dear. Care of Château St Martial. Catch me when you can and hold on tight. Don't come looking. I'll give you a buzz. Long short long short long.'

iii

'They're putting up the Taj Mahal out there. They're building the Great Pyramid. Who was it built the damned thing?'

'We were going to Egypt,' Pansy said, 'at one point. And then something happened. Or was that Thailand?'

'Look, Pansy, I hate to ask you, but can you possibly lend me ten grand?'

'You could have said you loved me first.'

'I do love you. Obviously. But can you?'

'My money's all tied up. Don't ask me why, or where, but it is apparently. Otherwise I'd have it.'

'Chops,' Roger said. 'Was that his name?'

'Brice has people who tell him where to put it, and he does. Which he rarely does when I do. Where are the Cayman Islands?'

'They've got no right to come and camp here. They've got no bloody right. What do you mean, the Cayman Islands?'

'Why don't you just go and tell them? It's where he keeps putting it. And call someone if they don't move. I would.'

'You might; I can't. All right then; daren't. If that's what you're thinking, you're a hundred per cent right. You had to be here, didn't you? You just had to be here.'

'What's ten grand going to do?'

'I haven't got it, have I? So it's not going to do anything.'

'I'm going to talk to them,' Pansy said. 'And get them to see some sense. And then when I come back, you can be nice to me again. Funny the way people's anger comes out in kisses. I've often noticed that.'

Quigley and Goldstein had canted the truck on the edge of the field beyond Rachel's garden. The orange tent had a pink, hooded terrace in front of plastic bay windows with integral mosquito netting over them. Goldstein, in black track trousers with a wide grey stripe, and a '69' khaki basketball top, was twanging the guy ropes as if he were tuning an instrument. Quigley was crouched, in the nylon parka, frying sausages on a camping-gas stove. He let

123

Pansy watch him for a while and then he said, 'Fancy a banger then, Pansy? Or are you here strictly for the exercise?'

'I thought you were vegetarians.'

'We're vegetarians with a difference,' Goldstein said.

'And what's that exactly?'

'The difference is, sometimes we're not.'

'Are you *anything* permanently, or . . . ?'

'We believe basically in give and take, don't we, Jonts? Live and let live, always with the proviso of a fair return on our investment.'

'What kind of sausages are those?'

'Those are your basic *saucisses du pays*, your *frichti*-type, I'm-basically-up-for-it-if-you-are brand of local banger, which we like for a change; sometimes between your *braguette*, sometimes not, as the mood dictates. Haven't we got a lovely evening for it and isn't this a lovely girl, Jonathan? They don't slip this kind through your letter-box, do they, very often?'

'You're having one,' Pansy said, 'I'll have one.'

'Reciprocity,' Quigley said. 'What a lot there is to be said for that under existing world conditions!'

Pansy said, 'You two evil sods're having quite a lot of fun, aren't you, one way and another?'

'You've slightly rumbled us there, I'm afraid. The eclectic mode very much appeals to Jonathan and myself. Is there any possibility it might do likewise with you, Pansy, by the look of you? You have a miraculous waistline and, so far as I can judge, thighs which could give pleasure to countless people. Evil sods, was that?'

Pansy said, 'Look, how long are you intending to stay?'

'As soon as I look, since you mention it, I want to stay pretty well indefinitely. You are an object of true aesthetic gratification. As Jonathan quite rightly pointed out when we was dwelling on it earlier, that is one of the world's three-star *tushes* you have there. Did he send you down here?'

'Of course he didn't.'

'I believe you. You know what is the most miraculous and certainly the most underestimated achievement of nature? It's got to be the packaging. Because look at this woman, Jonts, and what do you see? The perfect example of the untarnished ex-factory model ideal evening out, and later in. Why do you ask about our intentions? *Evil sods?* Is our presence turning the milk, is it?'

'And, possibly more important, in the short term at least,' Goldstein said, 'will you be wanting mustard at all?'

'What she needs first, Jonts, and it's a need well within our capacity to satisfy, is a nice chair. A chair worthy of the *tush* which you see before you, but are naturally too polite to want to do anything but cosset.'

'I can sit anywhere.'

'You *can*, dear, but why should you? Because look at that.'

'That's a very nice chair,' Pansy said.

'That is indeed. That's not a chair that's used to being associated with a tent in any way whatsoever in the normal run of things. That is a chair for a lady of quality. What we have kept under wraps until the right lady came along. Which she now done.'

'What else have you got in there while we're at it?'

'*Are* we at it? How time flies, doesn't it, Jonts?'

'All right,' Pansy said, 'a joke's a joke.'

'Not necessarily,' Quigley said, 'not necessarily. In the sense that –'

'*Look* . . .'

'Done that, darling; and very much enjoyed the on-going experience, as I hope it will prove to be. A joke can, however, also be more than a joke; you've heard of the part for the whole, haven't you? And may well have had some experience of it. Well, here it comes again. *De luxe* edition. In spades. That's a Louis Treize *fauteuil*, as you may well have recognised.'

'I've recognised a few other things,' Pansy said, 'including . . .'

'She sticks at it, Jonts, you can sense that. No use putting up signs in large letters for this particular lady. You can add courage to beauty in her instance, and still have something for another time. Including?'

'You amuse yourselves.'

'For example, insight. Always granting that she's got a good heart, because why else would she be bothering, quite frankly, in the circumstances? You haven't said a word about the *saucisse*. Is it to your taste? We have others. It's the best means available, dear, isn't it, comedy? There's your public media, which are shit in several colours, and then there's your independent nexus of private and personal associations if you're looking for day-to-day gratification. Which we ourselves very often are, we find.'

'What do you think he owes you? What's he done to you? And what are you trying to do to him?'

'You've heard of innocent fun, haven't you, dear? At your age, you must have.'

'This isn't innocent,' Pansy said.

'She's talking now like a girl who wears glasses. You've got this I would definitely call it a frown on that flawless face of yours, hasn't she, Jonty? I hate to see that, don't you? I thought my sausage would go down better than that. Life: if it's not laughs, what is it? I can answer that from my personal repertoire: disappointments. So now you know my driving philosophy basically.'

'You think you're funny,' Pansy said, 'and I think you are.'

'That's nice. Isn't that nice, Jonts?'

'Very much so,' Goldstein said.

'Because who else do we personally care about? The Happy Few and that's it, today; the rest can go jump.'

'Funny up to a point. Which has now been reached.'

'Our main object,' Quigley said, 'is to give pleasure all round.'

'Is it? And do you really think they want you here?'

'You want to make two questions of it then, do you? "They" being?'

'You know damned well. Roger and his wife. My sister.'

'I know *him* damned well. All too. *Her* we have yet to have the pleasure of meeting.'

'Did you come down here specifically to do this?'

'We have a wide range of interests, Pansy. Like yourself, in all probability. Which sometimes converge, as in the present instance, which brings us back to Rodge. Come here often, do you?'

Pansy said, 'I've been having a few problems at home.'

'Husbands and wives!' Quigley said. 'An old old story! And yet, at the same time, we must never forget that marriage is the source of so much of the world's stock of happiness.'

'You were married,' Pansy said, 'weren't you?'

'And am,' Quigley said. 'The Catholics are so often right, no wonder people flock to them from time to time.'

'Do you have children?'

'I've got Timothy and I've also, as perhaps you might expect, got Sandra. Jonty and I have decided to leave it at that, and I should advise you to do the same thing. And I should also advise you to keep that admirable little *tush* of yours out of other people's

126

business or range of interest. It's an asset, indeed it is, but like all assets it can be a temptation to others.'

'I think you should stop till tomorrow,' Pansy said, 'if you want to, and then you should pack it in.'

'It's always an option,' Quigley said, 'especially if you was to come with us, for instance. That would certainly keep it open, wouldn't it, Jonathan?'

'Very much so,' Goldstein said.

'Would you like to see inside the tent, dear?' Quigley said. 'It has many features which might amuse and conceivably delight a fun-loving person such as yourself.'

iv

The Harley-Davidson battled along a track which circled up and around Château St Martial and then dived, on the far side, into the deserted village. The ruined houses were grey and streaked with damp. The *lauzes* on their roofs had sagged or dropped into the exposed rooms, where they slumped in heaps, like a library turned to stone. Elder and fig and wild acacia possessed the streets. The burnt church, with its blind windows and notched stonework was a dead cavern behind thick twists of cypress. The porch was looped with brambles; lichened bullet-holes badged the walls.

The black Saab was parked with the driver's door half open with a foot on the ground beside it. The woman in black leather was reading a book. When Cator rolled into the square, she pushed the door of the car wide, finished her paragraph and then closed the book. She leaned over the front seat for a zippered leather pouch from the back.

'*La Fête des femmes!*' Cator said.

'You recognise me?'

'Should I?'

'I have been looking for you a little bit. I have some things to tell you. I am Yvonne Langon's daughter. I imagined you might have guessed. Where can we go?'

'Imagination costs nothing,' he said. 'Get on the bike, if you want. And hold tight. How's your father?'

She did not put her arms around him. They racketed past the burnt-out tank with its tired gun and through the dead village.

The road dipped and went along a tight valley with grape-vines strung on each side. After the vineyards had dwindled to scrub, Cator plunged down a track into uncut woods and turned off the engine. The Harley-Davidson rolled and bumped, on wheezing springs, over roots and flints down to the scaly roof of a cottage whose eaves reached almost to the ground. On the side where Cator leaned the bike, the grey blocks of the back wall rose no more than a foot before the slates began.

The woman hopped away from the machine. The fingers of her right hand were dented where she had gripped under the saddle. Cator tottered as he led the way down a glossy slope, one arm high, the other almost on the ground. It reminded her that he was old.

On the far side of the cottage, there was a higher façade with a plank door and two sash windows. An apron of grass and moss went down to a stone embankment, barbed with nettles. Below the wall there was a narrow, fenced vineyard. On the long hillside to the left, a snorting tractor was grubbing stumps from a recently felled wood.

The only room in the cottage had a rammed earth floor. A reddish cotton rug was lumpy with the unevenness of the ground. The single metal bed might have come from a boarding school. Along the wall, unplaned planks made shelves supported on beige bricks. The wood sagged under tins of food, sidelong books, warped boots, a game-bag and bundles of clothes. Walking-sticks and greening umbrellas and an alpenstock were holstered in a chapped leather tub by the door; one yellow cane wore a mackintosh hat. No pictures hung on the hard grey walls.

A gas hob, attached to a rust-scabbed blue cylinder by a rubber tube, was next to the broad fireplace. Split wood, braided with ivy, was stacked under a stone shelf. Cator struck a nervous match and crouched to the kindling in the grate. 'Tell me,' he said.

The woman unzipped the leather pouch and passed papers to him; they included several photographs. 'Is that man someone you know, would you say?'

'I no longer know anyone,' Cator said.

'This one was taken quite recently. In other words...'

'Other words you can spare me,' he said.

'He is almost certainly still alive. That woman you saw today, who was she?'

128

'Journalist. English. No importance. How do you know I saw anybody?'

'What did you tell her?'

'I gave her a cocktail; lies and truth, twist of lemon. Only pleasure left to me; never cared for spirits. Why bring me this stuff now? Damn you for it, if that's any sort of a comfort to you.'

'You do recognise him.'

'It's a face,' Cator said, 'that might belong to someone I once knew. They hang about, faces, don't they?'

'You're not surprised he's still alive?'

'Once you're wise to principalities and powers,' Cator said, 'what's left to be surprised about? Leaving aside common decency.'

'She asked you about him, I imagine. The journalist.'

'Rachel. Nary a word. Not interested, didn't know a thing. One-track Annie. Only wanted to know about myself and Yvonne. Your sainted mama. What's your name again, by the bloody way? Station identification, let's have a dose of that. Care for some tea? I used to know at one point.'

'Sabine.'

'It's mint; make my own; don't like it particularly, but I do get it delivered at the door. Mother Nature. A lot of this *paperasserie* looks like copies to me; could well be fabrications. No paucity of those. Normal life almost certainly one of 'em. A copy or a fake, where's the diff? Sabine, of course.'

'The last elements didn't come to hand till after Léah was dead.'

'Elements,' Cator said, 'did they not? Léah's dead? Didn't know she was alive! When was this?'

'A few weeks before my mother. All this stuff was lodged with Léah's lawyer. With instructions to pass them to Mother in the event of her death.'

'I.e., not a moment before. And what did she think of them, your mama?'

'They came too late for her to think much. That's why she said to give them to you.'

'What did she die of exactly, Evie, I mean?'

'Cancer. The breast, at first, then ... it generalised.'

'Hoped she might've been murdered,' Cator said. 'How's your father? Did you say?'

'Is this where you live all the time?'

'I don't live much of the time at all,' Cator said. 'Character left it to me; I use it. Services rendered; invoice to follow. Followed. You spend a lot of money on clothes. Where'd's it come from?'

'I am myself a lawyer,' she said.

'Then you're familiar with what hush money is. Not something we talk about.' He smiled at the joke she had missed, or because she had missed it, and poured boiling water into a buckled silver jug. He sniffed the mixture and then flipped the hinged lid shut. 'For almost fifty years, you're telling me, Léah knew that Félix had got clean away and told no one. If clean he could ever be. The corpse in the Borgward then, who was that?'

'Who knows?'

'Whoever isn't telling. Forty-seven years before little Léah turned honest, and she had to be a corpse to do it! Funny.'

'It was her pleasure, perhaps.'

'Forty-something years. Bit long to wait between sneezes.'

'To take her time. Does it anger you to think of a woman doing something merely because it pleases her?'

'Léah and Félix. Should have guessed; didn't. Little bitch. Never said a word. Very much her style, come to think of it. Spit in the world's eye. Loved it, I expect; never mind him, *it*. Take off your jacket, why don't you? You look like a lawyer.'

'I am.'

'I know. That's why. I wish you'd stop. Excellent English, *ergo* not English. You have a *petite spécialité*? In the law, I mean.'

'Divorce.'

'Took quite a fancy to me at one time, Léah, or so I imagined. Lucrative?'

'Sometimes. If you look, you will see: she was here and then she was here and finally...'

'Finally she married him! 1982. In Hyères! Lovely job! Why then? Ah, I get it: *en bonne Catholique*. Could only marry Monsieur Lévy when his widow died back in Sainte-Foy! Very moral, killers are, aren't they, sometimes? All the same, *quand même*, that's taking things a little far. If he's the man I think he was, and he was, that's a little mouldy, calling himself Lévy.'

'Mouldy is what?'

'Little Léah! One has to respect a woman who can do something so... so *singular* as to marry F. Argote Esquire, *whatever* he chose to call himself. Mouldy is rotten. Old English. We all had mould at school. Sugar?'

'As you wish.'

'Don't give the proverbial hoot. In synagogue, do you suppose? She and Monsieur Lévy finally tied the knot. You have a look of her, from what I remember. Evie. For Christ's sake take that jacket off. Preferably with a brisk movement.' He poured a long arc of tea, without a splash, into narrow earthenware mugs which he had set on the ground. 'You look like a secret policeman.'

'As you wish,' she said.

'All right,' he said, 'you're a woman; I can see now. Did she suffer much, your mama?'

'Yes, she did.'

'But she never talked.'

'She talked. About you. She said you were a scoundrel. She didn't understand how you could be so good and so bad at the same time.'

'Very decent of her, at a time like that. She nevertheless said to come and find me, though, did she?'

'Only to give you this.'

'This being "what for" under another name. Crime and punishment. I'm seventy-six years old, dammit; what am I supposed to do? File it in the miscellaneous gubbins department. Up the jacksie. Which I hope you don't understand. Monsieur Lévy, Alphonse. You do. Divorce lawyer; suppose you would. Was he there too, when she died, *ton illustre papa?*'

'Some of the time.'

'Man of importance,' Cator said. 'What did she say to you exactly, about this? *Exactly.* Don't lie; you're not under oath.'

'*Tu dois prévenir le Renard; il a le droit de tout savoir. Voilà.*'

Cator cupped the pale green heat between his fingers. 'The fox is dead, Sabine; don't hunt no more. Pass the word. Did for them both with his plan of attack. Poisoned chalice, this is; and she knew it.'

The woman lowered herself onto a crate and leaned against the short wall. An SW5 address marked on the plywood had thinned to the colour of ruined claret. She crossed her ankles and took a deep breath of his air. 'Tell me,' she said. 'About this Félix...'

'Félix? Cheery chap, very. Terrible thing, Sabine, when people want to be liked. He wanted to be liked. He didn't want any trouble and he wanted to be liked. You can go outside.'

'Excuse me?'

'Earth closet to your left. I piss in the weeds personally, but then I've got the pipe for it. Even your tailor doesn't spring to those, I imagine. Keeps the weeds down. I'll be here when you get back. Alternatively, if you've had enough and done your stuff, you can leg it back to the village, can't you?'

He stayed in the same position, but his face was creased with a series of expressions which passed like thoughts. He took the tea to his lips finally and let it warm his nose while she was outside. When she lifted the latch and came back into the cottage his brows went up.

'You could run me,' she said, 'couldn't you, to the car?'

'She never told you about those days, did she? She was right. Prize bitch. Perfectly right. I'll tool you back, if that's what you want, and you can go up there have a one-star meal, can't you, Relais St bloody J? *Or* you can stay here, bunk down with me. Do you like women or do you like nothing at all? Prefer to whistle while you work, do you?'

'What I like, if you must know, is not having men.'

'Her daughter! Recognise you now. She lived with Félix for forty-something years, Léah, is that the story? And just when — this is the interesting question — just when did she send word to her lawyer about what she wanted him to do when she had no further use for Félix? At the very beginning, or later? I'll give women one thing, but unfortunately I left it in my other pantalongs. What do we know? We know Léah lived with an officially dead man for over forty years. A man she knew'd done what he done. Very maternal, sometimes, aren't they? I give them that; the sex. They'll lend a tit to anything that sucks. It's the bub that gives the ladies the edge, dear, when it comes to feelings. *Too parse par lah, nesspa?*'

'My mother said you spoke good French.'

'Come on, *Maître*! Only a fool speaks the same to everyone, or only a saint perhaps. No claim to file under either category, me. Let's think about money. Let's get back to ground floor; street level.'

'It was a way of being sure of her pension perhaps. He had some money, didn't he? If she was the only person in the world who knew who he was, she had him where she wanted him.'

'Dangerous place to have people, in my experience. Situation in which it's wise to have a policy with the Prudential.'

'So she could never be safe from him, could she? Any more than he was from her. Unless his safety depended on hers. And *vice versa.*'

'QED. Léah was his jailer and Félix was her pension. Small surprise they never came to you for a divorce. Stay and have some supper; pot luck before it pots you. In another life I happened to live at one time, a man broke a branch off a tree and thrashed a girl called Léah and your mother watched it and knew exactly why he was doing it. And basically who to. And *vice versa.* All flows from that perhaps. Among other sources. "The world's equations always cancel out, / And all your certainties supply my doubt." Who said that?'

'The important question is, what are you going to do now?'

'Or is it what should we have done then? Do you eat tuna? I eat it all the time.'

'It's not important what I eat,' Sabine said.

'In that case, you've certainly come to the right place,' Cator said.

v

When Roger saw Pansy come back through the arch into the patio, he was on the telephone to a Mr Van Sluijs, in Leyden, about his renting a property called *Ecoute s'il Pleût* in July or possibly the first two weeks in August. Pansy was adjusting her hair with both hands; her neat elbows pointed towards the sky. She shook her hair straight and came on up into the house.

'They seriously had no idea you were that bothered,' she said.

'Cock.'

'And they'll be going in the morning, possibly.'

'And possibly not.'

'Or else after lunch. They're going and so am I is the full story.'

'Have you got a plane?'

'With them,' she said.

'With them.'

'Any objections?'

'Whatever for?'

'They're going the way I want to go.'

'They're a couple of poofs,' Roger said. 'What's Bricey going to think about his wife trolling around with a couple of poofs?'

'Are you going to worry about that? Because don't. They've both been married.'

'Which proves what? Which proves that you're . . .'

'Everything proves everything, if you're clever enough, as far as I can see, so why bother? It proves mainly you'll be done with all three of us by tomorrow night. Which is, as they say, a result.'

'Brice isn't going to recognise you. And I don't mean to be alarmist, but you never know with those people. Your trousers are inside out. The seams are outside.'

'So they are,' she said. 'They really like women. They often do, you know. And I like them. A lot. They make me laugh. All the time. I try not to, but they do.'

'They're a thoroughly dangerous couple of buggers, Pansy. Have you thought about that? And what about the car?'

'We can dump that. Quigs knows where.'

'Quigs!'

'Knows exactly where.'

'He's not really like that, you know. He's quite an educated person; he never used to talk like that. Where the hell do you think Rachel is?'

'She'll be all right.'

'I'm wondering what we're going to do for supper.'

'They want me to go out.'

'The hell they do.'

'I said I would. You don't want me here, do you?'

'I love you, you bitch, and you know it. I'd like to do you for supper, if you really want to know. You're not – repeat *not* – going with those two jokers. It's dangerous.'

'That's possibly what I like about them. They're very gentle and they're also dangerous as hell. Ideal combination really.'

'They actually *said* they were going in the morning?'

'Under certain conditions.'

'You haven't done anything with them, have you, at all?'

'At all? What's "at all" mean? I've had a sausage or two.'

'Meaning what?' Roger said.

'This is it,' Pansy said.

'If I was your husband, I can imagine beating you black and blue from time to time. Especially if you looked at me like that. You took them off, didn't you?'

'How else can you get them inside out?'

'What else did you do?'

'Tried to help,' Pansy said.

'You go with those two characters, do you think you're necessarily going to get away with it?'

'Don't get worked up. I don't go, they don't go.'

'I am up. Want to see how up I am? That's how up I am.'

'Oh Rodge, for God's *sake*.'

'Let's get to it,' he said, 'if that's what you want. Get these damned things off again and let's get to it.'

'You're being incredibly *prosaic*, honestly.'

'Prosaic? What's prosaic mean?'

'Oh I don't know. It's what Brice says sometimes. It sounds horrible when he does. Oh, all right: they've got this exercise machine and I tried it.'

'What kind of exercise machine do you have to take your pants off to try? Isn't that the car? I'll bet you that's Rachel now.'

'You row sort of a thing. They had it in the tent. We can *all* go out, if you want to. They told me I had to take them off, so I did. To use it properly.'

'Do you know what I'd like to do right now?'

'Of *course* I know. Only I was right: it *is* the car.'

'Kill somebody. I'd really like to kill somebody.'

Roger came out of the house with one kind of a smile on his face and replaced it with another when he saw that a white Peugeot Junior had parked under the solitary walnut tree. Sibylle Argote was re-closing the door. She wore soft flat shoes and a long grey woollen skirt and she was huddled in a white cardigan with large pink roses on it. She said, '*Excusez-moi, mais Olivier, il n'est pas là?*'

'Here? Certainly not. *Absolument pas.*'

'*Il a disparu et on prévoit soixante couverts ce soir.*'

'Carol and Denis!' Roger said. '*Peut-être il les a trouvés...*'

'*Non, non, non. Il est parti. Une fois pour toute. J'en suis sûre et certaine. Ici, c'était ma dernière chance. Il ne reviendra plus jamais.*'

'*Entrez. Prenez un verre.*'

'*Merci. Soixante couverts. Malheureusement, la vie continue.*'

Rachel spent the afternoon among the '*Archives de la Résistance dans le Sud-Ouest*' in the library of the *Institut des Anciens Combattants* in Caillac. By closing time, she had compiled a scribbled set of notes from a number of literary and journalistic sources:

'R.A.: Ch. Martial/ Réseau Victor (SOE directed). C mentioned as '*Renard*', also Captain (Major?) Cator, liaison with FFI (1943/4?), Montauban, Siorac-en-P. (weapons' cache, in ch., p.126). '*Contentieux*' with *réseau* Maurice (Communist?). Rescue of prisoners attempted, but death of Louis (sic) Lerclerc, Apr.44; Yvonne L. cited among successfully liberated prisoners, Rte Buissonière, May 44).

' "*Evènements dramatiques*" July 44 (cf. L.C.); capture and "deportation to Germany (???) of party of refugees sheltering in hotel cellar" (Jews? Not specified). Accusations (local press), after lib., by local Communists of official (London? Gaullist?) reluctance help "*personnes en danger*".

'Félix Argote mentioned as *hôtelier* accused by Communists, cleared by court; "*émeutes*", CGT-led, after 1946 (?) decision. Vandalism, "perpetrators unknown" at *Relais* (See Sud-Ouest, winter 46/7). March 1947: disappearance (kidnapping?) of Félix A. Discovery burnt-out car and calcinated body, Gorges du Tarn, winter 47. Communists hint at final settlement old debt.

'M.Z.: More detailed on Ste F. incident: 44 women and children, mostly Jews, "*cernés*" in "empty" (??) hotel cellar. Dawn raid by Milice/Germans, party rounded up, July 24th 44, driven to Périgueux, transported Lyons, destin. Auschwitz. Local Résistance said to have been outnumbered and/or indecisive (*Rés.* Maurice barred from action); Z. implies failure Gaullist/London nerve: *no move made get party out before German arrival all way from Périgueux* ("*no military purpose to be served*" says A.C. *in S.E.A.*). No survivors listed; but 3 local people released (Périg.) on "petition" (strong hint deal, payment, or both), inc. 1 woman called Léah (same or diff?)

'Félix A. accused 1946 – by which time owner of hotel – of complicity, prior contact with enemy, taking blood money. Strong denial; F.A. supported by some in village; PCF campaign against him + backlash. *Non lieu, début* 47; attacked by persons unknown, badly beaten up. Soon after disappears, leaving wife, infant (Olivier) behind.

Oct. 1949, F.A. officially declared identical with corpse in car; hotel inherited by wife Jeannine (d.1982).

*

'Apparent chrono. order of events: Luis/Louis L. commands *réseau Victor* (plus Maurice, or in alliance with) until summer (?) 43, when arrival L.C. Succeeds takeover, thanks London money, arms. But Luis "embarrassment" since local hero. Area of command incl. Ste F., V.-les-E.; very big for communic? *Relais St J* bar mentioned as used (sometimes?) by Frids, also L.C. + *amis*; arr. Félix Argote (archaeolog!) from where (before 43)?

'Attack on tunnel/troop train end May 44, just before D-day. Hence Leclerc dead well *before* Ste F. episode, July 44. Aug.44: *Renard*, Y.L. sd to have "watched helplessly" (A.C.). as SS attack and massacre Ch. St Martial, Aug. 44, during final retreat region; L.C.'s bravery there (cf. A.C. p.331) in diversionary attack; rescue of v. few survivors from unburnt school. Hence (aha!) L.C. decorated by de G. 1946, *never* by London; why? Said never have returned UK (A.C. again). Yet spoke of going Oxford *after* war.'

vii

'Now what is it?' Roger said. 'Now what is it?'

'Sorry to intrude, squire, but it's loo paper. We're out; one of those things. Been a run on it.'

'Very funny.'

'Unintentional. But, as a matter of fact, could Jonts possibly use your toilet?'

'What does "as a matter of fact" mean?'

'It means he needs to use the bog.'

'What have you been doing up until now exactly?'

'We've got facilities, but they're on the primitive side and seeing as we find ourselves highly adjacent to civilisation, I begged to presume...'

'It may have escaped your attention, but my wife still hasn't come home. I'm more than somewhat worried. She went out quite early this morning and she still isn't back.'

137

'Jonty only wants to use the toilet. After that, if you so wish, we can mount an operation to find the lady. We can then comb the countryside and beat about the bushes, but we certainly can't do it before.'

'You never used to talk remotely like this.'

'Look, mate, Jont wants to use the kazi. Can he, please?'

'I like it,' Pansy said.

'That's one hurdle cleared.'

'I'll find you some loo paper. Not that I see why I should. We're honestly against people coming and using our loo. Even friends.'

'Been a vote on this then, has there?'

'I don't know where she keeps it. I thought it was in here and it's not. What do you like, Pansy, exactly?'

'Old friends,' Quigley said. 'I thought we was. It's maybe not central, but it still constitutes a blow, what you just said.'

'We're not old friends. Never were and certainly aren't now.'

'Horrible thing that can be, honestly! The rug from under you, Pan; know what that feels like? I imagine you do, the way he was talking to you.'

'I know what it feels like *under* me,' Pansy said. 'Often enough.'

'Wonderful girl. Wonderful, wonderful girl. You're lucky to have her, Rodge.'

'I thought it was in this cupboard. I haven't got her.'

'They can use mine,' Pansy said, 'if they want.'

'Pansy,' Quigley said, 'you're a gentleman.'

'It's not *yours*; nothing here is yours. It's mine; it's ours.'

'And the shareholders',' Quigley said. 'Let's not be forgetting them. Because they're certainly never going to forget you, are they? Friends may be friends, or not friends, but a shareholder is always a shareholder.'

'I do seriously need to use the kazi,' Goldstein said.

'Ingest, digest, and the rest follows, I'm afraid, as the day the night; that's man for you. Beast and enigma, isn't he, dear?'

Pansy said, 'Why can't we all just . . . live and let live?'

Quigley gestured as a magician might to a sequinned assistant who had just been cut in half and did not have a scratch to show for it. 'Is this a woman with heart or is it not? Sound sense in an exceptionally well-cut and eminently practical trouser-suit. Not that the jeans were not equally flattering, if flattery is called for which, from this side of the house, it is not.'

'Stop this shit,' Roger said. 'Stop this bloody shit. And stop it now.'

The telephone rang. Roger made a little quieting gesture, as if someone else had been speaking too loudly. Before he could lift the receiver, Quigley had hooped his arms around Roger just above the elbows. Pansy put her head on one side and reached for the telephone, but Goldstein stepped across the room in two long paces and had it high above his head.

Roger said, 'All right, you know what this is, don't you? This is criminal. Think about that.'

'Wanting to use the kazi in a place you've been invited to stay is criminal? What've they got, half the population in clink out here, have they?'

'All right then,' Roger said, 'use the damn thing. And then you two . . . can get the hell out of here. Now let me answer that bloody phone.'

'Us two what? No, no; us two what? You've started, so why don't you go on?'

'It's all right,' Jonty said, 'it's stopped ringing.'

'All *right*? That could have been my wife. That could have been important. This is a blatant assault. Will you let go of me?'

'Us two what?'

'All right,' Roger said, 'all right. I'm sorry about that.'

'Would that be "monkeys" at all?'

'Will you please let me have that telephone now, Jonathan?'

'What colour is the material would you say, Pansy, in your ensemble? Is that cream or is it beige, or could it possibly be Naples Yellow, which I've always liked?'

'Jont went to Art College at one time.'

'If he wants to use the loo, he can use it.'

'They said it was buff.'

'Buff is nice,' Goldstein said. 'That always gives me ideas, buff does. Said it was buff, did they? They ought to know.'

'You've worked out a lot since I knew you, Quigs.'

'That's correct; I've found it's a case of work out or be worked out these days, isn't it, Jonts?'

'Very much so,' Goldstein said.

Pansy said, 'What do you want from him, you bastards? Why don't you bloody well come out with it?'

'I love her,' Quigley said, 'this one, I seriously do. Six months' worth. In whatever currency falls to hand. Work of a moment in the right conditions. Bastards! She doesn't mess about, is why.'

'Buff,' Goldstein said, 'that's a word gives me considerable ideas. It's got legs, has that.'

'You had the runs; you said you were desperate. Now I'm saying go in and use it, you don't even move.'

'I must be feeling better,' Goldstein said.

'I'm supposed to phone my husband,' Pansy said, 'if it's six o'clock. Is it all right if I do, Roger?'

Roger said, 'Why couldn't he phone you?'

'He wasn't sure where he'd be.'

'Then where are you going to phone him?'

'The colour of flesh basically, isn't it, buff? *Some* flesh. The best kind for me; that's a preference not a judgment. I don't think you'd best use the telephone, Pansy.'

'At home. I *beg* your pardon?'

'The phone. I don't think you should.'

'I want to call my husband, if you don't mind, who also happens to be a Member of Parliament.'

'In addition to what would that be?'

'There are things an MP can do, in case you didn't know.'

'And I'm sure the country would be very glad to know what they are. There seems to be an understandable measure of confusion just at present.'

'More things than you think, and could very well find out.'

'Spitfire, this one,' Goldstein said. 'How do these stay up? Simple drawstring affair, is it?'

'Leave her alone, Goldstein. I warn you. Leave her alone.'

'Tell me what I'm doing. Describe it to the court. Because am I hurting you, darling?'

'Car!' Pansy said. 'Car, Roger.'

'To my ear,' Quigley said, 'that's more your tractor. It went down and now it's coming back up again. That's life, isn't it?'

'Very much so,' Goldstein said. 'I love it. I honestly do.'

'You're criminals,' Roger said. 'What you're doing is criminal. I don't care who you are.'

'Am I hurting you, dear? If I hurt you, you say so. And until you say so, I'll assume I'm doing anything but.'

'It doesn't matter if you're hurting her.'

'That's not a nice thing to say, is it, Pan?'

'Assault is assault. And other things are other things.'

'Very true that,' Quigley said. 'How many bank accounts did you say you had?'

'I never said how many bank accounts I had.'

'And ditto forwarding addresses.'

'I was never asked for one.'

'Was anyone naive, would you say, in retrospect?'

'I certainly was,' Roger said. 'Trusting Tubby; trusting Lester. Especially trusting Lester.'

'Skin like velvet, Lester. Which is very much in my private plus department. So, no secret accounts in your name or in nominees' names either, is that what you're saying?'

'I'm not saying anything.'

'I keep hearing that.'

'All right; how much do you seriously think you're owed?'

'Leave it out, doll, the telephone, all right?'

'It's after six,' Pansy said. 'You're a couple of ... of *terrorists*, if you want to know what you're really a couple of. And I'm not afraid to say so. Well, I am actually, a bit, but...'

'That's a lovely face and that's a lovely bottie and I defy anyone to say different, and now she's got a tongue as well, which certainly adds interest to an already potentially tantalising, conceivably explosive cocktail.'

'You touch her,' Roger said, 'and...'

'That's the interesting bit, Rodge, what comes after the copular, as you might say.'

'He went to college. He went to a Poly. This is an act and we all know it is.'

Pansy said, 'What's Roger ever actually done to you?'

'That sums it up,' Goldstein said.

'Because whatever it is, you've had your fun.'

'Fun, have we? Is that what you'd call having your life ruined by someone? It's a matter for lively debate, that is.'

'You're also breaking your word. Just now, when I was down there with you eating sausages, you said you were going in the morning.'

'And is it now morning? How time does fly! But then again so do pigs; certainly in one quite notorious case I could mention. And who's going to stop them, now that they can open a bank account wherever they like? You know what would suit us, on reflection, don't you, Rodge, in the accommodation department, and that's this place.'

'Very funny,' Roger said.

'No humour intended, I assure you.'

'This is my house.'

'I always did admire your taste, Roger. That's probably why I fell under your spell.'

'You thought we were going to make a bomb, and so did I, and that's what Lester told us, and ... we both fell under a bloody bus instead, is what happened.'

'Except that I was the one the wheels went over.'

'Look at that,' Goldstein said. 'If that's not a pretty sight, tell me what is?'

'It's all right,' Pansy said. 'It's all right, Roger. He isn't hurting me.'

'I'll kill you,' Roger said. 'You do anything to her, *anything*, and I'll kill you. I know you're strong. I know there are things you can do, but you'll have to do them, all of them, or I'll bloody well have you. Sooner or later.'

'Sentiments that can but earn you a wide measure of respect, Roger. Towards your ... sister-in-law, isn't that right?'

'You know damned well.'

'Yes, I do; yes, I do. What I also know and you possibly don't is that Pansy and I have already reached a sort of, well, understanding. We've already had a meeting of the minds which carries the hope – I would never say promise – of meetings of a less mental character in the future. Do I summarise accurately, Pan?'

Roger said, 'You're a sadistic bastard is what you are. A sadistic bastard shit-head. And that's not all.'

'Well, she's out of her shell at last, this one, Jonty, isn't she? Took her time. Not all?'

'You go any further and I'll fucking kill you.'

'Come after me, will you? Sooner or later, that was, wasn't it?'

'You're a couple of sadistic fag bastards and you can do what you like about it.'

'Terrible thing about name-calling,' Quigley said, 'is that people remember. Mind you, they remember all kinds of things, like I remember this inquiry you was making about bank accounts in Switzerland. Used to be quite a serious offence, but that's all finished now, of course. Who wants to be serious in the end? Much better to have a bit of a party, bit of a knees-up in a general sense. You wouldn't object to that, Pan, would you?'

Pansy said, 'I do hate things to get nasty.'

'She hates that,' Quigley said. 'You know what's nasty in life today, don't you? What's seriously appalling actually, and that's how little of the wealth gets shared. And I'm not only thinking in your purely material terms.'

'I'm not joking,' Roger said.

'And, since nobody's laughing, it's just as well, my son. Only look at this lovely creature. Arms up, darling. That's it. That's lovely.'

'It's all right, Roger,' Pansy said. 'It doesn't matter.'

'I think it matters. And I think the police'll think it matters.'

'You know what's terrible with the police, as I found to my cost?' Quigley said. 'Once they start digging, it's dig, dig, dig. They want to get to the bottom of everything. Sods is right.'

'That's a lovely article. Lying so close to the surface is what is so incredible and yet normally we're denied it. Is that not a true thing of beauty?'

'I don't think you should say "sadistic", Roger, about me. Or Jonts. Because sadism, what's that exactly? As I understand the term, it's deriving sexual pleasure from other people's pain, whereas – if I read her attitude aright – Pan here is not in any sort of pain whatsoever. Look at this girl. This is a female person who looks as if she's getting what she deserves, which is our pretty well full attention. No, *look*, Roger. Because she's responding very positively. That little smile. That little frown. What does it tell us? It doesn't tell us it *hurts*, whatever it tells us. And then look at this flesh; that's blooming, to be honest with you, in my book. Step out of these, darling. Step out of them. You don't need these. Or these. What need when a girl looks like this? Tell me the truth, Roger, haven't you been thinking about this girl in this light ever since she decided to wash her hair, if not before? And where's the shame in it?'

143

10

I made my notes in the grey office where the dossiers of the *Centre de Documentation et des Archives de la Résistance dans le Caillacais* were filed. The clasps were rusty from dried dampness which had rotted the cotton waists around the folders. Even the more recently published material gave off a library odour when I opened the pages in pursuit of the few indexed allusions to Cator, Lionel; Langon, Yvonne; and Leclerc, Louis (sic). The fuzzy photographs and locally printed pages were of a piece with the uneven typing and fading manuscript in the dossiers.

There was something eerily touching even in the most shameful of the contemporary official papers, with their cross-referenced arrests and expenditures. I was dismayed, and excited, by the details of reprisals and executions in the months before the Liberation. How can I explain, or excuse, my complicity as I cribbed the schooled calligraphy of bureaucrats who conceived it their duty to minute the recommendations and decisions of a collapsing Fascist state in old-fashioned, republican handwriting? Even as I damned them, I was observing the callous delicacy of their script and the ignoble accuracy of their grammar. They turned me into the kind of school mistress whose approval I had craved in the days when good marks were my only consolation for the want of Pansy's good looks.

Vichy's clerks became creatures whom I had redeemed from their catacomb. They treated me to a visit to a world where I had never been, yet where I grew uneasily at home. I had no part in the '*transports*' and '*perquisitions*' and '*actions sanitaires*' whose reality was sterilised in the jargon of the scribes, but journalism had given painless lessons in the toleration of the intolerable.

As I surveyed the officially ruled pages with the '*Etat français*' heading, I began to distinguish one clerk's hand from another. I noticed the frequency with which one dipped his (or her?) pen, while another went on until the nib splayed. Were the writers as old as I was, or younger? The motion of my hand, as I summarised their verbosities, exercised me in how they could have confused honourable diligence with the tabulation of horrors. After all, they never initiated the actions to which their hands supplied an official warrant or assigned the funds. Who could say how many of them, like Cator's *père de famille* who turned keys in the prison in Périgueux, at the same time collaborated and passed information to the Resistance? And who could ever say why they had done one thing or the other?

When the part-time archivist, Monsieur Martinez, who is also a watch-maker in the Avenue Thiers and whose father was executed as a hostage in 1944, returned to lock the office, I felt that I had been revising for an examination which I was bound to fail. As I stood on the threshold of the Avenue Thiers, I knew and did not know where I was; I was certain only that I did not want to go back to *Les Noyers Tordus*. I was a diver with the bends, breaking surface into the present too fast after being submerged among the silent, barnacled wreckage of the past.

As I walked the streets of Caillac, with no new destination in mind, I saw that several of the parked cars carried Roger's flyers under their windscreen-wipers. I no longer thought of them as 'ours'. I wondered only why I had let Lionel Cator escape me when I had a dozen new things I wanted to ask him. His evasive garrulity was infuriating; I could now imagine using less inhibited means to puncture his defences. My desire was hardened by a strange, impersonal vindictiveness; it was as if I had caught some bacillus in that drab room with its notched tin shelves.

The clocks in the meshed window of Monsieur Martinez' shop told me that it was half past six. The present seemed as remote to me now as the last months of the war would have that morning, before Mike Lea's call had made them part of my day. As I thought about Lionel Cator, I detected a fund of undischarged hatred in him. For whom? For Yvonne? His pretended dismissal of her could be evidence of her importance to him. He had affected to resent my curiosity, but then why had he come fishing for it?

The nearest thing to what I wanted was a drink. I loitered

outside the *Café du Théâtre* (there was no theatre), but I could not think what I should order. I stood in the street and tried to believe that I could ever have done anything of the kind Yvonne Langon had done. I wondered how the good daughter of the nice people from Alsace could so quickly have learnt the use of weapons and conquered the fear of capture and pain. Perhaps she never had that fear; perhaps her desire for Luis enabled her to ignore it. Perhaps he simply enchanted her and enrolled her in a romance in which fear and pain were part of the pleasure. I had read about and around her all afternoon and I had no illusion that I had come within a mile or a century of her. I kept asking myself what could have been left of Yvonne's love for Luis after she knew that he had instructed her, in the event of his capture, to give herself to a rival with whom he disdained rivalry. What greater gesture of contempt for other people could he have made? Or was I misreading his motives? What if he planned her 'betrayal' because he needed to know exactly what she would do without him? It was a way of retaining control of her, and her actions, even when he was in German hands. Alone with his torturers, he could then enjoy a torture they had no idea was being inflicted. Don't they say that one pain shuts out another? I even wondered whether, when he told Yvonne that, if things went wrong, the first thing she should do was to give herself to the *Anglais*, he was not somehow – oh somehow! – contriving the ironic tragedy which would make him a kind of saint. He was a bit of a Spaniard, Luis Leclerc.

Standing there in the Avenue Thiers, I began to see in Luis a man whose shadow was darker and more substantial than that of Yvonne or the Fox. Yet there was little likelihood that Michael would want a word about him in the paper; even Gervase Bristowe had effaced the alien Leclerc and replaced him with a pair of legendary lovers who, in the years after the war, proved unable to sustain the burden of banality. Luis was a soldier compounded of cruelty and honour. The animus of Lionel's admiration had retrieved a surge of his virility from the past: I felt its heat in the evening street as if from the sprung door of some secret furnace.

'*Bonsoir, Rachel.*' Thierry de Croqueville was coming out from the *coiffeur* whose narrow shop was on the corner of the stepped alley which led up to the Chapel of the White Penitents.

I said, 'You're looking very chic, Thierry. Do I assume a *rendez-vous galant*?'

'*Ah, ma chère Rachel, vous me surestimez!* I am taking my mother to the *Relais St Jacques* for dinner. Do you have time for a drink?'

Thierry's usually artistic hair had had its extravagances curtailed. He seemed lighter and more efficient for the operation. I followed him to the Bar Montaigne and asked, without enthusiasm, for a glass of Alsace. He was wearing a light blue shirt and a white sweater under an unlined orange cotton jacket of the burly kind favoured by French television interviewers. He faced me with a smiling enthusiasm which chose not to announce its subject. Having married, unwisely, at an early age, and having divorced, wisely, a little later, he had a reputation as a Don Juan; I had heard from Sibylle Argote of a little black book in which he and an unprepossessing but well-connected local *foie gras* manufacturer marked the qualities of their conquests out of twenty, in the standard French scholastic style.

I said, 'Tell me about something.'

'You don't prefer to have a glass of champagne?'

'Of course I do. Sainte-Foy-le-Fort during the war. What happened up there exactly?'

'*Deux coupes de champagne, Baptiste.* Ouf! *Exactly?* So many things happened.'

'July 1944, to be precise. There was a big raid, wasn't there? A big *rafle*, wasn't there?'

'You must ask Manu Martinez. He knows these things. I'm an architect, Rachel. I may look old enough to have been in the war, but...'

'They came and took away some Jews, didn't they? What I want to know is, was Félix Argote involved in it, Olivier's father?'

'Why not ask Olivier?'

'You know that isn't easy.'

'*Tchin,*' Thierry said.

'Wasn't there suspicion that they'd been betrayed?'

'France was betrayed, some people will tell you. *Ma petite Rachel*, we leave these things on one side now, because who cares?'

'You did work at the *Relais*. Did Olivier not talk about those things?'

'Fifty years ago, his dead father hid people in the cellar; today he now wants to turn the cellar into a fast food *bistrot* for midday meals, because people are changing their *habitudes* and they don't

147

want big meals for lunch. Which of these two things do you suppose we talked about, exclusively?'

I said, 'How much did the *Relais* cost, do you think, when his father bought it?'

'You can ask the *notaire*, Lespinasse, you can check in his books. Pennies probably. As if it matters! It's finished, all that. It's for the old people; it gives them something to keep excited about. I like to be excited about things that are happening now. You are looking very … alive tonight. Very.'

I said, 'Is it true about your little black book?'

'Excuse me?'

'Is it true that you have a little black book that you write things in about girls? What they're like, what they do, and how well they do it?'

'You must never believe the things that the Caillacais tell you. The only little black book I have contains the names of people who owe me money, which is something much more important than girls. Old Félix, he was a smart one, I think. They talked about him, because he came from somewhere else and he established himself at the *Relais* after the war. People are very envious; they are envious and they resent strangers. They talk about me, why? Because I have this silly *particule*. They think I am some kind of an aristocrat. Ask me something else, please do!'

'How do you think Olivier's father got the money to buy the Relais?'

'He came from Alsace, I think. Or was it the Béarn? Perhaps he had money there. Who knows how people get what they get? We only know that no one likes them to get it.'

'Could he have sold those Jews to the Germans and got it that way?'

'Did they have to pay for Jews? Rachel, my dear, I don't honestly know you in this mood. Because what does it matter?'

'You don't know me in the least. Roger makes use of you and you make use of Roger and what's that got to do with knowing anyone?'

'These matters of what happened fifty-something years ago, they amuse you,' Thierry said. 'They are a way you know you can always make French people at a disadvantage. Let me tell you something, I don't know what happened at the Relais St Jacques and if I did know, I would not want to tell you. It is possible that bad things were done, but I did not do them and I do not, if I am honest, care if some old man did them. I never saw Argote, the father; I know Olivier, he is a friend, and I know Sibylle, who is beautiful and a little bit mad maybe, I don't know. I build houses and I repair houses and I do not, if I am honest with you, appreciate people who are not of our region coming here and conducting inquiries about what people did in the past in order to give us lessons whatsoever in the present.'

'I'm sorry.'

'I am explaining. I am not personally angry.'

'You are personally angry, Thierry.'

'We have had that bastard in the region for fifty years. Cator. He's been here, he goes away, he comes back. They give him medals and they make him a hero and he thinks he can do whatever he likes. Ask *him* who sold the Jews. Ask him who sold the French, if he's such a hero.'

'The English never gave him a medal. You did.'

'He drives me crazy, that man. What he says, what they say; I don't want to hear about it any more again. Understand something, *ma petite Rachel*: they did not give medals only to people who did something but also – I am not going to say more about this – to make it seem that things had been as they should have been. Cator, for me, he is just one more profiteer. I'm sorry.'

'You know him pretty well then?'

'Not at all. I know of him. Pretty badly! He came to my father's house once or twice, in St Martial.'

'You *lived* in St Martial?'

'Outside. We had a property there. A *château*, in fact. Château Croqueville. Which is not very big. The village was destroyed, you know, by the Germans. Our place is outside.'

'So they didn't come to your place.'

'They surrounded the village and that was that, luckily for all of us. They killed a lot of people there. "*Ils étaient rudes, ces messieurs*," that's the way our old *bonne* put it.'

'Why did Lionel come to your father's house? How old were you?'

'I have to go and collect my mother,' Thierry said. 'Quite small. Eight years perhaps. Perhaps nine.'

'You remember it though. There was a quarrel between them, was there?'

'A discussion. But I didn't like the way he talked, or smiled. Especially smiled. My father gave him a place to live. He lives there still, I think. I don't know how he got it. It's mine by rights, but ... I am sorry I cannot continue now. When someone gives his word, sometimes he keeps it. Another time maybe, I explain. Unless we find something more interesting to do.'

'That sounds good,' I said. 'When?'

'In truth, Rachel, I have nothing more to tell you.'

'This *château* of your father's, does he still live in it?'

'It was burnt down,' Thierry said. 'Some years ago. Accidentally. They say. Papa is, in any case, dead since five years. He did not die in the fire, but soon after it. Perhaps because of it. He lost many things.'

'Forgive me,' I said. 'When you have a moment.'

'Meanwhile, keep away from Cator. And above all, don't trust what he tells you. He did something, if you ask me, and that is why he cannot go home. He is not French; he should not be here at all.'

When we first met him, Thierry used sometimes to drive up to the house in his black Peugeot 205 GTi with the black windows and the radio-telephone just to have a glass of wine. I admired the trouble he took to seem friendly beyond the obligations of business. Roger was quickly his accomplice in authorising craftsmen to pad clients' bills, in return for a percentage. I could well believe that Thierry had a book of fucks; without appetite or shame, I could see myself figuring in it.

As I drove, slowly, back towards *Les Noyers Tordus*, Thierry became available to me, as a field of research. I turned him over in my mind like a pig on a spit. What shamelessness or ingenuity, exercised on what bit of his body, might prime him to give me good marks in his black book? I could even see myself introduced to the smug, uninteresting Bruno Bernet, who shared Thierry's bedfellows, and I wondered how my marks might prime his interest and what surprises I could spring on him. Without desire or disgust, I went on to imagine how a whole troop of men might be guided to my bed. It was as if, after having been a bad fit for so many years, my body had suddenly become available to me in a more comfortable form.

I was surprised but untroubled to see a tent in our field. A

150

Transit van, with English plates, was parked half on the verge. The wheels had gouged long grooves in the grass. I stopped the Cherokee and went over and stood on tiptoe to peek into the cab of the van. I then walked down our field to the tent. There was a small stove on the grass in front of it; a frying pan had a tilted glaze of fat in it. I called out, but there was no one in the tent, so I went inside. There were two sleeping bags on a waterproof sheet and a remarkable chair. I checked out the interior without annoyance or apprehension. The present seemed less alarming, and more remote, than the past. When I had seen all I could see, I drove on up to the walnut tree and parked next to Pansy's hire car.

The lights in the house made it seem darker than it had been a few moments earlier. I went through the arch into the patio and saw two strangers in the bright living room. A rather gigantic man with a black beard and a large white nose had his hand on Pansy's shoulder. She was naked, but seemed quite talkative. Roger was standing next to a man with cropped hair and a metal earring in his ear. I was neither astonished at Pansy's nakedness (she wore it like one more stylish item from her heavy suitcase) nor did I bother to construct a plausible reason for its parade in front of strangers. I found that I no longer envied my sister her jumpy, individual breasts or the shining belly. Her curly triangle reminded me of that crisp, greenish seaweed one gets in Chinese restaurants. There was a new Thai-cum-Vietnamese place in Caillac which might well serve it.

'Company,' the bearded man said.

'Here we all are then.' The man with the earring had put his fingers on Roger's neck and was caressing it lightly. 'This will be the missus, presumably.'

'Quigley,' Roger said. 'You remember Quigley I worked with at one time. He's been through a few changes.'

'And we know thanks to who, don't we? Because has he told you? Have you had a good laugh about it from time to time, have you, between you?'

Roger said, 'We've put it all behind us, all that, haven't we, Raitch?'

I did not care one way or the other why the men were there or what had induced Pansy to take off her clothes or what they all thought they were doing. I had the impression that it was both dangerous and irrelevant to me, like some once-compulsory game which I no longer had to play.

I said, 'And who are you?'

'Goldstein. Jonty Goldstein.'

'Jonty,' I said.

'Otherwise Jonathan,' Roger said. Quigley was still caressing his shoulder. 'We bumped into them in Caillac.'

'This is a very nice place, this,' Quigley said. 'You done well. You've definitely got the touch. We come up looking for somewhere to live, having seen your literature, saw this, and accordingly we was some way into a negotiation.'

'Balls,' Roger said. 'That's balls.'

I said, 'I think you should probably leave now, shouldn't you?'

Pansy said, 'We shall be all right, darling. Did you discover what you wanted?'

'Why haven't you got any clothes on?'

'No one's done anyone any harm. Brice sent the money.'

'There's a lot of it about,' I said. 'People just leave it everywhere, don't they?' Quigley looked at Goldstein, but without alarm. 'I liked the *fauteuil*. So what have you got in the van?'

'Let's leave it there, honey,' Roger said, 'shall we? Don't worry about it. We're more or less ... it's all going to be fine.'

'I had a wife, if you remember that,' Quigley said. 'I had a wife; I had a couple of kids.'

'They had Timothy,' Roger said, 'and then they had Sandra.'

'Who's telling this story? I'm telling it, all right?'

'I seriously think you should leave,' I said. 'Now.'

'The lady is a thinker. I had a house. I had a job. He was my friend. And then he done what he done.'

'Sad story,' I said.

'*Raitch!*'

'That's right: Ray-aitch! Because I went to bloody prison. I go to prison and you, you come down here. My friend, said he'd stand by me, said he'd take care of things, packs up in the middle of the night and buggers off. Is that your idea of sad, is it?'

'My idea of sad,' I said, 'is someone who does something he knows he shouldn't do, and then blames other people.'

'Why don't we all have a glass of something?' Roger said. 'Why don't we take the heat out of this?'

'Tell me something, Ray-aitch, which has always interested me.

Have you ever asked yourself, as a matter of interest, if he didn't possibly play much the same trick on you as what he played on me, with the odd variation maybe?'

'No,' I said, 'I never have.'

'Only this is a man knows all about moving money, isn't that right, Rodge? This is a man, once he's got his hands on a bit, it's here, it's there; it's wherever he feels like putting it and once it's up his sleeve, there's absolutely nothing whatsoever that anyone can see. I lost the lot, and I never even had the satisfaction of seeing where it went. You're not in the same boat, possibly, Rachel, if I can call you that, are you possibly? Rodge the dodge, what's in a name sort of a thing!'

'That too is a thought,' I said.

Pansy said, 'I was going to call Brice. Can I?'

'Of course you can,' I said.

'Christ,' Quigley said. 'CHRIST. You can see how it's done, can't you, Jonts? Never mind us. You can see how they do it, over and over again.'

'Very much so,' Goldstein said.

'Out the back, that's where we're supposed to go, people like you and me. The rubbish is what we are. Be careful though, Rachel. Because look at the man you spend your life with. I think *you're* sad. Because you don't see a thing more than you want to see, do you? Look at these women, Jonts, just look at them! Look at these fastidious creatures who pretend they just about tolerate the snotty bastards they have to share the earth with and then think about what they put where from time to time down the years. He cost me the bloody lot, your hubby. I trusted you and it cost me the bloody lot, trusting you did.'

'Balls.'

'You say something, Rachel?'

'I said "balls", and wasn't I right?'

Roger said, 'Are we having this glass or what?'

'Stay where you bloody are, bloody Roger,' Goldstein said. 'Or I'll 'ave you all the way in.'

'He owes me,' Quigley said. 'Plenty.'

'You've got more than enough,' I said. 'And you know you have. And we can all guess where it came from, can't we? That's a chair I happen to recognise.'

'She beat you up a lot, does she, this one, Roger? She certainly knows how. Biff, bang, wallop. Straight in. Doesn't know the meaning of fear, this one, does she?'

'Buff,' Goldstein said. 'That's an unlikely colour to suit someone, but it suits you. You've got this colour in your cheeks, is the great thing about you. Sets it off, buff does. Lovely cheeks they are too.'

'Put something on, Pansy. You two've got a lot less time than you think to be out of here before the police arrive. It's supper time and I hadn't planned on company.'

'No one's calling the police,' Roger said. 'Necessarily.'

'Thanks a lot, because he's the one shoulda been in the slammer. And if you want to talk about food...'

'If you shared a cell with Roger,' I said, 'you'd never've met handsome, would you?'

'Is she the cheeky one then, is she, your sister, or what is she?' Goldstein said.

Pansy said, 'You know what we could always do, don't you?'

'I was very much thinking along those lines myself, Pan my lovely, which is a funny thing for you.'

'Go out and eat something, all of us.'

'They're the business, aren't they, these women? I'm trying to get your sister to see something, if you don't mind, darling, before you start passing menus around. I'm trying to complete her education is another way you could put it.'

'She went to university,' Pansy said, 'and took a degree, didn't you, Raitch?'

'Are you hurting him?' I said. 'Is he hurting you, Roger?'

'Am I hurting you, darling? He hurt me, dear. He hurt me and you never even knew about it. You certainly never gave it a thought.'

'What do they seriously want, these two?'

'See that, Jonts?' Quigley said. 'Abstract problem, us, topic of bloody conversation mainly is what we are, if that. What I want – if I'm not interrupting anything – what I *want* is, well, what I want is ... my rights, is what I want.'

'No, it's not,' I said.

'He destroyed my life, if you happen to remember that. Or was you at university at the time?'

'No, he didn't. He didn't destroy your life in the least. And you happen to have committed a major theft in a country where foreigners quite often get the justice they deserve. He helped you do what you wanted. And you did what he wanted because you wanted to. Be honest, if that's not a ridiculous thing to say.'

'There she goes again: races down the wing, races down the wing, cuts straight in and – wallop! Straight in! Major crime? What you on about?'

'If it hadn't been for Roger, where would you be now? You'd be in your dinky little house, wouldn't you, with what's-her-name and the kids? Kevin and Sandra, you'd be with. Working with the same miserable people. Wearing your suit and your tie.'

'Some truth in that,' Quigley said. 'Isn't there, Jonts? Tim actually. We never had no Kevin.'

'Instead of which, you're what you always wanted to be.'

'That I question. What major crime is this?'

'All right, you're what you feared you never would be, until you were pushed into it. Roger never dumped you into the gutter: you fancied the gutter all the time. If you had any guts, you and Samson, instead of coming here and trying to terrorise people...'

'I like Samson,' Goldstein said. 'I like Samson very much.'

'That's funny,' Pansy said, 'because I said they were terrorists too.'

'No one's terrorising anyone that I know of,' Quigley said. 'That's totally out of order. Innocent fun is another thing. All I want personally is what you might call a little recognition. I refute the theft charge; that I totally refute, don't you, Jonts?'

'We bought some items, including the *fauteuil*, under reputable circumstances, and we can prove it.'

'And you'll almost certainly have to. And refute isn't the same as deny. You think you've come here for revenge, but I can tell you what you've actually come for, if you're honest about it. To gloat. To boast. You've come here so that we can see what a big strong man you've turned into. What Roger's done for you, so he can see that. *And* who you've come with. And how much better off you are. You've come to say thank you, basically, except that you haven't got the guts, and you certainly haven't got the manners to do it any other way except ... the way you've been doing it.'

'Brains,' Quigley said. 'I do like them with brains. Don't you like brains, Jont, in a woman sometimes?'

'I'm still a *tush* man myself,' Goldstein said.

'Can I take this thing through there and call Brice before it's too late?'

'You was leaving him,' Goldstein said, 'is what you told us down in the tent, in days gone by. Come on the road with us, would be my advice. I had in mind to show you a few things you might really like. Disappointing not to really.'

'All right, Rachel,' Quigley said, 'I'll give you this, which is, yes, there's some truth in it. But only up to a certain point. What, on the other hand, you may not yet know about, at all, I daresay, is Roger and me. Or did he tell you about Regal Court?'

'Quigley, you fucking sod. You fucking sod bastard shit. OK?'

'Manners,' Quigley said. 'You're supposed to be the host, remember. You talked about drinks. This is someone talked about drinks!'

'He told me absolutely all about it,' I said. 'Including the steam bath afterwards.'

'He told you about him and me and Lester before this whole thing blew up?'

'Of course. What do you think I am?'

'He never! He told you about Lester? You told her about Lester? I don't believe some people.'

'There you are,' Roger said.

'He told me everything. Always did, always does. That's the way we live. And always have. Full disclosure.'

'Bloody hell,' Quigley said. '*Regal Court*, he told you about, and you're still here? This is some woman apparently, isn't she, Jont? These two have lessons for all of us.'

'Very much so,' Goldstein said.

'Phew; seriously. Because that was never the impression you give me at the time, Rodgie. That she'd take it in her stride.'

'He probably didn't think you were ready for it,' I said.

Roger was looking across the room at me with eyes so bright and so grateful that he might have discovered that he loved me. 'I wouldn't ever do things I didn't tell her about,' he said, 'ever.'

'And you reciprocate, do you, Rachel? In that respect?'

'Not particularly. Roger likes me to keep things from him, so I do, sometimes.'

'Yeah? Such as what? I'd more than appreciate you satisfying my curiosity in that department. Not that you have to or anything.'

'Then I don't think I will,' I said.

'Excuse me, but ... back on the other point, you actually *knew* all along what him and me and later Lester was up to, when we was late at the office and everything? Including, when we was pushed, up in the room with the duplicating machine in it, did you?'

'I was glad to hear that he was doing what he wanted,' I said. 'And then again, I had my own agenda, obviously enough.'

'Talk about his feelings then, at all, did he? About me personally? What were they?'

'Feelings. He thought secretly you were rather afraid of yourself. Is that feelings?'

'Some truth in that, isn't there, Jont?'

'Very much so,' Goldstein said. 'From where I stand.'

'About this money you was talking about.'

'Money?'

'Of ours. That you was hinting about. Down below. It's all right, is it? Because anything happens to it, that's got to be down to you personal, darling. You won your round, but I'd leave it there. All right, you boxed clever, but don't overdo it, OK?'

'Look,' I said, 'I could've motored on up to the farm and called the police.'

'Don't elaborate. Unless you want a good spanking possibly. A clever girl wouldn't want to add to her problems, or ours, would she? Because how clever would that be ultimately?'

'And I still can. Call them. Now. Tomorrow. Whenever.'

'I've got to admit something,' Quigley said. 'I've got a soft spot for being threatened by women; up to a point.'

'I suggest you drive away while you're still free to do so.'

'She sounds like the fucking magistrate now; sounds like the fucking beak now, doesn't she, Rodge? Oh, sorry, you wouldn't know, would you? Take it from me, she does; spot on.'

'That's a nice smile, Roger,' Jonty said. 'For a change.'

'He thinks he's out of it, don't you, my son? Clear water you reckon you're looking at, is it?'

'You still haven't used the bog,' Roger said. 'You must be cured. Homeopathic. That's why they came up here.'

'What are you calling me exactly?'

'Homeopathic. When you get better without the use of drugs.'

'I do like this house,' Quigley said. 'I seriously do.'

'There are tons of them about,' Roger said. 'I could help you with. We could.'

157

'Be careful. Promise people things and they can sometimes take you up. Always subject to Rachel's say-so.'

My look willed Roger not to respond. We had to leave them with a way of making their defeat appear to be a victory. Like politicians who had been voted out, they needed the comfort of having their eviction appear to be the result of their own fastidious decision.

Pansy said, 'OK, I'm going to phone now, all right?'

'If you're seriously out of bog rolls,' Roger said, 'I'm sure we've got a spare one, haven't we, Raitch, they could have?'

I went to find the box of spare rolls in the cupboard at the back of the kitchen. I took my time; by protracting the break in conversation I might foster enough suburban embarrassment for the two men to be happy to leave. When I returned, Roger looked at me with deference, and a hint of apprehension. It quite primed my ambition to tell him my news. With a show of briskness – as if I knew that Quigley and Goldstein had a train, or a tide, to catch – I held out one green and one pink floral toilet roll. Give people the chance to choose between two things and they often have the grateful impression that they are being given more than one.

'Very nice,' Goldstein said.

'Could have happened sooner,' Quigley said.

I said, 'Is there anything else you want?'

Pansy was over by the television set, with the telephone bracketed between jaw and shoulder. Her voice was increasingly animated. She was already speaking at a length which made Roger frown. The long pauses cost money too.

'It's a seriously lovely bottie she's got,' Goldstein said, 'that one. I still wouldn't mind having it in the back.'

'You don't do lists at all, do you?' I said.

'Lists?'

'Of antiques. I'd be very interested to know what you've got on offer at any given time. And I know other people who might too.'

'Don't go too far, Rachel, all right? You done well; you know it, I know it. I'm not totally sure Roger knows it. Only don't go no further would be my advice.'

They stood around for a while longer and then they nodded, as if they had taught us enough of a lesson. Quigley threw the floral pink roll in the air and caught it again. After that, he opened the terrace door and, like swimmers into an evening sea, he and Goldstein disappeared without a splash, or a word, into the darkness.

Roger's look became sullen, and a little rueful. I could almost imagine that he wished that he had gone with them. Pansy was grinning and turning round and round as she spoke to Brice. Perhaps she thought that Roger was less likely to attack a moving target. He was glaring horribly. Then he stopped looking at Pansy and cleared his throat and found a more or less normal voice. 'By the way, Raitch, in case you didn't know: Olivier's disappeared.'

'Olivier? Since when?'

'Sibylle was here before and she's very worried. He never came back to the *Relais* after you went out with him.'

'Yes, he did. Because I saw him there. With the leather lady.'

'Sibylle's in a terrible state. I wish I had a gun. I really ought to have.'

'What would you do with it?'

'Pansy, he can call you back,' Roger said. 'Get him to call you back. PANSY! What was this about money they were talking about exactly?'

'They had a bunch of francs in a belt in the tent.'

'What were you doing in their tent?'

'What were you doing with Quigley in the room with the duplicating machine? And what's *Regal Court*, as if I hadn't guessed?'

'You were fantastic. The way you handled them.'

'You and Quigley, was it?'

'They absolutely had us. Until you turned up. I still can't believe they've really gone.'

'They didn't ... hurt her, did they? Pansy. Did they make her undress or what?'

'She wasn't all that bothered, that I know of. I thought they were an item when I first saw them, but they don't necessarily have exclusive interests. Quigley was winding you up. You saw through that, of course, which was brilliant, how you handled it. About him and me. Don't get any ideas, will you?'

'I don't need any more, do I? Was it just to get him to put his hand in the till or was it something less tender and true than that?

159

And then it was threesomes, was it? The duplicating machine, that's a nice touch.'

'It's all cock, Ray, is all that. How did you get on? See the people you wanted? Catch up with Cator? Article all written?'

I said, 'Roger, I don't want you to be upset . . .'

'I was,' he said. 'And more than. Just before. But I'm fine now. Too late to go out to dinner. And probably not very wise. I'd hate to come home and find . . . You think they're the people did the Schlickies then, do you? You do, obviously. I reckon it wouldn't hurt to make a leisurely call to the cops. Once they've packed their stuff. They can pick them up on the road. You were fabulous, Raitch. Wasn't she, Pan? Seriously the business.'

'And now for my news,' I said.

'Absolutely. Let's hear it.'

'I'm leaving you.'

'Is that them going or isn't it?'

'If that's all right with you.'

'It didn't mean a thing,' he said. 'Regal Court. If that's what's bothering you after all. It was business. You had absolutely the right attitude when you said what you said. You could see the stuffing coming right out of them. Wasn't she amazing, Pan?'

'Brice is going to meet me at the airport if I tell him what flight I'm on. He's discovered this Labour MP who's into totally enormous black ladies so he won't have too much trouble getting a pair. Can I phone British Airways anywhere?'

'I love you, Rachel. I honestly and truly love you. Now more than ever. And that's no lie.'

'It's got nothing to do with you and Quigley,' I said. 'I don't give a damn what you did. In fact, it comes very much as a relief. You can phone them in the morning; toll free.'

'You were very taken up at the office. At the time, I thought something might be going on with that editor of yours. It was strictly a reaction thing on my part. I'm not really that way.'

'Let's not go into reasons. I'm leaving.'

'You're not going anywhere,' Roger said. 'And certainly not tonight. Anyway, you haven't got transport.'

'You should've gone with them,' Pansy said. 'I was going to myself, but I don't seem to have, do I? Mind you, I hadn't packed, which might come into it. Bit sad possibly.'

'You fancy stuffing at both ends, do you, you silly little tart?

He's meeting you at the airport, you bitch. Your husband, that's why you've shoved Samson out the window. I liked Samson, by the way, Raitch. That was inspired.'

I said, 'Roger, please don't talk to my sister like that.'

'So did he. I bet he calls himself that from now on.' Roger opened the door of the refrigerator. The light from inside it seemed to cover him with faint icing. 'I had a suitable gun, I'd go down there right now and blast them both to hell. One-two! Self-defence, the frogs buy that, don't they? I seriously didn't know what was going to happen at one point.'

I said, 'It's all right. It's over. It's finished.'

His eyes were daggered with tears as he turned and looked at me. Those thin lips were trembling and moist. He was furious. '*I'm* finished more like, because you know what they've gone with, don't you, in addition to the bog roll? The crown bloody jewels, they might as well have. Bastards. *Bastards.*'

'Good news,' Pansy said. 'Because Brice wants to buy me one of these new Mazda convertibles which are absolutely brilliant apparently. It's amazing what it does to people, isn't it, showing them you can do without them?'

'I get it,' Roger said. 'Not very often, but I get it this time all right. Taking a leaf out of sis's book, are you? I might as well have given her one for all the good it did not doing.'

'I don't know about anybody else,' Pansy said, 'but I could really, really eat suddenly, couldn't you, Roger?'

'She tried to get me into bed this afternoon, your sister, in case you really want to know.'

'I don't,' I said.

'I don't remember it like that,' Pansy said. 'Anyway, I didn't, did I?'

'What have I done?' Roger said. 'What am I actually supposed to have done?'

'There they go,' I said. 'They've gone. Your troubles are over. You don't even have to buy a gun.'

'It doesn't mean they won't be back. The van! Did any clever person get its number at all?'

Pansy said, 'Is there a morning flight, early, from Bordeaux? There is, isn't there? You can come with, if you like, Raitch, but I would like to be alone with Brice when we actually get to London, if that's all right with you.'

'Shut up, Pansy. Shut up. Because Rachel isn't going with you. She isn't going anywhere. Me, I'd like to bloody well shoot you,' Roger said. 'All right: both of you. I'd like to shoot bloody great holes in both of you. I'm not going to, obviously, ever, but I'd certainly like to. Big as soup plates. And then sit down and have one bloody great quiet bowl of freshly opened Cruesli. With a sliced banana and tons of cold milk. And if there are any strawbs left, I'd be having some of them too. And like that.'

'I'm not going to London,' I said. 'I'm going somewhere else entirely.'

'Why are you doing this?' Roger said. 'For what conceivable reason? What am I ever supposed to have done, exactly?'

II

After Olivier had overflown Rodez and Millau, the horizon cleared. It might have been early on a different day as he came over the Cevennes and caught a first slatey view of the sea. He began to see other small planes over the coast and tuned in carefully to ground control's staccato babble as he entered the crowded Provençal air-space. His routine checks on course and fuel were carried out with impersonal calm. He observed the rules from a much greater height than anyone could suspect.

He enjoyed the flight to Ste Maxime as if no dark purpose had fuelled it. He landed with feathery ease and parked the Piper by the high hoop of a canvas hangar. He walked with his canvas hold-all across dry grass to the cracked concrete apron where a disused, camouflaged aircraft was braced on the two stiff arms of its undercarriage. The flat tyres made it seem that it had spent all its breath.

At the Budget desk in the commercial terminal, he hired a Renault 5 and asked for directions to Les Hameaux de l'Escalet. He had written the address which Sabine had given him on a hotel napkin. He drove with less ease than he had flown. He wished that he had further to go than only as far as the modern hamlet which adjoined the village of Escalet. He had to pass the cemetery of war dead where sprinklers were working over the grass. A slash of water flopped across his windscreen.

There were two *boules* pitches, side by side between the Café des Sports and a rain-streaked concrete church. The green bell in the square tower looked like a huge uncut cheese. Olivier consulted the map outside the *Syndicat d'Initiative* and then found his way to a colony of beige stucco cottages set among white concrete streets, dry *soir d'été* saplings, and grey kerbs. Number 43 had its brown shutters closed. An olive-green plastic table and two similar chairs were under the tiled eaves of the tight front terrace. Colourful publicity had been stuck in the mouth of the recommended post-box. The front garden was cracked and the leaves of the rose-bushes were the colour of dried blood.

An earth-covered roundabout at the end of the *Impasse Jacques Doneux* enabled Olivier to come back for another look at 43. It appeared deserted. He returned to the Café des Sports and went in and ordered a beer. The *patronne* told him that Monsieur Lévy was among the old men playing *boules* under the plane trees.

The bare knuckles of the branches carried no shade. Olivier took his *demi* out under the café awning and sipped it while he watched the game. The eyes of the old men measured the dusty ground where the shots they had already fired set them pensive problems. The players might have been framed in some provincial gallery. Although they moved, they remained within easy view, as though tethered for Olivier's inspection. If he had expected emotions, he felt none. He allowed the afternoon to shade into evening without impatience or an inkling of purpose. When the first lights went on in the café, he had been sitting there for nearly three hours.

He went inside and made another beer the excuse for starting a conversation with the *patronne*. Her hennaed hair was combed upwards to reveal a very white neck on which she wore a black velvet choker. Her green silk blouse was generously open on a cleavage which was used to the interest of visitors. Olivier mentioned that he had connections '*dans l'industrie hôtelière*'. The *patronne* was not optimistic about the future of her establishment; despite the *boules* players, there were few regulars in so new a village. More than half the houses were owned by people who came to them only a few weeks in the year. Most of the residents were retired people on fixed incomes; they were always worried, as Monsieur could imagine, about their 'ends of the month'.

Olivier did not say where he came from, nor what his reason was for his journey to Les Hameaux de l'Escalet. The *patronne* seemed to accept his story of being in the business, but then, as she was wiping the bar, she said, '*Vous êtes de la police, non?*'

She read his denial for confirmation and nodded, as if she

understood his reticence. He took a slice of wrapped fruit cake, of a kind he would never normally have eaten, from under the plastic dome on the counter. When he made to pay for it, she waved away his money; he was not sure whether it was because they shared a profession or because, in a way he recognised, she thought it a small price to pay in order to keep in with the police.

He walked out once again to the empty terrace. He almost hoped that the old men would have scattered. The puzzle of discovering which one was Alphonse Lévy would then be made more complicated and their meeting postponed. The players had finished their game, but they were still together. As they caged the *boules* in latticed carrying cases and walked towards him, they were talking in louder voices than before, still fingering the dusters with which they had been polishing their material. The pensioned faces were creased and weathered with the common marks of age. Despite his knowledge of the circumstances under which the name Lévy had been acquired, Olivier tried to discern which of the men had an appropriate nose. He fastened his attention on a tallish figure who turned his shoulders, not merely his head, when he went to reply to some remark of his late partner. Olivier's mouth tightened as he was reminded of his own way of retorting to criticism. It was like looking into a mirror of his own future.

Although the long terrace was now brightly lit, and largely deserted, the *boules* players sat only a few tables away from Olivier. He guessed that it must be their habitual spot. The losers pointed fingers at the winners in order to discover what they would like to drink. The *patronne* advanced no further than the door of the café. She already knew what they would order. The man of whose identity Olivier was as good as certain pivoted his head and shoulder again in order to ask for '*quatre Pastis*'.

Olivier monitored the old men's chatter without attending to it closely. They remained indifferent to him; like children, they could not imagine that anyone would care to spy on them. Olivier observed them without concealment; since he might as well have been invisible, there was no call for pretence. Once their drinks had come, the old men's conversation consisted of rehearsing random incidents and political opinions culled from the local newspaper. Time lay all around, and stretched ahead of them, like a desert. Their frailty was not that of men who had once been virile or who feared decline; they might as well always have been the same age.

Finally, one of them stood up and said that his wife was waiting for him. A second then said that he would walk along with Jojo. The man who seemed to be Alphonse Lévy looked at his watch, sucked his lips against his teeth and then glanced, for the first time, at Olivier. His remaining companion looked into his empty glass and said something about the gears on his bicycle. Their condition required him to get home in order to see his first cousin, who was a 'crack' when it came to *vélos*. The reason he gave for his departure was elaborate enough to sound like a lie.

The supposed Lévy sat alone for a while until the arrival of a pair of middle-aged lovers whose spare fingers were laced together as they drank their *pastis*. The uncomely couple treated each other with loving attention; the world was their private joke. From a few metres away, Olivier watched the old man with terrible affection. Something disturbingly akin to love inspired him, though he could not put a name to it: pity was too generous, curiosity too ardent. He simply accompanied the old man without being with him. Their situation afforded him a sort of disturbing comfort. It put an end to something, but he had no wish for it to end; he would have preferred it to be prolonged, although – or because – it was, in substance, nothing.

The old man's face had settled into long lines, three on each side, that hung from his familiar cheekbones. His forehead was ruled with what might have been forgotten thoughts; the grey eyes would have suited a discredited statesman who still hoped to bequeath some wisdom to a world of which he was wise enough no longer to have any expectations. His solitude was vacuous and austere; its defiance, like its pride, lay in looking neither for pleasure nor for compensation.

Olivier could not detect whether his presence had made any impression on the old man. He watched for some indication of effort in his companion's long impersonation of detached serenity. Why did merely sitting adjacent to him excite such angry patience? Olivier wished that he had spelt out to himself what he meant to say or hoped to hear. He had assumed that the meeting would generate its own drama. Now the surprise which he had come to administer seemed to be turned against himself. By saying and doing nothing, he postponed what he feared might become a defeat; he was a policeman who had mislaid his warrant.

The old man looked again at his watch, perhaps more out of complacency at its size than from any desire to check the hour. He then shuffled a few coins under the ashtray he had not used. Olivier wondered, like a tourist, whether he too should leave a small tip. He had not been rendered any service, but he did not wish to appear less generous than the old man. He dropped five francs on the table, as if he had been bluffed into doing something foolish. When he straightened up and turned his shoulders, the old man was considering him, like some unimportant puzzle. Before he could be bothered to solve it, he had shrugged and stepped out into the drab road.

Olivier followed, a few paces behind him. If he hoped to provoke even a mildly nervous response, the old man disappointed him. Did he truly not wonder in the slightest whether anything was being prepared behind his back? By what right could he assume Olivier to be as harmless as the moths which clustered on the amber domes of the wayside lights? He stayed in the middle of the empty street until he veered across a bald patch, where a set of yellow and green municipal swings catered for children of whom there was no other evidence.

Olivier followed precisely, but the old man was not teased into looking round. He walked down the *Impasse Jacques Doneux* and came to an early stop, at the door of a pavilion. He tapped on the brown shutter in a way that announced itself a habit. He waited, and Olivier waited, until the door opened. A woman with a North African face and tight black curly hair stood in the unsubtle light of the hall. She was holding two plastic supermarket bags. She put them down in front of the old man's feet and then she reached inside and came out again to count some change into his hand. He tilted his palm towards the light to check it. Then he put the money in his pocket, picked up the stretched bags and walked on.

For Olivier, it seemed offensive to arrive and leave without a word, but the old man's lack of grace conferred an air of stoic endurance on all his acts. He was alone in the world and he knew it; the existence of others did nothing to alleviate it. His previous willingness to talk to the other *boules* players became a sort of irony: he had conferred his presence on them in an apparently sociable way, but he could evidently just as well dispense with them. Indifference killed them all without a thought. Olivier followed him now as if he had been invited. He felt himself on the verge of becoming the old man's client.

The so-called Monsieur Lévy acted like a Monsieur Lévy. When he reached his front door, he put down his supermarket bags and took a ring of keys from his trouser pocket and undid two locks on the shutter and a third on the door behind it. He switched on a light in the *pavillon* and came back for the plastic sacks. When he had gone inside with them, he left the door ajar. His action offered Olivier a way in without even acknowledging his existence.

Olivier did not move for several seconds. Something in him was willing, even now, to walk back to his car and drive away. Out of some strange emotion, or its absence, he could imagine leaving the old man in peace, if that was truly what he was in. The bright doorway and the domestic sounds from inside invited him to do something which he had come a long way to do and would as gladly now not do at all. That he felt obliged to go in made him resentful, like a sulky boy who was going to have to admit something.

He rattled the shutter to advertise his entrance. The sounds came from the narrow, rustic-style kitchen at the back of the house. The old man was pouring oil into a frying pan with a hand which trembled steadily. The gas flared with a raucous gasp.

Olivier said, '*Bonsoir.*'

'*Bonsoir.*' There was no inquiring lift to the voice; it sounded like a routine greeting.

'*Je suis Olivier Argote.*'

'*Oui.*' The monosyllable did not doubt the truth of the assertion. The old man added a knob of butter to his oil.

'*Je suis venu de Sainte-Foy-le-Fort.*'

'*Oui.*'

'*Où j'ai reçu une visite de la part d'Yvonne Langon.*'

The old man appeared unsurprised at the news of Olivier's visitor. He knew that Yvonne Langon had died a few days earlier. He broke eggs into a plastic bowl. When Olivier wanted to know what he was preparing, he said that it was an omelette. Olivier could have one, if he wanted: there was no shortage of eggs.

Olivier pushed the old man aside, with peremptory gentleness. He seemed to feel the need to touch him, to confirm his reality. He turned off the gas and relit it. The flame was properly blue now

168

and made little sound. He broke another egg into the bowl and frisked the mixture.

The old man walked towards the kitchen door and, without turning back, said that there was also the possibility of a green salad. When Olivier asked where he was going, he called that he was going to '*pisser un coup*'. After a few seconds, Olivier heard the ring of the old man's stream against enamel. He poured the eggs into the hot fat and became the chef.

When the old man came back, buttoning himself with too many fingers, he asked, without any sign of anxiety, what message Olivier's visitor had brought. Olivier said that Yvonne had wanted him to know everything that had happened a long time before. In order to do what exactly? Olivier said that she had left no precise instructions. The old man inquired whether perhaps he had any ideas of his own. His lack of intonation was a kind of challenge. Olivier said, '*Argote. Je m'appelle Argote. Ça vous dit quelque chose?*'

The old man looked at Olivier and pointed a finger at the omelette and then he said that his own name was Alphonse Lévy and, in consequence, what did Olivier want of him exactly. Olivier tilted the omelette, and the uncooked mixture thickened in the fat, and then he looked at the old man with a sudden charge of rage, and relief. The relief was that he could at last feel rage.

When the old man repeated that his name was Lévy, Alphonse Lévy, Olivier said that, no, his name was Félix Argote and that he was his father. The old man said that he was sorry, and he might have been sorry for Olivier, but his name was Alphonse Lévy and that he was a Jew and that the omelette should come out.

Olivier said that he was a chef and that he knew about omelettes and that the old man was a criminal, and also rich, wasn't he? The old man watched him put the omelette on a plain plate and said that he was as Olivier saw him to be, a modest man; a modest Jew.

Olivier said that he was the old man's son and that the old man knew it, from the beginning. Or did he live with his door open to everyone? He said that the old man was playing a game and that he knew he was. What about Léah? Where did she come from and how was it that he had married her when he had married her?

The old man advised Olivier to stay calm. They were, after all, at table. He gathered that Olivier had come in order to get some information, to which he had no objection, but if they were going to eat, they needed to stay calm, for their digestions' sake.

Olivier said that he had come to confront the old man before he croaked. In that case, the old man said, they could take their time. Olivier stood up and took his share of the omelette to the corner of the room and began to eat it there. He said that the old man had no shame but that, despite that, he was also his father.

The old man said that he had nothing against that.

Olivier felt obliged to continue eating as he said that the old man was his father and that he was also Félix Argote and that he was also a coward and a murderer. He seemed to be feeding himself with the accusations. He was also a swine and a liar.

The old man said that that was a matter for discussion.

Olivier's plate was now empty.

ii

'At least explain to me what I've done,' Roger said. 'You owe me at least that much.'

'Why do you have to have done something for me to want to pack a suitcase?'

'Or haven't done. I married you, didn't I? I've got a right to know why you're doing what you're doing it.'

'Why does there have to be a why?'

'I don't mean to interrupt or anything,' Pansy said, 'but can I just say one thing?'

'Not if you're going to say that it's all your fault.'

'It's all my fault,' Pansy said.

'No, no,' Roger said, 'don't tell her it's not, because all right, if we're going to get down to it, it *is* her fault.'

'It's nothing to do with her whatsoever. It's nothing to do with either of you, if we're talking about me leaving. I will not accept that my life or my decisions are dependent on either of you. I also advise you strongly against trying to make me stay in this house for one second longer than I want to.'

'He stole your money, didn't he?' Pansy said. 'That Daddy gave you. And now where is it?'

'As for you,' Roger said, 'as for you ... if you hadn't bloody well come down here uninvited and unannounced...'

170

'I did try to telephone. Be fair.'

'Well, suppose you now try to fuck off. I don't know which one of you I want to kill more. It's seriously tight.'

'You need to see somebody, Roger,' Pansy said. 'He needs to see somebody; quite urgently, if you ask me. He needs help.'

'Imagine if I had a million pounds,' Roger said. 'Imagine if we'd brought it off, which might well have happened, and I had a million pounds. Half a million even. I wonder whether you'd all be packing suitcases then.'

'He's got the money somewhere, haven't you, Roger?'

'Money! You'd gladly have had one of them up one end and the other one up the other and you'd still be on the bloody telephone to bloody Bricey and butter not melting in your mouth.'

'You're very rude, isn't he? *And* you've got something to hide, if you ask me.'

'More than anyone could say of you after this afternoon.'

'Let me sit on it,' Pansy said, 'and then you can shut it.'

'I can manage,' Rachel said. 'I never liked this bloody suitcase.'

'Didn't I give it to you for Christmas?'

'I bought it and you gave it to me. And I never liked it.'

'*Sorry*,' Pansy said, 'about that.'

'You walk out of this house,' Roger said, 'and you're not ever going to walk back into it. Let's get that very clear, shall we? I'll bloody let them have it. I'll let Quigs and Jonty have it. See if I don't.'

'He really is a charmer, isn't he?' Pansy said.

'I wouldn't be surprised if they both had you in the tent. Did they?'

'Why would anyone want to surprise you, Roger?'

'You're not having the car. That Cherokee's mine. It's in my name. I bought it. Take it and I call the cops. That's a promise.'

'You can come with me, darling. We can go to that hotel you were talking about you say's so nice.'

'What have I *done*?' Roger said. 'What am I supposed to have done that's so unforgivable suddenly?'

'You stole her money, didn't he?'

'It's nothing to do with money,' Rachel said. 'I wish you'd stop talking as if it were. You haven't done *anything*, and you're not going to. This is something I'm going to do.'

'It is her fault. It *is* her fault. You would never be saying that, or anything like it, if she hadn't been here, if she hadn't put her bloody nose in the door.'

'In that case,' Rachel said, 'I'm very glad she did.'

'Do you imagine they'll have a room at this time of the year?'

'I don't know and I don't care. There's somewhere I intend to go and I'm not going anywhere else.'

'We'll go there then,' Pansy said.

'I love you, you fucking bitch . . .'

'Which fucking bitch is that then?'

Roger flopped across the banisters and hung there, panting, as if he had reached some breathtakingly high ledge. 'You, you fucking little cow. You married me. You said you loved me. What if someone calls for you? What do you want me to say? I'll kill you, if you do this.'

Rachel said, 'I might come back, and I might not.'

'What's that telling me?' Roger said. 'And what about that baby we were going to have? What about him?'

iii

The old man raised his finger. He could hear someone coming. Was Olivier expecting anyone? Olivier said that no one knew where he was and he was certainly not waiting for anyone. All the same, the old man said, someone was certainly arriving.

Olivier said that it was probably for the old man, which he admitted to be possible. The old man collected the plates and glasses from the table and set about washing them up under the tap. It was as if he were giving himself an alibi. The sound of the motorcycle engine was loud and then it died.

Olivier asked if the old man was afraid.

Of what for example?

As if time now pressed, Olivier asked about Léah: had the old man believed that she truly loved him? He replied that to speak of love was perhaps too much. And as for the truth . . . The truth was that they had coped with each other without asking too many questions. Wasn't that the best way?

They had 'coped' for fifty years, Olivier said. The old man agreed: it had been a long time. Olivier said that it was 'a lifetime'. The old man thought about that and then he said, 'A lifetime.

What's that, after all?' Had he regretted her death? Yes and no: she had, at the end, had several 'unhealthy habits'. If the old man heard the knock at the front door, he made no move to answer it. He thought it might be Jojo, or someone from Jojo; his partner had not been in form for the last few days. Probably he had sent to say that he would not be playing next day, which was a pity. He went, with a sigh, to answer the second knock.

Cator was wearing green oilskin overalls and black boots. He carried a canvas satchel which might have had tools in it. His black crash-helmet hung on the handlebars of the Harley-Davidson which he had wheeled inside the low gate of the garden and parked against the plastic table. 'Be all right there, will it?'

'*Vous risquez rien*,' the old man said. '*Entrez!*'

The oilskins made a creaking noise in the narrow passageway into the kitchen. Cator's hair was flat from the journey; it peaked on his forehead like a pressed leaf. His face was flushed and puffed; it took a moment or two to resume its wrinkles. He said '*Bonsoir*' and held out his hand to Olivier.

'*Bonsoir.*'

'*Drôle d'endroit pour un homme riche.*'

'*Comment?*'

'Funny place for a rich man.' Cator's English voice was loud and impatient. His face seemed to go through its programme of expressions before arriving at one of mordant derision. 'This is a miserable bloody bolt-hole, Félix, and I'm sure you know it.'

'He says that he is Alphonse Lévy. A Jew.'

Cator looked at the old man for a moment as if the silence which came from him were some kind of an explanation. He waited until a certain point, when the quality of what was not being said seemed to change. Then he slapped the old man across the cheek. He did not react or move. Cator struck the old man again, harder. 'You are Félix Argote. I know it; you know it; Olivier knows it. End of argument. Would be my advice.'

'*Vous avez faim?*' the old man said. '*On mange quelque chose?*'

'English officer,' Cator said. 'Don't eat on the job. You ate, did you, Olivier, with this person?'

'*C'est mon père.*'

'*Quand même.* She showed you the stuff presumably? Here to do what, are you?'

'To see. I came to see . . . if it was him.'

173

'You heard about the money. Or have you always known?'

'I was a little boy.'

'Useful state. Recommend it.'

'You are here why?'

'I am here why, Félix?'

'I am Alphonse Lévy. I am an old Jew.'

'*Il cherche sa claque, ce petit bonhomme.*'

'I am allowed to be. *Personne n'a le droit de me terroriser. Je suis chez moi.*'

'British officer. Why am I here? Any ideas?'

'*Pourquoi ne pas parler en français? On est toujours en France.*'

'Talk what lingo I like, me. British justice. British jurisdiction. Talk as I please. English money, English bullets, English justice. Fair enough?'

'It has been a long time,' Olivier said. 'Where 'ave you been these years?'

'Round and about. Up and down. Admitted it, has he?'

'I admit nothing,' the old man said. 'What do I have to admit?'

'You sold them out; you got the money; you bought the bloody hotel and then things got a bit hot and you legged it. Don't need three days of may-it-please-your-lordship to get that established, do we?'

'*Je laisse tout tomber,*' Olivier said. '*Tout, tout, tout.* The hotel, my wife, my family, all of it; I'm getting out. Forever.'

'Long time, forever, I'd say. Being as one who knows. But it's up to you. Not my part of ship, that. My advice'd be bugger off *instanter*, if not sooner, and leave me to it. Bugger off. *Allez*, pally, and don't look back.'

'*Je n'avais aucune idée avant l'arrivée de cette dame en noir.* As far as I was concerned, he was long dead.'

'My daughter apparently,' Cator said. '*Cette dame.* It's certainly the hour of the *retrouvailles familiales*, one way and another.'

'You are here to do what?'

'He knows why I'm here. I imagine you do.'

'*Il veut tuer un pauvre petit Juif de quatre-vingt-trois ans.*'

'Hole in one. Any questions at all?'

'It is fifty years,' Olivier said. '*C'est pas possible.*'

'*Vas-y, Olivier,*' the old man said. '*Il a raison. Tu n'aurais pas dû venir.* He should not be 'ere.'

'You're here for what exactly, *chef*?'

'I thought he was dead. Forty-five years. My life.'

'And now you're a man,' Cator said. 'Men have to know when to let things go. Likewise when not. None of my business, but I were you, I'd bugger off home and think no more about it. Get back to the pots and pans. Cédric.'

'*Vous avez une arme?*'

'We're not savages, unless the occasion warrants. Rules of war. *En gare comme à la gare.* And thence to a place of execution.'

'The war is over.'

'Some of the war is over; some of it, not. Got your car?'

'I have a car, in the square.'

'Saw it. Wondered. You're a bloody nuisance, Olivier. No business here. Understand your curiosity, but you're much better out of it, do you mind?'

'You expect me to go and leave you to ... do what?'

'I don't expect, sonny, to put it plainly. I'm telling you: on your way, two-three; surplus to requirements, you are. Nothing to be said, best not say it.'

'He's an old man.'

'Seen that for myself. And? Furthermore?'

'*Mentalement ...*'

'*Mentalement*, don't care one way or t'other. Decision of the court. Condition of soul, ditto other intangibles, not my concern. He sold those people; he sold my friends and assorted others. Long time ago; I heard you. Too long, is it? And when did it start being? Justice got a do-by, has it? Since when is this? When does this become that exactly? Wanting to hear from learned counsel? Not me; not much.' Cator pushed the webbing through the buckles of his tool-bag and they could hear metal fall over inside. 'Against ceremony, I am rather, after all these years.'

'And if I refuse to go? *Si je refuse ...*'

'Got the English bit, thanks all the same. You want to be here, you can be here.'

'I will tell the police,' Olivier said. 'If you do anything I will tell them.'

'Inadvisable,' Cator said.

The old man said, '*Je regrette.*'

'Facer, that one,' Cator said. 'Grant you that. He sold them at a price. Not for nothing. Not even out of dislike. Previous occasions, he was quite nice to them. Money, nothing else. He sold

175

them and we couldn't do a thing. Made fools of us; me. And Léah; made a fool of her. Good-looking, Léah, wasn't she, Félix, at that stage, in her day, and then she decided ... Understand that at all? Why she took up with him? Think I do. Much it matters. Didn't end with the Jews, did it, Félix old boy? Once you'd sold one lot of merchandise, you rather got in the way of it.'

'*J'ai payé*,' the old man said, as if speaking of an outstanding account to some ignorant clerk. He said that he had paid with his whole life for a crime which was not truly a crime. '*Et puis, maintenant...*'

'Had a whole bloody company up there, the Fredas, didn't they, Félix, that day? Make sure we didn't do anything courageous. Fat chance: Baker Street not interested in acts of chivalry; much to be discouraged in fact. Arms folded, two-three, very much the order of the day. But Félix saw us right, didn't you, m'sieur, just in case? Gave us every excuse. Odds for, odds against; good afternoon and thank you very much. Léah's hand in that, if I know anything.'

'*Je ne comprends rien.*'

'Yes, you do, matey, understand, very well. He took their money, he took our money, and here he is fifty years later and remarkably well on it. Going to tell the police, are you? On you go then. Think I care where I get handed my soup, do you? Not a bit. Not a damn. Suit yourself. Call it justice, suit yourself. And parleyvoo to you, m'sieur.'

Olivier said, '*C'est vrai?*'

The old man bent to put the dry plates in the cupboard under the draining board. He stood there with the check cloth in his hands, as he had with the duster he used to clean the *boules*. He clenched his fingers on the yellow cotton but he did not rub them. '*Tout ce que tu as et tout ce que tu es, c'est grâce à moi.*'

'He's right,' Olivier said. 'Everything I am, everything I've got; it's all because of him.' He stopped by the old man, at an angle which avoided his eyes. '*Adieu, papa.*' He turned to Cator and said, 'He's all yours. It's all the same to me. Do what you want as far as I'm concerned. I was never here.'

'No you weren't,' Cator said. 'And don't expect any thanks. If you really want to know, I'm more on his side than I am yours.'

The old man waited for Olivier's footsteps to lose their claim on his attention. The front door was shut quietly. Then he said, '*A nous deux maintenant.*'

Cator said, '*Vous vous souvenez d'elle?*'

'*Qui ça? Yvonne?*'

No, Cator said, the other one. The one who looked after the children. Her name was Monique. She had left with the children, when the children were driven away, she had gone with them, although she had the chance to escape. The old man said that, in all honesty, he had no memory. His name was Alphonse Lévy.

Cator made two little gestures of preparation before he hit the old man on the side of the face and sent him to floor with a pan in his hand. Monique, he said, had stayed at the *Relais* for two or three days and the old man knew it. He asked him why he wanted to die under a pseudonym when they both knew very well who he was. He said that the old man was ignoble to the last degree; that he was a piece of shit.

The old man said that it was not worth the trouble of insulting him. It was undignified as well. On second thoughts, he agreed: the woman had been a saint, but war was like that: one forgot things. And the money, Cator asked, had he also forgotten about the money?

About the money, the old man said, Cator knew as well as he did: whoever had profited, he personally had certainly not.

Cator said how strange it was that, even on the edge of eternity, an old man could bring himself to lie, presumably for the pure pleasure of doing so. It was almost an act of piety.

The old man said that they should not exaggerate.

'On your knees,' Cator said. 'On your knees. The sentence of the court. On your damned knees with you.'

The old man looked up and said, 'The money. You don't want?'

'I'm not interested in the bloody money,' Cator said. 'I'm interested in getting this damned thing loaded and you finished and me back home, two-three.'

The old man watched with interest as Cator banged the magazine onto the sten gun with the flat of his palm. He said that he supposed that Cator had enough money already. The old man looked around the kitchen, as if he expected to be gone for some time. He reached, still on his knees, and turned off the gas, which neither of them had extinguished after the omelette. It was worth the trouble, he said, of being prudent.

Pansy said, 'Now what happens? Where shall we go?'

'I want to go to one place and you want to go to another one entirely.'

'You're lucky,' Pansy said, 'if you know where you want to go. It's more than I do.'

'I don't. Or rather, I do, but I'm not sure where it is exactly.'

'Perfect time of night for finding out,' Pansy said. 'What do you want me to do?'

'All you have to do is put me down somewhere. But for God's sake, let's go.'

'You could always come back with me. I know someone who'd be pleased and that's Roley Savory.'

'I don't want to go back,' Rachel said. 'I want you to put me down somewhere specific. A village called Château St Martial. What did they do to you exactly, those two?'

'Nothing worth worrying about. They were a bit excited. He's going to be very unhappy without you.'

'Is that a promise?'

'I must say though, he has been a bit of a one, your little estate agent character. I suppose you always knew he was a crook?'

'He's a very proper sort of crook. Compared with those two anyway. That van must be jammed with stolen stuff.'

'Oh well. I thought they were heaven. I was really sorry not to go with them in a way. I rather fancied being a bit of stolen stuff myself.'

'Don't be so silly. There's no knowing what they would have done to you.'

'Of course there is. Is this where I'm supposed to be going? You don't know how seriously disreputable I could be, Raitch, if only I wasn't quite so presentable. What do I do if he comes after us? I can scarcely change gear on this bloody car.'

'He won't. Go on down here and I'll tell when to turn. Did they make you take your clothes off like that, or did you volunteer?'

'They love to force you to do things, don't they, men, even if you don't mind all that much doing them? The big Jewy one took a fancy to me rather. I think the other might have come round. He did show bulgy signs from time to time, but that may just have been because he was giving Roger such a hard time.'

'You know what you could do.'

'What's that? Assuming it doesn't demand a lot of preliminary study and stuff.'

'Tonight: you could drive to Bordeaux, or you could go up to the *Relais* at Sainte Foy, where our friends Olivier and Sibylle are.'

'Isn't she the one who came up this evening?' Pansy said.

'He must have got home by now.'

'She had sixty people coming to dinner. You won't believe this, but she thought he might be with you. That's why she came up. Do you know what I think they'd more than likely have done with me eventually, those two?'

'Turn left when you've got through the little village,' Rachel said.

'I think they'd have set me up. I don't know what else they would have wanted me for, really, do you?'

'And now go right. *Now*; down that little road. You've missed it. You've gone past the turning.'

'Sorr-ee. Why do you want to go to this village? I wonder what it'd be like. Being set up by someone. And two of them might have made it rather interesting.'

'For God's *sake!*'

'I thought that was reverse. I haven't used reverse. I hate reverse.'

'Look, pull up and over to the left and...'

'You can drive, if you want to. He did. He reversed without any trouble at all. Roger. Does he always jump people if he's alone with them?'

'I don't have any idea. Careful: there's something coming.'

'Oh. Shall I wait for it?'

'Yes, please.'

'I hope it isn't him. It might be *them*.'

'It's the police,' Rachel said.

'Well, we haven't done anything wrong, have we? That they know about?'

'*Bonsoir.*'

'*Bonsoir*,' Rachel said.

'*Vous n'êtes pas perdues?*'

'*On a raté le tournant, c'est tout.*'

'*Vous allez où exactement, madame?*'

179

Pansy looked at Rachel, who said, 'Sainte-Foy-le-Fort. *Eventuellement*. They think we're lost.'

The *gendarme* was looking into the back of the car as if he might find a topic of conversation. '*Vous n'avez pas vu une camionnette anglaise, blanche, assez grande?*'

'*Pas du tout.* They're looking for a white van.'

'Like theirs,' Pansy said.

'*Vous la connaissez?*'

'I'm not gettin' into it, orl right?' Rachel spoke to Pansy in what she hoped was an accent inaccessible to the *gendarme*, to whom she then said, '*Je connais très peu de camionnettes. Et pas du tout de cette description.*'

'*On a eu des cambriolages, parfois assez spectaculaires, dans le coin.*'

'*Je sais*,' Rachel said. 'He says they've had quite a lot of spectacular burglaries in the region.'

'I'm not surprised,' Pansy said, 'with those two on the loose! Aren't you going to say anything?'

Rachel shook her head. 'And nor are you, are you, Pan?'

'*Vous êtes Anglaises, toutes les deux?*'

'*Nous sommes deux soeurs anglaises et ... voilà!*'

'*Bon. Vous êtes en vacances peut-être?*'

'*Si on veut*,' Rachel said.

When the police car had driven on and round a bend in the road, Pansy said, 'Oh, I do rather wish that had been a close one, don't you?'

'If you'd done much more gabbing, it might well have been.'

'When there's nothing to feel guilty about, one feels such a fraud at the same time. Which is quite nice too.'

'What a fool!' Rachel said. 'What a fool!'

'Oh look at that,' Pansy said. 'It worked! I reversed. You did say left, didn't you?'

'I said right, and I still do. You know why he's tipped them off, don't you?'

'How do we know it was Rodge? Why?'

'Because now he's going to have to sell the house. Because it means he can't stay there, even if they get caught, and convicted. They'll come and find him eventually. He must know that.'

'Perhaps that's what he wants to have happen.'

'They'll kill him,' Rachel said. 'They're perfectly capable of it, if you ask me.'

'You're not sure. Is it all his then, is it, the house?'

'It's half his and half mine.'

'Then he can't sell it, can he?'

'He can make me let him. If I go back. Perhaps that's it. Now I'll have to. That probably *is* it.'

'You'll have to go back, or have to let him?'

'I wouldn't put it past him to have told the police about us as well as about those two.'

'Unfortunately, what is there to tell? They didn't exactly do anything, did they? You're a jolly good liar, Raitch, I must say, because you did lie, didn't you, about where you wanted to go? And in French.'

'You go on down here quite a long way, only be careful because it's very bendy.'

Pansy said, 'It's none of my business, of course, but where *are* you thinking of going exactly?'

'It's where someone lives,' Rachel said.

'Ye-es.'

'A man I met.'

'Often?'

'Today,' Rachel said. 'It's the one I'm supposed to be doing this article about. This morning. Heavens!'

'Is he expecting you? I mean, is this something you've fixed?'

'Not in the least,' Rachel said. 'Not in the slightest.'

'Fine. On we go, in that case. Did you ever meet Kosta at all?'

'I certainly feel as if I have.'

'He isn't all that Greek really.'

'Does it matter?'

'In the crinkly-hair, olive-skinned sense. He's not like that at all. Which is quite an advantage, because I'm not all that up for hair all over people, are you?'

'I've not given it much thought.'

'I have. Tons. His grandfather was some kind of a German. One of his grandfathers, and that's where most of the money comes from. Which is why he's so good-looking. Of course he is a *bit* of a Greek, but he doesn't talk it or anything, at least not when I've been around.'

'I thought you'd decided that you were going back to Brice.'

181

'Oh, I have,' Pansy said. 'I definitely have. That's what made me think about Kosta.'

12

I had one soggy suitcase and my portable Olivetti with the defective 'h'. I had put enough things in the suitcase to convince myself that I was serious about leaving, but since I knew that, without a car, I might have to lug it for considerable distances, I omitted several pairs of shoes and my more improbable clothes, not to mention my three-speed hair-dryer and all of my make-up. There were, no doubt, several explanations for what I had done, each one contradicting another, but like an inexpert thief I grabbed whatever was most easily accessible and left the rest. I now recognised that I had also left myself with good reason for returning. I suppose theft must be quite like shopping: there is always another time.

When Pansy stopped the car by the war memorial in the post-war village of Château St Martial, I was surprised to realise that it was no later than eight-fifteen. There were lights in the windows of several houses and I was able to obtain directions from a woman who ran the characterless café and petrol station. My English accent convinced her that I was the niece of Monsieur Cator.

Pansy was looking at her watch, like a taxi-driver who has promised to be home at a certain hour, but she drove on through the ruined village and past the burnt-out German tank, quite as if the antique desolation were no more remarkable than the new stucco houses which carried the name of the same community.

When we reached the track which led down to Lionel's cottage, I took pity on Pansy and suggested that she leave me there. I watched as she turned the car, with some difficulty, in the dark road and, with regret and relief, I waved her on her way to Ste-Foy-le-Fort.

The thought that she might miss the road was a petty comfort as I stumbled down the track towards the cottage which I had been promised was there. The bulging moon was hazed by low clouds and the branches of the woods. My behaviour seemed more peculiar to me, once I was on my own; it had been a performance which, without its audience, became unduly melodramatic. I did not wish that I was still at *Les Noyers Tordus*, but I could have wished that I had stayed in Pansy's company. She reminded me keenly of the England which I missed so little.

Did I really want to see Lionel Cator? Would he be anything but sarcastically hospitable? He was an old man; he might already be asleep. Even if it came as some kind of pleasant surprise, my arrival would be likely to afford him an opportunity to display how little he needed or wanted me. I could not imagine that he would confess to being flattered. The prospect of having to make room for a homeless woman was more likely to make him grumblingly courteous and patronising.

It was both an anti-climax and a relief to discover that the cottage was in darkness and, as I soon realised, empty. When I tried the door, it opened. I immediately felt myself to be smiling. The cottage was an unbaited trap; its unlocked door made a fool of whoever might have in mind to rob it or to surprise its owner. Even in his absence, Lionel Cator had the first laugh: an intruder, whoever it might be, was denied the pleasure of achievement.

I found myself in a dark, dank cottage without electric light. I frowned my way in the gloom, grateful for the vague light which came through the uncurtained windows. There was a box of matches in the grate. I hesitated before I tried to light the fire, which had already been lit once and lacked kindling. Then I spotted the gas-ring and used its blue glimmer to find more fuel and, in due course, a paraffin lamp.

I was disappointed and relieved at Lionel's absence. I sought consolation in imagining how disconcerted he might be to discover that the fox's lair had become host to the rabbit he had surprised at the mill. As the evening became night, however, I began to feel like a child who had brought an insolent gift and, unable to deliver it at once, became increasingly apprehensive of its suitability.

I had been nervous at first; every mild sound in the landscape could have been a slyly approaching footstep. By midnight, however, I was more inclined to fear that the fox was no longer using his burrow and, by dropping a trail which proved cold, had encouraged me to make a fool of myself. I sat on the bed and put the Olivetti on the packing case which Cator used as a table and set about writing my article. Bugger him!

ii

'Lionel Cator is a man of mystery. It is a mystery which this seventy-five-year-old recluse is not above wrapping in the enigma of eccentric behaviour and cryptic motives. It is not easy to track him in the recesses of the Périgordine countryside where he has lived, off and on, underground and, less often, above it, ever since he was dropped into France as a young British agent in 1943, but I finally found him in the territory which he has never abandoned for very long and in which he still has a heroic reputation, of a slightly dubious kind.

'I tracked him down principally in order to discover his reaction to the death of Yvonne Langon, GC, the heroine to whom he was married in the exhilarating days following the Liberation of occupied France. Following Churchill's famous instructions to "set Europe ablaze", Cator was – as he puts it – parachuted into the enemy-occupied Dordogne "armed to the teeth with a box of matches". In suggesting that he had to "make it up as he went along", the ex-agent exaggerates somewhat (and teases a great deal). At the age of twenty-three, he was, in fact, a captain in charge of a sophisticated operation in which arms and equipment were dropped to the Maquis under his command.

'I came across the still lithe and solitary Cator – despite the local ignorance of where exactly he lives – in a mill where a man suspected of betraying a section of the Resistance died of strychnine poisoning, well after the end of the war. It is typical of the man who is still known as "*Le Renard*" (the fox) that he was not quick to deny rumours alleging that the traitor was condemned by a secret tribunal, presided over by the fox himself. Local society is divided between those for whom he is something of "*Robin des Bois*" (Robin Hood) and those who regard him as a troublemaking psychopath who has refused to let bygones be bygones.

'When I asked him about Yvonne Langon, Cator's face broke into creases which implied both happy and unhappy memories. He and Yvonne loved each other when they were both young.

185

Love and courage and fear were all ingredients of an adventure which became a romantic legend, despite its dangers and its horrors. Yvonne was captured and tortured by the Milice, the Vichy Gestapo, before she was rescued in a daring hold-up by Cator and his men.

'Yvonne's and Lionel's romance was clouded by the death – a week before D-day – of Luis Leclerc, a mythical figure whose origins it is not easy to discover. He had fought in the Spanish Civil War and was replaced, on the orders of Colonel Gervase "Bisto" Bristowe, as commander of the "*Réseau*" (network) Victor by Lionel Cator.

'Even today Cator insists that Loulou, as they called him, was the bravest man he ever knew, and he told me that he and Yvonne might never have become close if it had not been for Leclerc's capture and, soon after it, his death.

'The marriage of Yvonne and Cator did not outlast the war by many years. Yvonne, of whom he still speaks with admiration, was eager to return to the "ordinary life" which still has small charm for Lionel Cator. "Reality," he told me, "had one meaning for Yvonne and another for me. We loved each other at a time when our realities seemed to be the same, but something happened at a given point and things were, as they say, never the same again. They rarely are," he added, with characteristic cynicism.

'What *exactly* it was that happened, he was not prepared to tell me. He is, in truth, prepared to tell outsiders very little, and often less than that. He lives in a small cottage, with an earth floor, on the estate owned by a man whose large *château* was mysteriously destroyed by fire but who, it seems, allowed Lionel Cator free use of the cottage where, among his books and his memories, he continues to live – at least during the time that he spends, so to speak, above ground.

'Yvonne Langon has left a deep scar on Cator. She reminded him of heroic days – of successes and of failures. The greatest failure was the death of Luis Leclerc, but there has to be more. Cator never returned to London, was never given a British decoration, and receives no British pension. It seems that there is some secret charge – or animus – against him, though it cannot be due to any lack of commitment to a cause which, even in old age, he is suspected of continuing, in his own way.

'Of his love for Yvonne Langon, he will say only, "Love is one thing among many, and it comes and goes, I'm afraid." His ex-wife – but not wholly ex-love – died a heroine, but a tragic one. Her second marriage, to the aristocratic Baron de Castillonès, who had not been in the Resistance, alienated her from wartime comrades. She had to be "dried out" several times after episodes of alcoholism and, although her courage in the brave days of the Occupation was never in doubt, her recent willingness to be associated with dubious causes excited vigorous comment. Two years ago, she signed an appeal for the reinstatement of a "revisionist" university professor who cast doubt on the guilt of the Vichy authorities in the deportation, and subsequent death, of French Jews, some of them from the region in which *Réseau* Victor operated.

'The marriage of Yvonne Langon and Lionel Cator was, perhaps, as doomed as it was romantic. It depended on the dangers which they faced together and the passions which such comradeship, quite as much as physical desire, can create. Its decline and failure coincided with the realisation that the post-war world was no epic poem. For most people, prosaic post-war realities are more insistent. The painful death of Yvonne Langon closes a chapter in the history of the war, but it cannot kill a myth.'

iii

I had no conviction that Mike Lea would want to print what I had written. The style seemed insufficiently caustic. I wrote with energy and even excitement, but I suspected that I was writing – I hardly knew why – for the spike. I sat uneasily on Lionel's bed and swore each time the 'h' on the Olivetti did its little leap and left only a tiny croquet hoop on the page. The petty disfigurement mocked my professional affectations and reminded me that I was rusty and ill-equipped. I wrote in a silence which the pecking of the typewriter keys did too little to breach. My ears were tuned for any sound which might allow me to regard the article as finished; its writing was an exercise in patience: I was a penny-a-lining Penelope, busking until the master's return.

I typed and I typed and I flicked the 'h' back into the bank of keys with increasing impatience, as if the machine ought to be capable of learning from its mistakes. I tried to sharpen the piece, through Mike Lea's borrowed eyes. I could imagine how he and Roley would scan my copy for signs of rust or softness. Should I hint that Cator was inhibited by his public school background or even, as he suggested, that he had been 'in love' with Luis Leclerc more than with Yvonne? Had I missed some evidence that Lionel had been guilty of a dereliction of duty which made it unwise for him to return to the UK? What kind of experience would lead a man to use the dated vocabulary and jerky diction which seemed designed to intimidate the curious? It made me think of my father; Mickey too had a way of hinting at what he was not prepared to tell. His kindness had that tinge of condescension which made any disclosure of his true feelings, or actions, double as their camouflage. Was he a weakling trying to persuade me that he was a scoundrel, or *vice versa*? And what about Lionel Cator?

I was tired. I told myself that I must not fall asleep, but that was the last defence of a lost cause. The moon had disappeared and the darkness thickened against the windows. The fire was an ashen husk; I had used the last of the available wood. Keeping my feet on the floor, between the bed and the packing case, I toppled to my right and put my elbows over my ears for a muffler and told myself that I was only pretending to be asleep.

Did I hear the approach of the Harley-Davidson or did I dub it, in angry retrospect, onto the dream which I threw off, like a skimpy blanket, in order to blink at the pink room? Lionel Cator was standing, in what looked like fishing clothes, frowning at my manuscript, which he was holding at arm's length. I was cold and ashamed.

'Morning,' he said. 'Been here long?'

'A few hours.'

'Cold?'

'I'm fine,' I said.

'Use this to light the fire, shall we?'

'Up to you,' I said.

'Too old for fiction, me. Don't mind my looking at it, do you? Sequel to *Ivanhoe*, is it? Ladies' night at the Crusades!'

'Help yourself.'

'Rarely find anyone else does. Know where I've been?'

'Of course not.'

'Why didn't you get into bed? A lot warmer that way.'

'I didn't really mean to sleep,' I said.

188

'Chucked you out, has he?'

'You must be tired yourself.'

'I've only been to the South of France.'

'Of course.'

'Don't you believe me? You don't believe me.' He walked out of the cottage, still holding my pages, and kicked the door to behind him. His crash-helmet was on top of the walking sticks. There was a canvas bag on the floor beside it. He came back holding a set of logs against his chest. My pages were between his lips. He had used his knee to push the door open and hopped into the room, let the logs thump onto the ground by the fireplace and took the pages in his hand. 'Could've done that yourself.'

'I didn't know where anything was.'

'Knew where this was, though, did you? The cottage. Got our spies, have we?'

'You told me. I asked for directions in the village.'

'And got a civil answer? They must've hoped you had some bad news for me. *Were* bad new perhaps. Why have I been in the South of France? Any ideas? Any rumours?'

'What do you mean the South of France?'

'Place called L'Escalet. Brief visit. Went to kill someone.'

'And did you?'

'Heads or tails, what do you say? Want some tea?'

'That would be nice.'

'Staying long? I didn't get your card.'

'I don't honestly know.'

'Forget honesty. Anything you do know at all?'

'I've left my husband.'

'Nothing to do with me, I hope. I didn't though. Kill anyone.'

'Good,' I said.

'Disapprove of death, do you, Rachel? In all its forms or just the ones that leave a mess on the floor? Less important than you think, death. And easier forgotten, in many cases, than a sore lip. All right if I use this for kindling then?'

'I'd probably sooner you didn't, as you very well know.'

'Good to see you've got *some* preferences. Not much of a Pauline myself in most respects, but I do share the apostle's distaste for Laodiceans. It was Laodice, wasn't it? Where they blew neither hot nor cold? Father would know, but luckily he's unable to be with us here tonight. He's in Abraham's bosom. Funny spot.'

189

'You've seriously driven all the way to and from the South of France since I last saw you?'

'You've pressed button "A", caller! The message has got through. Grinning like an ape some of the time. Caught myself at it. Call of the wild. Be that as it may, shagged to the wide, I was looking forward to my bed.'

'It's yours.'

'It damned well is that; it damned well is.'

'You can burn it, if you want,' I said. 'I don't suppose they'll print it.'

'Pack of lies,' Cator said, 'so they more than likely will.'

'You didn't tell me the truth, is that it?'

'Can't, dear,' Cator said, 'wouldn't know it if I saw it. Morning, Rachel Stannard. Cheer up, for *Christ's sake*. Failure of a mission; *I'm* allowed to be a bit blue, but you ... you're supposed to tell me that it doesn't matter. You don't know whether to believe me, that it? Afraid I've only been into Cahors for a glass? I've been to the South of bloody France to kill a man and ... I need a shave. No one's been here, have they? No company, no messages? Nil return to be rendered, Rachel. Well?'

'Nothing's happened since I've been here.'

'Common experience of yours, that, is it?'

'Do you want me to cook you something?'

'It'll have to be something better than this concoction. There's scrambled and scrambled, Rachel Stannard, and there's bad and there's worse. You know who was here before you?'

'Quite a few people, I imagine.'

'Yesterday. My daughter, she said she was. Who do you think you are?'

'I saw her, didn't I?' I said. 'I did. I saw her. She was driving a black Saab. She was up at Sainte-Foy-le-Fort. She looks like you.'

'That's her mother, not me. Do you want some eggs? I always have eggs. They're bad for you. What isn't?'

'I'm all right,' I said.

'What makes you think she was my daughter?'

'She looks ... she's got ...'

'My tits, has she?'

'She looks *like* you. Not her face, her ... character, her bearing. She looks like someone who ... wants something to happen.'

'And what do I want to happen?'

'I wish I knew.'

'Do you really? Your idle curiosity frequently remarked on, was it, by your headmistress? *Bloody* idle if this garbage is anything to go by. I don't know what she wants to happen, and I don't know she does. Look at this.' An egg in each hand, he strode across the floor. He laid the eggs on the ground and unzipped the canvas bag. 'Look at this bloody nonsense and then write home about it, if you've got the ink and the inclination.'

He pulled the sten gun out of the bag and reached in for a clip of ammunition. He banged the clip into the gun with the flat of his hand and stood up with his legs braced. He then leaned back and winced, like someone trying to open a can of beer. 'Bloody damned thing, to be honest. About as reliable as Tuesday week.' With an air of contempt, he pulled the trigger and bullets rattled on the stonework above my head.

'Good God,' he said. 'Look at that.'

The noise of the bullets seemed to go on after he had lowered the weapon. Perhaps they went on ricocheting from the hard wall. Fear, or amazement, prolonged the moment. It seemed that I could actually see the bullets spitting out of the black tube which Lionel Cator was holding and nattering against the stone. The subsequent silence was loud with what had happened.

'Bugger me,' Lionel Cator said, 'with a rich assortment of knobbly implements. Are you all right?'

'It didn't work, I assume. When you were there.'

'Assumption correct. Galling, that. Bloody things. Always were unreliable. Sorry about that. Not meant to happen, Rachel Stannard; meant to be a demonstration of what we were up against, British workmanship in all its capricious unreliability. Leading article to be written. Human error, its place in the divine comedy. I drove seven hours there, seven back.'

'And you didn't achieve *anything*?'

'Achieve. Saw an old chum. Dead man; lived down there for forty-something years, dead and buried. That's what she came to tell me. Daughter. Off you go, dad, as it were, and off I went. You know – except that you don't and can't – moment comes when feelings turn into something pretty well as dull as duties, and as dusty. Tally-ho no longer part of the vocab, Rachel, if the truth be known. It's not only old sodjers what fade away, it's also old appetites and allied trades. You can even forget how to do desire.

Told you: haven't seen a naked woman in eleven years. Not a boast, not a lament; *constatation*. What's that in English? Found his son down there, which rather put me off my stroke. Fact of life. Your friend from the *Relais*, Olivier with the flying machine.'

'Got it,' I said. 'That explains ... something that happened.'

'Does it so? Good to have something cleared up. Courtesy call on his dear old dad, if you don't look too closely.'

'And he stopped you...?'

'*Pas de* two; buggered off. Left the world to darkness and to dad. So what did? Stop me. Tact? Cowardice? Better things to do? Jammed bloody sten. The thing about the world, Rachel, is that it's sick of reasons, sick of motives, sick of the truth in any form. Truth itself's an impostor; fabrication, dear, a suit of clothes put on in a hurry or made-to-measure. I don't know why he went there, your friend, do you? Does he? Why did Sabine want him to know his dad was alive? Kindness of her heart, d'ja'spose?'

'Your daughter.'

'As she reports herself. There's a nice one for your article: heroine waits till she's pregnant, then makes alternative arrangements. She was probably shagging the noble Baron before she upped sticks, so whose daughter *is* the lovely lady in leather? Shall we ever know? Should we care? Science could tell; science won't be asked. Could be his, could be mine, could be ... well, yes, unlikely to be sister Annie's, but there might well be other candidates. What matters today? Not yesterday, we can be sure of that.'

'You never went to Oxford after the war, did you?'

'Paid a brief visit. The part for the whole, dear; happens more and more as time presses. Did I lie? I deceived. More fun; only fun that lasts. Keeps you company, deception, gives your day its belt and braces. Are you beginning to rumble me, do you suppose?'

'You knew damned well that gun was going to go off.'

'There we have it, Rachel, in all its beauty, all the beauty life is likely to supply. The proof that the truth is a dubious article, and a worse pudding, proving nowt. Because did I? Nope! Stack of Bibles, if to hand, would not cause my tongue to falter: hand smack on top; no hesitation, swear to God. Who He? Another question. Think I wanted to give you a fright more than I wanted to deal with unfinished business *là-bas*? Reasonable theory, but what's that got to do with the facts? Never know, can't know; life is a metaphysical category of being. Appeal to you, that, does it?

192

Time meaningless; see you next Tuesday? Ready when you aren't! Your friend Mr O. disappeared into the night, went to have a look at the condemned man, elected not to hang about for the execution. Went thataway, but don't ask me where that is. Left me alone with the subject. Know what the French call a condemned man, when he's due for the chop?'

'You're going to tell me.'

'*L'intéressé*. The interested one.'

'I gathered.'

'Clever Rachel. Resent my help, do you? Sooner be left to your own devices, wouldja? Being what exactly? What's your *projet*, now that hubby's no longer on the top deck?'

'I haven't truly the least idea.'

'Sounds ambitious. My biographer, how about that? Nil return with a vengeance, that. I tried myself at one point. Raining like buggery in our incomparable *paysage*, so I thought: write it down, make a small fortune, embarrass the national conscience, stir the old memory, salt and pepper to taste. Couldn't do it, dear. Wouldn't come. Rubbed and rubbed. Aladdin with very sore hampton; know the feeling now. He looked at me just the way I would've looked at him. Old Lévy.'

Lionel sat down on the bed and rubbed his hands in what was left of his hair. It stood up as if electrified. He bent and pushed the boots off his ankles and wiggled his toes. 'Got used to the stink at boarding school. Two, three weeks in the same pair sometimes. Education for life. He calls himself Lévy. Converted, like one of your cottages.'

'Why did you say you were circumcised?'

'Slipped out, that, did it, dear? You know what old fogies are like, tempted to expose themselves to selected targets. Why did I tell you that?'

'Is it true?'

'We can always have a look. Yes, it's true. You know what I dream about, Rachel Stannard, sometimes? School. School.'

'A lot of people keep taking exams all their lives, don't they? I do sometimes.'

'Bugger exams. Killing the father. I can never do it. Did it in reality, killed; can't do it in the imagination. Nothing you can't do in reality; almost nothing you can when you're dreaming. Sometimes you *have* done it, but rarely do it. Drive a lot of cars and the old Harley, but … Ever had sex in a dream? Can't say I have.'

'Why didn't they give you a medal? The British. What happened, Lionel?'

'Lévy. He said he was Alphonse Lévy. So what did *he* dream about? What's he dreaming about now? Olivier's father, dear. He knows it's not true; he doesn't even quite deny that it's not true, but he still says that that's who he is. England's in much the same case, wouldn't you agree? *Mutatis mutandis*; practice to be observed at all times.'

'I'm not going to write about this, if you tell me about it.'

'Then why the hell would I want to tell you? Put me down for some kind of a saint, have you?'

'Far from it.'

'Paradox of sainthood that, isn't it? Ask Batzan. Further you go, the nearer you get. What's a good man? The kind that won't be missed. Aristides. I half believed him, Rachel Stannard, that was the funny part. And so did my artillery. They never did work when you wanted them to, sten guns, famous for it. Made by trades unionists with a grievance, I shouldn't wonder. Serve 'em right department.'

'You should get some sleep,' I said.

'Jimjams, my mother used to call them. God, I was glad to go to war! Do I smell? Can't tell, to be honest.'

'Not that I've noticed.'

'Not even foxy? Sad, that. You know the funny thing? You don't know the funny thing. You went to war, but you weren't really there, in your heart. Jimjams; all part of the same thing. Was it a defence, as they say? More than like. But war is a form of abroad, you know; the tourists, when they come here, they think they're here, but are they? What does it mean when things happen to them, falling in love, falling off cliffs? Nothing real, does it? And that's what Europe is; Europe, Europe, Europe, because what is it? Who cares? In a nut shell. Cf. pig's arse. I kept thinking, dear, that I was getting close to the real thing. Might be scared, but it was bound to be worth it; end of the rainbow, dear. Crock of gold, crock of shit; not much in it. Are you going to sit there all night and look at me?'

'There isn't much of the night left,' I said.

'Bar of choc, dear. Nibble, nibble, nibble. Life's the same; hardly

194

begun, munch a few squares and *nox perpetua dormienda est*; elision at the end brings it sooner even than you think. Syllables like small change. Follow me? As a man grows shorter! I didn't invite it. Up to you. There's a blanket in the shelf, stuffed in a bag, stole it from the SNCF. Got to keep your hand in. Liberation came long before the end, dear; liberation was a bit of a fraud, half-time whistle, you thought, and they were all shaking hands, some of them, and it was all supposed to be over, getting ready to line their pockets, the ones that weren't lined already.'

'You're justifying something,' I said. 'What is it?'

'Oh no, I'm not; oh yes, I am. There you have it. The panto villain. All right, think about this possibility: you haven't any idea what really happened, who I really am.'

'I've already thought about that. A lot. What you were doing when, and more or less why.'

'Good girl. Top girl. Care to offer a *résumé*, or haven't you got that far yet?'

'What happened at the *Relais St Jacques* in July 1944?'

'Finger right on it. That's the spot, doctor. Want to see me without my clothes on? Is that a sight you want to see? Because that's what it comes to, Rachel Stannard. Visions of loveliness, and visions of another kind. Man's an animal fights to get 'em off, fights to keep 'em on. Never knows one thing from another, hence reason, with all its departments. Early closing Wednesday. *Caveats* a speciality, except that they never take care of nuffin'.'

He covered his nakedness with a heavy pair of faded flannel pyjamas with broad olive-coloured stripes and got into the bed and lay down with his hands behind his head, like a child who has been promised a story and is determined to hear it, however tired he may be.

'You did something that London told you not to do. And it led to something happening which ... annoyed them quite a bit.'

'Annoyance not really in it, not loggable, annoyance.'

'And it also had some effect on you and Yvonne.'

'On me,' he said.

'And not her.'

'Seven hours there, seven hours back and nothing done. I made him kneel on the floor and you know what he said, when he thought I was going to make noisy holes in him? Warned me neighbours might not like it. Smiled at me and, by Christ, I hated the little shit and I also – shouldn't say this – I also felt we were both doing this for someone else, third party, which we both of us felt the same about. Worse. There's worse. I'm sorry: I interrupted you.'

I shook my head and he grinned at me with an uneven grin, one side of which was a sneer.

'He said he was Alphonse Lévy. He knew he wasn't; *I* knew he wasn't, and yet somehow – that old stand-by! – somehow he still was and, this is the nasty bit, this is the bit between your teeth, when I was telling myself to pull the bloody trigger, when I was trying to give myself the old rooty-toot, it went through my head, like a fast train, bloody little Jew. I was my bloody father at that moment, Rachel Stannard. I needed to be to pull the trigger. I pulled it, thinking what a grisly little Yid he was, Félix Argote, and what are you going to tell your readers now? You know the old one, you can think anything you like, but don't, don't, don't think of a big black cat. In which case, can't think of anything else. QED, and thank you very much. Goes a bit further back than that though, if truth be told. Why do people persecute people, ever thought about it? Why do children?'

'They learn from their parents, don't they?'

'Keen to answer, Rachel Stannard, *bonne élève*, the girl. Do it because it's immensely enjoyable. Doesn't have to cost a penny. Sociable too. I used to get pushed through that green baize door and I'd be trembling, and then I'd remember: there's always Cohen. And so there always was. Nice enough chap, bright, quite spo-ey, as we used to say, and we'd give him regular hell, which is what he was designed for. Why the Rev. Papa had let him in, that and the fees, which were not to be sneezed at. Bit of a thing about the Chosen, my sainted pop; couldn't say Jew without a curl of the paternal lip; even Jesus had a touch of the four-by-two, unfortunately. Kick against the pricks? Would've if he could've, but not in curriculum. So there it was. Members of the family we never met, never spoken about; can't argue, can't approve. Hence upper lips, stiffness whereof. I'm going back, of course.'

'You should go to sleep,' I said.

'What about you?' Lionel Cator said.

'I've already slept. A bit. What did he say when you pulled the trigger?'

'And nothing happened? He looked at me. Understood my posish. Embarrassing for me, that.'

'What did you say?'

'All right! I said, "We seem to be out of luck," and he said, "Me or you?" I suppose that third person, the one I felt was there in the room with us, must've been my sainted *pater*, now I come to think about it. Happy to see me fail? I dunno. Know what he said next, Félix? He said, "*Vous permettez?*" Wanted to have a look at the gun. Bit of a *bricoleur*, apparently. Damn near let him; that's how far I was from doing it. He looked at me with his yellow eyes and then he said, "*Ne t'en fais pas – c'est pas vraiment la peine de tuer les morts*". Don't worry, it's not really worth the trouble of killing dead people. Oh, you understand. *Félicitations*. Also, as previously stated, risk of disturbing neighbours.'

'Wouldn't you have got caught, if it had ... worked?'

'Prob'ly. So?'

'You wouldn't have minded.'

'Proverbial ungiven toss, dear. At my age? Didn't know you were waiting for me, of course. There is perhaps a destiny that shapes our ends. I would put that in the fat chance department, but there we are. Amusing thought, so-called hero on trial for murder of dead man who supposedly shopped a few *Youpins* at out of season prices. Rich possibilities, e.g. sub-poena Bristowe G., Colonel retired. Never woulda 'appened, dear, is my bet. Never will is now a certainty. Didn't have the strength to strangle the little shit, did I? Kitchen knives too messy; didn't appeal. Put my gear in my old kit-bag and prepared to re-embus, two-three. Old boy said I could stay, but knew I wouldn't. "*Un petit café avant de partir?*" Some dead men tell their bloody tales all right. Know what, Rachel Stannard? I almost felt, well, *fond* of the little bastard. The clown has his place, his everlasting bloody place. I thought, you bloody little *Jew*; you bloody little Jew, I thought! You bloody are what you say you are. Didn't have the coffee though; joke's a joke, but enough is also enough. *Pari passu, nesspah?* Besides...'

'What exactly happened up there, Lionel?'

'*Un amour peut en cacher un autre,*' Lionel Cator said. 'But you know a funny thing, doncher, one of many, many? Masculine in the singular, *amour* is, and feminine in the plural. More than one and they go into a different category. Nothing in English like that, is there? The one and the many. I'm going to sleep, Rachel Stannard, and if you're still here when I wake up, I'll tell you a story that'll more than like make you bugger off and wish you'd never come here. If you're not still here, I'll put you down for a sensible female, better things to do.'

'I'll be here,' I said.

13

Olivier walked a longer way back to the Café des Sports than he had taken when he followed the old man to his house. The ochrous light of the street lamps gave the quiet hamlet an air of shadowless menace. There were lights in a few windows, but there were more closed brown shutters. When Olivier reached the café, it was still open. The last clients were waving to the *patronne*, with perfunctory cordiality, and left their empty glasses and walked past Olivier towards wherever they were going.

The *patronne* came and collected the glasses and went back into the café and shut the door. When she bent down to close the lock on the floor, her breasts tumbled forward in her silk blouse. She wore high heels and her feet popped out of them at the back as she leant her weight on the low bolts. She stood up and seemed unaware of Olivier as he watched her from the corner of the deserted *boules* pitch.

He had the keys to the hired Renault in his hand and then he was walking across the concrete to the café. He looked through the glass to see whether the *patronne* had a man to help her close the place up. She seemed to be alone. He tapped on the glass with his keys, quite quietly, as if it were something he did regularly. The *patronne* looked up, unalarmed, and felt for some strands of hair at the back of her white neck as she came to the door. She refixed them behind one of two amber combs. She looked at Olivier through the glass and then she bent down once more and unbolted the door. He stood with his back to her as she did it, looking towards where he had come from. It seemed they were on time for each other.

She opened the door and said, '*Vous l'avez trouvé?*'

He said that, yes, he had found the man he was looking for and that he had finished his business with him, for better or for worse, and that he was looking for somewhere to spend the night. He said that the old man was his father, but that he could not stay with him. He never expected to see him again. The *patronne* showed no surprise and only as much interest as she thought he might like. He asked her if she was married and she said that she was; her husband was a sailor, a master mariner in fact, who was often away, who was almost always away. They had not married when they were young. She imagined, without rancour, that he had other women, perhaps other wives, certainly children. She turned out the lights in the café and cleared the till without any sign of suspecting that Olivier might be some kind of villain.

She told him that she did not rent rooms and that she had no spare bed made up. He said that he would gladly sleep on one of the glossy red *banquettes* in the darkened café, but she said that that was a bad – and visibly unwise – example. In any case, he would be woken by the early sun. She gestured to him and he went behind the bar and followed her through a beaded aperture up speckled, uncarpeted composition stairs to the floor above the café. She unlocked a door with thick glass panes in it and indicated for him to go past her into the sitting room which overlooked the *boules* pitches. The windows were on a level with the green cheese of the church bell. As Olivier watched, the municipal lights went out. He thought of his father and Lionel Cator. When he turned round, she was opening a lacquered cherry wood cabinet. She took small glasses and a bottle without a label from the mirrored interior.

Olivier sat down as though he were in the habit of these visits. She filled the glasses with *eau de vie* and held one out to him with bright fingernails all around the rim. It was an unprofessional gesture which mimicked an intimacy it did not promise.

The room was tight with fringed velvety furniture and impersonal mementoes from foreign places. Several rugs overlapped on the parquet; there were silver-capped glass bottles and other brightly coloured jars, perhaps from Venice, with glass stoppers. A glass-fronted sideboard contained dishes and more glasses. On top there was a fat round alarm clock, both cheap and antique, which seemed to be a reminder of harder times. Next to it, four silhouettes, in oval frames, two of females, two of aristocrats with impressive wigs, leaned against the wall below a gilded mirror with a pair of angels officiating at the top. Double glass doors, with lace curtains over them, took up almost the whole of the facing wall.

He asked her whether she had had a good day and she said that she had not. She sat in a plum-coloured armchair of a heavy design and let her high-heeled shoes dangle from her toes before she removed them and tucked her feet beside her as if she did not need them for the moment. She told him that the *eau de vie* was given to her by an *ancien client* who had retired, by coincidence, to Gassin. It was better than anything she served in the café.

He told her that his father, whom he had assumed to be dead without ever being convinced of it, had dominated his life, although he had been absent since he was a small boy. Now he had discovered that the hotel which he had promoted to its present one-star status, in the *Guide Michelin*, had been bought with tainted money. What could he and what should he do? He had a wife and he had a child and he was ashamed to think of speaking to them again. As for his wife (when he mentioned Sibylle's name, he might have been reminding the *patronne* of what she knew already), he felt as if his attraction for her – he said nothing of her attraction to him – had been acquired on the strength of what now seemed shameful to him. She bore no responsibility, in justice, for their having based their lives on what was, in effect, stolen property, but – and he wondered if the *patronne* could understand this – the knowledge that Sibylle had been impressed by what now discredited him seemed also to discredit their love. He had become a chef, he said, without *being* a chef, entirely. He had always felt the urge to be something else (he would have become a *pilote de ligne*, had his eyesight not been slightly irregular) and, although he was a man of competence, and perhaps a little more, he had always had the fear that he did not have the sentiments, or the invention, of a true chef. He had inherited a *métier* which now seemed to him as tainted as the property in which he practised it. Could she understand his feelings? She understood them with a nod.

Now his situation was ambiguous. If he did not return to Ste-Foy-le-Fort, what would become of him? He was over fifty years old; he could not start again, nor did he want to continue. If he went back and sold the *Relais St Jacques*, would he be purged of his father's taint? If he gave away the money from the sale, how could he face his wife and his son, Cédric, who already had the makings of an excellent *pâtissier*? Perhaps he should simply never go home. Perhaps he should 'die' as his father had, leaving the restaurant and the future to the innocent members of the family. His present feeling towards Sibylle was indefensible but undeniable: he wanted to punish her for what she had not done and for what he had not. He knew, of course, that her sin was negligible compared to his; as a young and beautiful girl, she had accepted a man of standing as first her employer, then her lover and now her husband. He saw her as a woman who, precisely because she had put her faith in him, was undeserving of respect. Neither fairness nor justice came into the equation; his sentiments were as they were. Could the *patronne* follow what he was saying? She could, without a word.

He said that he was taking up the time when she should be asleep and that he knew that she would have to be up early. She smiled at that and the light from the lamp shone on her sidelong shins. So: either he could fly home and make it his business to resume his *métier* without apparent change of style or enthusiasm or he could do something else, though he could not see what it might be. There was also the possibility of suicide, which would be easy to contrive, since he had a small aeroplane at Ste Maxime; he could fly into the sun, like Icarus. She took the allusion, but found it distasteful. Why not find a job elsewhere?

He knew that she did not mean with her. The café needed no chef and there was no possibility of running a successful restaurant in *Les Hameaux de l'Escalet* for more than two or three months in the year. Besides, her husband might not appreciate his presence. She shrugged at that. Olivier leaned back in his chair and tilted his chin to the ceiling. There was a chandelier with green glass petals and four milky 'trumpets', each containing a bulb. He said that he had taken poison but that it had not, unfortunately, killed him.

After thought, or at least after quite a long silence, she said that she did not share his scruples about the sources of money. He looked at her and smiled as if she had at last made a confession which gave them something in common. It did not diminish her, what she had as good as told him, but it made them square. He asked whether she had worked in Paris and she said that she had been for a time in Paris, in the area of the Madeleine, and then she was in Nice, thanks to the man whose *eau de vie* they were drinking. He had not been her only client, as he very well knew, but he had been the most regular and the most generous. Unfortunately, he had been diagnosed as having a cancer of the prostate, which had required an operation that rendered him impotent, as is normal in the present state of things; one had either to be impotent or to be dead. There might, she agreed, be an evolution in time, but for the moment that was the situation. It was when Etienne was no longer able to be her lover that she had got married. It was too late to have children by her husband, but she had had two from other people when she was young. Her husband would, in all probability, not have married her, had he not needed someone to take care of the café, which he had inherited, quite unexpectedly and when it was far from complete, from a younger brother who had been killed, while drunk, in an accident on the road. She had a small capital which, rightly or wrongly, she thought would be safe, and provide something for her old age, and her husband's, if invested in the café. One would see.

She spoke in a sombre but practical tone. She had neither great hopes nor any self-pity. She had become a prostitute when her father, who was an *agriculteur* in the Sarthe, had refused to allow her to become a hairdresser. He was a man who worked extremely hard, from five or six in the morning, according to the season, until dark, year in, year out, and for whom women were no better than the animals in his stables, and rather more trouble. She was incapable of hurting him by anything she said or did. She had seen her mother become a tearful and pitiful object at his hands and she despised her weakness more than she did the brutality which exploited it. She had no recipes for the world or for herself. She had bad *notes* at school and no hope of a profession. She regarded it as a blessing that she grew beautiful breasts and not bad legs and a face that knew how to smile, and how not to. She made no pretence to herself when she hitch-hiked to Paris that she would become anything but what she did. '*La prostitution*,' she told him, '*c'est ce qui nous distingue, heureusement, des bêtes.*'

On the way north, according to plan, she was depucelated by a couple of Italians, one of whom was quite a chic type and offered to introduce her to some people in Paris. She met them, but she did not want to be exploited; she could have stayed at home if that was what she wanted. She worked for a while as a *femme de ménage* until she picked up a man on her day off and made her first *passe*. He took her to a hotel and expected her to know all the things which she had not done with a man. She found she did. She had saved a little money by this time and rented a mansard room in a tall apartment block not far from the Place des Grands Augustins. It was a long climb to the top, but the clients did not mind following her up the stairs.

That was that, until she met Etienne. When Olivier asked how she tolerated the work, she said, '*J'avais mes habitudes, et j'observais un certain rythme saisonnier.*' She took regular holidays, though she found that she did not like to go abroad very much. Tunisia was all right.

He asked her whether she had found pleasure with her clients at all. She moved her head at that and the four bulbs of the chandelier flared in her wide black eyes. He looked along his body at her and she said that it happened from time to time because, after all, there were men who did things better when they paid for them. He smiled for the first time and said that he found that he drove cars which he had hired with more flair, less apprehension than his own, which he did not even like very much. '*Voilà,*' she said. She had also, of course, had some bad experiences, but she had never been so afraid of a man that she was powerless to deal with him. On the other hand, she did not open her door to everyone.

He asked her what sort of men she refused. It was, she told him, more a question of avoidance. Sometimes, out of boredom or bravado, she almost involved herself with men with whom she was unable to go further. On one occasion, for instance, when she had not yet met Etienne, who somewhat changed everything, she was in a bar when a number of men with Languedoc accents came in. For a minute or two she was filled with a kind of nostalgia which was mixed with disgust. She recognised with affectionate loathing the tones and styles of the men with whom her father went hunting during the season. The men had been at the *Salon d'Agriculture*, at the Porte de Clignancourt, and they were quite drunk and bold by the time they came into the bar. She had been deprived of her sense of what was prudent by the smell and sound of them and she thought, to begin with, that it would secure '*une certaine libération*' to go with one of them. However, the two men who accosted her, '*non sans une brutalité familière*', wanted to bargain for her services and she guessed (it was not difficult) that their pleasure – in each other – was being derived from the process of bargaining.

There was something so vicious about their manner that she was reluctant to turn her back on them; they reassured her, in every gesture, of the rightness of her decision to make her own life in the way she had. By consequence, she was almost lured into a folly. At the last moment, she made an excuse and escaped from the bar by a back way which the *patron* had shown her, on another occasion, in return for '*un service quelconque*'. A few days later, a prostitute was found with her throat cut in her room not far from the Place des Grands Augustins. When he asked what impact that had made on her, she thought for a moment and then she said that she felt that she had been a little bit clever. Just!

What about now, he asked? Did she ever take men upstairs these days? She said that she absolutely did not. It was not that she thought her husband would mind, still less that she imagined him to be faithful to her, although he was a man who knew how to make her laugh when he was around; it was more a matter of habits and rhythm, which was how she managed her life. She said, as if it followed naturally from what they had both said, that she would be glad to make love with him, but that he was under no obligation. She would not be offended if he preferred to sleep with her '*sans m'approcher*' or if he wanted to stay in his chair. He said that he would like to make love to her. He would like to make love without going into the bedroom, if that did not displease her.

She went to the window and let down the shutters by a strap which was set in the wall. She adjusted them after they had fallen all the way so that the room was not entirely sealed from the night. He removed his shoes and sat there comfortably as, without fuss and without false moves, neither hurrying nor delaying, she rearranged the two combs in her hair before she unzipped her skirt and pulled the green silk blouse out of the waistband and began to display herself to him with a mixture of appetite and pro-fessionalism which, in the delicacy of its expertise, he could take for subtlety, perhaps even for tenderness. He had catered for the weddings of old friends in something of the same attentive spirit.

Pansy talked to herself as she drove in the darkness. Patches of light and, once, the flames of a bonfire which had not yet died down, gave the countryside a nervous and unfathomable depth. She told herself that she could not be far from the high lights of Ste-Foy, to which Rachel had directed her, and yet she could find no easy way through the maze of lanes and tracks. The alien place-names promised people and houses hidden in all directions, behind the woods and valleys which her headlights deepened and then flattened as she leaned through the curves in the road. She drove and drove until, suddenly, she came to a crossroads where Ste-Foy-le-Fort was indicated two kilometres away.

Pansy parked next to the covered market and walked, without her suitcase, to the gate of the *Relais St Jacques*. The hotel lights were out, but a bulb was burning in the bar. Pansy tried the door without expecting it to open. It did not. She made a typical face and walked round the side of the building, where the plastic tables had their chairs canted against them. The leafless cherry trees cut the moon into portions. She had no reason to think that she would find anyone on the terrace overlooking the long fall to the river she could not see, but something in her appearance, which was also her character, made her believe that she would always get something she wanted; not being *terribly* disappointed was part of what she was.

A whitish light shone from where an open door to the kitchen made a short fence between the hotel and the black world beyond it. Pansy's eyes were able somehow to carry the light towards the edge of the terrace, although it was fainter there. A double metal railing, solidly supported on concrete stanchions, ran the length of the hotel terrace above the gorge. A woman was sitting on it, with her knees over the void, quite calmly, as if she were a spectator of some amateur sport. She was rocking very, very slightly on her haunches, in a way which made only the up-and-down paddle of her feet, in flat black slippers, visible to Pansy. The woman did not move her head and Pansy made no sound, but Sibylle's failure to look at the stranger was her acknowledgement of her. Pansy considered the other woman's profile against the moonlit sky and she smiled to herself, and at it.

Pansy said, 'Hullo.'

The other woman did not turn her head even then. The motion of her feet stopped and the tiniest crease of a smile broke the impassiveness of her profile.

'Am I too late?'

Then Sibylle did turn. She smiled with all her even teeth and the grey eyes were vivid with welcoming vacancy.

'*Pas du tout. Vous êtes tout à fait à l'heure.*'

'I'm afraid I'm awful at French. Non-existent at it really.'

'What 'as 'appened?'

'What 'as 'appened? Well. I don't know if you recognise me.'

'You are ze sister. Ze beautiful sister.'

'Thank you. She came back. Rachel. Only a few other things also happened after you'd been. Above averagely dramatic actually. Is he back at all? Your husband?'

Sibylle shook her head, vigorously, but as though it were something she had decided to be happy about.

'Have you heard anything?'

Sibylle gave the same vigorous shake of the head; she might have been grateful for the chance to do it again. 'Nuzzing.'

'You speak English very well.'

'Not at all.'

'The thing is, I know it's late, but do you happen to have a room at all? Am I interrupting you?'

'Interrupting?'

'Are you doing something?'

Sibylle swung a leg back over the fence so that she seemed to be riding it towards Pansy, who was, in fact, walking towards her. 'I was sinking,' she said.

'What were you sinking about?' Pansy said.

'Life and dess. Nuzzing important.'

'I need a room is the problem.'

'Not a problem,' Sibylle said. 'A room is not a problem anyway.'

'Because it's all falling apart up at, you know, my sister's.'

'What does zat mean?'

'She's gone off somewhere. My sister. And I didn't want to stay with, you know, him. So ... I came up here. On the off chance.'

Sibylle looked again at Pansy with the broad smile and amused eyes appropriate to a woman who had been interrupted while thinking about suicide. She led the way, with an exaggerated swing of the hips. She was wearing a grey, pleated skirt and the same cardigan, with the roses on it, in which she had driven to *Les Noyers Tordus*. She walked as she might have if Pansy had been a man. At the door of the bar, which she had to unlock, she glanced back, under her brows, at Pansy, who appreciated the complicity.

'How did the dinner go?'

'Ze dinner.'

'For sixty people, wasn't it?'

'Wizzout incident. The *sous-chef* was very 'appy.'

'So where is he, do you suppose? Your husband?'

Sibylle shrugged. The shrug asked Pansy what else a wife could expect of a man if she was beautiful and loyal and faithful and worked very hard. It asked for no sympathy but it broached a sisterhood which Pansy was quick to grant.

Sibylle said, 'Do you have a baggage?'

'In the car. I drove up.'

'Shall we get him?'

'Oh, I can do that.'

'You want to eat somesing?'

'I wouldn't mind a nibble, if there is anything.'

'I get you,' Sibylle said.

'Have you tried the police, presumably?'

'No one knows anysing,' Sibylle said. 'I find you somesing.'

When Pansy came back with the suitcase, Sibylle had brought bread and *pâté* and a bottle of *Château de Cèdre*. She reached over the top of the bar, swinging one leg balletically in the air, for paper napkins.

'What are you going to do?'

'I will wait, I suppose. I have a son nine years old.'

'You must've been very young when you had him.'

'It was a mistake. But, like they say, where would we be wizzout mistakes?'

'You're very beautiful,' Pansy said. 'You have amazing eyes and brilliant bones and a wonderful mouth and I don't know what he can be thinking about.'

'I am not important,' Sibylle said.

'Has he got other people?'

'I don't know. Per'aps. Women are not much to him. That is why he married me.'

'Aren't they grim?' Pansy said. 'They are seriously grim.'

'*Grim?*'

208

'Men are grim. Miserable. Pathetic. Um...'

'*Nuls*,' Sibylle said.

'Sounds about right,' Pansy said. 'Have you got people staying?'

'Some.'

'I got lost,' Pansy said, 'or I wouldn't have been so late.'

'Do you want to go to bed?' Sibylle poured more wine into their glasses.

'I wouldn't mind,' Pansy said. 'It's been a funny day. Do you dye it?'

'A bit, yes, I do. Do you?'

'Quite a bit. You're so beautiful. You're so ... *neat*. I love that. You look so ... wicked. Are you?'

'Wicked?'

'You don't look as if you would ever ... disapprove.'

'Disapprove.'

'Oh, I don't know. Not like what people do. Disapprove.'

'I do not like what people do. I do not like what 'e does.'

'I've expressed it badly. I'm sorry. You don't *like* it, but you aren't ...' Pansy gave a comic shrug in the face of Sibylle's tic of uncertainty. 'A prude.'

Sibylle considered the compliment and then the brightness of her eyes, and the bulge of her lips, admitted that she was unable to understand it. The two women leaned towards each other and then Sibylle stood up and collected the plates and the glasses and put them on the bar. 'Would you like somesing else?'

iii

When the women had left the house, Roger stayed for several minutes flopped along the banisters in the attitude of angry help-lessness which he had adopted while Rachel and Pansy were on their way out. Although he heard the engine start and its sound dwindle as Pansy drove down the hill, he held the pose until it became quite uncomfortable. Only when he had to move did his rage find new expression. He looked around for something to accuse, but nothing quite filled the bill of being both vulnerable and unimportant. He was tempted to use the usual excesses which he had seen on film, and on video, but to throw the telephone through the window might affect its performance. He found himself in a torment of frustration; he could not even get his tears to work. It was only after looking furiously for some gesture which would show somebody something, even though there was nobody to see it, that he went and called the police and informed them, anonymously, about the *camionnette blanche.*

He did not conceal his identity out of fear of Quigley and Goldstein. He simply did not want the police quizzing him for further details. His good humour was slightly restored (against his own desires) by the Périgordine accent which he put on when speaking to the *Gendarmerie* at Ste-Foy-le-Fort. It hardly mattered whether it convinced them, since there were so many foreigners in the region, but such amateur dramatics reminded him that life was full of fraudulent possibilities and that despair was out of order. Yet he was desperate. He wanted Rachel to come back so that he could spend some rage on her. As for Pansy, he had been a complete fool not to give her one when she was absolutely blatantly asking for it. In many ways, he thought, he was much too moral for his own good.

He sprawled in front of the TV, one hand just under the kneecap of his braced left leg, and began to work his way through the satellite stations. Tennis was being played in German in some bright blue stadium. One of the players, with his head in a tight kerchief, was whipping at the court in a series of angry air shots. Roger was immediately eager for his opponent to win, although he sympathised entirely with the man whose ball, as the replay proved, had been falsely called out. He hated the patience of the other player, who was wearing classical whites, in contrast to the piratical style of his aggrieved opponent. At the same time, Roger recognised the cunning of propriety, and its sadistic rectitude, and he thought of the savage courtesies with which he would, or would like to, greet Rachel's return.

While the players were sitting in their chairs, the one with a towel over his face (he managed to appear to be glaring *through* it at the same time), the other sipping a paper cup of some cordial he had brought in his own bottle and looking around, as he did so, like a regular guy, Roger pressed the button to see what was happening on some other stations. Mostly, people were talking, in a variety of languages, into microphones as big as ice-cream cones. Nearly all of them had large audiences, ranged in rows, who were easily excited to enthusiasm or indignation. Roger changed his attitude to the screen from time to time, but he did not move his hand from below his left knee. He might have been waiting for the trainer.

Why, really, had he called the police? He needed to express his spite, though it was not now directed, in any way, towards Quigley and Goldstein. If they came back up the hill, he would certainly not run for cover. He would actually quite welcome them, assuming they were willing to be in the least reasonable. It was Rachel's fault, and Pansy's, that he had had to be so radical. The women had pushed him into defending them instead of looking after himself, which was typical in his experience. They had driven him into a corner, in order to defend them, and their interests, and then they had turned on him. If Quigley and Goldstein really had been involved in robbing the Schlickies, they must be looking for somewhere to offload the stuff. He listened, with waning hope, for the sound of their rumble.

When he returned to the tennis, they were just beginning the third set. The angry player was serving one ace after another, and each seemed to make him angrier than the one before. Winning was the last straw. After he had served a fourth ace, he flipped the spare ball over his shoulder towards the linesman who had offended him, but when he sat in his chair, he did not cover his face with a towel; he looked around energetically, as if he had just got into the office, and pointed out things that needed to be done for him.

Roger switched to another channel where, by chance, a woman – in a long black skirt and top – was leaning against a curve of ornate banisters in a spacious *château*, of a kind that might have interested the Greshams, while a figure in a dinner jacket was fondling her lips with long, gloved fingers. Another woman, blonde and very young and completely naked, came through some french doors, with dazzling light behind them. When she saw the other couple, she looked at them with generous envy and slowly bent her knees, as if in some compulsory gymnastic figure, until her legs were wide apart and the pale fuzz between them shone in the light from the bright window.

The woman who was leaning against the banisters lolled back and took the glove of her partner between her teeth and so helped her to ease it from her hand (it was now obvious, as if it had always been obvious, that it was another woman). The woman in the dinner jacket pushed down the top of the other woman's black outfit and revealed her breasts, which she began to caress with infinite slowness, watched by the naked blonde whose girlish innocence looked somehow *relieved* by the scene before her. The desire of the woman in the dinner jacket was cruelly controlled; she was more *thoughtful* than Roger could ever imagine being. She was positively instructive, in fact. She had time to look promisingly at the naked girl and her mastery of the scene was the same as her pleasure in the pleasure she seemed to be giving.

Roger sat round to watch more thoroughly. The woman whose breasts were being caressed looked so longingly, so pleadingly at the other that it was a relief when, with scrupulous slowness, and the kindest possible cruelty, she was offered the curled tip of the other's tongue. It was in the character of the clothed figure that it commanded in two places at the same time; she was easily able, as she kissed, to be looking attentively at the naked girl, whose offer of herself was as gauche as it was beautiful, while also displacing the long black skirt to reveal the slim legs and pouting purse of the woman who was her victim and her accomplice.

14

Lionel was sitting on the floor next to the crate on which I had written my article, one knee almost to his chin. I must have fallen asleep in the small quarter of the bed where I had curled up with his SNCF blanket. I watched him now, through sly eyes, as he reached into the crate whose lid was next to it and brought out bundles of paper and cardboard files at which he made a variety of faces. He was wearing an old boarding-school-style dressing gown, with a braided edge and a tasselled cord. I managed to look at my watch and saw that it was nearly ten o'clock.

'You slept.'

'Didn't you?'

'I slept and then I woke. What are your plans?'

'Plans,' I said. 'That's asking rather a lot.'

'Have you come to stay?' He had still not looked at me. He seemed more interested in his old papers. He was wearing horn-rimmed spectacles. I expect he looked like his father.

'Am I welcome?'

'You have. Why?'

'I've left my husband.'

'Is that flattering?'

'Do you want flattery?'

'You need somewhere, in other words. I'm not getting it, am I?'

'I've left him because of you. If that's flattering. I think it might be.'

'Never asked you,' he said.

'Meeting you, for reasons I don't entirely understand, made me realise something.'

'Viz?'

'I married him as a joke.'

'Joke, did you? What's wrong with that? I don't see anything wrong with that.'

'Jokes have their limits. Their laugh-by dates. After that...'

'You never liked him.'

'I liked it,' I said. 'And I don't mean that. Also he amused me. Because he didn't understand me, didn't want to. I was a prize, not a consolation. He thought he'd got lucky. That was the joke. Among others, including the faces of my friends. As you were: my sister's friends. I felt free. So...'

'What about "that"? Did you learn to like it? *Come to?*'

'I liked it happening, quite often. I liked the fact that it was happening to me. More and more. I liked the fact that I could ... take it and leave it, come and go. I never liked *them* for doing it, not even when I enjoyed it. The pleasure was something I had, not something they gave me. Perhaps it's always like that.'

'It isn't,' Lionel Cator said. 'Do you want some tea?'

'Is there some?'

'There's no coffee,' he said. 'If you're going to want coffee, that's something you're going to have to take care of. You seem to be used to taking care of yourself, one way and another.'

'You don't sound as if you like that.'

'It's not my part of ship, is all I'm saying. I'm a Cator but never a cater*er*. There is tea. There is yesterday's bread. Start as we mean to go on, shall we?'

'Definitely.'

'Heart sinking yet, is it?'

'No.'

'Wouldn't blame you a bit.'

'I'm disturbing you.'

'God, yes,' he said. 'I have to think how I look. Haven't done that for half a century, best part of. How do I look? Elderly schoolboy? Old boy. Am, really, aren't I? And what are you?'

'Probably the ugly duckling, aren't I?'

'Choose your fairy story and stick to it, soundest policy. British justice; human decency; survival of the fittest. *Au choix*. I was looking for some stuff I wrote at one point. Mentioned it to you. I was looking to see whether I still had it. Might amuse you. Amazing the amount of firelighters a man can hang onto. Why are you here? Can't answer, can you? Lots of reasons, no reason.'

'All right ...' I said.

'Sounds menacing. Getting down to business, are we?'

'I don't have a business.'

'Not what I read.'

'I promised to do something; I did it, for better or worse. I suppose I'd better send it off sometime. If I can.'

'Came on foot, did you?'

'I had a lift. My sister. My husband's got the car.'

'Throwing yourself on my mercy, is that the size of it?'

'I wanted to see you. I never thought about its size.'

He sat on the floor, with his legs crossed, and read the contents of his files as if it had required my presence, and the opportunity to ignore it, in order to find them interesting. He seemed particularly to like not looking at me. 'Bog's outside, turn left. Taste for the old and primitive, luckily, haven't you, Rachel? Bit of a disgrace, calling you that, but not to be held against you, is it? Spoils of war. I saw a good deal of that, and that is no lie. I wash at the tap over there, when I do. Shower ditto, but not to excess. You're not going to like it here.'

I went outside and faced the bright morning. A tractor was dragging the carcasses of felled trees down the hill towards a waiting truck with a crane attached to it. The neat greens of the countryside lent its beauty a purpose and a form. The anonymous men who were working together were both servants and masters: they groomed and pillaged the great mother they walked on in their thick boots.

It was my first day in a new school. I knew very well how unwise I had been, and I tried to calm my doubts by promising myself that I had no obligation to stay. Yet I was already determined, by my doubts, not to leave Cator. I neither loved him nor did I love being with him. He was a puzzle which I wanted to solve. If I looked forward to anything, it was making myself indistinguishable from someone who loved him; it was for that reason, if reason it was, that I wanted to give him pleasure and, in consequence, to have him make love to me. His age and his possible impotence did not concern me. It was not a physical matter.

I used his earth closet as if it were the first, not very displeasing, step towards the intimacy which, in a nicely calculated way, I had decided to create. I wanted to get to the bottom of the man and I was given licence, freedom, and a kind of strength, by the ruthlessness of that mild desire. I stood and watched the trundle of the tractor, spitting gobs of mud as its wheels worked in the raw ruts they had cut, and I admired the patient, orderly cruelty of the vegetarian slaughterman who stacked the bodies of the trees in their fat-tyred hearse.

If I was not yet happy on that first day in a new school, I was satisfied, by the time I lifted the latch and went back into the cottage, that I had come to the right one. When had I expected to be happy? Cator was standing by the window on the short wall, tilting pages to the light. Again he played the game of not looking at me as I came in, but he had taken the opportunity to put on his corduroy trousers and socks and sandals, though he still wore his dressing gown. I was touched by his refusal to look at me and, having told myself that I did not really like the man, I felt a stir of emotion; since it was unfamiliar, it may have been pleasure at the presence of someone for whom people were, in principle, of no use. There was involuntary kindness in his refusal to ask anything of me. But I remembered – of *course* I remembered – that it was eleven or twelve years since he had seen a naked woman, and that he had told me so.

'All right,' he said. 'Read a lot, do you?'

'I used to,' I said, 'before I got married.'

'Think you're on to something, do you?'

'On to something.'

'Stalling. Being attractive, is that what you're doing? *Think* you're doing? Henry James.'

'I'm sorry?'

'Read him at all?'

'Yes.'

'Publishing scoundrel. Always liked that story. Close to home?'

'I don't want to publish anything,' I said. 'If that's what you're afraid of.'

'I was rather looking forward to it,' he said. 'Come here to disappoint me, have you?'

'Are you serious?'

'Do I have to be to want something? What should I seriously want, *à mon age*?'

'OK,' I said. 'Why am I here?'

'OK, OK!'

'You interest me. You frustrate me. I want to know the truth.'

'And when you know the truth, whatever that improbable article may be, you will no longer be frustrated or interested. So now we have the basis of a relationship, don't we? And what is life without relationships? Peace and quiet. The monks were right; it's the margins that make the texts worth looking at. What do you think?'

'About?'

'Why I interest you, let's say.'

'You're a merchant of half-truths.'

'Half true,' he said, 'because I'm not buying and I'm not selling and what kind of a merchant is that in your experience? You're wishing onto me the qualities you fear in yourself. Well?'

'Why did you never go back to England, officially at least?'

'Never liked the place. Felt at home there.'

'You don't feel at home here?'

'Feel, no; am, however. In the sense that I'm not. Which is man's natural condish; ever since he found he had a tongue that could make lies his distinguishing mark. Art, politics, love; what have they got to do with the truth? Then again, as you were about to say, what's truth got to do with what? You see what you've done, Rachel Stannard? You've pulled my cork – halfway anyway – and let the gas out, the few remaining bubbles. I'll be flat in a few days and then you'll wonder how to get out of the door, which is open anyway.'

'You don't like me very much, do you?'

'Boo-hoo. Very much; that's a larger size than I generally stock. It's good of you to come and . . . do what? Supply me with a target. I never thought that damned thing would go off, but imagine if I'd actually potted you. Thank my father, the HM, you'd better: "Never point a weapon," he said. He wasn't exactly sincere, of course, because he never broke the rule: anyone pointed a gun – they did shooting, and archery, if you can believe it – he had their pants down and swished them black and blue. A man must have his pleasures, even in a just world, which was the British way, I always thought, at least until I began to think. If you're going to stay here, which no guidebook recommends, we shall have to do something about beds. You're not curling up on my feet every night and no more are you lying on the floor in an accusatory huddle. No debate on that score; guillotine applied. So . . .'

'I could go and get a bed from home.'

'Pick up thy bed and walk back here with it? No call, unless you fancy it. Got an old WD-style camp bed in one of my burrows. Go and get it for you if you don't ask me nicely. What're you going to do all day? Improve me? Wonder where I am?'

'I haven't thought about it,' I said.

'Change my ways? Discover my ways? My paths are the paths of solitude, *seule étude*, Rachel Stannard, and your big eyes aren't going to see anything as it woulda bin if you hadn't decided, a trifle high-handedly, to barge in here and lighten my darkness, oh lady, which will almost certainly mean that it puts on weight. I don't usually talk, you know, sometimes not for weeks on end. Reticence is garrulity that dares not speak its name. What we like about people, Rachel Stannard, is the first thing we set about changing, their strangeness. Best service I could render you'd be not to change my socks until you get out of here. But I lack that kinda kindness. Don't look for easy outs with me, dear; be careful or probably I'll twist you in the wind of my indulgence until you beg for a harsher fate. *What* a shame you're not a fortune-hunter!'

He gave me his foxy look, which I chose – with a feeling that things were beginning to go well – to ignore. He took off his dressing gown and threw it onto the bed, and his pyjama jacket on top. His chest was scrawny, with a few black and grey hairs, and his flesh looked cold rather than old: there was a raw redness to it, as if it had been exposed to the wind he had talked about. Deep creases ran from his collar-bone towards one of his arm-pits; he might have been wearing badly ironed flesh which had shrunk with use: the bones were coming through. His stomach was a bit of a pot, but less than I had imagined; could he be holding it in just a little?

'Right,' he said. 'Spot of choring, me. Don't know how long I'll be.'

'I really don't mind the floor,' I said.

'Not your place, is it?' he said. 'You need anything while I'm out, you either help yourself, go without or go out. What're you going to do for money?'

'I've got a bank,' I said.

'Everyone should have one,' he said. 'Good solution. Mention it to the minister, I should.'

He put the pages which he had been reading on the packing case from which they had come and tapped them, knock-knock, as though the gesture would remind them not to fly away. They were written on squared paper in somewhat blurred soft pencil. I was touched by the copy-book neatness of the script.

'Don't wait lunch,' he said. 'If you can find any.'

'Am I supposed to look at that?'

'You're supposed to make up your own mind. No easy form of composition sometimes, that. Beg, borrow or steal, what's the diff? No problem finding gold, is there? It's the rainbow that's elusive. Over and out, me.'

I said, 'Lionel.'

'Almost.'

'You're the Bluebeard who doesn't even bother to lock the door, aren't you?'

'Saving that for a rainy day, were you? It's not raining that I can see.'

'These pages.'

'Told you they weren't worth anything. Hence all yours. Publish, don't publish; up to you. Naked girls, naked men; different items altogether. The altogether; no such thing with males, in my humble. Try as we might. I got them out for you, I suppose; a slice of the mighter-bin, dear. Help yourself; butter and jam in the larder, if required.'

ii

'My father introduced me to Caesar and Caesar to Gaul and its divisions. The *pater* told us that we should look no further for a model as a stylist. Because Caesar was a soldier, he did not have time for periphrasis. The Gallic Wars came out as curtly as a series of appreciations and consequent orders. *Pater* said that he admired people who were not devious. That was why he admired Baldwin! Who ever admired people whom they resembled? The HM's reports were written in what he thought echoed Caesar's style, brisk, forthright and pitiless. He told us that he had learnt "*clementia*" from Caesar. Caesar's idea of forgiving people was to reward the servile and massacre the defiant. I was just about the only pupil at the school who was both things. My defiance had the appearance of servility and it was by seeming to be something that I learned how to be *and* not to be; I ducked Hamlet's dilemma from an early

219

age. I was educated to be a spy by my reverend father's humbugging advocacy of straightforwardness.

'Writing this down is not painful, but it is strange, like a kind of sleepwalking or painless drunkenness. I want to say certain simple things, but I am already finding reasons for postponement. Perhaps simplicity is only another form of evasion. Caesar is certainly the model there. His narrative style presented ego-centricity and careerism as forms of self-denial; that must be why he spoke of himself in the third person. I cannot do that, not because I am incapable of deception but because I cannot see myself clearly enough in public events; I should lose myself in the crowd, and I should probably not be sorry.

'There is no one here, and I expect no one, as company or as reader, but I am my own double, sitting across from myself in an attitude of scepticism, interested to see how soon I shall start telling lies, or what is not quite the truth. Does that mean that I actually know what is and is not the case? If I had a case to argue, I should do better, but I am merely trying to see myself, and what happened, with a clarity which is itself a doubtful means of dispelling obscurity. *Et voilà!* I am preparing to keep my secret from myself, who am the only person who knows it.

'Mimicry always came easily to me. It is a part of the character of all those who keep the rules, whether from conviction or from cowardice. No one is naturally obedient; it is a choice which was forced upon us, in the days when it paid a dividend to be a certain kind of Englishman. I was aware from the earliest age that I was pretending to be the person whose company I have kept ever since, not always with a good grace. I joined up when the war came and I was glad to go. The pretences to which I was accustomed enabled me to mimic competences which selection boards recognised as their own. I had no doubt that I should be an officer, which seemed less a privilege than a part. Because it did not *matter* to me whether or not I was commissioned, or even killed, since I had no independent ambition other than to pass for a creature indis-tinguishable from others of my breed, I appeared to be fearless; the anaesthetised patient watches the knife with a certain interest. He winces at what he might be feeling, but never at what he experiences.

'I learnt French as a result of my father's first attempt to run a school in the Riviera town of Hyères, which had quite a large

English population in the 1920s. His idea was to teach the English children French and the French English. In the event, he did not attract many pupils of either nationality, though we managed to survive in shabby gentility for several years, during which I went to a local school and became Francophone *malgré moi*. I hardly remember the teachers and none of my *camarades* became my friends. I enjoyed the place, however, because it gave me an early acquaintance with being indistinguishable from those with whom I knew myself to have nothing in common. When my father came into some money, we went back to England and I was enrolled as a pupil in the school which he started. Although I was now supposed to be among boys of my own age and race, I must already have been *spoiled*, spoiled for uniformity, I mean: I earned the temporary nickname, which I managed to shed later, of "Frenchie", perhaps simply because I was unwary enough to teach the French teacher a phrase or two.

'I remember my bemusement at the "leaving jaw" which my *pater* delivered to those who were due to go to their public schools (the educational bus left for no other destination). He spoke in forthright riddles, promising a candour which perplexed me, and assumed a manly equality with those whom he had swished and patronised during the previous four or five years. It seemed that "certain changes in our bodies" which we must have observed recently, entitled us to be aware of, if not to enjoy, new horizons. These changes might lead us into temptations and might tempt other, older boys in "the next place you go to" to visit their attentions on us. My father's circumlocutions inclined him to assume a frowning severity; any puzzlement which we might be showing was taken to be a form of obtuseness. Something in his attitude implied that he was telling us things which we knew already and that he knew that we knew them. He made innocence into a presumption of guilt. Why did I have the impression that he was asking, if not insisting, that he be forgiven for something?

'I enjoyed my public school. It was a beastly place. It was my pleasure not to be disgusted or surprised by anything, not even the code of "common decency" to which the victims of the bully appealed and which the bullies themselves imagined themselves to be upholding. The great lesson of my education was that the way not to be a criminal was to make sure to be among those who devised, and administered, punishment. I became a pitiless, mildly

221

spoken enforcer of school rules. If I had some notion that I was a hypocrite, that confirmed my conviction that I was doing my duty. I was particularly vindictive towards a boy in my House with rather a brown complexion. Although quite athletic, P.D. elected to take no keen part in the house teams and spent his weekends at a local swimming pool where he watched and, when opportunity arose, aboarded shop-girls.

'The watchful disapproval which I visited on Darling was not personal: I do not think that *I* disapproved, in my own right. *I* was neither here nor there; it was not in my gift to show P.D. understanding. My only proper contact with him was to exact payment for his transgressions; as a monitor, I was neither friend nor enemy: I was justice. In this way, we saw quite a lot of each other.

'There were stories of monitors who required their victims to kiss the rod with which they were to be chastised, but I found this repugnant; I never wondered why I felt it necessary to explain that I was obliged to make an example of P.D. or to seek his sympathy over denying him the leniency which I asked him dispassionately to recognise would have abysmal spiritual consequences for him and for the school. I realised later, and perhaps realised then, what heroic condescension was involved in his seeming to take me seriously. I was performing my father's part and I thought that I should escape the accusation of being a humbug by the defence – before what court I could not say – and that I deserved congratulations on the accuracy with which I parodied my *pater*.

'I look back on those days without shame or interest. They shaped my future life, rather as foot-binding determined the gait and mobility of the Chinese girls who were subjected to it. Everything which limits our prospects can be seen as a privilege. I became more interested in the illicit – especially in liquid form – during my last quarters at the school, but, by and large, keeping the rules was a form of perversity which more or less satisfied me. It was in this manner that I was prepared to go to war by a generation which, supposedly, would do anything to stay at peace.

'The outbreak of war came as a relief. I was about to go to Oxford. I was neither enough of a scholar to look forward to academic life, nor sufficiently lacking in wit to be unworthy of it. I welcomed Chamberlain's doleful declaration as a reprieve. My father had relied on appeasement, a policy which he never followed if there was a chance of taking down a small boy's trousers. I derived straight-faced amusement at his shattered faith in its champion.

'When I arrived in Cairo in 1942, having seen some action in the Aegean which did nothing to persuade me that I had done any *fighting*, though I saw some death, I was advised that certain brothels were much more reliable than others and that I should watch my step elsewhere. A Captain Peter Darling was the man to mark my card. As I had not bothered to guess when we were at school together, Peter had Levantine connections; although he had an English father and mother, there was a Coptic maternal grandfather of considerable wealth and culture.

'Peter had grown broader and braver in the few years since we were at school together. He greeted me with a shout of laughter and a smack on the back which seemed to say that we had been a pair of howlingly successful impostors. He was frightfully sporting. He assumed that our "Surrey shenannigans" had been a terrific joke on the school which we had hoodwinked by behaving exactly as the code demanded. His accent was very pukkah; perhaps he had been mixing with Etonians, or perhaps with his grandfather's elegant friends, but it was as if he had been to another school entirely since we had last met.

'P.D. seemed truly pleased to see me. I was embarrassed by the memory of my officiousness, which no doubt added to his pleasure. At first, I saw myself in such a measly light that I avoided his company; I was also mortified to find it so attractive. In that sense I fell in love with him at second sight. It was not a physical passion, though I could not – and did not need to – deny that it was a craving for his physical company. He played cricket for whatever HQ set-up he was involved in (I must have guessed it was Intelligence) and he also rode extremely well, horses *and* camels! His grandfather kept polo ponies in his country place in the delta outside Alex (I shall remember the name presently). His worldliness made me feel that P.D. had been in disguise during our schooldays. I was offended (i.e. humiliated) by his concealment of the qualities, and the money, which exempted him from routine English habits, sexual inhibition in particular.

'I should like to claim that I instantly divested myself of my own reach-me-down principles, but I was, of course, a British officer. As another kind of monitor, I was neatly tailored in a new set of proprieties. My admiration for Peter was crowned, you might say, by a lingering disapproval. He was incredibly nice to me. If he sensed my reluctance to presume on my previous cruelty towards him, he made a loud joke of it; I sometimes found it rather bad taste when he told people at dinner how I had given him six for picking up a tart in Guildford and six more for the extravagance of giving her a two-and-sixpenny cream tea. That was when Wendy, the Colonel's lady, began to take an interest in me.

'I did not know any better in Cairo than I had at school how to escape from deference to regulations which I found ridiculous. It was in deferring to them that I gave a sense of danger to a life which seemed already, when I was no more than twenty-two or three, to have gone beyond the point of revision. If Peter made me perceive the absurdity of my schoolboy attitudes, he could do nothing to alleviate the passion of envy which the perception triggered. I thought of him ceaselessly; it was not only my father's warnings against "unhealthy proximities" which fostered my obsession, it was also the feeling that I deserved the treatment (I was going to say "punishment") which Peter was uniquely qualified to administer. My father's pompous use of the word "proximity" was very exact, I realised: I wanted to be so close to Peter that there could be no way of distinguishing one of us from the other. It was for that reason that I applied to join the "Special Services" group for which he worked. I was now as eager to be under his orders, but in a military context, as I had been to reduce him to obedience as a schoolboy.

'Peter managed to be both a man about Cairo and someone who could vanish for days, or weeks, into a world of shadows. His charm was enhanced by his disappearing tricks; he seemed more brilliant by virtue of his absences, which darkened my days and filled my nights with unworthy fears of what might happen to him, and so to me.

'I begin to touch on what I have been postponing, not least because it is what I do not know. By trying to write about this part of my life, I have the illusion that I may stumble on some knowledge of what will, in fact, always be beyond me. I am running up to an abyss in the hope that the velocity of my approach will carry me across the void.

'I was surprised to find that Wendy Mac was interested in me. She made it known with a blatant game of footsie in the French admiral's house in Alex. I could hardly make a connection with what was happening under the table and the prim face she offered above it. It promised that she could handle the deception, I suppose. If I had had any emotional investment in her, I might have been shocked by her duplicity, but since my emotions were taken up by my feelings for Peter (which stood *between* me and him), it was more important for me to have a chance to prove that I wasn't a pansy than it was to have a mistress. Ham Mackinnon was a particularly decent chap, which added to the fun.

'I could not find out why Peter was arrested, or even whether he certainly had been, although the rumour was very strong. I asked Ham to do what he could to discover the truth and he said that he'd done his damnedest and that he had drawn a blank. Soon after Peter had "disappeared" (or "been disappeared" as Jim Scobie put it), I was interrogated by a panel of Intelligence people. They seemed so convinced that I knew more than I was telling them that they almost persuaded me that I did. Their methods schooled me in a new form of deceit, even though I was not deceiving them. My ignorance was turned into a form of courage. I wondered whether they would go as far as to torture me, but evidently I fell into the *non torturabile* category; maybe they were using me as a test-bed for their techniques – they may even have been trainees, some of them, and knew very well that I was innocent of any intimate connection with Peter. Why else would they accuse me of one?

'It seemed, however, and still seems, even now, that they had seen a version of myself who was bolder, more shameless and much more interesting than I had ever known myself. They were aware of my "mysterious" movements around the city, which had been designed only to conceal my meetings with Wendy. She enjoyed having me hire dubious rooms where, with a little giggle, she would ask me to perform precise services – not too soft, not *too* hard – with her husband's swagger stick. This ritual was preliminary to her pleasure, but so essential to it as to be, it seemed, its motive.

'My notion of honour prevented me from telling my interrogators the truth about Wendy. I was obliged to hint at something more mercenary. This, in turn, led them to assume that Peter had played the pimp on my behalf, which (as if it might help him) I did not deny. I do not believe that he was spying for the Germans, but I have never been able to discover what he was doing or what happened to him. One spicy memoir, which was not published till after the Suez affair, hinted that he had been some kind of a hero ("Lawrence of Arabia in reverse", whatever that meant).

'I knew almost at once that he was supposed to be dead and that it was "patriotic" to accept that he was. Were my interrogation and the dark rumours of his "treachery" all part of a charade which Peter himself had devised in the service of some subtle scheme? Who could say how far back his plans had been laid or what purpose they served? A drunken Philhellene promised me, in Homeric jargon, that he had been sent on a suicide mission in Greece (Peter spoke Greek and often rolled his eyes upwards, in unvoiced negation, as the Greeks do). I was also advised that he was made to walk across a minefield somewhere west of Alamein, but that no one saw anything blow up. It may be that no one actually knows any longer what became of him, still less why.

'I do not know whose eyes were supposed to be on me, or what they were intended to read into my abrupt eviction from the Middle East. I was told very sharply that I was to return to London on a troop ship. There had been believable rumours about certain unpopular people being dumped in the Med during such journeys home. I was glad to be allowed to keep my pistol. I spent most of my time in my cabin, with the door locked, reading difficult poetry. When one of the other officers on board knocked on my door and asked me what was going on, I called out, "Repeated buggery, if you don't mind", which seemed to do the trick.

'Peter's disappearance had had the instant effect of making me lose all interest in Wendy. I never said goodbye to her and was horrified when, after the war, she wrote me a letter saying how much I had meant to her and how cruel I had been and how much she would like to see me again, "if only for one of our Rue Awad-style afternoons". Perhaps that was why I felt a strong desire to keep out of England.

'I met Gervase Bristowe in "the French pub" in Soho. I seem to remember being advised to go there, perhaps by someone who had tipped him off about me. When he suggested that I "come over" to SOE, he did so with the air of someone whom I could trust as long as he could trust me, and no longer. He gave me the impression that he knew what happened to Peter and had no intention of letting on, at least yet. That, he seemed to imply, was just how trustworthy he was, and I had better be.

'I am coming to the part of my life of which I meant to be the Caesarian chronicler, the period I spent in command of *Réseau Victor*. I wonder why I am trembling and wanting to say nothing, even to myself. Bisto and I talked English while we were in the pub, but then he suggested we go to his flat in St Anne's Mansions. I suppose Baker Street had fixed it up for him. He produced some Rémy Martin and we started to speak French. He was fluent but his accent was not perfect; it may have been his excuse for never visiting what he called "the field". There was a certain comfort in having a CO whom I could suspect of being a little bit fly.

'I had done nothing disreputable in Cairo, unless you count cuckolding Ham Mackinnon, but I was evidently under some kind of a cloud which Bisto indicated that he was able to disperse, and might even turn into a halo, if I did my stuff.

'It is strange how telling oneself things which one presumes oneself to know already alters both their nature and one's attitude to them. I had not realised that there could be any connection between what I felt for Luis and the disappearance of P.D. (whose initials, in a French context, have a meaning for which my Hyères lessons had not prepared me). Now I see how Luis was, in a way, a substitute for Peter, although I do not find the observation significant. My admiration for L. was primed by the treachery which had been enjoined upon me by G.B. (more portentous initials!), though I am sure that I should have felt it even if I had not had Luis's demotion as my *raison d'être*. I want to say here, as if my evidence could ever be of importance, that I have felt more guilty concerning L.'s capture and death as time goes by. At the time, I consoled myself for not ordering him not to blow up the tunnel by telling myself that I was being clever rather than weak. Perhaps I was both. Yvonne did not enter into my calculations; I neither saved her for myself nor sacrificed L. in order to make her available. I never thought she would be. There may have been some kind of crime, but there was no passion in it. I did not even want to please G.B. *that* much! I thought the mission was unwise, but that L. could bring it off, if only because I doubted if I could. It is true that I was able to see a no-lose situation for myself, but that was a consolation, not a plan. In the event, I wanted to mount an operation to save L., but G.B. ordered me not to risk our strength so soon before "new calls" were likely to be made on us. I showed initiative in allowing Y. to see what she could do, but I fought shy of direct disobedience. Blind in one eye, I was a Nelson who could also squint through the other. Was I thinking of P.D., or was I just trying to have things both ways? *Qui sait?*

'It was a shock to me when Y. came and threw herself at me. I had not learnt enough from W.M. about the ways of women. I took her as a gift from L., and I loved her, for the weeks when I did love her, for his sake and under his aegis. I did not think it right to do what I did, but I thought it was what he wanted. After we knew he was dead, my desire for her was the only form of vengeance that eased my guilt. I did her for him and I did him through her. It was convenient, with so many other things to do, to call it love which, in French at least, it was.

'The rage which I might have directed against myself, had I been a civilian, I reserved for G.B., not that he knew. That was my pleasure, as usual. Typical L.C.! I allayed my shame and my grief by appearing not to give a damn. Having supplanted Luis definitively, I became a hell of a good leader; they can say what they like. I was fearless because I dreaded having time to think about what I had done, or not. Fearlessness, I discovered, is not at all the same thing as courage. I did not crave pain, but a spell of oblivion – though I did not know how protracted it might prove – had its attractions. Y.'s love seemed to promise that I could be as reckless as Luis; she demanded that I be hard. I was caught between what she expected of me and what G.B. required. Luckily, for several weeks at least, I had the energy and the vanity to manage both.

'It is true and it is not true that, as they say, I had "something to do" with Luis's death. I did not forbid him to do what he wanted to do. I connived and I also made it clear that, officially, I could not approve. To that extent, I repeated, and embellished, the pattern of behaviour I had followed with P.D., whose "death" may – repeat *may* – have had some very small influence on my decision to let Luis do, as they now say, his thing. It was as much my envy of his nerve as my obedience to Gerry B. that prevented me from preventing him. The thing seems complicated, but it remains quite simple: the Germans had a train coming, we had the means, though not the OK, to ambush it, and I thought everybody might be happy at the outcome.

'When it comes to what happened in Ste-Foy-le-Fort in July, it's a completely different kettle and entirely different fish. By this time, the Germans were preparing to pull out of the Périgord. A lot of their heavy equipment was already on the road. More people had joined our *réseau* – we actually had a full-blown camp in the woods – and we were now actively hungry for targets. It was the hunting season.

'I knew Félix Argote from early on in my time *dans le coin*. He had come from the Béarn, I think, and rented the *Relais St Jacques* soon after the surrender. He was a cheerful opportunist who wanted as little trouble and as large a profit as possible from whatever activities he followed. It was typical of him, and many others, that he would serve the Germans and members of our network in quick, and generous, succession. If it paid well, he was not above a measure of subsidised Quixotry. The hotel had a large cellar and a secret passage which gave access to some limestone catacombs where, it was said, early Christians had sheltered when on their way to St Jean de Compostelle. It was an ideal place to hide Allied personnel who were being passed down the line from the North to the Pyrenees. Félix had found quite a lot of archaeological curios while cleaning the place out. He was always digging around.

'It was part of our policy to compromise as many people as possible by implicating them, however marginally, in our activities; in this way, we both enjoyed their help and had something against them, which would disincline them to betray us. Félix was as reliable as any mercenary; he might not save the sum of things for pay, but he would certainly keep them in a fairly safe place. He wanted to be popular and he wanted to have enough money to buy the hotel when its owner came back from the wars.

'Since he had Allied soldiers and airmen in and out of his cellars quite frequently, we kept an eye on Félix and warned him, occasionally, of rumours of German excursions from Périgueux in his direction: there was no permanent garrison in Ste-Foy-le-Fort. German security became more and more porous as their local staff sought to establish that their only purpose in working for the enemy was to supply us with intelligence. It was in this way that we were advised of the raid on the *Relais* which was being planned for 24 July.

'Militarily, there was no sense in what the Germans did. In

the midst of their retreat, they were said to be coming in company strength to invest a hotel in a hill-village in order to arrest a party of refugees. No Allied personnel were involved. By this time, escapers were able to join us or move, with impunity, southwards into a region from which the Germans had already withdrawn. The party at the *Relais* consisted mostly of what remained of a Jewish school and its staff; there were also several refugees who had come down from Limoges, not all of them Jews. At the time, I did not consider the question of how the Germans had learned of their hiding place. I was more concerned to ambush a German party than to save the refugees from deportation. Despite my experience of Baker Street's Jesuitries, I assumed that my plans would be approved without question. They were not. I was told by Bisto (or rather by Mrs Marlowe, acting on his behalf) that a Panzer unit was said to be moving down from the Corrèze and that we should liaise with the Resistance there and allocate "all available resources" to impede the German progress. The rescue of civilians was not our part of ship. What had apparently happened was that *Réseau* Maurice had already demanded that an operation be mounted to remove the Limoges refugees (who included two members of the Communist-led CGT trades union) and had been ordered back in line. My innocent suggestion sounded like insolence. Its rejection annoyed me: I did not believe that our people could do much to cut off, let alone stop, a Panzer division fifty or more miles from where we were, whereas I had adequate men, at this stage, to mount an operation which would save the refugees, whoever they might be, and bloody the Germans. I could not disobey orders, but commanders in the field enjoyed a measure of autonomy, so I sent as many men as could be given transport to the Corrèze (where there was, in fact, no German column) and I took Yvonne, among others, with me to see what we could do at Ste-Foy-le-Fort, if the Germans were really on their way.

'They were. We had light arms, mostly sten guns, and they came in trucks and personnel-carriers, heavily armed and in full company strength. We were in the old quarantine hospital, beside the church. It was a very large stone building with walls a yard thick, and it had been deserted for years. As soon as I saw how many Germans there were (some of them were Ukrainians, in fact), I looked at Y. and I knew that we were going to be spectators. We had less than a dozen people and they were three times that number.

'We were up in the roof, looking under the eaves and down at the square where the War Memorial is, next to the *Relais*. I saw Félix Argote come out and play the innocent, but the Germans knew exactly what they were looking for and where to find it. They separated the Jewish children, and their teachers, from the half a dozen men (and one woman) who clearly did not belong to the school party. The woman was fair and she wore a black suit, with stiff shoulders, and a white shirt. There was a spotted handkerchief on her head. The children and the four or five Jewish adults were thrown into a truck which had been driven close to the gate of the hotel. A German officer pushed the fair woman towards the party of adults who had nothing to do with the Jews. He did it with a brutal courtesy which contrasted with the savage treatment of the children and their teachers. She wanted to go with the children and he was telling her to go with her friends. His words were more audible than hers.

'The German officer was angry and indulgent: he tried to explain to the woman that he was showing "correctness" and more than correctness. He asked her to be *"raisonnable"*: he was rendering her a service for which she should be very, very grateful. She insisted that she wanted to go with the children. When the German officer, with an expression of frustrated virtue, allowed the woman to run across and be boosted into the truck by two of his men, I happened to look at Yvonne. Her face was flushed, although we were deep in the cool shadow of the old hospital. It seemed to bulge, like a balloon with a new puff of air in it. She said, *"Elle est folle, la pauvre!"*

'It was at that moment, for reasons which will never be reasonable, that many things happened to me. The first was that I was filled with horror. The second was that I hated Yvonne with such a passion that I almost pulled the trigger of my sten (which would probably not have gone off). The third was that I was filled with a sentiment which had previously been unknown to me and which I had always assumed to be a fiction: as I watched the woman being tipped over the tailboard of the lorry, legs in the air, face to the sky, I knew that she had chosen to go with the children out of a purity of feeling which divorced love from desire. I loved her for

231

it. I loved her and I was powerless to help her. There was more: I knew all the things about myself which I had, as they say, *neglected* to know. I knew who I was and what I was not and that I could never reconcile the two, nor find a way out of my duplicity; my falseness was part of what I truly was.

'Did I look different? It seemed not. Yvonne made a sour face which seemed to endorse Baker Street's wisdom in not diverting a sufficient force to intervene. As for the blonde woman, was she a heroine or did she think she would be safer with the children? After the Germans had driven away, I ordered the rest of my people to stay where they were and then, still carrying my sten, I went down the loud wooden stairs and across to the *Relais St Jacques*.

'Félix was sitting in the bar with Martine, his red-headed wife. He said, "*Tu as vu?*" He was a great one for the second person singular. I said, "*Et vous?*" "*Les pauvres,*" he said, "*n'est-ce pas?*" I had a strong desire to shoot him and his wife, who had said nothing. "*Et vous?*" I said again. "*Nous?*" he said. "*Nous, ça va.*" I asked him why and he seemed, or pretended, not to understand what I meant. Why had he and Martine not been arrested? "*Ils sont comme ça, les Fridolins, ils sont comme ça.*" I said, "*Ils étaient juifs, non?*" "*Les pauvres,*" he said. If they had not been "*pauvres*" they might have been elsewhere, mightn't they? My sarcasm inspired Félix to make the face which I always think of as "*entr' hommes*". It recalls the merit of inertia and the good fortune of being called upon to do nothing above the parapet. I wonder if Frenchmen ever looked like that before 1917 and the *Chemin des Dames*.

'I asked him who the blonde woman was. Her name was Monique Touvian, he told me. She was, he said, "*courageuse*" and Martine said that she had been "*gentille comme tout*" with the children, who had been kept quiet by her stories. When I asked Félix how much he had been paid for revealing the refugees, he stood up and hit the table with the flat of his hand. "*Vous n'avez pas le droit,*" he said. Had I not been in the state I was, I might have killed them both. I had killed people and I would kill others; I hardly remember how many. I remember better the moment when I came across my last German. He was a Don R riding a Harley-Davidson, which he must have stolen from some garage. He stopped by the side of the road near Villefranche-lès-E. and walked into a copse where I was supposed to meet some Australians who were late. He eased his pants and I saw that he wanted to take a shit. I waited till they were down and then I put the barrel of my sten just by his ear. I can still see the way his eyes came round to look at me. He was a blond youth, probably about eighteen, with a pink, hairless arse. I could smell his fear, which also had the sweet flavour of curiosity: he thought I might want something, which gave him hope. I told him he was dead. He looked hurriedly around the copse, as if he might have to give evidence about it. I asked him, in a friendly voice, if he had ever been in Ste-Foy-le-Fort. He said, "*Je crang que non*". He seemed to imagine that it would have been to his credit if he had been. What he feared had condemned him was his salvation. I moved my hand on the sten, but it was pure sadism: I was not going to kill him and I knew it. I told him to pull up his pants. He did not seem very keen. Perhaps he thought that I was squeamish about shooting a man with a bare bum. He might have thought differently if he had known my father.

'When he had pulled up his trousers and made time by having problems with his buckle, I said that he didn't have to die, what he had to do was shit himself. He looked at me as if the reprieve was more painful to him than execution, but perhaps that was a luxury. I told him to shit himself and hurry up about it. He shook his head and then his face went a bit pink and he was, as they say, going through the motions. I pointed the sten at his balls and I told him to get a move on. He made a serious job of it then. He did what he could and then he looked at me. I thought that his trousers were probably full but I made him open his belt so that I could be sure. Then I told him to sit down on the ground and squish himself. He gave me the same look as before, but did so. I hauled him up again and told him to start walking and not to look back until he reached the next village. Off he went. And I was left with the Harley-Davidson. I wonder if he ever thinks about me.

'One more detail remains with me from that day in Ste-Foy-le-Fort. It was when the children were being herded into the truck that one of the Germans (or Ukrainians) pulled down a small boy's shorts and, with a laugh I could not hear from where we were hiding, but with a face I shall always remember, pulled out his penis between thumb and forefinger and showed it to a flat-faced corporal as if it were a berry to eat. It is on account of that memory that I went to a specialist, some years later, and arranged to be circumcised.

'I do not know what it means to be a Jew, or when someone of Jewish origins ceases to be one. Is a tomato a fruit or a vegetable? God knows. When I discovered that P.D. had an Egyptian grandfather (his wife was, I think, Greek and spoke French in the guttural Alexandrian manner), I felt as if I should always have known it. When Yvonne said *"Elle est folle"*, it was also as if she too had told me something about myself which I always should have known. I was aware not of my identity, as if I could step out of my self, like Kinsgley's chimney-sweep, but of the falseness of what remained part of me. I was irredeemably English, but I was also unredeemable for England. Can it be that the moment was so charged that I realised, as the trucks moved away from the *Relais St Jacques*, where the children were going and what Monique Touvian had done in insisting on being their companion?

'I had nowhere to disclose my rage or my shame. I had changed utterly and I went on almost exactly as before. The difference was that my desire for Y. was a desire for vengeance, not atonement. It did not express itself in any new way that she could recognise; it was my amusement to exact her pleasure from her in a way which would make her more in need of me. When the public war ended, I continued privately to be at war with her.

'It would be nice to leave the impression that I hated Y. because she had smirked when Monique Touvian was pitched over the tailboard of the German lorry. It would be equally pretty to claim that I pursued the war against the now retreating Germans with a new dedication. I could sustain the claim by reference to the battle in which we rescued the Allied airmen. It was quite a nasty little skirmish and Y. was exceptionally brave in the course of it. *"Tu es folle,"* I remarked afterwards. I had been wounded myself, in the shoulder, but it healed quite soon. I think that was the day that I shot a man in German uniform whom I suspected of being a Ukrainian but who turned out to come from Alsace. The part of the Alsaciens in the destruction of Château St Martial, and in the massacre of its inhabitants, was an embarrassment to the French. My *Médaille de la Résistance* was alleged to have been earned in the action we fought to keep the SS from further outrages, but it was in fact my reward for obeying an order to conceal the origins of the unit responsible for the massacre. My other reward was the little cottage in which I am writing these words. It was given to me by Ferdinand de Croqueville, who owned the *château* which I had made my headquarters during the battle. He believed that I had deployed my force in order to protect his property. In fact, since he had been a Vichy enthusiast of notorious proportions, I had chosen to use his house so that we might have the compensation of seeing it burnt to the ground if our operation was a failure or if the Germans came back later in punitive mood. The Baron de Croqueville had been among the subscribers to the *Action Française* who, like the sainted Charles Maurras himself, thought it a patriotic act to give the Germans details of where Jews were hiding.

'Two days after the *rafle* at Ste F., I was told that Félix was nearby, trying to get in touch with me. We were back in our camp in the *Double*, which was some distance from the *Relais*; I was very busy with claims for arms and official recognition from a variety of belated resisters. However, if Félix had displaced himself all the way to Villefranche, it must be important, though it might well be important only to him. I gave him elaborate instructions, through a runner, about how to get to the *Moulin de l'Enclos*. I had him shadowed all the way and he seemed certainly to be alone.

'I hated him so much that it was a pleasure to see him. It was a hot day and he was wearing blue overalls, like a peasant, and a beret, which was often the mark of a collaborator. Félix wanted to look like everybody except himself. He appeared shorter than usual, as if anxiety had made him lose height. I told him to come to the point. He did: the German commander in Périgueux wanted to do a deal. He could arrange for the party of Jewish children, or at least some of them, and their escort, which included Monique Touvian, to "lose their way" during transportation "towards The East", if I could come up with "the necessary". It required small wit for the German Major to see that the war was lost and he wanted to make "certain arrangements". If I could give him a hundred thousand pounds in sovereigns, he would – on his word of honour as a German officer – ensure that the convoy took a wrong turning and ended in our hands.

I asked Félix whether the whole operation to arrest the Jews, and the others in Ste F., had been mounted in the interests of this blackmailing exercise. It would be interesting to see what kind of a show of innocence, or ignorance, he could put on. He did pretty well. I could still have killed him without a shred of regret. He said, of course, that he knew nothing about the German motives; he had been made the emissary because he too was being black-mailed: if I did not agree to supply the sovereigns, he was going to be arrested and shot, Martine as well, "who has done nothing," as he put it. I was quick to spot that that implied that he had done "something", but the point was not worth making. The question was what to do now. I had kept my war-chest a secret, but everyone knew that large sums of money, always in gold, were part of the ammunition with which Baker Street sometimes had to prime the fighting spirit of its allies. In the case of minor disbursements, it was left to commanders' discretion to decide with what generosity to distribute funds, but the present situation was hardly of that order. I said that I should have to refer to London. Félix's green face was evidence that, in some regard at least, he was not bluffing. There was, he promised me, no time to lose. I believed him.

'Strange as it seems to me now, I did not wholeheartedly welcome the opportunity to save the children and their companions. At the time I was trying to organise the surrender of a small German SS detachment, still well armed, who were holed up in St-Médard-de-Mouleydier, a village in the valley of the Dordogne where they had already committed a number of brutalities. I was trying to negotiate not only with their commander but also with our "friends" in *Réseau* Maurice. Their (Communist) commander was not in favour of allowing the SS men to pass under British control and so, as he put it, "escape the just consequences of their earlier acts". He had a point, but I favoured *clementia*, if only because it would send a message to other German groups in the region that they could save their skins by surrendering. If they did so, in numbers, it would deprive the local collaborators and their *Milice* of German support. In addition, I wanted to avoid a massacre by the SS men in St Médard of the villagers who were still in their power. If I could achieve a bloodless surrender, I was prepared – much further down the line – to be compelled by *force majeure* (and official French demands, with the right kind of stamps on them) to hand over the SS men to the men from *Réseau* Maurice. *Ce n'était pas magnifique, mais c'était la guerre.*

The matter of saving the party from Ste F. was more complicated. I should be using a packet of money in a cause which London would regard as dubious. I was, however, resolved to do it. It was not that I "loved" Monique Touvian, certainly it was not *simply* that I loved her. As if a locked door had flown open in a gale and given access to something which had been hidden, yet always there, I had realised that my father's maternal grandmother, whom I had never met, was an embarrassment to him because her name was Rachel Moser. Although she was a concert pianist who had played for the Prince of Wales, she was never acknowledged as a member of the family and my father did not go to her funeral, which took place, luckily for him, in Melbourne, Australia, where she had re-married in old age.

'I cannot say that I had become a different man in the two days since that look in Yvonne's eye – and my reaction to it – evoked knowledge which had been there all my life. I had certainly not acquired a set of beliefs or a new sort of loyalty. It is more accurate to say that I· had learnt who I was not than to claim that I was suddenly aware of who I was. My *raison d'être* derives, even today (14.8.77) from what I am not.

'I had a problem: I might save the children and the others by giving the German commander what he asked for, but I might also enrich Félix, whose affectations of martyrdom did not prevent me from guessing that he was likely to be on commission. If I refused to do anything, I should be acting in accordance with my responsibilities to Baker Street, but devotion to duty was a very unamusing prospect. My hatred of the Germans spilled over into a universal anger which made me very lucid and entirely without faith in any human institution.

'I told Félix that I should have to speak to my masters in London and that he should inform Manfred Leitner, the German officer in question, that I agreed to his demands, but that he would have to be patient. Meanwhile if the convoy were to be moved, by rail or road, I should hold him personally responsible. Félix told me that he would be grateful to me forever for what I was doing. I took pleasure in assuring him that that was the only thing which made me hesitate.

'When I got through to London, I spoke of a party of "prisoners" who were held in Périgueux. Yvonne, who was still my W/T operator, looked at me with a complicity which agreed to admire whatever motive inspired me, so long as it was not altruism. She may even have believed that I had been made some promise by "the Jews" or that I was in their power. Nothing that happened in the war altered the influence of her parents on her way of thinking about the world; she became brave, but she remained brainless.

'London replied that I should on no account disburse important sums "unless Allied personnel or recognised fighters were at risk". When I was told that a full account of the use of funds would be expected of me, I could hear Bisto's voice and I could see the look in his eye. They did not quite say the same thing.

'I had a fat satchel of sovereigns hidden in the workings of the mill. I had had it there for months. It made me happy to think of it dangling, unknown to anyone, among the stone wheels and the wooden cogs. Not trusting another soul is the only true form of liberty.

'I gave half of what he asked for to Félix Argote and I told him to tell Leitner that he would get the other half when the refugees were safely in our keeping. Félix said that Leitner might not like that. I replied that even my sheltered life had taught me that one did not give a German officer the benefit of the doubt, especially if he mentioned his honour. I enjoyed the fear on Félix's face; it promised that something of his story had to be true. I decided to trust him as far as I could throw him, which might well be to the wolves. Meanwhile he so needed me to take him for some kind of a noble character that I almost felt sorry for him; contempt can be quite a friendly sentiment. In that spirit, I told him that he would be watched all the time that he was in Périgueux and, just for fun, that I would shoot him myself, if I could find the time, should I find that he was lying to us; otherwise I should depute one of our johnny-come-lately *franc-tireurs* to earn his spurs by making holes in him. I noticed, as if from a distance, that my public school education had not been wasted: when roused, I could still be a righteous bully.

'Félix handed over the money that night. Leitner came to see him in a *hôtel de passe* in the old quarter of the city, near the cathedral. I was bluffing about how closely we were observing them; it was not possible for our people to check precisely how much of the money Félix handed over. Subsequent events suggest that he kept a certain percentage. In the circumstances, it was just as well.

'Félix reported to me in the mill promptly next morning. He was eager to tell me what he assumed I knew already: the children and the other prisoners would be sent along a route to be communicated to us ahead of time. In the nature of things, Leitner could not simply surrender them. It was up to us to neutralise the small escort. I took this badly: it was not my responsibility to watch Leitner's back for him and I could not be expected to risk my men in an ambush unless the escort was forewarned to surrender. There was no way in which I could take his word that this would happen. Félix shrugged; he understood and he did not understand. He was a middle-man all right. He understood my anxiety, but he did not understand what he could do; we could hardly expect a refund. Besides, time pressed. Leitner could stall, but not indefinitely. Félix had to take the rest of the money that night and he would bring back the route map on his return. Otherwise...

'I was in the trap I had wanted to avoid. My concern was less to save the refugees than not to be deceived by Félix and his German manipulator and, I suspected, fellow-conspirator. I had already breached my orders, though I was not very worried about a formal inquiry; I knew enough about other little affairs to be vulnerable, it might be, to a spot of quiet assassination but not to a public grilling. The question was how to win the game, and whether it could be won. I had some sense, even then, that there were always conditions to unconditional surrenders.

'The crocodile had half my arm, in a fairly genial grasp. If I appeared to concede the other half, he might open his mouth wide enough for me to extract myself with both honour and advantage. It is strange to reflect how little Monique counted for me at this stage, but it is the truth. I wanted to get the refugees out of German hands more because I disliked Yvonne than because I cared about Monique, or the children. It occurred to me that I could distract *Réseau* Maurice from its vindictive concern with the SS men in St Médard, and so get them to surrender quickly, if I could syphon off some of its strength to "ambush" the trucks with my party on board (and their Limoges friends). Furthermore, in this way I should also turn what might have been a misuse of funds into a legitimate *ruse de guerre* against our allies. I could claim that I feared (as I did) that the Communists were not averse to some French civilian blood being shed, if it embittered local opinion and secured them a brave reputation. If all went as I planned, Maurice would be covered with a certain glory, but the Communist *main-*

mise on the region would be further limited. That kind of two-facedness would certainly convince Bisto of my integrity.

'I decided to supply a belt to my braces. I told Félix that, so far as I was concerned, as a British officer, the sovs were not payment for the delivery of the civilian refugees but a response to Leitner's threat, through another channel, to arrest a number of our people in the region, whose names were known to him from a very reliable source. He was to tell Leitner that any further arrests in the region would be regarded as treachery on his part. I had sound reason to want to append this to the main issue. It was routine procedure to assume that any captured agent, even Luis, would have been forced to tell all he knew, especially the names and addresses of anyone who had helped us. To hold out under torture was more than could ever be expected, even of heroes. Silence was noble, but it was pointless, since we always assumed the worst.

'Félix had no difficulty in believing that he was being used in a more devious game, not least because deviousness was his natural style. He probably felt better for being duped. That night, he delivered the money to Leitner, who, according to my sources, appeared to be satisfied with the transaction. If Félix was taking something off the top, as they say, it cannot have been much. The next morning he brought the map when he came to me at the *Moulin de l'Enclos*. Since they were keen to have their CGT comrades back on side, *Réseau* Maurice agreed to mount the ambush. I impressed on them the need for a large enough force to procure a quick surrender. We did not want the prisoners caught in crossfire, did we? While Maurice's men were on their way to the spot selected for the ambush, I was able to negotiate with the SS men at St Médard. After they had been brought out, I moved them smartly southwards, out of the immediate region. They were already on their way to Montauban before M. and his people reported back to me that they had waited all day and all night and that no vehicles, with or without the refugees and the children, had come along the supplied route.

'A few days later, we discovered that Major Leitner had been arrested on his return from his second rendezvous with Félix and immediately shot. The transports had left, by a different route, and had passed "safely" into the area still under firm German control.

'A number of things followed. I was able more or less to convince

240

Bisto, who arrived in our region in the autumn, after our little action to save the Allied personnel, in which Y. distinguished herself (and I made a modest contribution), that all the sovs had been honestly, if ignobly, disbursed in order to avoid a massacre. It was possible that we had been bluffed into spilling HMG's gold for no valid reason, but I could hardly be blamed, considering the kind of poker we were playing.

'All went smoothly until, over a bottle of liberated Schnapps, Bisto congratulated me on keeping a cool head and obeying orders on the subject of "Christian acts". Striking a senior officer and close friend while pissed to the nines was not a formal court-martial offence, not least because neither of us was in uniform at the time, but it contributed somewhat to the advice I was given not to manifest myself, least of all with my hand out, in post-war London. To what extent did my allegedly having misled *Réseau Maurice* dispose London to adopt a genial, not to say insistent, attitude to the prospect of my marriage to Y.? It was certainly conveyed to me that this would be a *very* good thing "in many regards"; Anglo–French relations could do with a dose of romance. No one was prepared to go so far as to mention any disability award on account of my wounded shoulder. "The Almighty can please himself," Jim Scobie reminded me, some years later, "but HMG very rarely helps those who have helped themselves."

'I had persuaded myself that Yvonne's GC, like Bisto's blessings on our union, was evidence that Baker Street had forgiven me, but as the years went by I came to suspect that it was as likely to be a refined form of revenge on Gerry's part. He never did tell me what happened to Peter Darling. I am quite prepared to believe that he never had any idea.'

iii

I must have fallen asleep on Lionel's bed. I was woken by the sounds of him assembling a khaki camp-bed made of canvas stretched on metal rods which had to be pushed together to make a rigid frame. The mild noises he was making could not be assimilated into the dream I was having, which involved Roley Savory (in a skirt) and Mike Lea.

'That looks ... intricate,' I said.

'Wodja think of it? My little essay?'

'Very revealing,' I said.

'Gross indecency, did you reckon? Or merely a spot of Phyllis Dixeying? Revealed what, did I? The truth, do you think?'

'Some of it.'

'I thought so too *à l'époque*. Find some holes in said account, did you, nonetheless? Viz?'

'You write very well.'

'The lady's surprised. I write English. Brought up that way. Old dog, old tricks. Oldish dog even then. Muzzle whitens; prose style endures. Couldn't be sure who was scribbling half the time, me or Thucydides. Could really. Wodja mean, "some of it"?'

'I believed the stuff about Ste Foy. It explains a lot.'

'Satisfied your curiosity, did it? When you can't satisfy anything else, you might as well. Believed it myself.'

'I wouldn't say "satisfied".'

'How about piqued? In the curiosity department. Any piquing going on at all?'

'I ought to send my piece off, if I'm going to.'

'Moral obligation, followed by the conditional. Very modern, that. Meaning you want to shelve further discussion. *Sine die?* One of history's favourite rendezvous.'

'I wonder why you stopped where you did.'

'End of paper, end of pencil, end of story. So I supposed. Hence why not?'

'Meaning it wasn't?'

'You could've worked in Baker Street, Stannard R., if the timing'd been right. Got the vocal equipment, incha? D'you want me to run you somewhere so you can bung 'em your soft soap?'

'I really need to get a bicycle,' I said. 'We also need some provisions, I daresay.'

'Dessay, do you? We are "we" now, are we? Going to improve my diet, are you? Cosset me into an early grave. All right, give you that one: left it a bit for one of those. Is he going to come after you, is he? With or *sans* shot-gun. Or is he after bigger game? He's not going to want to have it out man-to-man, I hope. I haven't the puff for that kind of nonsense. You wouldn't expect me to put up a fight for you, would you, Rachel?'

'That won't happen,' I said.

'You want to bunk here, you can bunk here. You want to read

and write: all yours. You want to organise me, *improve* me, or – worst of all – bring me up to date, that's the door. Kindly shut it quietly after you. Any queues? *Questions*, woman.'

I said, 'Did all the children die?'

'No lead up,' he said. 'Both feet, in she dives! Probably. No precise documentation to hand. Happy ending certainly not. Sound of Music not to be heard. Common decency not a war aim, dear.'

'Félix,' I said. 'How much did he get away with?'

'He got away with the lot, didn't he? *Ipso facto*; as reported. For more than fifty years.'

'I meant money,' I said.

'There's a bit of a funny one there, Rachel, as you mention it. Enough to buy the *Relais*, set himself up, though not from the sources what I always assumed; until last night. When he swore to me, on his knees, literally, he never took a single sov. Found I believed him, unfortunately. He also thanked me, which was a dirty trick, for letting him play the postman with Leitner. Knocked twice and all. See what happened, don't you? Using him as a go-between with the Herr Major gave him a cover story, *in parvo*, at least. A shred to cover his shame. Played the hero, didn't he, in a cringing sort of a way? Not his fault it didn't pay off. Saved his bacon for him, I did, his *jambon de* bloody *pays*. Not with every-body though. The Commies were furious, of course, when they found out that in the much-obliged-to-you interim we'd spirited away the St Médard SS boys. Litvaks *de pur sang*, a lot of them. Mixed bag by the end, your master race. Shades of Boney's *Grande Armée*, most of whom couldn't speak frog to save their lives, and most of whom didn't manage to do the latter either. For want of a nail et cet*erah*! So! Félix: Cocos gave him a hard time in the *épuration* and hence – always an equal and opposite force, isn't there, *per ardua ad astra*, not forgetting all stations to Cock-fosters? – the Gaullists and our good and brave selves interposed our persons, *pro tem.*, though not, finally, so's you'd notice. Rough game, politics; change of trump suit in the middle of the hand is all part of the fun.'

'What did happen to the money?'

'The money.'

'The sovs, as you called them.'

'Swift Hebrus, dear. Down to a sunless sea.'

'Bit of a confusion there, isn't there?'

'Natch. Spoils of war, never a pretty sight. What about this shopping and allied trades? Are we doing it or what? And if what, when?'

'Now,' I said, 'by all means. If you're up to it.'

'Change of subject there. You'll want to go all the way to Caillac, I suppose, to buy this bicycle.'

'If that's not ...'

'That is, that is. Much better learn to ride the H.D., source of all good things. You'd be surprised. Lesson one in Jew course. I'm not a jealous man, but if you smash it up, I'll put you over my knee. Not meant to be an incentive, that. Beware of warnings; because they don't arf procure the desired result. Think of Eden.'

'Alternatively, I could buy a small car. Second-hand.'

'Do, or don't, far as I'm concerned. Department of Total Indifference, Chief sec. your 'umble. Don't give the proverbial what you do, dear. Hope that's understood. Suits you to look tired. Interesting creases, nice eyes, slightly bruised-looking.'

'You wish I hadn't come, don't you?'

'Survived for years without a spare tin-opener,' he said. 'Can't say I've missed one. I don't do wishes; too close to regrets. Right, was I, not to go on with it? Story of my life?'

'Not at all,' I said. 'If there was more to say.'

'More to say, less to do. England since forty-five. Fishing's your thing, is it? The bait, the hook, the patient sit-it-out on the grassy verge. Suppose I told you, what then?'

'Told me what?'

'Told you what, told you when, told you who. The whole thing. *Tout le baz.* Make you sit up yet. Wouldn't hurt you to stick your tits out. They're nothing to be ashamed of. Outside, on the double, shall we? Pick 'em up, pick 'em up.'

I did not like him as much that morning as I had hoped. He had collected the pages he left for me and put them in tighter order than they had been before. The way that he tapped them even on the top of the crate, before putting them inside, seemed to warn against disturbing them again. I might have been reading them without his permission. Yet the look he gave me, however grim, had a conspirator's gleam to it. He dared me to question him further, and would be disappointed if I did not.

He made me wear the crash-helmet. It was, he told me, required by law. He himself would be happy bare-headed. He might have enjoyed being stopped by the police, but luckily, he said, he was invisible. The Harley-Davidson was an antique, but he told me that it was all right: it was not the same machine which he had taken from the SS despatch rider whom he had obliged to shit himself. Or had I skipped that passage? I assured him that I had not skipped anything.

'And you still want to send this stuff of yours? Of course you do. Opinions are sacred, facts are what people want to hear. Hence all aboard, two-three!'

Was I afraid of seeing Roger in Caillac? I presumed that Pansy was already on her way to Bordeaux. London seemed closer now and more real to me than it had during the years in *Les Noyers Tordus*; I could even imagine resuming a life, or at least a career, there, though I had no appetite for it. Perhaps that was why I could visualise myself as a full-time journalist again; in my dream, as I now remembered, I was being borne upwards on the shoulders of Roley (he was also wearing pearls) and Mike Lea towards some detestable eminence. I leaned my face against Lionel Cator's PVC back and took comfort in the unfriendliness of its surface.

While I held onto Lionel, my mind rode on ahead. I wondered by what ruse he would manage to keep his eye on me when he was dead. I certainly had the illusion that, with his back to me, he could see me perfectly well. As if in petty evidence, I caught his eye in the Harley-Davidson's mirror when he hefted the machine onto its stand and we drew breath before dismounting. Did I imagine that he looked at me in the wry knowledge that I would be in command of his story when he died?

The French have a form of house purchase which Roger and I discovered soon after our arrival in the Périgord. It involves buying a property at below the market price, on condition that the owner (who must have no direct heirs) is allowed to live in it until his death and receives a regular annuity. The purchaser must supply in patience what he saves in expenditure. Some friends of Thierry de Croqueville had been waiting seven years for an old lady to die and yield possession of a large river-side property on the road to Souillac which they had assumed to be a bargain until her longevity began, and continued, to exceed all actuarial expectations. Strangely enough, they did not feel any animosity towards Madame Grangier and almost relished her tenacious hold on life.

Thierry promised me that her death would be quite a blow to them. I had a feeling that I should see Lionel out with the same mixture of relief and dismay.

I faxed my pages to Wapping from the *Centre de Télécommunications* in Caillac. Since I could leave no number for them to call me back, I had no means of verifying whether Mike and Roley liked the piece. I could not quite convince myself that I did not care.

In the Casino supermarket, on the modern edge of Caillac, Lionel suddenly said, 'All right. Evidence is what stands between us and the truth. Your comments, if any?'

I chose to say nothing. He did not take it very well. He looked closely at me, rather as Toni did during my adolescence, when she still hoped that she might detect some signs of Pansy's beauty on my pouty person. She usually touched my hair, and rearranged it slightly, before she offered me the smiling sigh which postponed definitive assessment. Lionel's look was seasoned with suspicion; a pinch of generosity perhaps.

I said, 'Did you ever find out what happened to the woman?'

He was putting our purchases into the saddle bags of the Harley-Davidson. 'Monique? Ravensbrück. The woman!'

iv

I was living with the fox. Although I did my best to play the unobtrusive female, I appreciated that I was a charge on his energy. He was unaccustomed to attention; it demanded – however discreetly – that he give a continuous performance of himself. I did my best to respond in kind: I played the woman. I spent the afternoon cleaning the cottage, bringing in firewood, making arranged sense, like some domestic archaeologist, of the accumulated detritus of his solitude. He watched me with an ill grace. I sympathised. In my inquisitive presumption, I had assumed that I should be doing the old man a favour by my presence. Had he not hinted as much with his talk of not having seen a naked woman in more than ten years? I had taken him for a lonely soul, with a past but no future. Belated vanity told me that my presence would bring pleasure, in extra time, to tired eyes.

In the event, his manuscript had put an enlightening veil between us. Its attempt at terseness had not deceived even himself: he was a complicated man who had elected to parody the military style. It sanctioned what would, in clear, be too painful to recall; by putting on the mask of Caesar or Thucydides, he could go in disguise, even to himself. In the same spirit, by turning his back on England, he had been able to remain, or become, an Englishman of his own invention: he was a living criticism of the world which he had chosen to abandon because it had abandoned him. He had adopted a sort of imperial self-reliance which, today, could be lived only in mockery.

I had bought lamb's kidneys and broccoli. Lionel peeled potatoes from a big sack, accusingly, as if he feared my menu might be intended to deprive him of them. He had picked up bread and *Roquefort* (*Papillon*) and Balkan yoghurt, which he fitted into his small gas refrigerator. He chose not to have electricity or the telephone, although I could not help listening for its ring. I had also bought mushrooms and a small carton of long-life cream, with which I made a sauce for the kidneys.

We ate them in silence. If he was waiting for me, I knew better than to make idle conversation. I was waiting for him and I was determined not to sponsor the postponements I was ready to endure. I was happy that he should enjoy my cooking and suffer a little at the same time; my presence was an implied question: I was, I thought to myself, a one-person queue.

'Money,' he said. 'Funny stuff. No smell, said the emperor. Beats "Jesus wept" for brevity. Always imagined Félix must've got his hands on some of the sovs, despite *indications du contraire*.' He looked at me and I tipped the last of the kidneys towards him; his reluctance admitted that he had liked them. He shrugged, the smallest possible compliment in the French style. 'Pikestaff-plain in fact. Hence not observed until I had him on his knees, last will and test-your-ment, far as he knew. Said there was something he had to tell me. Waited fifty years, couldn't wait any longer. Didn't want a cigarette, wanted to spill some beans. Beans on your conscience, make a lot of wind, those do. So: the money; his money. Came from guess where?'

'You always thought he sold the Germans the people in the cellar, didn't you? *And* took some of the sovs. Which means...'

'Quite: didn't. *Said* he didn't. Last words can be famous without being true necessarily. However: no profit in delation. Only a moral glow. Dead children make some people's day. So: someone else got through to the *Kommandatur* one cheerful morn. Anon, anon, sir; some patriotic spirit with a disguised voice. Many birds, one stone; national sport, denouncing people, *chez* the frogs. Telling tales is no small part of their literature, *après tout*! La Fontaine runneth over. Cheese? Why not? Félix told me he *told* Leitner it was him, the *corbeau*, to save his skin, to get in good, as they say; unnerstannable! So. Didn't mean he done it, only means he *said* he did. Diplomatic, Félix; long-view merchant. Capital offence in my little book, but well out of print, that one. Archaeologist Félix also. Clue there, Stannard.'

I said, 'You really don't drink coffee?'

'Dirty stuff, my view. Help yourself, if you've got the will and the way. Mint tea me. Mother nature brings it to the door.'

'He *found* the money he needed?'

'Struck gold? So he told me. And so I believe. There was a lot of it about.'

'It wasn't the sovs, it wasn't from the Germans...'

'They were collecting, not disbursing. Makes sense. So?'

I said, 'I didn't come here to get your story out of you, I want you to know that.'

'After my body, that it?'

'I came because, all right, smile, because I thought you were...'

'An interesting case. *Car*-case, to be prescient, am I right? Better than ... *Roger*? Roger! More mysterious. Roger and out. Think of Monte Cristo.'

'In the *cave*,' I said. 'Good God.'

'In the *cave*,' Lionel said, 'by whatever agency. Swears he didn't know it was there. Credulity wears thin in that department, but maybe. *Credo quia etcetera*. He was digging around, wasn't he, after the Fredas had done their damnedest, and what did he find?'

'The Jews!' I said. 'They'd buried their stuff and he found it.'

'Reward of the just. Might well be true. But only in part. Because what else happened?'

'Meaning you know.'

'Meaning I like to see a clever woman with a frown on her face, wanting to get something out of me. Like chess problems, don't you?'

'I don't even play,' I said.

'Don't have to. Chess problems have to honour the code, if they want to deceive you fairly. So: principle is, all the pieces on show have to speak to the plot, even if only to mislead. Otherwise you get your money back. Which is what certain people wanted to do. Suggest anything? Because think carefully about Félix and his squalid history. This is what convinces me he was telling no lie, as they say, don't they, these days? I'm not greatly in favour of them, but ... So: he stayed in Sainte Foy, got the hotel with the money from his digs, let's say, and then – come forty-seven – he decides to – what else do they say? – do a runner. He decides to do a runner. It *seems* like it was quite soon after the war, but in fact things were calming down; he wasn't in any noticeable trouble with the law and Félix wasn't the kind of man who'd pass up the main chance because a few Comrades roughed him up on the way from market. He had his friends as well as his enemies. *Et alors?*'

'I want to get something clear. This money he found. It must have been quite a lot. Are you saying that these Jewish women, and men, I suppose, who were escorting the children, they left a fortune in the cellars of the *Relais St Jacques?*'

'Did you hear me say that?'

'I don't have to hear you,' I said, 'for you to say things.'

'Appreciate the compliment,' Lionel said, 'but you didn't hear me *and* I didn't say it. Try again, Stannard. You're warm, but you're not there.'

'He found some ... some *Roman* relics? Some *staters*? The pilgrims! He found a cache of coins left there by some of the people on their way ...'

'Cold as an English tart, you are,' Lionel said. 'Because who are you missing out?'

'Tell me.'

'You come here, you move in, you can bloody well use your head the way I want you to use it. Think, dear. Apply the faculties.'

'Not the Jews.'

'Not *only* the Jews, let's say, to be safe.'

'There were some other people, the people Monique ... Monique ...'

'Touvian.'

'... Touvian was with. From Grenoble.'

'Right, except it was Limoges.'

'Limoges. Communists?'

'*Important* Communists. *Je souligne.* Emphasis added.'

'Was she one herself?'

'Gaullist courrier, from Paris. *De passage*. Monique had no idea about what had happened. *Ante quam.*'

'How can you be so sure of that?'

'I can. I am. *Touche pas*, Rachel dear, all right, for the moment? *Ein* thing at a time. She arrived after the others. Caught in the same trap, not always the same species. Far from it.'

'Did she die in Ravensbrück?'

'*Hors sujet*,' he said, '*pro tem.* at least. Eyes in the boat, dear.'

'After they'd been taken away, and killed presumably, Félix found ... Party funds! Red gold. Hidden in his cellar? Really?'

'Strike out note of incredulity, dear, all right? Why not?'

'The Party had that sort of money?'

'What sort of money was that?'

'Enough to buy the hotel...'

'And?'

'And.'

'And what?'

'I'm not with you.'

'Yes, you are. *And* it was your choice. Being with me. Thinking caps to be worn.'

'Got it! And keep him in modest style all the time he was supposed to be dead.'

'See what you can do if you try? Didn't have to be that much. Tin, whatever form it took. Enough to interest the charming Léah, however. With whom liaison broached well before departure. So: a sizeable sum. Journalism; interesting trade yours. Full of people trying to have no illusions, am I right? Trying to know it all, thinking it all has to be there to be known. Continue.'

'Have I started?'

'Like you, Rachel! Cheeky-to-sir something of a habit with you. What happened next?'

'Do I take it I'm supposed to know what this money was?'

'Not reely. Party funds covers it. But special part of said funds. Mistake to suppose our late lamented Comrades from Limoges weren't *French*, you know, and couldn't recognise a main chance when they saw one. One or two of them at least. Brave men, don't deny it; why bother, when not seeking office? Reds. I liked them. Luis; goes without saying, though *he* wouldn't'ta lasted long in the *apparat*, probably knew it. What a character! Not in our problem, *mais quand même*. Are you going to take your clothes off for me, are you?'

'Probably.'

'Nice of you. Don't have to.'

'I wouldn't if I had to.'

'You don't know what you're saying, but I like the spirit it's said in. When?'

'At the right moment.'

'You can wait all your life for one of those. All right: most efficient organisation, most widespread, *admettons*, were the Reds. We were fighting a campaign; they were fighting a war. Knew the value of money, needed it, knew where to extract the stuff. *Sans problème*. With me?'

'I'm slightly lagging behind,' I said. 'That's me puffing. Where to extract it?'

'Illusions, Stannard; brush them away lightly, with an archae-ological touch, and – lo and behold! – there are the eternal verities, as nasty a little cluster as Karl Marx ever drew the world's attention to. No smell, has cash, maybe, but sticks nicely to the fingers, dunnit? Majority want a quiet life, Rachel, especially in noisy times. And are willing to pay for it, through the nose and other parts. With me? Nineteen forty-three, -four, began to dawn on a lot of people, depending on speed of mind, that collecting tins could be profitably rattled at bourgeois doors; worse the con-sciences within, the bigger the contribution. No one wanted to be in bad books, did they? Especially red ones. Rattle, rattle.'

'Of *course*.'

'Easy when you know how. And there was them as knew very well. No disrespect to the Cocos. Coffers are coffers. Bravest of the brave sometimes, on record as saying so. Which leaves what?'

'Why Félix waited as long as he did.'

'If waiting is what he did. He bought the hotel, he took a mistress who was, as they say, *sore* with me, with Evie, with slow service generally, and he – yes, you're right – looked like settling down. It didn't look like waiting. Two, three years went by. And then what?'

'He lost his nerve.'

'Come on, Stannard. You did better in the earlier part of the term. Had plenty of nerve, Félix. Not much else, in fact.'

'Why did he call himself Lévy?'

'Stick to the problem in hand.'

'Something happened.'

'Good point, though: probably did find some Jew money. Hate that way of talking, don't you? Probably doesn't bother you. Not being of the blood. Sarah, Rachel; they even stole their names when it was all over, didn't they, your friends? Mustn't be bitter, must we? Never got anyone anywhere.'

'Someone found out. Léah.'

'Knew all the time, betcha. Hence liaison, although she did have handsome rear end, as previously noted. And other parts.'

'Someone else found out.'

'Not "*out*" exactly. You're there, dear. Finger's hovering over it. Well?'

'Someone ... Ah! They didn't find out because they knew about it all the time. They knew about it all the time. Who did?'

'I'm enjoying this,' Lionel said. 'The kidneys were good, but this is better. Who could? Excellent sauce. Who did?'

'They came back from ... wherever they'd been and ...'

'They? Why they?'

'One of them. One of them survived and came back to look for the money.'

'One comrade chose freedom. Needed dibs. Been in Christ knows where, place Stalin sent the faithful, once he'd rescued them, to remind them not to do it again, whatever it was. Got him out of frying pan, gave him a taste of the fire. Which he did not, in the long run, appreciate. Decided to leg it across Europe. Arrived just as Félix thought he was 'appy as Claudius. Here are the pigeons; enter the cat. Walking very much alone. Highly incog. Because?'

'He'd escaped from ... wherever ... and he was no longer all that keen on the Party. He didn't want any of them to know he'd survived; didn't want *anyone* to, in view of ...'

'*Très bien! Félicitations même!* He was going to take the money and walk quietly away to a new life. Instead of which?'

'The body in the ... the Borgward, wasn't it? That they assumed was Félix. Burnt to a cinder. Felix killed him and ...'

'I think you've cracked it,' Lionel said. 'You're home and dry. Félix killed the poor bloody revenant, in cold blood or hot, and then he saw that a threat can also supply salvation. Old human plot, that, much favoured by divines. Outdid Latimer and Ridley, did friend Félix, put the body in the boot, made an RV with Léah in some Riviera frock department, and orf he went to the Landes, up she goes, followed by v. long life after death. QED. Never have known any of it if the bloody sten hadn't jammed on me. Miracle, you might say, if you worked for that sort of outfit.'

'And you let him get away with it.'

'British justice, dear. Killed him once, couldn't do it again. Let him sweat; he's been doing it for years. Alphonse Lévy. Took a name instead of having a conscience. Peerage principle. You're possibly right: he also found some jewels or something, baubles that he decided to apologise for, in very small measure. Unless it was the children. You haven't got any. Why's that?'

'It was never quite the moment.'

'Not looking to me for that, I hope. Not at all sure I've got any more of the necessary in stock.'

'I'm not in any hurry.'

'Never had a son,' he said. 'So I've spared somebody something. Square root of minus one; interesting cove, not that a square root's likely to make a lot of friends among those with round holes. Not appreciated?'

'What about you?' I said.

'Had a daughter, probably; odds favour that view, no other known progeny. A tart or two might tell you different, but...'

'I didn't mean that,' I said. 'I meant money.'

'Money?'

'We now know how Félix Argote got through the last fifty years; what about you?'

'Not on the board, that problem, Stannard. Where do you want to sleep? I'm not promising not to snore, nor promising to. You can always bunk down through there, in the *remise*, if you want to shift some wood. Not tonight, I don't mean necessarily, but...'

'You didn't get a pension and your father doesn't sound as if he was a rich man.'

'Think about it, Stannard, if that's your pleasure. Mull of Kintyre, why not? Haven't needed much. Live orf the land, me.'

'Doesn't mean you haven't got any, does it?'

'Reflexes sharpening up, aren't they, lady? Are you going to give me a *show*, or what? I've supplied the *quid*, so what about the *pro quo* sometime sooner rather than later, on the grounds that later may well be too late?'

'What's good for the Party is also good for members of HM forces when not under tight surveillance, is that it? Hence Jim ... Scobie, hence his little quipigram.'

'Mrs Marlow come again, Rachel, you are, but with rather more promise of pneumatic bliss.'

'Not all that pneumatic; don't get your hopes up.'

'It's probably the one thing that I can get up; imagine you'd already thought of that. Trust the sex. Trust the sex and ... no, I don't really mean that. I did once love a woman, Rachel. Not promising not to do it to you, but one love I did have. Pure and simple.'

'Yvonne, was that? Before...'

'Ever been bathed by someone, Rachel? Apart from mummy or the nanny, have you?'

'Bathed. I had my appendix out once and they ... sort of washed me.'

'Bathed. You want to know what I've lived on, is that it?'

'I was making conversation,' I said. 'I don't really care. You're welcome to it.'

'Inspector of Taxes, are we now? Possible wrong 'un, am I?'

'I only asked to see what kind of a face you made.'

'And what kind did I?'

'One that said you could probably kill somebody quite easily.'

'Easier than a lot of things. More difficult than others. Morally, I mean. Physically, it's ... a knack. Like riding a bicycle. Once learnt ... You don't really want to do that, do you?'

'It doesn't matter for the moment.'

'Wrong. For the moment is why I mentioned it. You're slipping, Stannard. All the facts are before the court. Only the truth escapes. Implicit in the narrative, dear. Jim Scobie, as you say. Went blind, poor chap. All right, I'm cheating a little. I'll nudge a piece or two, or will that spoil it for you?'

'I don't know,' I said. 'Will it?'

'You don't trust me an inch. Very decent of you. Very Christian. 'orrible suspish went through your mind, didn't it? No, I'm not in the woodpile. Not *that* woodpile anyroad. No, no, Rachel; don't be *that* clever, please. I'm not an informer.'

'I wasn't thinking that.'

'No? Negation always at the heart of knowledge, am I right? The unthinkable is always just down the road. No mood for a thousand and one nights like this. No time either. So: put it this way: I knew, as soon as that Urian heap Félix told me, that he was telling *der Trud* about the sovs he took to Leitner. Now: how? I never called you a brown cow, so don't look at me like that. Mint tea, 'avin' some or not?'

'I'd like some,' I said. 'Because you already knew something that more or less confirmed his story. Except that you never put that particular two and two together.'

'Identify which two, or four, and – like Holmes's cabbie – you shall have a *sovereign* for your pains.'

'Another clue. But I still can't . . .'

'Or won't?'

'I don't believe it.'

'Very touching. And also correct. My hand has been in a lot of tills, but never in a German glove. Oh, even that's not entirely true. But not in the sense you hope and fear . . . So?'

'You kept back some of the cash that you hid in the mill?'

'Did I? How did I? Why did I? When did I?'

'You didn't.'

'Pouting doesn't help, Rachel. No one ever taught you that?'

'Everyone did.'

'Same thing. I didn't keep it, cast it on the waters, as previously indicated. Destiny that shapes our ends, smoothly on occasion, but not to be taken for granted, ever. The bicycle, dear, the bicycle; one thing leads to another, rule of nature, however regrettable at times. H.D. not merely a poetess of renown but also, initially speaking, vessel of redemption. More luck than lucky Félix, me. Out of a clear blue sky.'

'The Harley-Davidson.'

'Often on my conscience. Fits like a glove.'

'The German who you . . .'

'The English hesitation. I'd go a long way for it. To get away from it. Whom I made shit himself. And walk stickily on his way. No wonder he looked back; fared better than Lot's lady, but never came back to have a word. No idea who I was. Or why. I can still remember straddling that little beauty. My *not* going home present, I thought at the time. Do me, as they say. No idea that *une fortune pouvait en cacher une autre*; did though. I parked the damn thing down at the *moulin*, in a little shed – always useful *remises* is – thought no more about it until I went back. Had me lunch with me, thought I'd take a spin in the woods and wait for a call from home, opened the saddlebag ... Up to the top, dear. Danae would've considered herself overtipped. Remember her?'

'The Golden Rain lady.'

'Passed your School Certificate all right, didn't you? Kid was taking the sovs home to his *Mutti* maybe. Or his *Fuhrer*; who's to say? The good and the bad use the same facilities, don't they, very often? Duplicity part of the system. "Nature's vile economy", whose phrase is that? Leitner's little insurance policy turned out to be negotiable. Catch as catch could. What should I have done?'

'Is there anything?'

'That's exactly what I did. You don't have to do anything you don't want to do, Rachel Stannard. In the *pro quo* department. Nothing incumbent, dear. No Jew date.'

'You really have a Jewish grandmother?'

'Everybody does today. No saddlebag without one, is there?'

'You really went and had yourself circumcised?'

'Yes, I did. But that was *suite* to another story, wasn't it?'

'You said.'

'Entirely.'

'No one ever suspected? About the money?'

'Why ever should they? Who was to know? Or guess?'

'Jim Scobie?'

'They all thought I'd had a nasty attack of altruism; cast HMG's war chest on the waters. Never imagined it had floated back to me. Never bought a flashy car. Aged p. gave the bucket a nudge in Jew course, which supplied adequate cover story. I was a wrong 'un, dear, best forgotten; misapplied funds was bad enough to supply smirk screen *in saecula saeculorum*. Did I complain? Not I!'

'You didn't do much with it exactly, did you?'

'Damned if I would when Evie was around. If I had, she still might've been, mightn't she, till death did its part? My little *bagage*, that, when I was trying to make the war last and having difficulties with the physical. No smell, limited powers.'

He stood up, as if he had suddenly gone too far. His eyes were confused with tears, which seemed to make him angry. He took the dishes to the basin and began to wash them as if they deserved it.

I said, 'I haven't come here because I want anything. More because I don't. Because I can't believe I do.'

'Roger,' he said. 'I never thought he was a good idea.'

'He wasn't even a bad enough one. I used him against people who I don't even want to know.'

'Whom. Decline of the relative, decline of the body politic. *Qui* and *quos*; get 'em right, basis of empire; hence Lenin's "Who whom?". Hole in one. Unfortunately for some, however, there are two holes. *Hinc illae lac.* Am I right?'

'I've upset you,' I said. 'And I truly didn't mean to.'

'Apple carts always were uncertain articles. You've done nothing, Rachel. Not you. Monique. As you mighta guessed.'

'She came back?'

He seemed to be washing more dishes and pans than I could remember us dirtying. He was old and I loved him. It was a casual, not a deep, emotion; an enlightenment almost, in the double sense that it also alighted as weightlessly as a butterfly. I had been waiting for something of the kind, but what I felt, when it happened, had no expectations and involved no desire. It was something I never felt for Mickey, and now I thought that perhaps I might learn to feel it for him, if he were old enough one day.

'I saw her,' he said. 'In a mag. Years later. Forty-eight. September Forty-eight. In *Paris Match*. Piece about Israel, just been founded. No thanks to HMG, you may recall; if not, be belatedly advised, no thanks at all. Suited the FO better if they'd all been nabbed, wooncha say so, while the mad Mullah was about it? Raaather. Saw this woman's pitcher in *Paris Match*. You know what they say about me, don't you, round here?'

'Not all of it, I don't suppose.'

'Comes and goes, isn't that what they say?'

'Oh, I have heard that,' I said.

'Treated Evie like a swine, Rachel. Don't deny it. Right to go. Pushed her out. Filled her up, according to some accounts, and then gave her the boot, general direction Castillonès. I saw this thin blonde woman in a group of people, soldiers and ... and others. Went back and looked again and should've wept, of course. Didn't; went crazy with it. Rolled the mag up and swatted Evie. Bloody hard. Anywhere I could find a vacancy. Shades of Looloo with his elder branch, but *he* was doing it for a reason, for a purpose; I did it because I daren't do worse. Beat her silly with a magazine. *La pauvre.* Hadn't done a thing, objectively speaking, comrade. Can you see me? Mad thing I was. She thought it was because she'd been up and down with her bloody baron. *Au contraire!* My salvation, he was. Year later, I went off to Israel. Year and more. Why? Can't remember a thing I did. Got her pregnant possibly. Can't have taken that long, but ... Had myself circumvented and off I went; that way, no problem getting in, I thought. You're looking at me.'

'Of course.'

'Think I'm lying?'

'Is that how I look?'

'You look as if you're getting ready to do something sympathetic. Because otherwise why would you be here?'

'There's that,' I said.

'You're the girl swerves to avoid a dead cat, aren't you?'

'So it says on the charge sheet. I never admitted as much.'

'She'd been in Ravensbrück all right; and come out of it, not all right. Weighed nothing, couldn't put it back. I'd seen it in the photograph and I still didn't go for a year. Worse things to do. As stated *supra.* Been separated from the children, of course, soon as they were round the corner. Toodleoo from the brave *cheminots de France,* never a train delayed on its eastward *trajet.* Songs at twilight. Never seen me in her life, remember that. I'd seen her. Found her in Tel Aviv. Concrete flat. Bloody awful spot. Wanted to get her out, bring her back to France. Didn't belong in France, she said. Nothing Jewish about her, Rachel, bit like you. Didn't belong there. She couldn't do much, of course, even before things got worse, but she was happy; she said. Relative term. She was content. Where she wanted to be. I had a stack of sovs, Rachel, and none of 'em could buy anything that would do any good. Today, I dunno; then, not a thing. Couldn't even put a name to what killed her. She wasn't sorry; almost annoyed me that: she was the next best thing to happy. Perhaps the next best thing higher up. No. She was dying, where she wanted to die. She was very kind to me. Very kind indeed, while she lasted. As she got worse, I could actually do things for her. I don't think she ever loved me and I don't suppose I deserved it. Didn't matter a damn, Stannard. What she felt for me; not a damn. She let me love her, which was the thing. Her days got shorter. When I first saw her, she used to go to an orphanage in the mornings. By the end; know

258

what I used to do? I'd wake up early and go and sit with her while she slept. She slept deeply and when she was asleep she was clear of all pain. I never wanted her to wake. I lie; I wanted her to wake, because as she woke, she'd open the eyes I remembered and she'd smile at me. She'd smile and her white lips made the shape of a word she didn't have the strength to say, "*Bonjour*". And that would be the end of the day. It was over as soon as it began. At the end, I sat with her and she never opened her eyes at all. Then I came back here and did a few things I shouldn't. Not much of a help really, but there you are.'

I said, 'I may well love you, Lionel Cator, but please don't worry about it.'

15

'Darling Pan,

'Found your letter at the house when I went to try and sort it all out with Roger (fat chance!). Trust him to hang onto things. He behaved like a total bastard, which is rather a relief: proves that he's not lost his sap. He tried to lose some of it, on me, as a matter of fact. We had a ridiculous wrestling match; I'm still not sure which he was trying to do, kill me or Charlify me. First one, then the other, probably. He wants to sell the house because he thinks I don't, so I let him believe that I was very upset, when I don't really give a monkey's. Loved the place at one point, but I'll never go back there. Keep it to yourself. As if you ever could. Roger swears that we are going to divide *everything* exactly in half, so I should obviously be watching him like a hawk, except that I can't be bothered to do that and *still* be swindled, so I told him to be *bloody* careful and looked as though I really, really meant it. I expect he saw through it.

'He hasn't heard *anything* from Quigley and Jonts, which is another sore point with him; he's bought a hunting rifle which he says is meant for bores. Names on a postcard? Every time we go to the supermarket, I find myself thinking that he may confront us with the thing sawn off. *The gun.* And want our money or our lives. Us being Lionel Cator and me. That was who I was going to see the night you dropped me off in the middle of nowhere. The ex-spy character. He wasn't actually there when I got there, but he came back and I decided to love him. I don't know how long he'll live; I don't even know for sure how old he is. He's certainly old, but not *kaput.* I shall stay until whenever, because I like it. When I first met him – that day when you were there – he told me that he hadn't seen a naked woman in eleven years. He has now and seems quite in favour. He likes to watch me wash. He likes the water on my flesh. It doesn't make me self-conscious at all; quite narcissistic in fact.

'We went up to the *Relais St Jacques* the other night, where Sibylle remembers you *very* fondly. She thought you were *magnifique* – eyes like saucers when she said so! You must've added a lot of service or something. He's back. Olivier; her husband. She calls him "*Monsieur*", as if it were some kind of a title, but with a lot of irony. I now know where he went, and why, but I don't think you'd be madly interested. He's shaved off his moustache. Dumped the cavalry, it seems.

'The Mazda sounds fun. Trust you to have a white one. I can imagine you leaving it on double yellow lines all over town. L.C. has taught me to ride his motorbike, which roars like a game park. I trundle along with *great* trepidation when I have to go shopping – prefer it when he plays the chauffeur. He says he's going to leave it to me in his will, along with his millions.'

*

'Dear Mickey,
'A difficult letter, so I've been putting it off. Not because I didn't want to say happy birthday to you. That's what made it *essential* to delay no longer. So: happy birthday. And that is *not* meant to be the bad news. You're a year older; we're *all* a year older. Ask not for whom the candles toll. No, the difficulty lies in the fact that I haven't got anything horrid to say. Quite the opposite, though perhaps you won't think so. No, I haven't re-married. I am not even sure that I've got divorced, because the papers have been all over the shop. Roger has gone to live in Spain. A place with ten golf courses, which he says is heaven and I hope it is, since I'm not likely to be going there. I am still living with L.C., who says, without any sort of enthusiasm, that you'd be welcome here. The cottage is very small, but we have now sprung to a double bed. I hope you're not 'orrified at my living with a man who is actually old enough, very nearly, to be *your* father. I'm not boasting and I'm certainly not apologising. *Ever*.

'Which brings me, I suppose, to the news: I hope you're sitting down, because you're going to be a grandfather. No, not Pansy; me. I'm telling you before I even tell L.C., who may not care all that much, and may care a great deal. Don't imagine that I'm shacked up with some antique satyr; he isn't at all like that. But we are – sorry the

261

word's so lame – fond. We're very fond and rather British about it; reticent, what?

'I have no illusions about being the love of his life; I know exactly who she was and I know that I can't, and shouldn't, have the smallest hope of "replacing" her. In fact, if it hadn't been for her, and the things she did, I don't think he would have any time for me, and I might not for him. They never had sex; I'm not even sure they ever kissed. He fell in love with her without her even knowing that he existed and he nursed her through some horrible disease which he won't give a name to. She was in a concentration camp (*not* Jewish) and never really got over it physically. I think I help him to feel that she's still slightly alive, because he talks to me about her, which he never has to *anyone* before. Do you think that sounds rather ignominious? I hope you don't, Mickey, because I think you're brighter than that, even though for some reason you don't want to be thought so.

'What I wanted to say here is that you mustn't be afraid of what I think of you any more. And it's not that I don't think of you. Nothing so glib. I thought of you when I got married to Roger, which was a disaster that was (now I think about it) probably designed to match yours, though it didn't leave any deep scars that I can see or feel. Not feeling anything bad about you and Patricia any more – and realising that Toni and you were simply never married at all – is what I wanted to convey to you herewith. Not much of a prezzie, but I'll manage that when I next see you. Of *course* I want to, but I'm not leaving here until I have to. Can't explain. There it is; here I am. But this is the funny part: I think of you a lot, and I *want to*! Many happies, Mickey darling. I wonder if Pan remembered. If she did, it's *not* because I reminded her.'

*

'Dear Roley,

'I've been living with a man in France for the last three years and now he's died. He was very old and I always knew that we did not have long together. It was a love affair of a kind that I don't think you'd understand and might not sympathise with. I had a child with him, Louis; he's almost two. It's not a name I expect anybody to like very much, so don't worry about it. I'm living down here by myself and thinking of writing a thriller, which is the real point of this letter.

I don't need the money, but that doesn't mean that I don't intend to get as much as I can for the book.

'My idea is to do a modern *Count(ess) of Monte Cristo* – a sort of who's-she-going-to-do-it-to about a woman who comes into a fortune and decides to use it in order to bring justice, in small ways, to an unjust world. If you're willing, I'll send you a couple of chapters and a synopsis and if you could show it to some agent you think might be sympathetic, or simply greedy, I'll buy you and Lindsey a gargantuan feast at any local hostelry at which you might like to make a disgusting exhibition of yourself (I mean *your*self, since I'm sure Lindsey would never do such a thing). Did you ever use that piece about Lionel Cator because – you may as well know – it's all your fault that I had his child? It's all right, you can tell anyone you like, because I shan't be coming back to London. I'm going to do this thriller, aren't I?'

*

'My dear Rachel,

'You can probably thank Léah for this letter. If she can do it, why can't I, after all? No, I have no more secrets to offer you; no wild geese that need to be chased, because I think I've just about done that. I want to thank you for what you will have done by the time you read this. I know it was a strange thing to ask of you to sling my bones in a ditch. Byron, for whom I've always had a bit of a *faible*, asked for no ceremony, though I can't be sure that he meant it; part of the beauty of a poet is that he doesn't have to mean a thing. You've gone off on the H.D. and I'm writing this in the silence, scribbling like a guilty person, as if writing to you after my death were a kind of treachery. I don't flatter myself that you chose to love me because I was anything very special. No, I do not. I think you needed to love almost in the abstract and I'm about as abstract as a man can be and still not have closed his bracket. You filled – are filling – difficult things tenses, in the present situation! – a time of emptiness in my life, and if I pretended that I liked it that way, be sure that I like it much better *this* way. A woman is a beautiful thing, and you know the beauty of the earth closet: you can't even hear her splash, which I never liked and always listened for. Sad article, a man, especially with a middle-class education. I know I shouldn't, but I'm glad that there's somebody in the pipeline for you to use the sovs on. You'll have a little change for yourself, which also pleases me. Poor bloody Kraut, he's a millionaire philanth. by now, if he got home without his master catching up with him. No, nothing special to say except that the improbable always was my *modus op.* and I wouldn't have had it any other way, or you. You're a bit of a beauty, Rachel Stannard, so far as I can see, but then you know my eyes these days. You remember what Scobie said, don't you, when he was on his way? "To wave goodbye to the world as presently constituted, two fingers will generally be found to be sufficient." But then, he hadn't lived with you at all, duckie, 'ad 'e now?'